Persevere

....

Vincent Rough

Contents

One

"Keep your face to the sunshine and you cannot see a shadow."

Today is my birthday...

Well, today is the day I decided would be my birthday a few years ago, I'm not actually sure when the real one is.

I'm aware that is generally something people know about themselves, but when your parents think of you as shit on the bottom of their shoe, they tend to forget the little things.

Sitting on the floor of my room, scrubbing away at my favorite t-shirt, I tried as hard as I could to at least have the blood stains fade. I had just stitched up the many holes littering the back and it was safe to say that it no longer resembled a shirt.

Shit.

I'm down to my last good shirt and I'd really like to put off asking my mother for another for as long as I can.

My room is simple. It may seem a little run down to most people with the cracked bed frame, heavily scratched floor boards and the window that, after a little accident, now consists of saran wrap, but it's mine.

I put a lot of effort every day into making it clean and homey. It would be so easy for me to just come in and crash, leave the place a mess, but this is my safe space. My parents never come in here, probably thinking it's below them. It is the one place I have all to myself, where I don't have to worry about watching everything I do and where I don't have to worry about always being on the lookout for danger.

"ELLIE!" My father yelled from downstairs and I instantly jumped to my feet, still frowning down at my messed up shirt. My father was the alpha of our pack, the Blood Thunder pack. Who chose the name? I don't know, seems a little off in my opinion, but I guess that's what this pack was, off.

It was easily the strongest pack in the United States, so people ignored what happened within it. They ignored that the alpha abused his own child. That the Luna joins in when she's had a bad day. That when they're done with me I get passed around the pack so everyone can have some 'fun' and release their frustrations.

I was born deformed. Both of my parents are alpha wolves, very strong and highly respected. Perfect genes. No one knows how its even possible that I look the way I do, all anyone knows is that I never should have ever existed.

I'm smaller and leaner than most werewolves, I don't grow as fast as the others either, and still look like a pup when I shift. My ears are round, not pointy and my facial features are just not right.

I am very obviously a curse and a disappointment, sullying the pack's reputation, so I'm not surprised everyone hates me. I would hate me too. I'm a disgrace to the mighty pack.

One of the reasons I probably grow so slowly is because I am severely undernourished. Its been weeks now since I've had a real meal. They give me just enough to survive, and I really couldn't ask for more. Just being alive is selfish but I keep holding onto the hope that one day I'll find my mate or I'll stop being deformed and everything will get better.

I scrambled down the stairs and to my father, trying to get there as fast as I could. I don't really know why I try so hard to please him, it'll never work, but I still have this silly fantasy that one day I'll be enough. "Yes, Alpha Green." I said in my perfectly rehearsed, non-threatening voice.

"Why aren't you making breakfast yet?" He bellowed angrily, his chubby cheeks tinting red slightly, small bits of saliva flying out of his mouth.

I looked at my feet, avoiding eye contact at all cost, "I was just coming down, I apologi-" Before I could finish the sentence I was falling to the ground holding my cheek. I was weak from the lack of food, making the effect of the little punch much worse than it should've been. My head was spinning and my eyes were blurring.

"Breakfast, NOW!" He said, shaking his fist slightly

I just nodded calmly from the floor, sure to stay silent. Thankfully he was in a good mood and that seemed to satisfy him because he shook his fist at me one more time before stomping off. I scrambled back up to my feet before dashing to the kitchen to start breakfast. I whipped up some pancakes, eggs, french toast, bacon and sausages. The hunger pains were always so much worse while I was cooking but I knew better than to try and steal anything. Last time I did that I couldn't walk for a week.

I should have fast healing like werewolves, but mine is almost as slow as a human. I should have the speed and strength of a normal werewolf, hell, of an alpha, but I was a mere runt. I should be strong and dominant and impossible to mess with, but I was the pack's pushover.

Once breakfast was ready I waited for the bell to ring which signaled that I could enter the dining room to put all of the food on the table.

As soon as it rang I picked up all the plates, balancing them on my arms and even shoulders and promptly brought them into the dining room. I was only allowed to do one trip and if I dropped anything I got whipped.

I carefully placed all of the plates onto the table, ignoring the pack's judgmental stares, but just as I was about to put down the last one one of the pack warriors stuck his foot out, tripping me and causing me to drop the plate of strawberries. I heard the alpha's chair dragging, letting me know that he was standing up.

I laid on the ground silently, closing my eyes as Alpha's footsteps quickly approached.

My father grabbed me by my neck and stood up addressing the room politely. "I apologize for the inconvenience, eat your breakfast, I will go take care of it."

They all nodded gratefully before diving into the delicious food I made. The alpha dragged me by my neck outside, bumping me against the walls and several rocks once we got outside purposefully. About 10 years ago he built me my very own platform that was used for public punishments or whippings.

Today, he placed my head in the collar with spikes on it. If I moved or passed out I would stab myself in the neck. The spikes were small enough not to be fatal but let me tell you, they hurt like a bitch.

My father proceeded to whip me, but it wasn't just any whip. No, that would be too generous of him. This whip was coated in a snake venom, the venom of the benvo snake, known for being able to make the victim experience some of the most excruciating pain known to man. It was generally used in small doses for torturing our prisoners, they got the information they needed every single time, but they had an entire stash dedicated to yours truly.

"Count." He said before diving right into it.

Crack

"One"

Crack

"two"

Crack

"Three"

People were now gathering around to watch, like it was some sick form of entertainment. I guess after watching it happen this many times, it had become entertainment for them.

After 64 whips he finally stopped. Today was worse than usual but nothing I couldn't handle. My pain tolerance has seriously increased over the years, but of course so did the punishments.

Honestly at this point all I could think about were the new ugly scars that would surely mar my back, and the fact that this was my last decent shirt.

I guess I won't be getting food today.

I've never gone to school with the other kids, never got to watch television or gone on a pack run, but things could be worse. I could be a rogue with absolutely no food and no home at all, living my life on the run, just trying to stay alive. I'm lucky really, things won't get much better for a deformation like a me.

Once he was finally finished whipping me he poured a pan filled with boiling water on my back. The raw flesh that was exposed during the whippings was now burning and bubbling.

Fuck.

I held my breath, biting my tongue until it bled but I didn't let a single sound pass my lips.

Never show them how much they've hurt you. Never give them the satisfaction.

Once they were finished I went back inside and cleaned the entire house again. If it wasn't spotless they would beat me again and I didn't have the energy to endure another round today. I've been wearing the shirt I was whipped in all day because I officially have no more to change into.

It was very counterproductive to clean floors while simultaneously dripping blood onto them. This paired with my extensive injuries caused the usual house cleaning to take at least three times longer than usual.

Because of this I was in the alpha's section of the house much later than I would have liked to be. As I was cleaning I noticed one of the pack warriors entering the alpha's office.

I know I shouldn't eavesdrop, but what could really happen if they caught me? They kill me? Fine, go for it. They whip me? Not like I've never had that before. Might as well risk it. I pretended to be dusting a nearby lamp and moved close enough to the office to overhear them.

"Alpha Green? I have a request if you don't mind, sir."

The conversations were usually pretty boring, but it was also my only for of entertainment so I was in no position to be picky.

"What is it?" My father asked through a growl.

"Well, as you know I've just recently found my mate"

"Yes, I am aware. You better not be wasting my time, boy."

"Y-yes, of course Alpha. W-Well I- apparently she isn't ready to fuck yet, which I completely understand. But, she isn't really meeting my needs, sexually..."

"Continue" My father said, seeming to become a little more interested in wherever the conversation was going. I could hear the anticipation in his voice and that caused my stomach to instantly fill with dread.

"I was wondering if I could use the little runt. I have a couple buddies who would be happy to join in too, so it wouldn't just be me."

My stomach dropped along with the duster in my hand when his words processed.

"You want to have sex with my daughter?" My father asked, his voice swarming with excitement.

"Y-yes sir." The warrior spat out and I didn't even have to hear my father's response to know how screwed I truly was.

"20 bucks per person, and do me a favor and don't be too gentle."

There it is...

"Of course, Alpha. Thank you."

"maybe you could-" I stopped listening at that point, I'd heard more than enough to know I needed to get out of here.

I knew my father hated me but I never knew I was THAT much of a disappointment. I couldn't take it anymore, they've reached a whole new level of cruel.

Every time I think I've reached my breaking point they push me some more.

Before I knew what I was doing I ran. I ran out of the house and out into the forest as fast as I could, tears streaming down my face, branches cutting up my already battered body. There was not point shifting, my form was even slower than me so I persevered on foot. I somehow made it out of the woods and onto a Main Street. I walked along it until the squeaky sound of old breaks filled the air.

I didn't know anything about the world outside my pack, I was beyond sheltered. I would probably die alone within an hour of escaping, but even if it was my last hour, I'd know I tried. At least the last thing I did was brave.

A large city bus pulled up right next to me and the door swung open.

"Hey hun, are you ok?" The bus driver called out, her peppered grey hair falling into her face as she tilted her head a little at me.

"Uhh" I mumbled, glancing around nervously, unsure of what to say. My body was still pumping with adrenaline and at the first sign of danger I was ready to sprint away.

"Want to get out of here?" She asked softly and I nodded frantically, "Hop on."

I got on the bus, thanking the bus driver quietly, my body still shaking as I took in the empty seats. Thank god there wasn't anyone in here, I'm sure I was a sight, covered in bruises and blood, my oversized shirt almost falling off of my skinny frame.

Who knows what people would do if they saw a weak and helpless girl all alone. I shivered at the possibilities.

"What's your name sweetheart?" She asked, her voice soothing enough to calm me slightly.

"E-Ellie." I stuttered, still on high alert.

"What a beautiful name. How old are you Ellie?"

I shrugged, biting my tongue in embarrassment.

"Do you want to explain to me who you're running from?"

Was it that obvious that I was running from someone? I glanced behind me nervously, still worried they'd somehow find me.

"Home." I whispered, still in shock from the conversation I had overheard.

"You're telling me you lived in the forest?" I hesitated for a minute. Right, they don't know about the pack lands, no human did.

"Ummm" I sputtered out like an idiot, completely prepared to jump off the moving bus if the conversation got any worse.

Great job Ellie, make this situation more suspicious.

We came to a stop and she leaned over and whispered in my ear, "Werewolf? Blood Thunder Pack?" My eyes widened in surprise as I nodded and she just nodded her head along with me.

"I'm guessing you need a place to stay?"

I nodded again, not trusting my weak voice. Where could I go? I wasn't strong enough to hunt for myself and I had no money. Maybe I could find a human homeless shelter to stay at until I figure things out.

I can't die now. My life can't just be that abuse. If that's all I will ever had then they should've just killed me when I was born, saved us all the trouble.

"Well you're welcome to stay with me sweetheart. We're not exactly rich or anything but we could still help if you need."

"R-really?" I asked, shocked by her kindness.

"Of course."

"That would be wonderful." I managed a small smile. They'll kick me out when they find out I'm Alpha Green's deformation of a daughter, but maybe by then I will have a plan figured out.

"Okay, its settled" She said with a large smile, her slightly crooked teeth and display. "I have to finish my rounds before we head over to my house so make yourself comfortable."

"Thank you" I said, my voice filled with relief, the adrenaline starting to wear off. I limped over to one of the empty seats and sighed out as I finally got to sit down, my body screaming at me.

"I'm Jamie by the way." The lady called out and I smiled slightly.

I leaned my head against the window, fighting to keep my eyes open as I watched my life become farther and farther until it disappeared.

The scary part was that I wasn't sure whether to be happy and relieved or terrified.

Two

"Stay positive, all other choices are pointless punishments to your psyche."

- Joe Peterson

Her house was a quaint little townhouse that looked slightly worn down, but to me it was the most beautiful thing I had ever seen. I saw it as my safety, even if it was only temporary.

Jamie glanced over at me hesitantly, her face looking slightly embarrassed. "Look, I know its not much, but -" She said, nervously glancing at her adorable home.

"No, its amazing!" I cut her off bravely, shocking both her and myself.

She smiled widely at me and nodded, "Well, let's head on in and I'll show you around."

The house, as small as it was, was beautifully decorated. None of the items were expensive, but they were amazing all the same.

"I'm guessing you don't have any other clothes?" She asked, cringing a little at my ripped up shirt and jeans. I shook my head.

Our pack house was overly fancy, you couldn't even live in it without messing it up. It was too perfect and I was mostly to thank for that. This place was much much more comfortable, not to mention it had MUCH less to clean.

"Okay, well make yourself comfortable and I'll go find you something to wear."

I was still taken aback every time she was kind to me. I kept thinking this was some sort of dream. I sat on the floor next to the rug and made myself comfortable like she instructed.

She came back out with a pile of clothes in her arms.

"Oh sweetheart, why are you sitting on the floor?" My eyes widened in realization. "I'm so sorry!" I said, standing up and moving to stand to the side.

"What are you doing?"

"You said you didn't want me sitting on the floor." I said nervously, numbing with my fingers as I shifted from one foot to the other. It's not like I can just start levitating, I need to be somewhere.

"You can sit on the floor if you want but don't you want to sit on the couch?" She clarified and my breath got caught in my throat.

"The c-couch?"

"Yes"

I stared at her with wide eyes. The couch... I've never been allowed to sit on the couch. She looked at me with pity in her eyes as she handed me the clothes in her hands. They were beautiful, new clothes.

"Now I know these aren't the nicest clothes and they're a little worn, but its the best I can do for now."

"What?! These clothes are amazing! Actually, I can't take these. I'm sorry." I exclaimed, thrusting the pile of soft fabrics back into her arms.

"Why not?" She said sternly, refusing to take the pile back.

"They're too nice. Clothes don't last long with me, it'll be a waste." I explained, trying to give them back to her. I usually didn't argue this much but she needed to understand.

"Put them on." She said with a finality in her voice that left no room for argument. I sighed heavily before stripping off my shirt to put on the new one and I heard a little gasp.

I turned towards the little sound and found Jamie with her hands clasped over her mouth. Her eyes started to fill with tears as she took in the train wreck that is my body.

I squirmed a little more than uncomfortable with all the attention.

"Oh, Ellie, what did they do to you?" She whispered out and I just continued my awkward shuffle, throwing the new, oversized shirt on.

"Its fine." I said, waving my hand slightly but she quickly shook her head, a small tear flowing down her cheek.

"Its not fine." She spat out, her voice harsher than I'd ever heard it and I flinched slightly. She looked at me sympathetically before speaking more softly. "Let's get you some food shall we? When's the last time you've eaten a proper meal?"

"I-I don't know." I said, embarrassed.

"What?"

I had half a burnt piece toast someone didn't want a couple weeks ago, that was pretty good but it didn't seem like Jamie would be happy with that response so I just shrugged. Alpha was in a good mood that day.

If I were human I'd be long dead.

"So how do you know about werewolves?"

"My mate's a were." I nodded, surprised. Werewolves very rarely had human mates. It happened probably only 1% of the time.

"Where is he?" I asked curiously, noticing an old picture of Jamie, a large man with red hair and a little girl I guessed was their daughter.

"He belongs to the pack up north, the Belle Foret Pack. He commutes pretty far every day but there's no human settlements down there. He needed a pack, even though I couldn't, and he wasn't about to join the Blood Thunder one. He should be home soon actually."

I felt my heart rate pick up once she said that. In my experience, men were easier to set off than women. I can't feel the pain anymore but it would be a shame to ruin these clothes.

Right in that moment I heard the door open and suddenly I was being held against the wall by my neck.

I struggled against the hand pinning to the wall but I was weak. I kicked and slapped the man that was holding me but he didn't even budge. I started to panic. After all this, after I finally escaped I was going to be killed by some random guy for a reason I don't even know.

My vision was starting to go black from the lack of oxygen as my lungs burned. Just as I was about to black out the hand was removed from my throat and I fell to the ground, gasping for air. I could feel my neck begin to bruise, but at least I wasn't dead.

I felt a hand on my shoulder and jolted away, backing up as quickly as possible, scrambling on the floor in panic. I can't die this way. My vision was blurring in panic as I sat in the corner, hyperventilating.

After a few minutes, my vision started to clear and my breathing began to slow. Once it did I could make out a worried face in front of me. It was Jamie and she looked extremely concerned. Her face calmed me and I felt myself relax again. I was safe with her. She saved me.

I finally relaxed. "Sorry." I said.

"Oh, my dear why are you apologizing?! I am so terribly sorry for that, I'm so sorry!"

This was the first time someone had actually apologized to me, it was weird.

"Its fine, don't worry." I assured her, its not like I haven't had worse.

"Its not fine, and I'll make it up to you."

After that I finally noticed the presence behind her, making me tense up again. I looked into his face and it seemed to be filled with regret.

Jamie noticed me staring and took the opportunity to introduce us. "Ellie, this is my mate, Henry." I gave him a small smile, which he returned, a little relief washing over his face.

Now that I saw him up close, he definitely looked like someone Jamie would be with. He had red hair and green eyes. He had a little scruff over his jaw and freckles across his cheeks. He looked like he was a nice guy, which Jamie truly deserved.

Jamie helped me up, even though I didn't really need it, she seemed to have a need to help in some way, so I let her think she was making a difference. She brought me to their dining room, which was beautiful decorated, again.

"Your house is so beautiful, who decorated it?"

Jamie blushed a little, "I did." She said a little quietly.

"Wow, if I ever get my own place you are definitely decorating it."

Jamie was about to say something when she was cut off by Henry blurting out, "I am so sorry Ellie!" His eyes were wide, his cheeks tinted pink and he was speaking much louder than necessary.

"Its fine, really." I replied calmly and at a normal volume.

"No its not, look at the bruises on your neck, I'm surprised you're not in more visible pain!" he continued.

I poked it a little, shrugging, "Thank you for letting me stay in your home." I said changing the subject since it seemed like Henry wasn't planning on letting this go.

"You're welcome anytime, Ellie. Do you mind if I ask who your parents are?"

I shifted uncomfortably at his question, horrible memories coming back up.

"Ellie, come here." Called my mother.

I scurried over as fast as my tiny feet could take me. I had turned 4 three days ago, maybe I would receive one of those presents I'd heard so much about.

"Yes Momma?"

"What did I tell you about calling me that?"

"I'm sorry, I just-"

My sentence was cut off by my mother slapping me. I fell to the ground in pain, holding my cheek. Why did Momma always hit me? When I see other kids their parents protect them. They were always shielding their children from me, keeping them safe.

"How old are you, runt?"

"I just turned 4!" I said proudly, holding up four fingers.

"Good, you're old enough for whippings now then."

Momma took a hold of my hair, like she often did when she guided me places, I don't know why she did it, I really didn't like it, but when I would complain she'd just pull harder.

She brought me down to the basement where she hung my hands from the ceiling, it was really uncomfortable.

"What's 3+82?" She asked.

"96?"

She whipped me. "Wrong. What is 37+95?"

"100?"

She whipped me again. It hurt so much I let out a scream that time. Why was momma doing this? It hurt a lot more than the slaps did.

"What's 88+24?"

"I-I I DON'T KNOW!"

She whipped me.

"WHY ARE YOU DOING THIS?" I screamed, crying in pain.

"Im doing this for your own good, Ellie. My child is already a runt, I won't let her be an idiot too."

This went on until I passed out. I woke up in the basement with the door locked. That was the first night I ever spent in the basement.

I was brought back out of my thoughts by Henry. "If you don't feel comfortable talking about it, don't worry. I didn't mean to upset you or push you in any way, I just want to understand what's happened, maybe see how I can help."

I looked to him but before I could say anything he cut me off, turning frantic again.

"Shit! I just keep fucking up! Of course you don't want to talk about it I mean look at you!"

My eyes widened and Jamie smacked Henry across the back of his head. Giving him a look that said shut the fuck up before you dig yourself into a hole.

"No, its fine, I can tell you." I took a deep breath. "Alpha and Luna Green are my parents."

They both looked at me shocked for a long while. They finally closed their mouthes when I cleared my throat, conveying how weirder out I was by their reaction.

"I'm sorry, I just- you're the deformation?" Said Henry, earning himself another smack over the head from Jamie.

I flinched at the name and nodded my head, looking at the table, "Yep, that's me. The great Alpha Green's runt. I guess the whole world knows about it, huh?"

Henry nodded, what he said finally dawning on him. "I didn't mean to be rude, I'm sorry... again."

"Don't be sorry, its the truth."

"I don't believe that." Jamie said sternly.

"trust me, its true."

"You must be starving." Jamie changed the subject. "Dinner?"

I nodded my head, standing up and heading to the kitchen. It was a quaint kitchen, but I could work with it. I immediately started pulling out ingredients. I didn't have a lot of energy, but when I did something too simple, like pasta, I got beaten. I had to find that sweet spot between time consuming and simple.

I landed on an easy chicken parmesan, noticing they had all of the ingredients. I pulled out enough for the two of them, and a little extra just in case and began preparing.

Jamie walked in, looking confused. "What are you doing?"

"I was thinking chicken parmesan, but of course if you don't like that or if its too easy I can make almost anything."

"I thought you went to the bathroom, honey, why are you cooking?" She asked again.

"I'm sorry, I don't understand."

"I was going to cook, why would you take it upon yourself to do so?"

"You are going to cook?"

"Yes, of course."

"Wow, I never get help, you are so nice."

"Honey, I'm saying you don't have to cook, I'll do it all, unless you want to cook of course."

"I..." It took a minute for what she was saying to sink in. "I don't have to cook?"

"No, of course not. You are our guest of honor! Now go get yourself comfortable on the couch and watch some television or something. If you need anything don't hesitate to ask Henry or me." She said shooing me playfully.

I confusedly walked into the living room and sat on the couch. Television. I've always dreamed of trying it. If only I knew how...

I tried to think back to the pack members using it, but I was always so concentrated on trying to remain invisible and finish up my cleaning for the day so I never really saw how it worked.

I looked at it, completely and utterly confused. I walked up to it and poked the screen but nothing happened. I even tapped it firmly a couple times and it still didn't turn on. "Uhhh, hello there tv, uhhh on? Tv on?" I said to it, trying to figure it out.

"Need some help?" Came a voice from behind me. I turned around to reveal Henry standing there, looking concerned yet slightly amused.

I smiled sheepishly at him. "I've never used a television before." I confessed.

"Ya, I got that once you started speaking to it" He chuckled softly to himself. "Here, let me help."

He pulled out what I then recognized as a remote and clicked a button. Next thing I knew the screen was lit up and there were people playing sports on the screen.

"Wow" I said, completely enthralled by the tv.

While Jamie prepared dinner, Henry told me all about the tv. He explained the remote to me and what each of the buttons do, he explained the sport they were playing on the screen and he told me all about commercials.

By the time my lesson was done, Jamie came out with two plates that smelled like heaven.

"Dinner's ready!" She called. Henry and I both stood up. He went and sat down at the dinning table while I stood just outside the room by the door, my stomach growling loudly at the sight of the delicious food. She had made the chicken parmesan I had gathered the ingredients for. Maybe there will be scraps and I'll finally get to try some, it was a lot of pack members favorite.

Alpha Green never let me have any of this, he said it was too good for me and sent me to bed without food. He never fed me nearly enough, I don't know how the hell I'm still alive.

Jamie came back in with a third plate of food which made my face twist up in confusion. Was there another person joining that I didn't notice? I looked around the room again to see if I missed something, but no, no one was there.

"Well, come on Ellie, don't you want to eat?" Jammie asked, finishing setting up the table.

"There are leftovers?" I asked, excitement filling my face. I finally get to try chicken parmesan. It smells so good!

"There are if you're still hungry."

"Still hungry?" I muttered to myself.

"Come on, now, sit down before it gets cold." It finally dawned on me that that third plate was meant for me and that they were going to not only give me food but let me eat it with them.

This was the best day ever. Tv and food! How can it get any better?

I smiled a huge smile as I joined them. They seemed a little confused by my happiness, but I didn't care. It had been so long since I'd really honestly smiled.

The dinner was amazing. I couldn't finish it, my stomach being too small, but it was even better than I had ever imagined. Jamie kept pressuring me to eat more, but I had eaten so much I felt this strange sort of bursting feeling coming from my stomach. I'd never eaten so much in my life, it felt amazing.

"You must be exhausted." Henry spoke up. I've noticed he's a little more on the quiet side compared to Jamie, but he seems like a genuinely good guy. Sure, he almost choked me to death, but so have dozens of other people.

"Yeah, I'm pretty tired if I'm honest, its been a long day." I said carefully, unsure if what I was saying could come across as offensive.

"Why don't I show you to your room?" Jamie asked and I coked my head slightly.

"Shouldn't I clean the kitchen first?" I asked.

"No dear, that's not your job, Henry will clean the kitchen. I cook and he cleans, it's our arrangement. Now, let's get you all set up for tonight, ya?"

I nodded my head, giving her another grateful smile. I had smiled more tonight than I had in the last year. She led me through a small hallway and opened a door to an absolutely stunning room. It had a nice big window on the back wall and all of the walls were painted a calming white with navy blue accents. The bedding looked like it were fit for a queen.

"Th-this is for me?"

"Of course, dear, like I said, you're our guest of honor."

I looked around amazed. Jamie noticed this and spoke up, "What was your old room like?" She said carefully.

I just stayed silent, figuring again that she wouldn't like may answer. She accepted that as answer enough for today at least and continued on, shaking off her concern at my silence. That would be a problem for another day.

"Now, I feel like this shouldn't have to be said but I want to make absolutely sure. You understand that I want you to sleep on the bed, right?"

Three

What if I told you that 10 years from now, your life would be exactly the same? I doubt you'd be happy. So, why are you so afraid of change?

--Karen Salmansohn

I have been living with Jamie and Henry for about 4 months now. They taught me all about life, which apparently I wasn't living. They told me all about themselves and I occasionally told them about my old life. I didn't like talking about it, it always seemed to make them sad.

It turns out they have a daughter around my age who lives at the pack house up north, they were even talking about transferring me up there. The way they describe it makes it seem like heaven, but I don't exactly have the best experiences from my last pack house.

"Hey Ellie, can I talk to you about something?" Henry asked, jogging down the stairs, a small frown on his face.

"Ya, of course, what's up Henry?" I said confidently making him smile a small proud father smile before frowning again.

"I made an appointment with my alpha to see about you joining our pack. The situation is really complicated though, he's not sure if he can help us out. It'll be hard for you to officially join a pack because they will then be at risk at going into war with your old pack. The thing is, the Blood Thunder pack is one of the largest and most powerful in the area, it could be devastating to go to war with a pack like that, and Belle Foret just doesn't have the resources for that kind of thing."

"I understand." I said, trying to smile through to make Henry feel better. "Thank you for trying." I added.

He put a lot into talking with the alpha and trying to find a place for me and I couldn't be more grateful to him and Jamie.

He nodded, pity in his eyes. I've really begun to hate when people look at me like that. It doesn't help me in any way, just makes me feel pathetic.

"So what's the count today?" Henry said, changing the subject. I've been weighing myself daily to make sure I'm gaining enough weight.

"105 lbs" I said with a smile. When I arrived I was way underweight and Henry has been working with me to fix that since I got here.

I'm almost 5'7, so still a little under average, but heavier than I ever thought I could be.

"That's amazing!" He said, a giant smile on his face while he picked me up and spun me.

It really was amazing. I looked and felt a million times healthier than I ever had. My senses have gotten so much better too, I felt like a whole new person.

The only thing weighing me down, cuffing me to my old life was my deformation.

I hadn't shifted once since I arrived here. I don't want them to see my form, once they do, I know they'll abandon me. They think I exaggerate when I tell them I'm a disgrace to my parents but if they were to see me I'm almost 100% sure they'd agree.

Apparently Henry used to be a pack warrior but retired early for his mate. Now he occasionally gets called in for emergencies but rarely fights.

They brought me to the stores for the first time a couple weeks after I'd arrived and bought me some clothes. I made sure to pick out the cheapest stuff I could find, I knew they didn't have a lot of money and taking up any at all made me like I was being strangled with guiilt.

That's the main reason I wanted to get into this pack. I couldn't live with Jamie and Henry forever. It takes a lot of money to take care of a whole other person and I've even noticed them both taking a bunch of extra shifts which made me feel even worse.

I would get a job if I could, but I have no experience and I haven't quite worked through all of my issues with strangers.

Henry would bring me out into public as often as he could and it definitely helped more than I could say, but I still had that lingering fear that wouldn't seem to let go. Every time someone raises a hand near me, even if it's to simply grab something on a high shelf a flinch really hard and back away.

One time some random guy saw that we had the same shoes and tried to high five me. It was so embarrassing when I accidentally threw myself into a clothes rack, knocking everything down. Everyone was really nice about it and the guy felt really bad, but that just made me feel even worse about the whole thing.

I couldn't even go shopping without making a scene!

There were a few setbacks, that example brought on one of the worst but we've worked through it and there are less and less incidents.

"The meeting will be in 2 weeks. My Jen (his daughter) has actually decided to come down and meet you and help you prepare." He said, lighting up when he brought her up. I couldn't help but envy how proud he was and how much he loved his daughter. I was so excited to meet the person who could make her parents so happy.

I hope the girl knew how lucky she was to have such kind parents.

A few hours later I heard the door open and a girl's voice fill the air, "I'M HOME BITCHES!" She yelled. I immediately knew it was Jen, Jamie had warned me she might be a little loud. I made my way towards the door slowly, to say I was nervous was an understatement. I really wanted this girl to like me, I wasn't ready to go out on my own and I'm sure if she wanted to she could get me kicked out.

"Jennifer, language!" Jamie scolded with a smile on her face and went to go hug the little redhead that was at the door. She looked a lot like Jamie in her facial features, they were delicate and cute, but she had her father's bright hair and green eyes.

She didn't look like a threat but the worst ones never did. It was the little ones who hit me the hardest, probably trying to make up for their size.

As Henry went to go hug his daughter Jamie noticed me standing by the door. "Come on in, Ellie, come meet my daughter. Don't worry, she wouldn't hurt you." She said, waving me over.

I cautiously walked over, my eyes never leaving Jen. Once she finished hugging her father she turned to me. "Hi there, I'm Jen!" She exclaimed excitedly with a big smile on her face, extending her hand. She looked nice which made me relax a little but I was still very prudent.

"Nice to meet you, I'm Ellie." I said while shaking her hand, my voice a lot more confident than I felt.

"Its crazy that I'm finally meeting you! I've heard so much about you I feel like I already know you!" She said and I felt myself begin to relax slightly. She seemed nice.

We all moved to the living room while Jen continued to talk to me about all kinds of things.

"So, the alpha's coming soon and we have to get you ready. I am one of the top warriors in our pack, taking after my dad, so I know just what the alpha wants to see. We'll get you completely ready in the next couple weeks, so don't stress, I've got you bitch."

"Language." Jamie muttered for what felt like the millionth time today.

Jen put her hands up in mock surrender before returning to ranting about how ready I'm going to be for the Alpha.

****

The next morning I was awoken by Jen bursting into my room. "Wake up sleeping beauty, it's time to get moving! Let's get this shit on the road!" She yelled while opening the blinds. I groaned a little, but didn't dare complain.

Beds were so comfortable, how did people get out of these every day? I sometimes wish I could just spend the entire day in bed and just never get out. The bed I had at Blood Thunder was really squeaky and hard, but this one felt like a million pillows stacked underneath me.

"Training day one! Gotta whip you into shape to impress Alpha James!"

I cringed slightly at her wording before reluctantly stretching and getting ready for the day. Jen instructed me to wear workout clothes so I threw on my new grey sweatpants and a black long sleeved top, just about enough to cover the scars that were finally beginning to fade. It was a gorgeous day out. I lived in a suburb of New York. Its August right now, so its starting to get a little cold but as my health was ameliorating, that was becoming less and less of a problem.

Jen was waiting for me by the door when I came out.

"Oh my god, you're so gorgeous!" She exclaimed, her eyes wide as she placed her hands on her face, feigning shock.

"Thanks" I said awkwardly, "so are you."

Yikes, I'm awful at this.

"I know right! Its just one of those days I guess! You know, when you wake up and you're like damn girl, okay I see you! Alright anyways, so I just want to see where you're at real quick then I can build a training plan based on your abilities, that way you'll for sure be ready in two weeks."

I looked at her, impressed that she could do all that.

"I know, I'm amazing right?"

We started with a run, and I actually found it really easy. I was keeping Jen's pace with no problem. Sensing this she picked up her pace. I burned out pretty quickly but it was definitely better than I was expecting. We ran about 3 km and it took me about a half hour. Not great, but not terrible.

"Bitch that was amazing! Much less work than I was expecting!" She said with a smile.

Next we did a ton of planks and some really slow lunges, pushups and squats. They definitely burned a lot and at one point my muscles were actually shaking under the strain, making us laugh a little.

Jen was amazing at all of these things, she must have trained a lot. We finished off the workout with some hand to hand combat and some knife work. I was completely awful at that, I never realized someone could be so uncoordinated. It was safe to say that I had a long way to go before I was ready.

We did this same routine every day. Each day we picked up the pace and distance of the run until I physically couldn't continue.

Once we had exhausted that we started hand to hand combat. The knife training was Jen's best area. She was amazing with them, moving around me in fluid movements, occasionally doing little tricks. A smile plastered to her face the entire time we worked with them.

We had really bonded over the last couple of weeks too. I was no longer nervous around her, she was such a nice person, just like her parents. I could only imagine how great my life would've been if I was born into this family instead of my own.

They already felt more like my family than my real parents ever did. I even saw Jen as the sister I never had.

The night before the alpha came I could barely sleep I was so nervous. There were a lot of reasons for the pack to not let me in and they seemed to be building up. I couldn't stay here anymore, I could see them starting to stress about the money and I could never do that to them. If they didn't let me in I would figure something else out, even if it meant returning to my old pack.

I would gladly be unhappy to let them live happily. It would be selfish of me not to.

Four

- -

Never confuse a single defeat with a final defeat.

--F. Scott Fitzgerald

Today's the day.

The alpha will be here in about an hour and everyone is hectic. My life could go either way now, either it will get much worse or impossibly better.

I'm obviously hoping for the latter but I will deal with whatever I get. I'm not stupid, I realize that the likelihood of me getting into their pack is slim to none. I won't let myself believe that it all goes right because from my past experiences that's only ever brought me pain.

We were all running around, cleaning the house, making sure it was spotless for the alpha. Henry's been in the kitchen all day, cooking, it smells amazing and my stomach won't stop growling. I hope I eat before the alpha comes because with his alpha hearing there's no chance he won't hear it, which would be so embarrassing.

My stomach growled again but even louder, causing Jamie to speak up. "Ellie, go grab some food before the alpha comes. If I can hear it I can't even imagine how loud it'll be to the alpha." She said, laughing at the blush that formed on my cheeks.

I went into the kitchen and just as Henry was about to kick me out my stomach made another super loud growl that stopped the words just as they were about to leave his mouth. He pulled a leftover burger out of the fridge and handed it to me.

"Thank you so much" I said softly, digging in. I definitely wasn't eating like a 'lady', thank god Jamie couldn't see me.

I gulped it down in 30 seconds, thanking Henry again. He just laughed at me, nodding. While I was recovering my appetite was humongous. It wasn't at all cheap to feed me which was another reason why whichever way this meeting went, I'd find a way to unburden Jamie and Henry.

I was dusting a corner when I heard a car drive up. It was the alpha, I could already feel the power coming off him. My heartbeat was flying out the window as we went to meet him outside, the familiar presence bringing back bad memories.

He gave a small smile and nod to Henry. "Good to see you Henry, Jamie, Jen." They all dipped their heads submissively in return.

The man was huge and had impeccable posture. His gaze was calculating as he looked me over. I couldn't help but cower, slouching and tucking my head slightly. Henry and Jen had tried their best to help me gain more confidence, but there was only so much the could do with the short amount of time we were given.

The hope is that one day I grow into my Alpha genes, but there's no way to be sure whether the damage I've accumulated over the years is permanent or not.

"You must be Ellie." He said authoritatively and I nodded, shaking ever so slightly.

"Y-yes, and you must be the famous Alpha James I've heard so much about." I said softly, cringing at how pathetic my voice came out.

"I have to admit, you're not what I was expecting... You're Alpha Green's daughter, correct?"

"Yes s-sir." My voice was shaky as I shifted from one foot to the other, nervously biting my lip.

"Very interesting..." He said, eyeing me up and down making me even more uncomfortable.

"Alpha, won't you come in. We can sit and have some food." Jamie chirped. Since she wasn't a werewolf she wouldn't feel the power rolling off of the alpha, so she happily stepped in to keep everything moving smoothly.

"Yes of course, let's go." He said with a nod, his lips twitching up into something that resembled a smile.

We all sat around the couch and like always, I made sure I was the last to sit. The alpha was the first, of course, and I was the last.

"I was told you were a runt, or, to put it nicer, a deformation?"

Not sure that's 'putting it nicer' but okay.

"Yes sir." I said, nodding my head slightly. I could feel that Henry wanted to intervene but I shot him a quick look to shut him up. Him trying to stand up for me wouldn't do any of us any good. We didn't need to be on another alpha's bad side, especially since he hadn't actually insulted me. He was just stating facts.

"Could you shift for me? I'd like to see what all the fuss is about. I've only ever heard of such things but never actually had a chance to witness it for myself." He said and I saw Jamie's face turn red, her hands balling up.

For some reason seeing how angry Jamie was, and how much she wanted to stand up for me calmed me.

"I would really not be comfortable with that sir." I said a little more confidently. He couldn't push me on this point.

"I understand." He said, surprising me. You are going to have to answer some personal questions though." He added, a warning in his voice.

"Of course, sir."

"Why did you leave the Blood Thunder pack?"

I paused for a minutes, thinking how to say this less bluntly but decided to just get out with it. "They were torturing me which I could deal with but then they... well I overheard them discussing raping me so..." I said and we all cringed collectively.

"If they hadn't threatened rape, do you think you would have left?" He responded carefully. I could tell he didn't want to be asking these questions but he had to keep his pack safe. That was more important than avoiding an uncomfortable conversation.

"Alpha, is this really necessary?" Henry cut in but I shook my head at him.

"Its fine Henry." I said and Jamie grabbed his hand in hers, her face tinged red.

He shot me an unsure look but I continued.

"Probably not, just because there wasn't a life for me to run to outside of the pack. Even when I did decide to leave I-I second guessed my self and debated it a lot. I - um - I thought my only other option was to be homeless and I wasn't at all healthy enough to survive. However, that being said, I want to make it obvious that I don't believe in anything the pack does. The fact that I was beaten in public because I was born different is an obvious problem, yes, but it was more than that. The alpha was extremely controlling. He used to control the food for the entire pack and withheld it as punishment. He's killed countless people for no reason and started wars that never needed to be started. He was greedy and it showed in the way he ruled and the environment I was raised in. "

I'd talked a lot about this with Henry and Jamie, that was the only reason I was so easily able to put my experience into words. When they said they would get me ready for this interview, they didn't mean just physically. Every night Henry and I would sit down and discuss the things the alpha might ask me so I'd be as prepared as possible.

The alpha looked a little shocked by my little speech, as did everyone else. We were all surprised I was being so forward with a total stranger.

"Well put." He nodded, "As you probably know, the Belle Foret pack is very small. Every pack member between the ages of 15 and 85" (werewolves age faster until they reach 20 years old, stop, then at around 85 begin to age much quicker) "are required to fight. Are you willing and capable?"

"I've been working on it." I replied unsurely, ringing my hands together nervously.

He frowned, "You'll have to do and pass a mandatory fitness check, not only for the pack's safety but yours as well. I don't want you going any-where you're not ready for."

I nodded, looking at my shoes. It was all going too well, I just knew something had to go bad. He silently stood up and walked out of the door, all of us automatically following.

"We'll start with running." He said sternly then gestured for me to start. I immediately raced off faster than I ever had. After 2 weeks I was already starting to see an improvement, but it's impossible to tell whether or not it will be enough.

After 20 minutes I was breathing hard, my vision blurring and my pace almost walking. I tried to push on but the alpha grabbed my arm, making me jump back in alarm and shield myself.

Alpha's eyebrows scrunched as he frowned at me, taking in my exhausted body, sweat dripping down my cheeks so thickly it looked like I was crying.

We walked back to the house in silence and I knew that was a bad sign. A part of me hoped I'd still get in but once I saw the alpha shake his head gravely and I saw Henry, Jen and Jamie's faces fall I knew that I had failed.

Once the alpha left everyone was very quiet. I think we had all hoped that by some miracle I'd be let in but we should have known better.

As soon as we all settled back in, digesting the news, I began my plan. I'd be long gone by the morning.

I couldn't tell Jamie or Henry, I know they are too nice and would insist that I stay, but I also know that I can't do that. It just isn't fair to anyone and I have already overstayed my welcome.

We all went to bed, no one really said anything, I think everyone was still processing. While I would've liked to say goodbye and have one last happy evening together this was probably better.

Once the clock hit 2am I decided it was safe to assume everyone would be in a nice deep sleep. I grabbed a bag full of necessities, trying to leave as much as I could, only taking what I absolutely needed to survive.

I climbed out of my second story window, somehow scaling down the side without dying. I smiled sadly as I took in the adorable little town house. My safe space.

I didn't want to leave, but I couldn't stay. I left a note on my bed so I didn't need to worry about Jamie and Henry freaking out. Everything would be okay, they didn't need a little runt ruining things for them.

I'd find my place, my safety, my happiness. It's easy to let myself believe that this is the only option, but in reality this is the only easy option. There are plenty of less self centered choices and when it came down to it I'd chose their happiness over my own every time.

I could take the pain, I was used to it, but I would never wish any on anyone else.

I walked off into the streets, my bag strapped onto my shoulders tightly as I began my journey. Tears burned my eyes but I didn't let a single fall. No.

Even if my life was going to be a little harder, the relief I know Jamie and Henry are surely feeling made it all worth it. They were getting too attached to me, and that wouldn't end well for anyone.

I walked down the long, winding quiet streets, trying to remember the route Jamie took when she brought me here.

I was no doubt going to get a good beating from my parents for leaving like I did, but if I survive I will make the most out of my situation and go on as best as I can. Henry and Jamie have taught me so much, but the thing I will hang onto the most while I'm back at that pack is that I am worth something to someone.

I may not be worth a lot, but Henry and Jamie would be sad if I died, and they deserve so much more than crying over me because I wasn't strong enough to hang on for them. Until the day comes when there is absolutely no hope and I am worth nothing to anyone, I will go on. I will fight and I will persevere.

I heard a car starting to head down the road and glanced up at it, hanging onto my back pack a little tighter as the car slowed down to a stop next to me.

Next thing I knew there was something pressed to my nose and I was forced to breathe in whatever soaked the fabric.

My vision started to blur and my ears began to ring as I swayed on my feet, trying to make sense of what was going on.

All I saw was dizzying darkness before everything faded and I was plunged into a restless sleep plagued with nightmares.

Five

"A single thread of hope is still a very powerful thing"

- Unknown

I opened my eyes to be met with darkness. I blinked a couple more times to be sure but nothing was making sense.

As my senses returned to me I realized I was sitting in a chair but as I went to get up I couldn't move my arms or legs.

It all came crashing back to me as my memories replayed in my mind like a movie. What the hell?

I now put all the pieces together and realized I was cuffed tightly to a chair, a blindfold blocking my vision.

I tried to yank and pull at the restraints but there was no use, they were very well built. This clearly wasn't an amateur job, I really wanted to be impressed despite the shit I seemed to have landed in.

As if someone sensed that I was awake I heard the door opened and listened closely as heels clicked towards me. They came to a stop and my blindfold was ripped off my face roughly.

I had to blink my eyes a couple times to adjust to the bright white lights that were illuminating the room harshly, but once I did it revealed a beautiful tall blonde who shot me a bright smile when she noticed I was awake.

"Hi there!" She said as she came in, taking a seat in the chair across from me, her curls bouncing with each movement. My hair was curly too and I wondered if it did the same thing when I moved. I looked down at my hair with a frown and the girl tilted her head at me.

I was contemplating the bounciness of my hair when I realized she was waiting for me to respond.

"Uhhhh hi?" I said, narrowing my eyes a little in her direction.

"You must have a lot of questions." She said right off the bat, twirling one of her curls around her finger while pursing her lips slightly.

"Ya, no shit." I said, rolling my eyes. I have no idea where the confidence was coming from, but I wasn't complaining.

I'd seemed to reach a numb state where I was just too tired to care. If she wanted to torture and kill me she could go right ahead. I couldn't be bothered to watch myself. I was done.

"Okay, well basically your father, Alpha Green put a bounty on your head, its worth a five hundred thousand dollars! Can you believe that?!" She said, with the same cheery attitude. "We've been watching you for months but those stupid caretakers of yours never seem to leave your side. I was starting to think we'd just have to take the messy way and get you through them so you can imagine my elation when I heard you had taken it upon yourself to leave and offer yourself right up to us on a platter!"

I knew I should be scared or shocked but her voice was just too nice. It's not that she didn't seem threatening, I'm sure she could do some serious damage, but I just couldn't find myself wanting to cower in front of her. She seemed, friendly? But not friendly.

I really don't know how I could explain this paradox of a person.

"So, you're turning me in to my father?" I asked, bored. I mean, I was heading there anyways. She really just saved me the long trip.

She tilted her head a little, narrowing her eyes at me. "Your father also said that if he got you back with a few new scars he'd up the price to seven hundred thousand." She said, a smile still gracing her lips as she told me she was about to torture me then hand me back to my dad.

I rolled my eyes. Classic. "That's dad" I said casually. I was honestly kind of surprised he bothered putting a bounty on me. I really had no idea I was worth that much to them.

She scrunched up her nose and I was kind of satisfied with how taken aback she looked. I doubted anyone ever really one up-ed her craziness. She was probably used to people cowering from her wrongly placed cheery attitude, but my aloofness towards my own father torturing me seemed to top that.

She was silent for a second before she smirked. "I like you." She said, a devilish smile on her face.

I tilted my head, frowning a little.

"I'm sorry, you're really pretty and all and I'm sure plenty of people would be very excited, but I'm straight." I explained and she snorted, leaning back in her chair.

"So, tell me. What did you do to make your father so angry? Steal some-thing? Kill someone?"

I laughed sarcastically. "I was born." I deadpanned but the girl didn't show an ounce of pity.

"I haven't called your father yet, I thought it would be some nice mental torture to call him while you're in the room. However, I'm starting to think I won't call him at all..." She continued to swirl a curl around her finger before nodding to herself, as if she had just decided on something she was debating. "I like you, and I don't like a lot of people."

"Okay? Can I go then?" I responded skeptically and she rolled her eyes.

"No. I've decided I'm going to keep you."

There was a beat of silence before I responded, "no."

"You're clearly homeless, shouldn't you be like, I don't know, groveling at my feet?"

I thought foe a second. "No." I shook my head and she smiled widely.

"Okay. I like you even more now. You've convinced me, I'm keeping you."

I shook my head, done with her bullshit.

She sighed, leaning back in her seat. "I guess you could say I'm part of a mafia of sorts. I'm one of the lead bounty hunters. People like your father offer a lot of money for me to kill their enemies or catch their delinquent children. Once this parent actually asked me to fake kidnap his child so he would appreciate home more. Do a few of these a week, five hundred thousand to a million a pop and boom, you've got a place to stay and food to eat, not to mention a couple extra thousand in your pocket.

I stared in shock because this sounded too good to be true. I didn't trust my voice so just nodded slightly.

She smiled proudly, "So, you in?"

I hesitated for a moment before swearing under my breath. Take the risk with this crazy chick or go back to Blood Thunder?

I took a deep breath before nodding, "I'm in."

The entire situation was all really completely out of nowhere, but it saved me.

None of the situation even made that much sense but I did know that this was a million times better than going back to Blood Thunder pack would ever be.

I spent four years traveling around the US and Canada. Sidney was in charge and always made sure that all of my cases were moral and that they couldn't trigger whatever was left of my PTSD. I got payed extremely well too and it felt really good to be supporting myself for once in my life.

I could just go out to a store and buy myself new clothes without asking for anyone's permission and I could have as much food as I wanted without feeling guilty about how much it costs.

I trained long hours to become both physically and mentally fit, even going as far as seeing a therapist a couple of times. It didn't really seem to help, especially since he was a human and wouldn't understand what had truly happened, but I'm still proud of myself for making that step.

I was able to acknowledge that there was something broken inside and actually did what I could to try and be the best that I could be.

I still had a long way to go, but every day I could see myself transforming into the strong and confident alpha I was meant to be.

I couldn't thank Sidney enough. I don't even want to think about what would have happened if she had overlooked my case and brought me back to my father, or just left me to die on the streets.

About a month into my new job I had a case near Jamie and Henry and, after a lot of thought, I stopped by their house.

They were definitely shocked at first, they thought I had succeeded in returning to Blood Thunder and were even trying to convince their alpha to somehow make a plan to get me out, even though they knew there was no way they could.

They were mad at me at first, which was completely justified, but they ended up understanding and forgiving me for 'scaring the living hell out of them.'

I went and checked in on them and Jen often, but the job always kept me busy. I was so grateful to be independent and working on myself, but I couldn't help get a little lonely. Sometimes I would go an entire day without talking to anyone and being left alone with my thoughts is not the safest thing.

After 3 years of training and working on myself I started negotiating with the new alpha of Belle Foret, Jack. He had slowly begun to take over for his father and ease into the alpha position. After a lot of compromising he decided he'd let me stay in their lands, in the pack house with Jen.

Since he was younger, he was a lot more flexible and open to the possibility of not doing things exactly by the rules. I think he was using me as a way of showing he is his own person.

I won't be considered an official member of the pack and if I bring any problems, whether it be my old pack or myself, I'll be kicked right back out.

I was beyond grateful for the opportunity to stay at a pack and finally learn about pack life. I was ready now, both physically and mentally. I may not be perfect, but I'm ready.

When I pulled up Jen was already leaping down the front steps of the grand pack house, a giant smile on her face.

"ELLIE!" She exclaimaed and I smiled.

It had been a while since I'd last seen her. She'd become like a sister to me over the years.

I knew the bounty hunter life couldn't last long, it wasn't for me like it was for Sidney, but I wished it would just last a little longer. I wish that I could put off getting a real life together a little longer and just have fun with my friend.

I turned back to Jen and smiled widely as I hugged her.

"I missed you so much sister!" She exclaimed and I laughed lightly, squeezing her one last time before letting her go.

"I missed you so much too. I'm so excited! This place looks amazing."

"Come on! I'll show you around!" She chirped suddenly, hooking her arm with mine. I just barely was able to grab my bags before she was yanking me towards the steps of the giant mansion pack house.

It would be very strange being back in a pack again, but it was something I needed to do. I just wanted to be normal. I just wanted to get a normal job, have normal friends, find a normal mate and settle down to have a normal little family.

I think I could maybe accept my deformation, my abnormality, if everything else was more stable and more... well, normal.

Six

"Anxiety happens when you think you have to figure out everything all at once. Breathe. You're strong. You got this. Take it day by day."

– Karen Salmansohn

Jen showed me all around the beautiful mansion, but I cut off the tour a little short because I was feeling strangely tired all day today and didn't quite have the energy to keep up with her extremely excitable attitude.

I didn't understand why I felt this way. For a few weeks now I've felt like I have a leak or something and all of my will to do anything other than sleep and occasionally watch Netflix was just leaking out of me.

I just shook it off and took naps but the worse it got the more concerned I couldn't help but be. Normally I would endure long, excruciating hours of torture and then proceed to clean the entire pack house and cook diner. I was becoming soft and I was very unsure whether or not it was a good thing.

Today I felt a little dizzy too and decided maybe it was because I was hungry. I hadn't eaten in a little while and my body was much more used to getting food regularly. My appetite hadn't been great lately but I managed to force down a sandwich before heading to bed.

It was about 4:00 in the morning and I was lying awake, unable to sleep. I was sharing a room with Jen who was sleeping peacefully beside me. Even though my body was screaming at me for sleep I just couldn't bring myself to drift off. It was like I was overflowing with caffeine and my mind wouldn't shut up, but the only thing I'd been drinking was water and the only thing I'd eaten was half a ham sandwich.

I tried everything; counting sheep, singing to myself, even synching my breathing with Jen's to try and relax but just couldn't fall asleep.

Getting frustrated with my inability to fall asleep I wanted to scream, but deciding that wouldn't be a good idea, I made my way down to the kitchen. Luckily, I easily remembered exactly where I was going. Part of bounty hunter training was working on your sense of direction and quickly being able to adapt to your environment and blend in.

I was hoping some water would help, maybe a decaf coffee.

Luckily I've always been a quiet walker, never wanting to anger my parents. I easily crept through the house and down the stairs, not one floor board cracking, and not one door screeching.

I filled a glass with water and settled down at the counter, trying to force some down. Water is the answer to everything, it really could only help. I couldn't help but feel repulsed as I felt it glide down my throat and the next thing I knew I was sprinting clumsily over to the closest bathroom where I threw up everything left in my stomach.

I sat on the cold tiled floor, trying to breathe through the nausea, resting my head against the nearby cupboards.

What the hell is going on with me? I couldn't have been poisoned, I have an extremely high tolerance to almost every poison imaginable thanks to both my parents and bounty hunter training. I weakly hobbled my way back to bed, holding my burning stomach, and I finally drifted off into an uneasy sleep.

****

I opened my eyes to find myself strapped to the whipping block back at Blood Thunder pack. It was completely dark outside and I could feel my father's presence creeping up behind me. I breathed, preparing my body for the inevitable torture.

My father laughed maniacally behind me.

"This is what you deserve. You're an abomination, a disgrace. A deformation and a curse." He said softly in my ear, making me shiver in fear.

"I don't know why the moon goddess would curse me with a runt like you for a daughter, you're a mistake, you should never have been born. You are nothing and will continue being nothing until the day that you're begging for death, which I will never grant you. "

I heard the crack of the whip as Alpha Green tested it out before the pain enveloped my body.

****

I woke up, shaking and sweating, fantom pain making my entire body seize up in fear and shock. I sighed shakily as my body began to relax, recognizing that I wasn't in any immediate danger. Seeing Jen still in a deep sleep next to me I rubbed my face in frustration instead of letting myself break down.

I hadn't had nightmares in a while. I sat up groggily, my body still trying to come back from the nightmare that was my life. I checked the clock which showed it was 5:30 am. At least I got a little sleep.

I rubbed the sleep out of my eyes, stretched out my neck and shoulders and got ready for the day. I changed into my black leggings and tank, deciding to go for a run.

I was still a little nauseous from the incident a couple hours prior, but pushed through it, making my way outside quietly. I knew most of the pack would still be asleep, but they were werewolves with overly sensitive hearing, so I had to be extremely careful not to wake anyone up when opening the heavy front door.

Once I got outside I took a huge breath, filling my lungs with the amazing feeling of fresh air, feeling my nausea and uneasiness from my nightmares fade. I still didn't feel as good as I should but it was certainly an improvement.

I listened to the sound of the birds flapping their wings, flying up ahead. I could hear the leaves rustle gently in the wind and the sound of wild animals living peacefully within the forest surrounding the pack house.

It felt really good to be in a pack, to be one with nature instead of living in a dirty, loud, bustling city.

I pushed through my lingering symptoms and began my run along the small, windy path through the trees. I ran at a fast pace, probably about 50 km/ hour, leaping over fallen trees and around the peaceful bees and lady bugs flying through the air.

I felt amazing and free until I suddenly felt a presence making me stop dead in my tracks. I looked around, trying to identify the threat.

I saw a quick blur through the trees, almost imperceptible but I caught it. I silently moved towards it. The dizziness tried to claim my vision once again but I pushed it away, squinting into the morning darkness.

"Hello?" I asked, hoping it was just a lost harmless person or something.

Next thing I knew a wolf was jumping out at me. I quickly side stepped him but my dizziness held me back and they managed to scratch my face deeply. I could taste the blood leaking into my mouth but nonchalantly spat it out before descending into a defensive fighting stance once again.

We began to fight, but my experience seemed to outweigh theirs as I quickly got the upper hand on the fighter.

Just as I thought I had a chance in beating the large wolf, 6 others stepped out from behind the trees.

Shit.

I started to panic which I knew they could sense. It wasn't doing me any good but once half of them shifted, all I could think was that after all that I had endured, this is how I die?

The all lunged at the same time, biting and clawing, punching and kicking anywhere they could reach. With my added dizziness and weakness I didn't stand a chance.

I could feel everything as they tore my body apart slowly and viscously. I knew there was only one option if I wanted to even have the possibility of staying alive.

I shamefully shifted into my form, it had a slightly faster healing capability and tougher, thicker skin. It wasn't much but I was desperate. The wolves immediately stepped back when they saw my small black deformation laying in the grass. Just when they were about to attack and finish the job off I could hear yelling in the background. I wanted to think that someone would be saving me but as the wolves that attacked me shifted back I recognized them as the Belle Foret guard and knew I was screwed.

They obviously weren't aware that the alpha was letting a rogue stay on their land, and I was going to pay the price. I slowly lost consciousness, bleeding out onto the forest floor as different loud voices started surrounding me completely.

****

I woke up to a soft beeping. It took me what felt like all of my strength to pry my eyelids open. When I finally managed to crack them open the tiniest bit I was blinded with bright white lights.

I groaned, trying to adjust to the light and figure out what was going on. The last thing I remembered was slipping into my form.

It was easy to figure out that I was in some sort of hospital. I had cleaned enough in my day to recognize the sound of the heart monitor and the bright, white, clean walls.

My heartbeat started racing audibly when it dawned on me that I had shifted in front of several pack members.

Ah Fuck.

I looked down to see my body pretty mangled, but nothing I couldn't handle. I had had much worse throughout my years and wasn't scared of a little pain.

I sat up slowly feeling my energy returning to me. It was dark outside, I must've been out for the day.

Peering down at the medical things in my arms I felt the urge to pull them out. Just before I did the door opened up revealing what I recognized as the doctor in a pristine white coat, smiling politely at me.

"Ellie, I'm glad to see you recovering so quickly!" She chirped before glancing down to where my hand was wrapped around the wires, ready to pull them out.

"Don't touch those." She scolded, making me smile sheepishly before letting go.

"Sit back and relax, you're not completely healed and there are some things we need to talk about."

I just nodded, sinking back into the bed.

"I have some good and bad news."

I had watched enough tv shows with Henry to know when they said that it meant that they had some somewhat okay news that they shared to compensate for the devastating news that followed.

I could feel myself shift uncomfortably as anxiety took over me.

Breathe In, 1... 2... 3... Hold and out, 1... 2... 3... I repeated this calmly in my head as I turned my attention to the doctor, urging her on.

"The good news is that you're almost completely healed. Your body is working at an incredible pace, faster than anything I have ever seen before."

I nodded along. Okay, that was pretty good news, the bad must be pretty bad then.

"You are doing outstanding considering the shape we found you in. You were on the brink of death, I had to inject you and force shift you back into your human state so that I could help, but the damage was deep."

I shifted uncomfortably again at the thought of her seeing my horrid form. Wanting to change the subject I asked: "What's the bad news?"

She took a big breath, her smile slipping from her face despite her best efforts.

"Well, although your incredible strength and healing are what saved you, it is also the thing that is killing you." She said, all of her features turning tense and melancholy.

I just stared at her, trying to process her words. What does she mean it's killing me?

"Your abilities are so strong that your body is not able to keep up. That is also the reason your form hasn't been able to mature, why you still look like a pup. "

I stayed silent, processing her words.

"I can give you medication to stop the symptoms that you've probably already been experiencing, such as nausea, extreme fatigue and dizziness, but according to these tests..." She trailed off.

"Just say it." I said as straitly as I could, trying not to let my voice crack.

"You only have about a year left to live."

Seven

"We can complain because rose bushes have thorns, or rejoice because thorns have roses"

- Alphonse Karr

I only have a year.

A year.

12 months.

365 days.

8,760 hours.

525,600 minutes.

31,536,000 seconds.

And then I'll be dead.

I just sat there in shock. I could feel my heart started beating irregularity as soon as the words left her mouth as did the doctor as she watched the heart monitor with open concern in her eyes.

"I'll give you some time to process the news." She said softly, scribbling down a couple of things into her chart after checking my vitals. "I know its hard. When you're ready to talk more or need anything just click this button and I'll come back..." she said, motioning to a little button right next to the bed I was on. "I've worked with a lot of people in these types of situations and I'm capable and happy to help in any way I can." She said seriously, clipping her pen back to her board.

I just nodded, not daring to look at the pity she appeared to be like drowning in, trying not to react in front of this lovely doctor. I didn't want her to feel worse than she already did.

As she was leaving she turned around at the last second, "I'm truly sorry Ellie. I'll never understand why the worst things happen to the best people." With that, she left me alone. I know that she didn't know me and I'm sure she said that to every patient, but I couldn't help but smile slightly at her kind words. There haven't always been that many people who've shown me kindness throughout my life and now I'll take anything I can get.

It's not like you make a lot of friends when you're a deformed, runt, bounty hunter who ran away from her pack and was denied entry into another.

I knew I should be crying and breaking down but I couldn't. I just sat in disbelief the information refusing to sink in as it swirled around my brain chaotically.

My life hasn't even started yet and now its going to end. I'll only ever see the seasons one more time. It was spring right now and I might not live to see another.

I took a few shaky breaths as everything I'm going to miss out on sunk into my bones, beginning to weigh me down.

I'll never be normal.

I'll never have a normal mate or a normal house or a normal life. If I'm unlucky, which I always am, I might not even ever have normal friends.

I'm going to die alone.

I'm just glad I won't be dying a virgin, that ship sailed a couple of years ago thanks to the few short term things I've had over my time as a bounty hunter.

I escaped that hell hole of a pack for nothing.

I truly am a disgrace to my mother and father who are both strong, powerful, and healthy, even in their old age.

I sat there on the oddly comfortable hospital bed overthinking for while. Thinking about all of the things I had never done and would never get the chance to do.

I probably wouldn't have had a mate since I'm so fucked up, but now I would never find out. I would never get married or have my own children. I would never have a real family.

Don't get me wrong, I absolutely love Henry, Jamie and Jen. I am beyond grateful for what they've done and I don't think you need to be related to someone by blood to be family, but they aren't really my family. They didn't adopt me or raise me, I only lived with them for a few months before getting a job.

It's nice thinking of them as a family, but they don't really know me and now they probably won't ever get the chance.

Just as my life was starting to look up the universe just turned around and went PSYCH!

FUCK.

I was so stupid to think I deserved anything more than to be the pack runt. They should've just beaten me to death, what's the difference if I'm just going to die anyways? At least then it would have been quick, I wouldn't wither away, all alone and looking desperately for love and happiness, trying everything to feel complete before my body's timer runs out.

I laid there for about an hour before clicking the little button and calling the kind doctor back in.

She explained to me that there is medication that can alleviate all of my symptoms until the last month when it will be too much to fight off. That's how I'll know it's the end.

"Is there anyone you want me to call in? To support you or share the news with? Your roommate? Your family?"

I shook my head. "Please don't tell anyone. I don't want them to worry. I will not be a burden."

"Ellie. I'm sure you wouldn't-"

I cut her off by raising my hand. "Please stop. I'm the one dying and this is what I want, you can't change my mind."

"Okay." She said, lowering her head in defeat, picking at her nails anxiously. I felt bad that she had to have these kind of conversations for a living, no one should have to endure this. "I'll need you to stay here for the night for observation, but otherwise everything looks good and you should be able to leave tomorrow morning."

"Thank you doctor. I really appreciate it." I said shooting her a gentle smile that she didn't even try to return. I'm the one dying, you'd think she could at least pretend to be a little less upset.

After that I went back to sleep, still recovering from my near death experience from which I learnt about what will be my sure death experience.

When I woke up I could smell the faint scent of Jennifer and Henry. I spotted the new vase with fresh little yellow flowers on the table next to me and smiled. I knew it was from them. I picked one from the bunch, a smile crawling onto my face as I twirled it between my fingers.

It was yellow, my favorite color. It had always brought me happiness and hope. Even in my darkest days when I found a yellow flower in the woods I couldn't help but smile.

I never got any yellow hand-me-downs, Alpha always saying the color was too good for me. I only ever got browns or weird beiges, occasionally stained white. It was not convenient for the blood that was almost constantly trying to seep its way through and see the outside world.

The little daisy seemed to brighten up when I smiled, telling me it was happy to see me too. I shook my head a little too myself, this attack must've left me a little loopy.

Taking a deep breath I got up to get ready. I found some clothes all folded up by the bathroom that Jen must've laid out. I entered the bathroom, stretching out my slightly stiff limbs. I felt perfectly fine already, barely affected by the near death experience just 24 hours before.

It was crazy that I was so excited about how fast my healing had gotten, but now it was the thing that was going to bring me to Hades.

I pushed those thoughts out of my mind, scolding myself mentally.

I decided last night to act like I had never heard it. If I got caught up in the reality of my situation then I would just be torturing myself for the rest of my short life. It has always been my defense mechanism and it's really helped me up until now. I needed to live, and if living happy meant living in denial then so be it.

I'm perfectly fine with pretending to remain ignorant in this particular situation.

I looked in the mirror to see my seemingly healthy face glowing slightly under the bright lighting. I had taken the drugs to prevent my symptoms and was already looking and feeling much better.

The bathroom was extremely nice considering it was a hospital. Henry had told me that pack hospitals were much higher quality than human ones, but I never expected this.

To my right was a gorgeous rain shower with glass doors. There was a large, double counter in front of me with a luxurious sink and even a small tub to my left.

I opted for the shower, slowly peeling off my hospital gown, simultaneously checking for new scars. There were still quite a few but not nearly as many as there should've been.

Most of my scars had faded and it was definitely strange. Only the larger ones still hung on but those were easy enough to hide.

The shower had amazing yet gentle water pressure, making me feel completely relaxed.

I gave my hair a good wash with the shampoo and conditioner provided, marveling at the warm comfortable sensations of being clean.

After giving my body a good scrub I hopped out, not wanting to waste a lot of water despite how good it felt. I changed into the beautiful clothes Jen picked out for me. She wanted to go into fashion at it clearly showed in every outfit she made. No matter how simple it seemed to be, she put tons of thought and planning into it and it would look exactly how she wanted it to.

She just brought me a simple black top and black sweatpants with multicolored stripes. I was extremely comfortable, but it all fit me perfectly, accenting my waist, hips, ass, boobs and legs perfectly. She somehow made me look runway ready, and I knew this wasn't even close to her best. A little makeup and a few accessories and I'd be turning heads.

I let my hair down to air dry, adding in a quick, loose braid that wrapped to the back of my head where I secured it with one of the yellow daisies.

My hair was naturally curly and went down to about my mid back. I wonder how many more haircuts I have left. I've found that there's nothing more relaxing than when the hair dresser washes your hair and thoroughly massages your head.

Sighing I left the hospital. Time to face everyone.

Everything's okay, nothing's wrong just smile. I repeated in my head until I actually began to believe it. Everything will be okay, just smile.

As soon as I entered my room Jen was jumping on me, pulling me into a bear hug.

"OH MY GOD ELLIE I WAS SO WORRIED ABOUT YOU, YOU BITCH, ARE YOU OKAY?!"

"I-"

"OH MY GOD DAD AND I VISITED BUT THE DOCTOR LADY KICKED US OUT! CAN YOU BELIEVE THAT?!"

"I-"

"DID YOU GET THE FLOWERS? I WAS REALY UNSURE ABOUT THEM DAD SAID WE SHOULD'VE GOTTEN PURPLE BECAUSE ITS GIRLIER BUT I DON'T KNOW I JUST HAD A FEELING YOU'RE MORE OF A YELLOW GIRL"

"Jen, I-"

"WHY AREN'T YOU ANSWERING MY QUESTIONS I'M DYING HERE! ARE YOU NOT OKAY! OH GOD, OH GOD, OH GO-"

"JENNIFER!" I finally snapped, getting her attention.

"Ew don't ever call me by my full name again. I'm so not a Jennifer, I'm a Jen."

"I'm completely fine," I said, ignoring her previous sentence, "stop worrying, and the flowers were perfect. Thank you."

I tear slipped down her face shocking me as she pulled me into another tight hug.

"I'm so sorry. I thought you were dead, I was so worried. I couldn't lose my sister. You're my family and I couldn't even save you!"

My heart melted completely at her calling me her family, making me feel a little guilty for keeping such a huge secret, but I just pushed through it hugging her back just as tightly.

There's no point in making her share my burden. It'll be easier for everyone if no one knows.

Once we were done hugging we decided to go down and get some food. I swear this girl is always hungry!

We were sitting around the counter in the kitchen. She had a bowl or cereal while I ate a bowl of corn and some grapes. I know, I have weird eating habits.

"I still don't understand how you can eat those things together." She said, shooting me a disappointed shake of her head, making me giggle and shrug, shoving another spoonful of corn into my mouth. It's not like I was eating them in the same bite.

"OH MY GOD!" Jen suddenly screamed, startling me.

I threw my hands up in shock, throwing myself off of my chair. For an ex-bounty hunter I was easily startled.

I just laid on the ground with my hand over my heart as I tried to regain my breathing.

"What the fuck was that, Jen!" I exclaimed, as she fell on the ground next to me laughing. "What?" I asked, looking at her, bawling her eyes out on the ground.

She didn't answer, just continued laughing.

That's when I heard someone clearing their throat from behind us.

I looked up to see the old Alpha looking down on us with an amused smirk on his face.

Jen's laughter completely sobered up as we both stood, straightening our-selves out in front of our leader.

"I'm glad to see you're feeling better Ellie, you gave us all quite a scare there" he said, walking around the table, cringing slightly at my meal choices.

"Thank you sir. I'm doing much better thanks to your amazing hospital staff. "

The alpha just nodded his head, grabbing a water bottle from the fridge before leaving without saying another word.

Once he left I turned to Jen, my face lighting up red to face her matching one. As if on cue we both burst back into laughter.

After we finally finished our outburst we sat back down to finish up our snacks.

"So why did you yell 'oh my god?'"

Jen looked at me confused for a second before her eyes lit up. "RIGHT!" She yelled a little, making me jump again.

She put down her food facing me. Oh it must be important for Jen to stop eating.

She took my hands in hers as she faced me, a goofy smile climbing onto her face.

"I completely forgot to tell you somehow! In a week our pack will be hosting the mating ball!" She screeched, waiting impatiently for my response.

"The what?" I asked utterly confused.

Her face deflated a little when I said that.

"You're kidding right?"

I shook my head no, my eyebrows scrunching together.

"The mating ball? It happens every 5 years? Everyone has to attend? Any of this ringing any bells?"

"Oh god, is this some sort of a sex party thing?" I asked.

She cringed as soon as I said that. "NO. JUST NO. " She said, shooting me a disgusted look, making me shrug innocently.

I mean come on. A 'mating ball'?! Don't tell me that that's not immediately what comes to mind. I swear I'm not gross.

"A mating ball is the party we throw every five years so that everyone can try and find their mate! All unmated wolves must attend and that means you! There will be party stations all throughout our entire pack ground as millions of wolves from all the nearby packs will be visiting! "

"Oh!" I said, faking excitement.

I really doubt I had a mate, but even if I did I would never wish that upon someone. It'd probably be better for them if we never met. I will only be here for another year, I don't want anyone getting too attached to me. I'm already so stressed out about Henry, Jammie and Jen. I don't want them to get hurt.

I would hate to meet the person who was cursed with a dying runt like me for a an eternal life partner.

"I haven't even told you the best part yet!" She exclaimed. "The royals attend all mating balls for oversight and since we're hosting it they'll be staying here for the entire weekend!"

I was shocked when she said that. The royal werewolf family were the ones that ruled the entire world. They were the strongest and largest pack not to mention it would take more than 50 wolves in order to kill just one of the royals. They are warriors. A lot of people like to challenge or try to murder the royal family to prove themselves which is just utterly stupid but it does mean they have to be constantly on guard and protected.

"How? Isn't that a little risky?"

"No. Everyone knows that during this party we all are required to put our differences aside. If they do anything rash or violent their entire pack will be banned from the mating balls forever. It sounds a little harsh but these are supposed to be peaceful events holding the sole purpose of finding your mate and we really don't want to risk people not attending. "

I nodded. "That must be why I've never heard of it. I wouldn't' be surprised if someone from my old pack decided to do something stupid and get themselves banned."

Jen just nodded along, completely agreeing.

I guess it's kind of exciting. I might get to see Jen meet her mate! That would be so magical. On top of that she'd have someone to help her through my death...

Eight

"Don't be pushed around by the fears in your mind. Be led by the dreams in your heart."

– Roy T. Bennett

After our snack we decided to go train.

Jen had shown me the training area when I first arrived but with the sickness and the attack I hadn't gotten a chance to use it yet. It was pretty much empty because by the time we had gotten there it was almost 11:00 pm.

I never actually got any apology or explanation for that incident... everyone just seemed to let it go so I did too.

As soon as I walked in I felt a little better. There's something about the sight of wolves really pushing themselves and training as hard as they can that makes me feel peaceful. Working out was one of the few things that managed to slow my mind enough to understand it and process all of my chaotic thoughts.

After a couple years of training as a bounty hunter I had really grown into my alpha genes and had started to secrete overwhelming amounts of alpha dominance. I hated the way people were always nervous and uncomfortable in my presence so I quickly learned how to reign it in and blend in, but it was always there, waiting to be released.

Because of this no one really takes notice when I enter a room, it allowed for me to easily fade into the background until I wanted to be seen. It was beyond convenient when I was following people or doing recon on new areas.

Something weird is that even though I'm a rogue I've never smelt of it. I should have a strong smell of mold and rotting but everyone's told me I smell nothing like that. Normally if a rogue were to enter any place within a mile of wolves they will be noticed, but luckily I've never had to deal with that.

All werewolves have at the very least three scents. One smells distinctly of their pack, another of werewolf and the last of their own personal smell. Because of this we're all very easily identifiable. For example, if Jen meets any other werewolf they should be able to easily know she's a werewolf from the Belle Foret pack and by the levels of power rolling off her at any given second she's a strong warrior.

That's why I'm very confusing if anyone were to pay attention to it. I never smelt like my old pack, Blood Thunder, I don't smell like rogue and I don't even smell like a werewolf.

Pair that with the fact that I can reign in my aura and on first encounter its almost impossible to figure me out. I like that. If I want or need them to know something, I'll tell them. Otherwise, I'll leave them guessing.

The only downside to this is that I can easily be percepted as a threat. this is probably why I was attacked on my first day here. Not only did they know I didn't smell like their pack, but I smelled like and entirely different sort of threat. The threat of the unknown.

Jen and I walked through mats of people sparring. Wolves were throwing each other to the ground, pinning them and attacking until one of them taps out. People rarely actually damage their opponents too badly but if anything happened the miraculous werewolf healing would take effect and they would be as good as new within a couple of days at worst.

"Gamma Heeler!" Jen exclaimed cheerfully, earning herself a nod from the man I now assumed was the gamma.

A gamma is in charge of training their pack and played a large part in battle strategy.

"Gamma Heeler." I nodded to him politely. He did not look like someone who's bad side you wanted to be on.

He turned to me and confusion swarmed his eyes, a natural reaction when people first met me.

"I'm Ellie. Your pack has graciously taken me in and I was hoping you would let me join your class and train with your warriors." I said professionally, bowing my head politely.

I'd met quite a few people you wouldn't want to mess with while being a bounty hunter and have learnt that this was the best way of dealing with them. They all loved having their egos stroked and throwing in a little mindless compliment could make all the difference.

"EVERYONE STOP!" He bellowed out of nowhere, bringing the entire room to a halt.

"We have a new member. You know the drill, let's see what she's got, shall we?"

The entire group muttered excitedly, making their way to the side lines to watch. Some of them were smirking, eyeing me up and down viciously.

They thought I was a weak little wolf because of my lack of power, but little did they know that there was a storm brewing beneath this innocent exterior, and one little broken window could let it all out.

I was dressed in an oversized sweater, completely hiding my strong, battle built form from them. I would have no problem taking them underestimating me for granted.

I made eye contact with Jen and knew she was thinking the exact same thing. It's time to show them all not to underestimate me.

"Would anybody like to challenge Ellie?"

At that multiple wolves stepped forward.

"Ellie, you will fight your way up, starting at my the lowest ranking volunteers, making your way up. Once you are defeated you will have your rank."

I rolled my neck getting ready and stepping onto the mats. "Who's up first?" I said gently and calmly, not showing weakness but not revealing how confident I felt.

I small girl stepped forwards. She was probably about 5'3 but I could tell she was fairly in shape.

I nodded at her with a friendly smile before removing my hoodie. I was now standing in merely a sports bra and leggings, leaving my light abs and lasting scars on full display. I heard gasps all around when they saw my beaten body but no one said anything. Little did they know that the majority of my scars were faded and this barely represented a hundredth of the shit I'd endured.

I was pretty self conscious about my body suddenly but tried not to let that break my concentration. I was a fighter and the scars have shaped me into the person I am today. I wouldn't be me without it.

Sometimes I wonder if that's actually a good thing but quickly try and push those ideas away. Self love was more important than anything else and it was something that I've constantly been trying to work on.

I got into my fighting stance, one leg slightly behind the other, both bent slightly and my hands up, ready to block or strike.

"You will continue fighting until someone taps out. Any mortal wounds will not be accepted. Kill someone and you will be sent to the dungeons and tried for murder."

He continued to lay out the rules as I scanned my opponent. I could tell that many probably underestimated her. She looked like she had a little fire building within her that was ready to blow as soon as she allowed it to.

We were pretty similar in that way, the only difference is that I had acquired the skill of a bounty hunter and had pure, untainted alpha blood running through my veins. My ancestry line was know for being purely alpha for at least the last 5 centuries, leaving us nearly as strong as the royals. As we circled each other I noticed that she was right side dominant and that her left shoulder looked a little tight.

"3... 2... 1... FIGHT!" Gamma Heeler shouted, his deep, commanding voice easily filling the room.

At that the girl immediately leaped at me, surprising me a little. I almost got hit but swiftly ducked under her swing. I faced her again but before she had a chance to react I had grabbed her wrist, pinning it behind her back, forcing her onto the ground.

She immediately tapped out.

I looked up to see everyone looking at me in shock while Jen was just smirking evilly.

Just like that almost all of them stepped to the side, no longer wanting to fight me leaving only three warriors left and Jen. I had taken a warrior down with incredible precision and skill and in only a few seconds. They were smart to know that they wouldn't stand a chance against me.

The gamma scanned me, cocking his head at me, clearly impressed with how I handled myself.

The three fighters left were two very large men and a tall lean red head that was shooting me dirty looks.

The red head stepped up first, obviously ranking lower than the other two. She did not give off any strong aura and didn't look very threatening but I knew better than to underestimate people.

She stepped up smirking at me as I calmly prepared myself for the fight.

"I saw your form, freak. Why they even let someone as weak and pathetic as you on our pack grounds is beyond me. You must be the pack whore, I don't see how else you would get in here."

My face lit up in sheer embarrassment when she said that. My form really was my weak spot and she knew it. I'd been through a lot of shit and had come out stronger each time but it still hurt.

Jen immediately stepped behind me standing tall and looking down on her. Before she could say anything I answered.

"Maybe, but to me it looks like the position's already been taken." I shrugged descending into my fighting stance.

I knew that it was cheesy and way too easy, I never pretended to be witty, but it was right there and Jen seemed to be satisfied as she said laughed and said, "Damn right, Ellie, okay"

"YOU BITCH!" Was all the red head I was fighting could yell making everyone laugh under their breath a little.

The whole situation was lame and immature but whatever. It got her to shut up so mission accomplished.

"As a red head, we do not claim her." Jen mumbled and I snorted.

The girl lit up red as she shook in rage, also getting into her own wonky stance.

"3.. 2.. 1.. FIGHT!" Everyone yelled together this time, probably excited to see me beat this girl's ass.

Before the bitch even had a chance to move I already had her pinned to the ground by her neck.

She refused to tap out so I squeezed a little tighter.

"Tap out." I said calmly, not wanting to hurt anyone any more than necessary.

She still refused so I squeezed a little tighter and she started to turn red from lack of oxygen.

"Brooke. Tap out, now." The Gamma commanded, shaking his head at how ridiculous she was being. There was no way out of the hold I had on her so I'm not sure what she was waiting for. Did she want to pass out? Because I'll happily oblige.

She finally listened and I released her neck. As soon as I turned my back to her she grew her claws on her hand and tried to rip my calf up. I easily avoided it but punched her right in the face, giving her a nice little shiner to remind her not to mess with me and to play fair.

She instantly broke out into tears, sobbing on the ground. "WHAT ARE YOU ALL JUST STANDING AROUND FOR?! THAT BITCH JUST TRIED TO KILL ME! ARREST HER!" She screamed making a scene. I could see Jen rolling her eyes exaggeratedly out of the corner of my eyes.

Some random girl in the crowd sighed walking forward shamefully and picked Brooke up off the ground, despite Brooke being perfectly capable of doing so herself. "I'll take her to the pack doctor." She said, clearly not amused by Brooke's childish embarrassing exaggerations.

I fought the next man. It took me a good two minutes to beat him, he even got a couple of good punches in but in the end I won. I should be out fighting other alphas, not normal pack warriors so these fights weren't exactly fair, but it was the only option.

Next up was Jen. I smiled at her as she winked. I honestly couldn't care less if Jen beat me. She was the one that trained me at first after all, but it was worth a try.

We both took our stances and began fighting. We swirled around each other, gracefully ducking and avoiding each other's hits. After about 5 minutes of only small hits and kicks here and there I finally saw my opening.

She swung her fist at my face and as I ducked I grabbed her wrist, twisting it and she fell to her knees in front of me. I swung behind her and pushed her to the ground, so that she was unable to move without dislocating her shoulder.

She quickly tapped out, sending me the proud smile of a mama bear. God I love this girl.

We hugged each other tightly.

"I'm so proud of you!" She whispered to me, jumping a little in god hug. As soon as we separated she was slipping her heels back on and lining up with the others to watch the final fight.

She was such a great person. She didn't care that I just beat her and now ranked higher than her, she was just happy for me. She was one of the least selfish people I knew, I don't know what I did to deserve such an amazing friend.

The next and last man stepped up to the mat. He was gigantic, a 6'4 giant wall of muscles. We took our stances as I tried to analyze him. He was definitely strong but probably slow, and I would try to use that to my advantage.

When the fight started we both took a moment to circle each other, thinking over a strategy of some sort. I decided he was taking too long and took the first approach.

I ran right at him before at the last second sliding under his arms so I was behind him. I jumped onto his back, trying to bring him down with my weight but he was too strong.

He grabbed me by my shoulder and threw me off him. I landed a few feet away on the mat with a thud and quickly scrambled back up to my feet. This was going to be an interesting fight...

We fought for another half an hour, neither of us wanting to give up. It helped a lot that I could easily handle the pain from his hits but I was definitely starting to tire out. Both of our moves were becoming sloppier and slower as well as our reaction times but we both pushed through. The crowd had dispersed for a few minutes out of boredom but seeing that it was going to end soon they all gathered around again, cheering louder than ever.

Some cheered for the man I was fighting but a good amount also cheered me on, especially the females.

After another five minutes I finally saw my move. I slid between his giant legs, grabbed both his feet, throwing him off balance and sending him tumbling to the ground. As soon as he landed on his stomach I leaped onto his back so he couldn't get up, pinning all his limbs but the hand he needed to end the fight.

After a moment of shock all around he finally tapped out. As soon as he did I fell to the ground beside in exhaustion.

The giant slowly sat up, smiling, also trying to recover from the fight. I was extremely relieved he didn't seem angry. I really didn't need anymore enemies. He seemed a little disappointed with himself but the nod of respect he gave me showed he didn't hold it against me.

After a few minutes I was almost at full strength again and got right back up, noticing a few people eyeing me in confusion.

I started stretching out my muscles again when I saw Gamma Heeler approaching me. I stood up a little straighter, addressing him with a nod of respect.

"That was some very good work out there Ellie." As soon as he started talking the entire room went silent. Clearly their gamma was a man of very few words so this was a little shocking for them. "Its too bad you're not an official member of this pack. We could use some amazing warriors like you. Being the best warrior in my class you will begin training with myself, the beta and our new alpha. Be here tomorrow morning at 6:00 am sharp and don't be late."

I nodded, letting a smile slip onto my face at that. Although I hated the idea of having to wake up that early I was proud of myself for having gained that level of respect. It was a very prestigious invitation and I was really proud of myself.

As soon as the gamma left Jen came over to me, making me spill all of the details of what just happened even though she'd witnessed it all.

The rest of the day flew by easily. I got to know a few of the pack members after the fight, they all seemed very friendly despite the fact that I'd knocked them all down in the rankings a little. This was nothing like my old pack.

Just as everything seemed to be looking up, queen bitch herself decided to step in and make sure I didn't enjoy myself.

"Hey slut!" Brooke yelled across the room. A few people looked to watch the commotion as she came up to me, making me roll my eyes in exasperation.

"Why are you here? This is a pack meal and last time I checked, you weren't part of the pack."

I could year Jen growling from behind me protectively. What is this? High school? This girl is ridiculous. She must be in her late twenties, even older than me, but she was acting like a 13 year old brat.

"Its no wonder your last pack kicked you out, I would've kicked out a runt like you too, or just killed you before you could go around infecting everyone with your runt disease. Just stay out of my way, okay? The prince is visiting soon and I don't need you going around and messing everything up for me now. got it?"

Wow, we've now gone from high school all the way down to kindergarten. Runt disease? Really? She's pathetic, trying to make other people feel worse about themselves because she's too insecure to admit that someone might be better than her.

I don't care what's going on in people's lives, making other people feel worse about themselves is never okay. Misery may like company, but does it actually ever make anyone feel any better?

With that she just walked away, too much of a coward to stay for Jen's perfect comebacks. I'm sure she's been planning the day she could use some of them, in her head for years.

"Why didn't you stand up for yourself!?" Jen exclaimed.

I just shrugged. "I mean, honestly, I feel like the more she talks the more she embarrasses herself. I just couldn't give less of a shit about her. She's gonna do what she's gonna do, there's no point in starting a stupid feud. I mean, there's clearly something going on with her, no one puts others done for no reason or just for the fun of it. She needs help and me being petty and fighting back is not going to help anyone."

"Okay, grandma. I'm going to go but a whoopee cushion on her seat now." Jen replied, confidently striding off in her stilettos, making my giggle under my breath.

Nine

"Each smallest act of kindness, reverberates across great distances and spans of time --affecting lives unknown to the one who's generous spirit, was the source of this good echo. Because kindness is passed on and grows each time it's passed until a simple courtesy becomes an act of selfless courage, years later, and far away. Likewise, each small meanness, each expression of hatred, each act of evil."

—— Dean Koontz

Just as promised Jen put a whoopee cushion on Brooke's chair. It's safe to say she wasn't happy about it. When she sat down everyone looked at her and instead of calmly saying it wasn't her and figuring something out she literally leaped off her chair, threw her food at the wall and ran out of the room screaming.

It was pretty entertaining if I'm honest, not to mention we didn't have to deal with her all dinner. I did feel kind of bad though, she clearly had anger issues and it was starting to look like she had no really friends, just fake girls hanging out with her to gain popularity.

The rest of the pack was so nice and welcoming. I talked with a bunch of them, gamma Heeler even winked at me from across the table making everyone stare in shock. After that I could've sworn I saw his cheeks tint red slightly but I can't be sure.

My whole life I dreamed of being part of a pack meal. It felt so amazing to be with them, to eat with them, not forced to serve them and watch them enjoy what I slaved over from a distance, trying to imagine the amazing feeling of a full stomach. Of course by now I've figured out that being too full sucks, but that's besides the point.

The servers were mostly older teenagers or young adults doing a part-time job and the cooks were payed well and loved what they do.

This pack was so much better, so much less archaic than Blood Thunder. I just wish I could truly be a part of it. I'll never be able to join a pack. I'm an alpha, a threat to everyone whether I like it or not. They would be risking war, not to mention there is always conflict when two alphas live in one pack. I wouldn't mind being under someone that I could potentially beat, as long as I could feel a sense of belonging, but I would never belong.

I'm an alpha runt. I shouldn't even exist, but here I am. I don't belong anywhere, not with the runts, not with the normal wolves, and certainly not with the alphas. I'm just kind of there, alone.

That night I couldn't sleep, too stressed about training the next day. At about 4:45 I got sick of trying and decided to go for a walk.

I walked through the house as quietly as possible but I had a hard time concentrating and kept messing up. At one point going down the many flights of stairs I somehow managed to trip on my own foot and went tumbling down, rolling awkwardly trying not to wake anyone up. I'm surprised no one came bursting out of their rooms seeing what all the commotion was about.

I was usually amazing at being silent but I felt really out of it today.

Once I finally made it outside I took a giant breath of relief shaking out my shoulders.

I walked into the forest, thoughts running through my mind when I came across a yellow daffodils. I smiled, kneeling down to stroke it.

Everything seems better when I smile, I realized. Nothing seems as detrimental when you're smiling. Bad news seems slightly less tragic, people's harsh words don't hurt quite as much and everyone around you is affected by the positivity.

If I were to smile at one person and they return the smile, other people might see them smiling and maybe even smile themselves. One little effort can create such a chain reaction and could make the entire pack's day slightly better. It's the butterfly effect.

I sat on the ground, surrounded by the few bushes of beautiful yellow flowers.

"Okay. I'll make a deal with you guys." I said to the flowers, definitely looking like a crazy person. "From now until the end I will do my very best to always smile."

I will smile through the pain and maybe it will feel better. I will smile to make other people happier. When I pass by strangers I will smile at them and when I am given bad news I will smile to console them for having to be the ones to share it. I don't want to drag anyone down with me, I want to make my death as easy and painless as possible.

It might not be the best for me, I should definitely talk to someone and cry and let them support me, but I don't want anyone to carry that kind of weight for me. I only have to stand under the weight of the burden for one more year, then I can let go. I'll let myself feel the pain when I die, not a second sooner.

I will be happy. There's not enough time to dwell on the bad things when there are so many good things to concentrate on. Like these beautiful flowers.

I gave the flowers a big smile before picking 5 of them, braiding one into my French braided hair and putting the other four in a bundle.

I looked down at my watch. I should probably start heading down to training now.

This is going to be so hard. They are such good warriors and-

I stopped myself.

No more negativity and overthinking, I'm done with that.

It is an honor to be a part of their training sessions. I can't improve without working for it. This is going to be great. If I'm not good enough, then I was never meant to be a part of this and I will find where I am meant to be.

I just hope that place isn't too bad.

****

I was the first one to arrive in the training area so I decided to start off with some warm up. I settled on one of the matts, reaching out and readying my muscles with some basic stretches.

I was dressed in a giant hoodie again, hiding my body until we started training. When I was working out people were less likely to pay attention to the scars that would be on display and ill instead pay more attention to what I'm doing. That's what I hope at least.

As I was stretching out my legs I heard a small bang from behind me. I turned around to see a giant man completely covered in tattoos that I could see very clearly since he was shirtless.

I didn't even realize I was staring until the man snapped in my face a little, bringing me out of it, making me blush profusely.

"Hey, little girl, this is a private training time. Out." Okay, that was a little rude.

"Little girl? I'm-"

"Look I'm not trying to hear your life story right now, okay? Now get out." He said, growling a little at the end.

What crawled up this guys ass and laid eggs? He was a pretty intimidating guy and almost anyone else would be shaking in their boots but I did not like his attitude. It was just irritating. It was early in the morning though, I'll give him that.

I stood up staring him down, or up seeing as he was at least a foot taller than me, keeping my small smile on my face although I'm sure it didn't look as welcoming as it usually did. I mean, little girl? We look like we're the same age!

"Sorry, I don't know who you are, but you're not the alpha and you can't go around insulting people and ordering them around rudely for no good reason!" I said in a sweet voice shrugging a little but not completely hiding my annoyance.

He looked a little surprised at my calm demeanor. I'm sure he's been yelled at hysterically a lot and I'm also sure that's done nothing but annoy him. I was pretty sure this dude was the Beta considering I'd already met Alpha Jack and Gamma Heeler and there was only one more person I'd be training with today.

"I'm your Beta I can do whatever the fuck I want to do, little girl. Now get out before I make you, don't think just because you're all cute and innocent

I'll let you do whatever you want." He bared his teeth, taking an aggressive step forward.

Little girl? Cute and innocent? This bitch.

Just as I was about to respond, probably with something stupid, I heard a familiar voice from behind us.

"You're not actually her beta." I looked back to see an unsurprisingly indifferent looking Gamma Heeler. I gave him a big smile and a wave which he returned surprisingly. I mean, from what I've seen, he was such a stone faced man, never showed any emotions but just because I smiled at him he actually smiled back! It does work!

"Did you just smile?" The beta asked, a shocked look on his face, making the gamma return to his stoic facade as he made eye contact with him, tensing slightly.

"This is Ellie. She was the strongest warrior in our pack training and therefore will be joining us today. She may be on pack grounds but she hasn't officially joined it so you are not her beta and can't really order her around. Idiot." The Gamma said sternly, not even bothering to try to. be respectful even though the beta outranked him.

The beta nodded along, shooting me a wary look. he almost instantly changed from a scary looking tense warrior to a big confused harmless oaf.

"Why don't you smell like rogue?" He asked innocently making me shrug.

He looked me up and down, seeming a little unsure and Heeler noticed this.

"I would seriously warn you not to underestimate her." He said, earning himself another surprised look from the beta and another smile from me.

Heeler actually started to blush a little, making the beta look at him like he had just told him he was changing his name to princess Shirley.

After a couple more seconds of the beta and gamma staring at each other intensely the beta nodded, turning to me. "I'm Christopher, but you can call me Chris." He said, giving me a small smile which I happily returned.

"Ellie." I said shaking his hand.

"Oh ya, I think I actually heard about you briefly. Alpha Green's daughter? I have to say you're not what I was expecting." He said curiously.

The new alpha, Jack, burst through the doors. He was probably around our age too, maybe slightly older.

"That's Alpha Jack." He said pointing his finger towards the very buff, very tall man.

Alpha came up to me, sizing me up a little, checking for threats but once I smiled he relaxed and shook my hand.

"Hey, I'm Ellie, How's pack life treating you?" He asked seriously. He had apologized profusely after he heard about his warriors attacking me. They saw me and thought I was some sort of spy since I didn't smell like a rogue. He assured that it would never happen again and a few of the warriors that attacked me even came and apologized.

It was all okay, it was just a misunderstanding.

"All good Alpha, your pack is beautiful."

"You can just call me Jack. No title necessary." He winked at me "Heeler told me all about how amazing you did in training. He wouldn't shut up about it actually." He said cheekily, looking over to Heeler with a mischievous smile.

I could see the gamma begin to blush a little again, making me laugh a little under my breath, trying not to embarrass him.

"Alright Ellie, why don't we show them what you've got?" Heller spat out, trying desperately to change to subject, "You'll spar with Chris while Jack and I observe." I nodded my head, beginning to mentally prepare myself.

My face fell a little to concentrate as Chris and I circled each other which he visibly tensed at. I mean, I can't be nice and kick his ass at the same time. The only person I know that can do that is Sidney, I don't know how she managed but it was definitely terrifying.

We did a couple of cases together and people would freak the fuck out when she would mile sweetly at them as they tried to threaten her. Sidney really was something else...

Chris lunged at me first but I saw it coming, quickly ducking and spinning my leg underneath me, kicking out his legs from beneath him. I saw the shock in his face as he fell to the ground. I was about to jump onto him pinning him but he rolled out of the way at the last second, springing back onto his feet.

I could see Heeler smirking out of the corner of my eye but managed to focus all my attention on the now very serious Chris.

We sparred for another 15 minutes before he finally managed to pin me. I mean he was a very experienced Beta and I was a dying deformed alpha runt. It was to be expected. Honestly I held up better than I thought I would.

Afterwards Heeler and I went over what I needed to work on and he gave me some pointers while Jake did the same with Chris.

We spent another two hours doing exhausting exercises, sparring, talking and laughing. Turns out I really like these guys. They were really surprisingly sweet, nothing like my old pack, and they seemed to accept me. Not that they'd ever seen my form, but still.

After training we all went to the kitchen for food and I could feel all eyes on me. It wasn't every day the three ranking members walked around with the random new girl who wasn't even officially allowed to be part of the pack. Chris seemed to sense that and put a protective arm around me pulling me closer.

"Just ignore them." He said softly in my ear, making me relax as he shot death glares to anyone who stared. He felt like the overprotective big brother I never had.

I wondered what it would've been like if I'd had a sibling. Would they be deformed too. If not, would they have helped me or joined my parents in hating me?

I could see Heeler glancing at us a lot, probably thinking I couldn't notice. He had a frowns on his face and almost looked jealous as Chris led me around. I don't know why though, I mean I clearly wasn't any of their mates. We had touched plenty, trust me, and no tingles, there was no electricity or voice in my head yelling MATE MATE.

Not to mention I'll be dead soon so it wouldn't matter... SHUT UP ELLIE! POSITIVITY!!

As we walked back into the pack house everyone was openly gaping at us and it was getting very uncomfortable, Jack's glares could only do so much. We walked through and I tried to ignore it but it was definitely difficult. Because of my werewolf hearing I could hear all of their nasty comments...

"Isn't that the runt girl."

"What the hell is she doing with the high ranking males? Should we try and save them?"

"Urgh, another whore I see..."

"Who the fuck is that bitch and what is she doing with my future husband?"

"They should get vaccinated. She could be contagious." I didn't even need to see Brooke say this to know that it was her. She was weirdly obsessed with the whole cooties thing.

"There's obviously a reason she wasn't let into our pack. She's probably a psycho and they're just pitying her."

Ouch.

That one hurt a little.

They continued on until the three large men stopped. They turned around to face the crowd that had formed. Some tried to flee once they realized they were pissed but one growl from Jack and everyone stopped in their tracks.

Chris held onto me tighter as Jake and Heeler stood in front of me protectively.

"If you've got something to say about Ellie, come say it to me. See how that works out for you, otherwise, shut the fuck up." Jake followed the statement with a huge growl.

Total big brother energy.

I stood staring at him in awe. He stood up for me, why would he do that?

I was so lost in my thoughts I hadn't noticed that everyone in the room was now on their knees bowing to their alpha. Everyone except for me... Shit.

Everyone was staring at me, making me freeze where I was standing which was definitely the exact opposite of what I should've done.

Shit. What the fuck do I do?

BOW YOU IDIOT!

I can't. I won't.

BOW, BOW RIGHT NOW! EVEYRONE'S STARING!

He won't control me.

WHO CARES! THIS IS NOT HELPING WITH THE WHOLE EVERYONE HATING YOU THING!

Welp. Too late now, might as well embrace it.

I gave the alpha a smile and his hard face softened. He walked up to me, slinging an arm around my shoulder before leading us to the kitchen, everyone in the other room debating whether or not to stop bowing yet.

That went much better than expected.

Thank god Jack didn't question the fact that I didn't bow. He at least knew I was an alpha so probably understood my internal struggles.

He was emitting enough power for even Chris and Heeler to have to bow, that takes a lot. A beta and Gamma don't submit easily. But me? I felt nothing. No urge to bow, in fact I felt the urge to stand taller.

At least the smiling thing works. I'm telling you, its the secret to life.

Jack and I sat down with a tub of ice cream and two spoons.

After a couple minutes of silence I looked up to see him observing me.

"Do you mind if I ask you a question? It's kind of personal."

I shrugged, "You can ask, I might not answer."

"Why aren't you still at your old pack? We discussed that you ran away but I never actually knew why. I know Blood Thunder is very old in their ways and your parents aren't the warmest people I've met, but what pushed you to leave?"

I was dreading the question but I knew it was coming.

"I'd prefer not to answer this one if you don't mind, Jack." I replied , throwing on a small smile and pushing back the tears.

Suddenly Jen came bursting through the doors, saving me from this awkward moment.

"ELLIE, BITCH, THERE YOU ARE!" She exclaimed, throwing her arms up in the air.

As soon as the words left her mouth Alpha Jack had her pinned by her neck against the wall, suffocating her.

"What did I say about talking shit about Ellie?" He threatened as Jen tried to pry his hands off, panic flooding her features as she struggled.

Next thing I knew I was grabbing Jack and tossing him across the room with a growl, standing protectively in front of Jen.

He stood up and I growled lowly at him, daring him to push me.

He stopped dead in his tracks, shock covering his face.

I could feel my breaths get shallow and my teeth and claws come out, ready to attack if I needed to.

My family was being threatened and that was all I could process in that moment.

I felt Jen's hand on my back making me flinch.

When I turned around to look at her she jumped back putting her hands up.

Ten

"Don't be pushed around by the fears in your mind. Be led by the dreams in your heart."

– Roy T. Bennett

After a moment of awkward silence the reality of the situation finally hit me.

Shit.

I just threw an Alpha across the room and threatened him on his own territory, not to mention he was just trying to protect me.

SHIT.

I stood up straight, retracting my claws and teeth a blush forming on my face. I brought my hands to my mouth in shock.

"Oh my God, Jack I'm so sorry! Are you okay?"

He nodded slowly, eyeing me with wide eyes. We all just stood there in an EXTREMELY awkward silence before Jen thankfully decided to break the tension. Thank god I could almost always count on her to get me out of the awkward shit I was always throwing myself into.

"I'm sorry I interrupted you two, Alpha," She started hesitantly, glancing around the room nervously, playing with her fingers as she attempted not to make eye contact with the potentially explosive alpha. Setting him off right now would be a very very bad idea. "I just came to get my sister here to tell her something. I didn't mean to offend you or her in any way nor did I mean to threaten either of you at all." She finished, giving her best innocent look which was honestly kind of scary.

I really love her but she was more of the resting bitch face, don't fuck with me kind of person, unlike me who was almost the exact opposite. I always looked younger than I am and excessively innocent and sweet. It was kind of annoying because on the rare occasion that I really did get angry no one really took me seriously.

He looked between us with his eyebrows furrowed.

"Well not sister sister like by blood, I just consider her my sister. Like, not just because we're good friends either, but my father is Henry who I'm sure you know took her in. I'm not like Green, I have nothing to do with the Blood Thunder pack I swear! I'M INNOCENT!" She babbled nervously and I had to smack her lightly in the stomach to get her to shut up. "Ya." She finished out nervously, making the entire situation really awkward all over again.

"Alright," Alpha Jack spoke up, smiling tensely, "I'll leave you two to it, see you in training tomorrow." he said before leaving. He looked a little unsure about the whole situation as expected since I threw him across the room by accident but he seemed like he could move past it pretty quickly. Or at least I hope he can.

As soon as the door closed Jen turned to me with GIANT eyes.

"ELLIE MOTHERFUCKING GREEN!" I cringed at her using my full name. I hated being associated with Alpha and Luna Green.

"Oops?" I said softly and she awarded me with a short little yelping sort of screamish grunt.

"YOU HAVE GOT A LOT TO EXPLAIN YOUNG LADY!" I sighed, nodding with a sheepish smile stuck on my face as we sat down.

"OKAY! I have so many question holy shit like, what happened earlier? I've been hearing rumors all day, why didn't you tell me?! Does it have anything to do with that sexy ass alpha that clearly has a thing for you and OH MY GOD DID YOU JUST THROW A FULL GROWN ALPHA MALE ACROSS THE ROOM?!!!"

I cringed at all her questions and tried to answer her the best I could. She demanded for basically my entire day in full, agonizing detail, yelling at me if I skipped anything. I swear this girl wanted to know if I sneezed.

"So what did you want to talk to me about?" I asked.

"OH YA! I GOT THE DATE FOR THE MATING BALL WRONG! ITS THE DAY AFTER TOMORROW!" She squealed jumping up and down.

Panic set over me.

"TWO DAYS?! HOW DID YOU LET ME RAMBLE ON ABOUT THE GUYS' BODIES WHEN YOU HAD REAL NEWS?!" I may have described their abs in great detail... What can I say! They were shirtless! Training! Sweating! There's only so much self control a girl can have.

"HEY! THE RATING OF EACH OF THEIR BUTTS ON A SCALE FROM 1 TO PLUMP IS REAL NEWS!" Oh ya... I might have done that too...

We decided to go shopping for outfits tomorrow after training. It would be tight but it would have to do. I mean, It was already 5:30pm by the time Jen and I were finished ranting and the malls would've been about to close by the time we got there.

I decided to go for a jog through the forest with my extra time, being extra careful this time, despite the fact that I knew there were new precautions to ensure it wouldn't happen again. On my way out Heeler caught up to me.

"Hey, you going for a run?" He asked, smiling slightly.

I nodded with a full smile on my face.

"Mind if I join you?" He shuffled a little, staring at his feet while he waited for my answer. The big guy could be pretty adorable.

"Of course, I'll wait for you to go get changed."

He was wearing a nice shirt that he certainly couldn't run in with grey sweatpants on the bottom. The combination was a little odd but he managed to pull it off.

"No need." He said then proceeded to slowly peel his shirt off, showing all his muscles flexing and his gorgeous abs stretching. Fuck he's good looking. Let's just say if he was my mate I wouldn't be complaining, except for the fact that I would be dead soon and wouldn't be able to spend any time with him and then he'd be alone for the rest of his life because I'm probably sterile and can't have a child for him - stop. Positive. Reset. Happiness. Okay.

He smirked at me when he noticed me staring away from his face a little too long and I felt a little heat creep up my neck making his smirk annoyingly large. I glared at him, well two can play at this game.

I smirked confidently, resulting in a confused expression falling onto his face.

"Good idea!" I said brightly then proceeded to pull off my own shirt, leaving me in my fairly revealing sports bra. I borrowed Jen's which was little small for me, which is why I originally out a shirt on but fuck it. Everything important is covered up. Most of my scars had disappeared by now too. Gotta love werewolf hearing, sure it's killing me but at least my skin looks nice.

He immediately shut up, his eyes going wide as he stared really intensely at my face, clearly willing himself not to look down.

I laughed a little before taking off.

I felt his eyes stray to my chest halfway through. I looked over, trying to hold in my laughter. I gave him a firm look and snapped in his face. "My eyes are up here." I said, making him blush.

Payback is sweet.

On our jog we came across a stream and decided to stop to dip our feet in the water and cool off a little from the hot sun that was beating down on us, even through the trees of the forest.

As we sat down I could hear his gentle panting that he was obviously desperately trying to hold in. His mouth was closed but he was breathing really loudly through his nose and his chest was moving really quickly. Poor guy is probably embarrassed that I can outrun him. He shouldn't take it to heart, I've always been good at running.

In all senses. I'm fast, but I never seem to stick to anything too long. I already know that's going to get worse now that I'm dying. I can't stay anywhere too long or people will get attached and my death won't be nearly as easy as I had planned.

I was stretching my arms out, jumping in place a little, feeling a little restless but I knew Heeler needed the break.

"How the fuck are you still energetic?" He asked, exasperated, squinting at me in jealous irritation. "This morning's training was rough, even for Jack. No one ever feels the need to do a second work out, let alone a long run through the forest after one of my trainings."

I laughed a little shrugging.

"You're tired?"

He nodded stiffly, a little embarrassed. "I pushed myself hard this morning." That was definitely true. I noticed it, he really pushed himself to the limit.

"Then why'd you come with me?" I asked curiously, not wanting it to seem like I didn't want him here. It was nice to have company, it was hard being alone all the time sometimes.

He shifted uncomfortably, giving me a sheepish smile and I was immediately wary.

"I uh, know about what happened the last time you went for a jog and well..."

"Well?"

"Well, I wasn't comfortable with you going alone again. I figured you'd be safer with me around..."

I smile lit up my face and I made a little 'aw', making his flush slightly. He was adorable.

Before I could thank him he was already switching up the subject.

"Come on, lets head back, it's already dark." He said, standing up and brushing himself off. We ran for hours, through the sunset. I've always loved to run but the it has kind of grown into an obsession since ai left Blood Thunder. I could do it for days without getting tired of it. It just felt so freeing and so good to let out all the extra energy.

My only problem was that I was still a little uncomfortable in these woods, every once in a while the memory of my last run would flash through my mind and ruin my fun. The only upside is that I was a pro at pushing away things I didn't want to think about and focusing on the positive in every situation.

If I hadn't been attacked I never would have known I was dying. I would have let myself think I could have a normal happy life and when I died I wouldn't be prepared. So, it's good I was attacked, it was a positive and essential part to my journey, and I wouldn't be me without it.

By the time we finally got back to the pack house Heeler looked like he was going to pass out. I lied, pretending I needed to take a break a couple times on the way back, when in reality, I was doing it for him. I kept noticing him puffing and his form was deteriorating noticeably as we went.

I felt kind of bad for taking him out as far as I did but he didn't protest at all so I just assumed he could handle it.

Clearly I was wrong... My bad.

In his defense we ran about 250 kilometers, to the other side of the territory and back, making it 500 km total in only 6 hours. That's counting the hour break at the lake though.

I felt good, a little more relaxed, I had gotten most of my excess energy out.

"Ellie!" I heard from behind me. I turned around to see Chris jogging towards me. I gave him a large smile which he happily returned. He picked me up into a hug.

"You're just so cute!" He replied swinging me around. We had gotten pretty close weirdly fast during our training sessions. He felt like the best friend I never really had. Jen was my sister, Jack my brother, Chris my cuddly, golden retriever energy best friend and Heeler... I don.t know what Heeler is yet."You're like a little baby bear!" I let out a little laugh at his affection, hugging him back. I honestly love hugs and he clearly does too.

He put me down and a frown took over his face and he walked away.

"Ummm what the fuck?" I mumbled to myself.

He came back 2 seconds later and his eyes were two shades darker as he stared at me intensely. He looked around and fury took over his face.

I followed his actions, looking around and found that everyone was staring at me. The girls giving me death stares and the guys' eyes filled with lust. That's when it hit me. I'm still in my very revealing too small sports bra...

Oops?

I felt my face heat up a little then turned to Chris with a sheepish smile on my face, which, thank the lords, made his expression soften a little. He threw a shirt at me, pretending to still be annoyed but I could see the smile twitching at his lips that he was pushing down.

I slipped it on and he put a protective arm around me, giving everyone else a death stare, silently telling them to mind their own business which they thankfully did.

"I just saw Heeler, he looked like he was goin to pass out, what the hell did you do to him?" He asked with a playful smile.

I just shrugged letting out a little laugh. "I guess our run did a go a little bit longer than he had anticipated."

"I heard you two ran 500 kilometers in five hours... "

"Ya, I guess we did..."

"How the hell are you still standing?"

I just shrugged. I needed to stop before my shoulders started cramping up.

"I also heard you threw Jack, an alpha, which I know you know but I feel is an important piece of information, across the room like it was nothing and then proceeded to threaten him..."

"Ya, about that- uhm- I didn't really mean to! It was instinct! He was attacking Jen, and nobody except me is allowed to attack my sister."

"It was an instinct to throw a fully grown alpha male across the room?"

"Uhmmm, well..." I shrugged innocently, rubbing my shoulder that was starting to spaz from the recurring movement.

He chuckled, shaking his head.

"You really are like a little baby bear. You look all cute and cuddly but it would not be a good idea to piss you off."

I squared up my shoulders, facing him playfully.

"I am not cute! I am scary!"I said in my most threatening voice, narrowing my eyes and pouting slightly, crossing my arms in an intimidating way.

This just made him laugh harder.

See? No one takes me seriously when I'm mad. Mind you, I'm not actually mad right now, but this is exactly what I would look like if I was. I've always been good at faking my emotions.

"Prove it." He said, a cocky smile on his face.

With that I leapt at him, grabbing the arm he flung up to block me with, leaping over his shoulder and gracefully throwing him to the ground, pinning him immediately after he hit the ground. Heeler's pointers and training were already starting to transform my fighting to get even better. It was finally starting to show that I was an alpha.

My bark was pathetic but my bite was not.

I was straddling his waist as he just continued to laugh, making me punch him in the shoulder which he pretended not to feel. At this point everyone was staring at some girl pinning their beta to the ground.

"Exactly what I'm saying! Don't piss off the little bear! She might be cute but she's feisty. By the way, I like feisty." He winked making me roll my eyes, get off him and help him up as he wiped his tears.

"I'm not cute." I mumbled angrily but he just made an 'aw' face as I punched him again.

"Dick." I mumbled.

"Bitch." He responded and stuck his tongue out at me childishly.

Suddenly the play-fullness slipped off his face and with one good look from Chris everyone went back to their lives but I still noticed them sending me mixed looks.

"You've got to teach me how to do that." I said in awe. It would be so convenient if I just needed to look at someone to get them to leave me alone.

We turned around to see an exhausted looking Heeler staring at us, his big frame sulking as he watched us.

"Are you even tired at all from our training AND run?!" He groaned and I shook my head sadly. To be totally honest I was ready to go right back out, but this time without Heeler so that I could run as fast and as far as I wanted. I'd never admit it to him but he really held me back.

Chris and I burst out into laughter as Heeler continued to sulk, though I could see the smile he was desperately trying to fight back. I don't know what happened to the stone faced Heeler I first met but its safe to say that I'm liking the new him a lot better.

"Awe Heeler, come 'ere" I said, opening my arms out for a hug.

Heeler finally let the smile slip onto his face as he came to hug me but before he could Chris swept me up bridal style and proceeded to run away with me.

"NO! SHE'S MY BEAR, I WANT THE HUGS!" I laughed at their childishness, shaking my head a little. I'd come a long way since Blood Thunder pack.

I felt so happy, I finally had friends, but every time I realized just how good my life was getting, I'd remember just how soon it was all going to end.

"NO! YOU CAN'T JUST STEAL MY HUGS!" Heeler boomed, his voice loud and intimidating but Chris just giggled like a child, running away happily, bouncing me lightly in his arms.

"I CAN AND I WILL! I AM THE BETA!"

Heeler ran towards us, knocking Chris onto the floor just as he let me down.

I just watched them wrestling, fighting for nothing, tears of laughter streaming down my face.

It was so nice to have friends again. I really liked these guys and couldn't help but be a little nervous about how things might change when they get their mates.

Our friendship would be different, whether we wanted it to be or not. Its just the way it was. To other people it might look like they were into me or I was falling for them but we knew that it just wouldn't really be like that. They all had their mates and they deserved so much.

So much more than a dying runt could offer them.

I felt a tap on my shoulder and turned around to see a smirking Jen.

"I saw the whole thing." She said with a knowing smile.

We just laughed together as the boys tired themselves out wrestling.

Chris of course won, he was the Beta and Heeler was still exhausted from our run.

"We should probably get to bed, we're going to start shopping as soon as the stores open. We've got a lot of work to do." I nodded along, following her to our room and we both fell asleep almost instantly.

Eleven

"When you are joyful, when you say yes to life and have fun and project positivity all around you, you become a sun in the center of every constellation, and people want to be near you."

– Shannon L. Alder

I was woken up by a loud, pig-like squealing.

"ELLIE! WAKE THE FUCK UP ITS SHOPPING DAY BITCH." Jen yelled loudly, her voice filled to the brim with excitement.

I just groaned and rolled over, burying my head further into my pillow. I was having an amazing dream!! Not that I remember what it was about now... Shit, but I knew it was good!

She went silent for a second and just as I thought I was going to get away with going back to sleep I felt my amazing, warm, cozy cover being yanked off my body.

I sat up quickly and glared harshly at Jen.

"Ya, ya, fuck you too, now go get ready we're leaving in 20. " With that she skipped out the door. SKIPPED. IN THE MORNING.

I swear if she wasn't my sister.

I quickly got ready and finished in exactly 19 minutes. Shit, I have on minute to get to Jen before she kills me. I darted out of the door and through the mansion, trying not to run into people as I weaved around the overly confusion hallways.

I was honestly so excited about shopping. Now that I had money I could buy whatever I wanted, but I never knew what to get. Sydney had taken me shopping a lot during my time as a bounty hunter, and I always enjoyed it, but I just never knew what to get and what I could pull off.

Sydney always yelled at me that I could pull off anything but I had a hard time believing that. No one can pull off everything, and if it were someone it definitely wouldn't be me. I'd have to have a certain level of confidence that I just can't seem to reach.

I ran into the kitchen to see the 3 guys, Heeler, Jack and Chris.

"Hey Ellie, we're joining you shopping today!" Jack exclaimed, no asking for permission or anything out of politeness. Typical alpha.

"What?" I asked quickly, checking the clock excessively and eyeing the door.

"Well, you told us you couldn't train this morning because you and um..." Chris stumbled a little.

"Jen." I filled in, rolling my eyes.

"YES! Thank you. Jen. You and Jen are going shopping and we all decided that since we might be finding our mates tomorrow we all want to spend one more proper day together! No jealous mates to stop us! Not that we do anything to be jealous about..."

He turned a little red as everyone gave him a look so Heeler quickly saved him.

"So we decided to come shopping with you today, if that's okay with you?"

"Of course!" I gave them a big smile. "I'm sure Jen will be fine with it too but I should warn you, she gets a little intense when it comes to shopping..."

"We'll be fine" Jack chuckled, "We are the 3 ranking males, other than my father, after all. I think we can handle her."

"Ya, sure." I mumbled, knowing damn well no one could handle Jen when she shopped.

We walked out to see an impatient looking Jen. "I TOLD YOU 20 MINUTES! ITS BEEN 21! NOW I'LL HAVE TO SPEED!"

She noticed the three shocked looking idiots behind me and raised her eyebrows.

"They're coming with." I said, gesturing behind me since they were all suddenly mute.

"As long as you all stay out of Ellie's and my way." She said eyeing them all.

Normally Jen wouldn't have the kind of crazy confidence it took to speak to a high ranking wolf like the but when it came to shopping nothing would stop her.

Nothing.

They just stood there, shocked at her change in demeanor.

"WELL, STOP STANDING AROUND LIKE A BUNCH OF LOLLIPOPS STUCK IN SOME TAFFY AND GET YOUR ASSES IN THE CAR!"

We all literally sprinted to the car, pilling in as quickly as possible. Jen drove, Jack in the front while I was squished between a giant Heeler and Chris in the back. I decided to leave the front to Jack since he was by far the largest out of all of us.

"Buckle up." Jen said darkly, making the guys' eyes widen noticeably.

That's all Jen had to say for all of us to lunge for our seatbelts, buckling up as fast as possible. Once we did she gave a quick nod before slamming on the gas, going flying to the main roads towards the mall.

I failed at holding in my laugh when I noticed Chris and Heeler had tensed up on either side of me. Jack up front was gripping onto the handle like there was no tomorrow, his knuckles turning white. I'm honestly surprised he didn't crush it under his grip.

I wasn't that scared. I mean, I'm going to die anyways, this wouldn't be the worst way to go. I just linked my arms with Chris and Heeler who were pressed up against me, giving them a reassuring squeeze and a smile.

I felt them relax but they were still a little on edge. Halfway through the ride Jack looked back, panic still painted on his face.

"Hey, no fair! How come I have to sit up here in the death seat while you two get to sit back there being comforted by Ellie!" He whined, making Chris and Heeler stick their tongues out at him while I gave him a sympathetic shrug.

"Chill out you big baby, we're almost there." Jen instructed from the driver's seat, making Jack turn back around to face the front and behave.

I tried to unlink one of my arms to give Jack a comforting pat but they both just held on tighter, not letting go. I gave them each a scolding look before settling back down.

When we finally arrived at the mall I could hear everyone let out a relieved breath but I knew better. As soon as the car stopped Jen was leaping out, yelling at us to 'get our motherfucking lazy, slow, fat asses out of the ,motherfucking car' before she comes to get us and 'yanks the lollipop out of our bodies' whatever that means.

I don't know what her sudden obsession with lollipops were, and it might not have made a lot of sense but it definitely had the four of us leaping out of the car.

Jen immediately strutted ahead, power walking as I dragged a shocked Heeler and Chris behind me, their arms still locked with mine while Jack trailed behind, trying to keep up without having to jog.

As soon as we entered the mall Jen started telling us her detailed plan, listing off each of the shops we had to go to and when. She even scheduled in lunch, snack and mandatory bathroom breaks to keep us shopping at our best.

We entered a gorgeous looking dress shop and Jen shooed the boys away, linking her arm with mine instead.

"Okay Ellie, this shop has the best dresses at the best prices. We will buy our dresses here, I guarantee it."

The shop was humongous, probably about the size of a Macie's if you've ever been in one, with multiple floors.

Jen got the attention of one of the workers who looked like she'd rather be anywhere else. "Hey you, we need dresses for a gigantic event tomorrow!" She was clearly a human so we couldn't say exactly what it is.

"We want fun and sexy as well as graceful. Got it?" With that we all started picking out dresses for both ourselves and each other. The boys were wandering around looking lost so Jen gave them the job of carrying the dresses. Jack carried mine, Chris carried Jen's and Heeler helped pile it onto each of them so they could carry it properly.

I gave them all an apologetic smile, which they all returned, their moods brightening a little bit. THE POWER OF THE SMILE!

After about 2 and a half hours of picking out dresses we had been through the entire store and headed to the dressing room. Chris and Jack were carrying mountains of clothes so high I couldn't even see their faces anymore, and they were big guys.

We each headed into the fancy changing rooms, Jen somehow getting us the big ones with the mirrors, and began trying stuff on. I looked at the giant pile and was immediately intimidated.

I tried them on one by now, leaving the change room and going into the sitting area where the boys were waiting. Jen and I would come out together, examining each other's dresses and looking at them in the gigantic mirror. We would all rate the dresses, even the guys, though they would almost always give it a 10 unless it was truly hideous.

After 2 hours of trying on dresses I was down to my last one few. The first one looked a little odd on the hanger which is why I had left to to last, but you never know. I had a few good contenders anyways. Jen had finished a few dresses back and chosen out a gorgeous green dress that complemented her red hair perfectly.

My dress was red and flowy with a low v cut and a slit to show off my long tanned legs. I put it on and instantly felt more confident. I smiled at my reflection. This is the one, I thought to myself.

I stepped out of the dressing room and everyone stopped talking. Jen squealed a little, jumping up and down.

"THAT'S THE ONE!" She yelled, making my smile even wider.

The guys just stared at me, looking me up and down, making me shift uncomfortably.

"Stop staring at her like that and tell her how gorgeous she looks!" Jen ordered them.

They all muttered some complements, each one turning a little red as they continued to stare.

I just rolled my eyes and went to get changed so we could stay on schedule.

After we paid we all headed to the food court for some lunch, thankfully we finished the longest part. Now we just needed to find shoes and jewelry to match.

The guys were still wary of shopping Jen, clearly trying very hard to stay out of her way which I'm sure she didn't mind.

We all sat down with our hotdogs, trying to gain back all the energy we lost from the long process of choosing a dress.

We sat down and I had Jack on one side and Heeler on the other.

Chris warily sat next to Jen, trying his best not to bump her or annoy her or slow her down in any way.

"Can you guys believe that we might find our mates tomorrow?" Chris asked, making conversation.

"I know man, its crazy, I wonder if everything they said was true." Heeler said, digging into his fourth hot dog.

I just nodded along, thinking about the fact that I'd never know. A dying deformation would never get a mate. At least that's what my parents used to tell me all the time.

They used to repeat, "You're nothing, deserve nothing, the moon goddess would never curse someone to have a mate like you. You were never and will never be loved."

Ever since I was old enough to understand properly they've been telling me this and honestly, I hope no one is forced to be suck with me. I'm a lot more confident now then I've ever been, but some things really stick with me and, despite what everyone says, I know I'm not normal, and I don't deserve to be that happy.

my entire existence ruined my parent's lives, casting a shadow of shame all over my pack. There are no other heirs other than me, and there's not chance I'm taking over, so it may even be the end to the entire pack.

Just me being born ruined so much, I can't imagine the damage I've managed to do, some of which I might not even be aware of, over the years.

I just ate my food and smiled through the pain.

"What do you think your mate will be like?" Jen asked and we went around the table answering, Chris starting.

"I have a feeling she'll be small and cute and sweet but have a feisty side to her"

Jack followed, "I hope mine is nice and caring and strong, she needs to have the qualities of a luna for obvious reasons, and as long as she's shorter me I'm happy."

"I bet my mate will be kind and gentle, someone I can take care of and protect from the world." Heeler added in, staring off dreamily.

"I hope my mate is strong but has a soft spot for me, and I'd love to have kids. He has to be able to deal with and love my crazy side too." Jen blushed as she gave her answer.

Then everyone turned to me and my heart rate sped up. I was the only one who hadn't answered yet.

"I-I don't know." I stuttered, "I guess I've never really thought about it."

All of their answers were so heart felt and perfect and I totally ruined it. Classic Ellie. Always ruining things.

SHUT UP ELLIE POSITIVITY!!

They all accepted that answer, turning back to their food, but they were all clearly disappointed. I felt guilty, but I truly didn't have an answer. I guess I just wanted someone who made me feel happy, and made me feel like I'm enough.

Ya, if I were ever to get a mate that's all I would ask for. I don't care what they look like or if they're a little nerdy or geeky or something, as long as I'm happy and feel wanted.

I couldn't eat my food as my depression hit me.

Sometimes everything really hurt.

I always tried my best to stay positive and push it away, but sometimes there was nothing I could do. I just took deep breaths, trying not to let anyone see the tears that were burning my eyes as I swallowed constantly, trying to hold myself together.

Now was not the time to cry. I was just being dramatic, plenty of people die al the time, I'm not special and I don't need any special treatment. I just have to stop being weak and pull myself together.

As we were leaving the food court Heeler pulled me aside as the others went ahead.

"Ellie and I are just going to go to the bathroom real quick." He announced.

"WHAT?! YOU GUYS JUST HAD A BATHROOM BREAK! You know what, whatever, but you better go faster than you ever have before! Meet us at the shoe store." Jen said with a warning look before stomping off with a scared looking Chris and Jack trailing behind her, sending us pleading looks.

Once they were out of ear shot Heeler turned to me.

"Ellie, something's been off with you since our mate discussion. What's wrong?"

My heart beat sped up and tears sprung to my eyes despite my best efforts.

Shit.

"N-nothing, I'm fine."

Heeler gave me a knowing look and I couldn't stop the tear that slid down my face.

"Ellie... You can tell me anything. Truly. I won't tell anyone."

Fuck it. I really needed to share it with someone, I couldn't hold it inside and keep it to myself anymore. I hated the thought of anyone having to share my burden but I couldn't care about that right now.

"I-I..." I took a deep breath, trying to force the words out, "I don't have a mate."

"What? Why do you say that? Is this because of your form? Ellie, that doesn't matter you'll still get a mate!"

"Yes that, but that's not the only thing. I-I, I'm dying."

There was an uncomfortable pause before Heeler spoke up, "What?"

"I'm dying." I repeated, more strongly this time.

"What the fuck do you mean you're dying? You can't just go around saying, 'I'm dying' without explaining." He said, running his hand through his hand as h began to pace slightly.

"I have about a year left. I'm sick and, its kind of complicated but I'm dying. Why would the moon goddess curse someone with a mate who is not only a deformation, but dying! That would just be cruel. Even if I did have a mate I never want to have to meet them. I never want them to have to lose me like that... Look, I know I don't have a mate and I have accepted that I'm just..." I took a deep breath, "tomorrow's going to be a little hard."

Heeler pulled me in for a hug but not before I noticed his eyes shimmering with tears. It broke my heart even more to see that I'd managed to bring even this strong, confident man down. I shouldn't have told him, it was so selfish of me.

There was a reason I didn't tell anyone, and this was it. Now he'd have to carry this around with him. Not only was it a heavy burden, but now it's also a secret that's going to force him to lie and leave him feeling guilty and horrible.

I really am a horrible friend. Maybe it's a good thing I haven't had very many throughout the years.

"We should probably get back before Jen kills us." I said softly, trying to get away from the horrible situation before I made anything worse.

Heeler nodded, "Look, I'm here for you and I love you," He paused, "as a friend obviously but still. Who else knows?"

"No one." His eyes widened.

"You should really tell-" He started but I held up my hand to stop him.

"Heeler, you said you could keep this a secret. "

"I-I can I just-"

"Heeler." I wanted and he nodded reluctantly.

"Okay. I won't say anything, I promise."

"Thank you." I breathed out.

With that we met back up with Jen and the others in a comfortable silence.

Heeler held my hand and I wanted to let go because I didn't want his pity but he wouldn't let me. I just wanted to stop concentrating on my problems, but his warm hand encasing mine, squeezing every few minutes was just reminding me of everything that was wrong.

I get that it was supposed to be a comforting gesture, but it did nothing but make me feel worse.

'Just smile, everything will be okay' I repeated to myself in my head, forcing to take deep breaths.

But would it?

Twelve

"When you have exhausted all possibilities, remember this: you haven't."

- Thomas Edison

The rest of the shopping trip went pretty well. We all just followed Jen's orders and managed to finish just as the mall was closing at 11pm. The guys were exhausted but I think we all had a very good time in the end.

It was funny watching full grown men so scared of pissing off a fairly harmless little wolf. It would be hilarious to see if her mate could handle her. I just hoped I would live long enough to see it.

We all went straight to bed once we got back, utterly exhausted. Jen said I had to get at least 9 hours of beauty sleep and this was one thing I definitely wouldn't be fighting her on.

****

It was 10:00am and Jen and I were finally making our way out of bed. I decided to go for a quick run to get out my nerves then we would spend the rest of the day pampering and getting ready for 5:00 when everyone would start arriving.

Yesterday at the mall we had mani pedis, facials and got waxed from head to toe. The hair stylists would do my hair at 12:30 and the make-up artists scheduled me for 3:30, leaving me just enough time to change.

My run was going to cut it a little tight to my appointment, but I desperately needed to get some energy out.

I only had 45 minutes of running before Jen would murder me so I made the most out of it, sprinting the entire time. I was probably running at about 400 kilometers per hour. I had gotten pretty fast throughout the years and nothing felt better than whipping through the amazing forests at these incredible speeds.

Something just felt so right about being out in the forests, under the sun and the moon, everything dancing around me, everything in harmony. Sometimes I couldn't help but feel like I was part of the forest, no matter how stupid it sounded.

I thankfully got back just in time to hop into my shower and clean myself thoroughly. I got out, changing into my sweats and made my way to the hair dresser area.

There were frantic girls running all around, desperate to get ready on time. They basically ignored me which I was very thankful for.

Jen was already getting her hair done when I walked in. It looked like she was curling it and braiding the top part to look like a waterfall. Safe to say she looked gorgeous already.

"Ellie!" One of the hairdressers called and I scurried over to him.

"Hi there, sweetheart, well aren't you gorgeous!"

I loved him already. He just had that kind of bubbly, happy energy about him that made me want to spend time with him.

"So what are we thinking today?" He asked, running his hands through my wet strands, careful not to mess with my natural curls.

"I honestly have no idea. You're the expert, you can chose." I decided, trusting the man's sense of fashion.

"Oh, honey you won't be disappointed, now sit your pretty little ass down while I get some things we'll be needing." He winked at me and strutted off, the long, colorful patterned jacket he was somehow pulling off flowing behind him sassily.

He came back with an entire cart full of things different products and machines, some of which I didn't even recognize.

What did I just agree to?

"Darling, I'm going to get creative here so it might take some time. Just relax and enjoy! You'll be perfect in a few hours!"

I did as he said, rolling my shoulders a little as I settled in. There was something so relaxing about hairdressers doing your hair.

"Do you mind if I trim the dead ends a little? Clean it all up" He cringed, holding up my dead ends for me to see.

"Of course," I cringed along with him. I really needed a haircut, "do what you do, I trust you." I laughed.

We shared a smile before he put on a concentrated face and started examining my hair, no doubt deciding exactly what to do.

I closed my eyes, relaxing as he did what he does.

A few hours later he was finally finished. "Okay darling, you can open your eyes now!"

I looked in the mirror and was shocked. My naturally curly hair looked so silky, shiny and soft, healthier and I'd ever seen it. He had given it a bit of a trim and seemed to have put some kind of treatment on it to fix the slight dryness. He then pulled it up out of my face but left it classy, not overdoing it and making it overly complex looking.

"Its perfect!" I exclaimed, marveling at it. "

"I know, I'm amazing!" He exclaimed, pretending to flip his non-existent hair.

We laughed together before I checked the time, "Oh shit, I have my makeup appointment in 5 minutes!"

"Don't run it'll ruin the hair!" he yelled after me, panic in his voice.

I just laughed and speed walked off to the makeup area that was inconveniently set up at the other end of the house.

I got there just as one of the artists called out my name and rushed over to her. She was taller than me by a couple inches and so gorgeous. She wore natural looking makeup and looked amazing.

"Hi there sweetheart! This shouldn't be too difficult." She complimented and I laughed a little, looking down nervously. I'd never been good at taking compliments. I loved giving them but couldn't take them.

"Look at yourself! I'm surprised someone so naturally pretty would be so amazing with makeup!" I deflected and she just laughed.

"You're so sweet. Sit down so we can get this going."

I did as she said and she went right in. She cleaned and moisturized my face, making sure it was as soft and glowy as possible before she started on my makeup. I closed my eyes to let her do whatever she was doing because she wanted it to be a 'big reveal'.

Once she was done she spun me around to face the mirror and I opened my eyes. I was shocked at my appearance. She seemed to put fairly minimal makeup on but my eyes and lips looked bigger and my cheekbones and jaw more pronounced.

"I absolutely love it!" I squealed to her, sounding more like Jen than myself.

"You look amazing! Now go get changed people have already started arriving!" She said and my eyes widened.

"What?! What time is it?"

"6:45, actually most people are already here..."

"Shit, thank you! Jen's gonna kill me! Pray for me!" I squealed to her waving as I quickly made my way back to our room.

I entered to a frantic looking Jen.

"There you are!!"

"Look Jen-"

"NO TIME FOR TALKING, GET YOUR ASS UNDRESSED NOW!" She yelled as she unzipped my dress, preparing to slip it on me. I quickly threw my clothes off and Jen helped my slip into the dress and zipped me up.

"You look absolutely incredible Jen." I said once I was zipped up and had a moment to appreciate her. She looked beyond amazing in her green dress that matched her bright green eyes. Her makeup was minimal but perfect and her hair flowed gorgeously down her back in soft curls.

"I know right!" She boasted, doing a little turn, "You look stunning." She finished and for some reason we both started tearing up a little.

"Shit our makeup!" She exclaimed as we hugged.

"Ready?" I asked.

"Ready." she confirmed.

We linked arms and headed out. This was it. This was the moment Jen could meet her soul mate, the man she would live with for the rest of her life. Everyone was outside all throughout the pack lands. We would have to just walk around the grounds and we should be able to catch our mates' scent at some point. Then we could track each other and find each other.

My plan was to just stick by Jen and hopefully see her Happily Ever After moment.

We walked arm in arm outside and we both took a big breath, searching for the scent of our mates. I just went along with the motions, playing along for Jen's sake.

The pack lands were beautiful. There were fairy lights hung from the trees, giving it a magical feel. There were food and drink stations set up all over the place and small tables for two placed along around for the new couples.

We walked about three steps before Jen gasped. I looked to her and her eyes seemed to be locked on something. I looked where she was looking and saw a man from across the fields staring right back at her.

Jen dropped my arm and ran to him while he ran to her. They met in an embrace in the middle.

The man took Jen's face in his hands, staring at her face, looking like he's trying to memorize every detail of it.

I teared up a little bit at the happy moment but refused to let them fall as I watched the beautiful scene unfold in front of me. I was so beyond happy for her.

To my left I saw Jack and Chris both with girls in their arms doing similar things as they swayed to the slow music that was drifting through the air.

I let a huge smile slide on face as I watched how happy everyone looked. I just wish I got to see it happen. The moment of shock and happiness where an ear splitting smile spilt over their face and they ran towards each other.

I felt a tap on my shoulder and turned around to see Heeler.

"Walk with me?" He asked and I nodded, still trying to keep the happy tears down.

"Still haven't found her?" I asked, slightly choked up.

"Not yet... I'm pretty nervous honestly." He whispered out the last part and I couldn't help the small laugh that escaped my lips

"It'll be amazing, don't you worry."

Heeler and I started our trek through the gorgeous forest. We strolled together, arms linked as we watched all the other couples.

After about a 15 minute walk in complete silence I heard Heeler start to sniff the air next to me. He froze.

"You found her?" I smile lit up my face.

"I-I think so, but I don't want to leave you here alone."

"Go."

"No, I won't leave y-"

"Heeler I swear to god if you don't get your stupid ass to that beautiful mate of yours I will-"

He put his hands up in surrender, smiling widely. "Okay, okay" and with that he ran off.

I was alone.

I decided to continue my walk, happily watching the couples unite and trying to keep the dark thoughts out of my head.

P - O - S - I - T - I - V - I - T - Y

I was so incredibly happy for all of them. I got to see my friends meet their partners for life. I knew none of them would be alone when I died and I felt much better about the whole thing.

I felt more peaceful.

I closed my eyes and took a deep breath, finally relaxing, when I smelt the most amazing smell in the world.

What the fuck?

I opened my eyes as I sniffed it again. Words couldn't describe the smell it was so amazing. It was familiar but I had never smelt anything like it before.

Then I met eyes with the most beautiful man in the world.

What the actual fuck ?

He came running towards me but all I could do was stand frozen, watching the large, burly man barreling at me.

As soon as I was in reach he grabbed me and embraced me, putting his face in the crook of my neck and inhaling. My heart was beating so fast I'm sure he could hear it.

I looked at his face up close and I almost fainted. It was perfect, looked like it was sculpted by the god of beauty himself.

I ran my finger along his sharp jawline resulting in a deep growl from him. I looked into his eyes and felt complete, the last words I wanted to heard echoing through my mind. I couldn't even try and deny what had just happened. I found my mate.

FUCK.

I knew I should tell him to get away from me, that he couldn't want me and should begin moving on but I couldn't. I felt selfish and couldn't tell him to do anything but hug me tighter and kiss the shit out of me. Somehow I already felt like we were one and to take him away from me was to rip my entire being apart excrutiatingly slowly and painfully.

He stroked my cheek then spoke to me in the most mesmerizing voice I'd ever heard. "What's you name?"

"E-Ellie."

"Ellie." He repeated, a small smile on his face, "Absolutely perfect. Ellie, what?"

I don't know why but I felt compelled to tell him the truth.

"Ellie Green."

As soon as I said that he tensed up and took a step back, a look of shock covering his face.

For some reason everyone was staring at us now.

"You're Alpha Green's daughter?" He asked, disgust lacing his voice.

"Y-yes." I said nervously, my heart racing at his sudden, unexpected change.

"Shift." He growled out and my heart almost started flying away it as beating so fast. I had never wanted the ground to come to life and swallow me whole more than I did in that moment.

"What?" I asked, panic starting to set in.

"I said shift. Now." He seethed, steam practically coming out of his ears as he stood taller, a malicious look in his eyes.

"B-but" I said, shaking my head and beginning to back away.

"GUARDS!" Next thing I knew there were 8 guards on me, grabbing me and pinning me on the ground. Suddenly I felt a sharp pinch in my arm and knew exactly what just happened. He was forcing me to shift.

Not only that but I now knew exactly who he was. Only one man had that many guards following him around, listening to his every order, and only one man could invite this much attention.

He was the prince. The one everyone was dying to meet, the one everyone wanted to be mated to was destined to be mine.

I started shaking, trying to hold back the shift but they just just injected my three more times, until I couldn't hold back anymore and was forced to shift.

My father had used a dose or two before to torture me. The shift that results from the serum is excruciatingly painful. Some people die from the pain alone, their hearts not able to deal with the strain of the torture. One dose could do that.

I was given Four.

My pain tolerance was extremely high, but even I couldn't handle this. It was a whole new level of torture that I had never experienced before. All I could see was bright white as I felt a scream leaving my mouth. My body felt like it was burning and bubbling from the inside out. No one had ever survived this high of a dose. No one had ever lived through such torture.

I could feel my body shaking and my mouth fill with bloody foam.

When I stopped shaking I was in my form and I cold hear gasps and even crying all around. I was still in an insane amount of pain, unable to move or even see, but that didn't stop the shame from overwhelming me as my tiny, limp black deformation laid in a pile of my own blood in the grass, in front of my mate.

I could only hear one thing, one voice that could cut through anything. The voice of my mate saying one of the only things that could hurt me almost as much as my parents had my entire life.

"I, Prince Jacob Kaden Lunar of the werewolves reject you, Ellie Green, rogue."

With that, the pain finally took me and I was released into the empty serenity of the darkness.

Thirteen

"You only live once, but if you do it right, once is enough."

– Mae West

It was dark. I couldn't move nor could I see, but I could faintly hear voices in the background, echoing through the silence as I floated through the numbness of my mind.

"Ellie! Please come back to me." I frantic voice said, interrupting my serenity, "You'll be ok-kay. Y-you will! Oh god, oh god what did they do to you?" It was Jen. Her words were said in between sobs, making me desperately want to get up and hug her and hold her and tell her I was okay, but I couldn't move, I could barely even think before everything went blank again.

Why was I here? What was happening?

I heard soft shushing and Jen's sobs were muffled. I smiled when I realized it must be the man I'd seen her meet at the ball. Her mate.

After that everything faded away again, but a little later another voice filled the void in my head. "Hey Ellie, I don't know if you can hear me but I just want you to know that we're all here for you. Jen called your parents, they're going to come and see you soon. Just hang in there, we love you."

Heeler.

Later Chris came and sat with me. "Oh E-bear, I'm so sorry. Please come back to us. I could really use one of your amazing hugs and I want you to meet my mate! Her name is Jade and I already know you two will get along so well and I just... I miss you. We all do. You can't let go, okay? You have to fight like the little bear you are. You show them how strong you are, okay? And-"

He was cut off by an angry sounding female voice that I went ahead and assumed was his new mate Jade. I hope they're happy together.

They argued for a few seconds, but I couldn't make out their words. Chris let out a loud sigh before they both stopped.

"Bye." He said softly and I couldn't help but wonder where he was going. I didn't want to be selfish but it felt good having him here. It felt good not being alone in my dark, empty mind. Why would his new mate make him leave?

A little later Jack visited but he sounded a little more awkward than the others. "Hey Ellie. I'm so sorry I couldn't stop him. I may be an Alpha, but he's a prince! I wish you were here with us. I found my Luna, her name is Jasmine, and we're going to take over the pack tonight. I wish you could be there to share in the joy with us. Just know we'll be thinking of you and praying for you. You're so strong, I know you can fight through this." With that he left.

They all sounded so happy about their new mates and I hated the jealousy that bubbled up in my chest. I wasn't jealous that I couldn't be with them, I was jealous that they all had someone there with them, not matter what.

For some reason thinking of mates made pain shoot through me, stopping my thoughts in their tracks but I couldn't' remember why. All I could remember was pain.

They were all so sweet and caring. I was constantly fighting to try and get back to them, they sounded so sad and I wanted them to be happy again. I don't know how many days I was out for, but everyone would come and visit me pretty often. Jammie and Henry even moved into the pack house temporarily so they could be here if I woke up, or stand by me while I die.

I could feel the darkness tugging at me every day, trying to tempt me and drag me down into peace but I fought through it.

The excruciating, paralyzing pain never left after I passed out, I never got a break from it though I could feel it fade a little every day. I could't remember why it was there, but I couldn't forget it. It was getting harder and harder to carry on. I was getting tired. Things were getting better, and easier, but I didn't know whether or not it would be fast enough.

I prayed that it wouldn't be, It was not time yet. I got a year. I would not die yet. Not yet.

****

Come on, open your eyes, you can do it. I gave myself the same pep talk I'd been giving myself since the pain wore away enough to allow me to think. Finally, it actually started to work.

My body was finally listening to me and my eyes began to very slowly peel open.

It took so much effort that I almost gave up but I fought through it. Once I did I was met Jammie and Henry cuddling on the couch across from my bed, small tears trailing down their cheeks.

Once they noticed I was finally waking up they leaped up and were at my side in seconds.

"Come on honey, you can do it!" Jamie encouraged, petting my hair in a motherly way.

"Oh my god, thank you, thank you, thank you, she's okay." Henry muttered, pacing excitedly back and forth from my bed, running his hands through his short red hair.

I immediately forced a small smile onto my face, making them sigh in relief. I could hear Henry call the doctor as I blinked the blurriness away and even managed to sit up the slightest bit.

"Stop crying." I rasped out dryly, immediately being met with a small cup of water to my lips. I took a few more sips before trying to speak again, "I'm okay." I said, this time a little more clearly to Jammie which only seemed to make her cry harder.

Next thing I knew the familiar doctor was rushing to my side, pushing my parents away.

She started doing random tests on me, asking me questions about pain and such and I just answered my best, keeping my smile firmly on my face. I was exhausted and had a hard time keeping up with everything that seemed to be moving so quickly around me, but I could feel myself getting better by the second, my healing doing what it did best.

After a couple minutes I sat up straighter and began stretching my limbs.

"How long have I been out?" I asked quietly but everyone seemed to hear me just fine.

"3 weeks. Its a miracle you're awake at all, let alone sitting up on your own. You truly are incredible." The doctor said fondly, proud but sad smiles forming on Jamie and Henry's faces.

I swung my legs off the bed and stood up stiffly making everyone gasp.

I looked around in confusion, stretching a little more but decided to shrug their reaction off.

I knew it wasn't normal that I was walking, but I was sick of sitting around. I didn't have that much time left and I refused to spend it unconscious and pitying myself.

One dose of force shifting concoction can keep you in a coma for 3 months with a 6 month recovery period before you can even think about walking. No one's ever lived through 3 doses. Being rejected can put you into a 2 month coma, usually taking years before you can smile again and even begin to try and be happy, but I'm not even sure this was the worst thing I had endured. My body had really built itself up strongly, which was the entire reason I only had a year left.

It really was both a blessing and a curse.

My physical pain form the shifting was gone, already healed, but I could still feel my heart throbbing weakly in my chest, filled and weighed down with sorrow and betrayal.

Every part of me begged for me to fall onto the floor and just cry. Part of me even considered suicide, just to escape the overwhelming pain, but I immediately just pushed down those thoughts, like I had been doing my entire life. I shot Jamie and Henry a smile before asking them to walk with me. We went outside and onto the path through the forest that lead to the pack house.

"So, tell me, what have I missed?" I smiled at them, pretending nothing was wrong when in reality I just wanted to drop to the ground and scream and cry and brake things.

They looked at me shocked for literally 2 minutes and 43 seconds before Henry finally spoke up.

"Uhm, are you sure you want to know? You know, being rejected and all." Henry spoke up earning himself a good whack from Jamie as I held back my cringe.

"Alpha Jack found his mate, Jasmine, and they took over the pack, they've been running it for about a 2 and a half weeks now and are doing a wonderful job. He is a natural alpha and she is a natural caring Luna." Jamie said, taking over and probably trying to make up for her husband's bluntness. "Jen found her mate, Brian, and they are a perfect match. He is calmer, more down to earth and can handle her energy perfectly, they both keep each other in check, but they also seem really happy together."

"It's sickening." Henry muttered and Jamie nudged him making him shrug indifferently.

"It's cute." Jamie corrected but Henry shook his head before continuing the explanation for his wife.

"Your friend Heeler found his mate but she wasn't in the best shape. Her parents had died and her foster home was abusing her, but Heeler is taking care of her. We were thinking that you could help given the fact that you were abused by your family and rejected and all that."

Jamie hit him even harder this time making him flinch. "That's it. No more speaking for you. How you make it through life with out constantly getting beat up I will never know."

Henry scoffed, "I'd like to see them try and beat all this up. One look and they'll go running for the hills."

"Oh honey, don't worry, you aren't THAT ugly." Jamie said softly, rubbing his arm mockingly before turning back to me.

"I think you could do a lot of good in helping Sarah, and I'm sure Heeler would be very grateful. He's already pretty infatuated with you though, so don't get too close to the situation."

I ignored the end of her sentence, rolling my eyes, "Ya of course, I'd be happy to help." I said sincerely and both of them just smiled proudly, hanging onto each other, sharing secret looks before staring back at me.

It was a little weird honestly but their hearts were in the right place so I moved past it.

When we exited the forest and arrived at the pack house I could hear gasps all around. They all saw me, they all know what happened and they all saw my deformation.

I just walked though it, I kept my head up and a smile on my face. I really wanted to run back into the cover of the forest and cry over all of my losses, but I couldn't. I wouldn't. I already wasted almost a month in a stupid coma, I would not give that man any more of the limited time I had left.

Jen came running out of the house, her mate trailing behind her, tears streaming down her face.

"ELLIE!" She screeched as I met her halfway and gave her a long, tight hug and let her cry on my shoulder. I looked up, meeting eyes with her mate and gave him a smile as Jen stepped back.

"This is Brian, my mate. Brian, this is my sister, Ellie" Jen managed to get out through her sniffles.

"Nice to meet you Brian. You better take good care of my sister or I will hunt you down and kill you." Even in my slightly weakened state he knew that I was perfectly capable and in no way kidding. I would follow through. His eyes widened and he quickly nodded.

Jen gave me a bit of a death stare for saying that but she looked more amused than anything, even though she tried to hide it.

Brian laughed onerously, hiding behind Jen slightly which just made the whole situation more amusing to her and her parents that were still lingering.

"Jen told me all about you, I feel like its very important that you know that I would never do anything to hurt her nor let anyone hurt her. I'd really like to keep my head on my shoulders" He explained nervously, a British accent obvious as he spoke.

I narrowed my eyes, "I would never behead you for hurting Jen." I shook my head and he visibly relaxed but the rest of us knew exactly where I was going with this and they all held back laughs as I tilted my head innocently at him. "That wouldn't be nearly fast enough. I was thinking paralyzing snake venom, maybe ripping limbs off slowly, maybe I can even whip out my whip or-"

"Okay!" Jen stopped me, laughing. Brian visibly gulped and grabbed Jen's arm tightly.

I glared at it and he dropped her arm, backing up with his hands up.

I liked him, he and Jen would be good together, I could tell.

"Ellie, I actually need to talk to you.... alone" Jen spoke up, a sad tinge to her voice.

With that everyone said their goodbyes, leaving us to talk.

Henry and Jammie hugged me tightly before heading back to their house. They had to go back to their lives. They couldn't stay here any more, after all, Jammie was a human. I was sad to see them go but wouldn't be selfish and try and make them stay.

Brian went inside, shooting me a sad smile, clearly already knowing what this chat was about and by the look on Jen's face I knew this wasn't going to be a happy conversation.

We sat down on a bench nearby, surrounded by yellow flowers that instantly made me feel slightly better. The sun on my face and the nature surrounding me made me feel safer, less alone.

"How are you doing? You seem okay but I can't even imagine what you're going through." She said softly, trying to hold her tears in and appear strong. I knew right there that I'd have to be strong for her. She couldn't handle the truth and she didn't need the burden that seemed to be crushing me every second I tried to breathe, taunting me and trying to pull me into the darkness.

"I'm totally fine." I lied, shrugging slightly. I was starting to think it was becoming a nervous tick of sorts. If anyone payed attention they'd see that every time I was lying or hiding anything my shoulders lifted in an effort to appear nonchalant. "What's up? You looked like you had something important to tell me."

"Well, I do." She took a deep breath, "It's Brian he's well... He's the gamma of a pack in England. He was visiting his cousins here and decided to come to the event for fun. He never thought he would find his mate here but well, here we are. The thing is..."

"You're moving to England with him." I finished for her. That's how it worked, since her mate held a ranking position in his pack it would have to be Jen that would move. If Jen had been a Beta or Alpha or even Gamma he would've moved to her pack but she was just a pack warrior.

She looked at me, tears streaming down her face. "I-I can't leave you."

I wanted to cry but I could tell she needed me to be happy and okay for her, otherwise I'm not sure she would go. She needed to go. This would be amazing for her.

"You're going to be the best warrior there, they're so lucky to have you." I said smiling proudly at her and she broke down in my arms again.

I held her tightly while she cried, refusing to let her go. To anyone else it would just seem like I was hugging her, but really I did it so she couldn't see the single tear the managed to slip down my face.

After about an hour of sitting and catching up we headed back inside.

I was instantly met with a smiling Chris picking me up and spinning me around in a big bear hug. "E-BEAR, YOU'RE BACK!" He exclaimed happily and we both started laughing a little.

Next thing I knew I was being grabbed by my hair and was thrown onto the ground.

I was still pretty weak from everything but thankfully was still strong enough to remain conscious. I sat up, a little dizzy, holding my head in confusion. I looked up to be met by some girl yelling at me, baring her teeth.

"WHO THE FUCK ARE YOU AND WHAT ARE YOU DOING WITH MY MATE!" She yelled.

Chris grabbed her from behind as he looked at me apologetically. The girl I knew as Jade, Chris's mate fought his grip, trying to lunge at me.

"I am so sorry, Ellie." Chris managed to say, his tone worried as he took in my confused, dizzy state and I shrugged at him, trying to force out a small smile.

Jade froze when he said that turning to him. "This is THE Ellie?" She asked loudly, dread in her voice. He nodded and she turned around, bringing her hands to cover her mouth.

"Oh my god! I am so sorry!" She exclaimed running to my side. When she reached me I couldn't help the flinch that took over. My anxiety, confusion and temporary weakness mixed together was not a good combination I wasn't strong enough to fight my old instincts. This seemed to make her feel even worse, which really wasn't my intention, as she looked at me with wide panic eyes.

"Chris told me all about you and what happened to you and I am so sorry! How the hell are you up so soon! I just saw Chris with some random girl and I lost my shit! I have some anger issues, I know" She sighed aggressively, her fists clenched tightly, "but I'm really working on it, I really really am, I am so, so sorry."

"Its okay," I waved my hand with a small smile. "I understand." I finished softly, shrugging nervously, holding back my groans and fighting to the dizziness as I lifted myself back up to my feet.

"Oh my fucking god, of course you're as sweet as they say. I really fucked up. CLASSIC JADE, GOING AND FUCKING EVERYONE OVER AC-CIDENTALLY WITH MY BIG ASS MOUTH FUCK FUCK FUCK FUCK FUCK!" I saw tears start forming in her eyes. "What the fuck is wrong with me?" She she whispered but Chris was immediately by her side, hugging her and rubbing her back. Shushing her softly as she hung onto him sadly.

They were really adorable together.

Right on time Jack came around the corner with his new mate, Jasmine I believe Jamie said her name was.

"Ellie!" He exclaimed, walking over to me and embracing me, surprising me a little. Jack wasn't usually as joyful and affectionate as the other two. "You're okay?" He asked, wrapping his arm back around his beautiful mate.

"I'm totally fine." I said nonchalantly, shrugging my shoulders. I've got to stop shrugging goddammit. I'm starting to look like one of those weird puppets.

"What's happening there?" he asked, pointing to a hysterical Jade.

"Nothing really, don't worry, I think Chris is handling it."

"WHAT DO YOU MEAN NOTHING?!" Jade then screeched from Chris' grasp. "I JUST THREW YOU ON THE GROUND BY YOUR HAIR AFTER YOU JUST CAME OUT OF A COMA! WHY AREN'T YOU REPORTING ME?!"

"I'm fine" I said with a soft smile shrugging, trying as hard as I could to make it genuine. I really wanted it to be genuine, she seemed like a nice person and I hoped we could be friends one day.

"Anyways..." Jack said changing the subject, "This is my mate, Jasmine."

"Its nice to meet you Luna Jasmine" I greeted. "Congratulations to you both I heard you guys are doing amazing already."

Jasmine came and hugged me. "I've heard so much about you and please, just call me Jas."

"Okay Jas." I said with a smile.

"Heeler is just in the kitchen with his mate. I'm sure he'd love to see you but he doesn't want to leave her alone." Jack explained and I nodded.

"Lead the way!" I said, a little too enthusiastically. I had to tune it down a little.

I really missed them all but I couldn't help but notice how much everything has changed. I hated the fact that I felt a little jealously build up inside. I didn't want to be mated to any of the guys or anything, but everyone had someone and I couldn't help but struggle to breathe under the crushing loneliness that managed to crush me despite the fact that I was in a room full of people.

Fourteen

"Life is like a box of chocolates. You never know what you're going to get."

– Forrest Gump

We headed into the kitchen where Heeler was sitting on a stool with his face in his hands. He lifted it briefly to look at me but looked absolutely exhausted and sick. It looked like he hadn't slept or eaten properly in weeks.

As we walked in further I saw a small, clearly underweight girl sitting curled up in a ball under the counter.

"Ellie. Thank god you're okay" He said weakly and I smiled softly, shrugging against my will. I really don't know where this shrugging thing came from but I've got to stop. People are definitely going to notice and then my otherwise perfect facade will fly right out the window.

I went over to him and gave him a big hug. He smelt pretty horrible but I fought through it, he looked like he needed it.

"Is that your mate?" I asked to which he nodded his head slowly.

"That's Sarah."

"Do you mind if I go say hi?" I said gently.

"Be my guest. I trust you completely, but I should warn you, she hasn't spoken eaten or slept yet."

I just nodded before making my way over. I sat next to her on the ground and she looked up at me. Her eyes looked a little dead, and deep down I felt like I was staring into a mirror. She looked exactly how I did all those years ago, before I had accepted the reality of my life, before I pushed it all down and put up all my facades.

"I'm Ellie." I said my name softly. She seemed to relax a little when I smiled at her, holding onto her knees a little less tightly.

Heeler was watching us carefully but thankfully Jack and Jas had already left. Sarah didn't need anyone else staring at her.

I turned to Heeler. "Go take a shower and get as much sleep as you can. I know its hard but you need it, we'll be fine together and if we're not I'll call you immediately. I promise."

He paused for a moment, clearly debating it before finally nodding and slowly making his way upstairs. I could tell that he had lost a weight too and I made a mental note to change that.

I was a little hungry myself.

I turned back to Sarah.

"Sarah. I'm craving some spaghetti." With that I got up and head towards the stove. I wasn't trying to force her to talk or treating her like she could break at any little thing. I was treating her like I would have liked to be treated, like she was normal.

God, I would've given anything just to be treated like I was normal.

She warily got up and I could see her debating whether or not to run, probably to go to Heeler.

"My name is Ellie Green. Daughter or Alpha and Luna Green of the Blood Thunder pack. The strongest pack in America. I know what you're thinking, I must have lived a lavish, comfortable life, with servants doing anything I want them to anytime I wanted them to. The reality was much darker of course, I feel like most are, the only servant in that house was me." I turned away from the pasta bowl, letting it come to a boil as I faced an intrigued Sarah.

"Take a seat." I said gesturing to the counter which she thankfully complied, even though she seemed very hesitant.

"I know what you're thinking, what you're going through. I know that it's hard to believe since your experience was unique to you and I don't seem like someone who's experienced a lot of trauma, but just because my outside wounds have healed and the visible scars have faded doesn't mean that I have."

I poured the pasta into the pot and grabbed the sauce from the fridge. Sarah was listening very intently, seeming to relax with me a little more.

"My parents beat and tortured me every day of my life. All the ones I was conscious for at least. I was starved. I did their cooking and their cleaning. I was their punching bag on their bad days and their way to celebrate on their good. I ran away after I overheard them planning my rape."

She gasped a little at that but I just stirred the pasta.

"I'm not telling you this to get you to pity me or to guilt you into speaking up and telling your story." The pasta felt soft enough so I drained it in the sink then threw it back into the pot with the sauce to warm it all up.

"You deserve to take as long as you want to open back up. You need to move at your own pace and you can't let anyone push you to do otherwise."

I poured the pasta into the bowls, giving each of us a nice generous serving then sat across from her.

"I'm not trying to claim that I know exactly what you've been through. No one can know that but you. All I can say is that it will get better. I'm here if you ever want to talk without judgment, and if you're willing, I might be able to help lessen the pain a bit, just like my new family did for me. Your mate, Heeler, is an amazing person and I can absolutely guarantee you that he will never hurt you. He loves his family and you are now his family. He's here for you, as am I. We all are. When you're ready, we'll be here."

She picked up the fork and took a bite of the pasta I gave her. I gave her my most genuine smile before digging hungrily into my own. I was still a little nauseous from my coma but I knew my body needed sustenance. I had already began to lose weight despite the feeding tubes and knew if it got any worse I'd have to deal with an angry Henry.

"E-Ellie?" She spoke up after about 5 minutes of eating in silence. I just looked up at her and smiled encouragingly.

"Thank you." She whispered and I just nodded silently, letting her let out whatever she wants to let out.

"I really l-like Heeler, and I-I w-want to t-trust him" She stuttered, "I'm trying I j-just." She sighed loudly, running her hands over her face. I stayed quiet, letting her work through it. "I'm scared."

I nodded, not having anything to say. Sometimes silence is better.

I noticed she was done eating and picked up the plates and put them in the dishwasher. I put the remaining pasta in a a Tupperware for Heeler.

I grabbed a little pink sticky note and scribbled down a little message on it.

'Please eat this. Sarah is fine, we're going to go for a walk. Take care of yourself a while. Don't disturb us, we need our girl time. I will bring her back to you when we're done and I've felt you've had enough time.'

I stuck it on the Tupperware and extended my hand to Sarah, "Come on." I said and she stood up, holding onto my hand. I led her upstairs to Heeler's room where I carefully left the pasta outside his door.

I then brought Sarah downstairs, our hands still attached. As soon as we stepped outside I knew exactly where to take her.

We walked through the paths until we reached the field of flowers I discovered once on one of my runs. It had every kind of flower you could imagine. It was beautiful, more than that. When we arrived let out a little gasp, momentarily stopping in her place. A smile lit up her face as she ran out into the sunny field, twirling around in the flowers. She turned to me.

"Its beautiful." She said, happiness, relief and freedom taking over her features.

We laid in the middle of the field for hours, taking in the comforting sun, getting some much needed vitamin D.

I told her all about Heeler and everything he's done for me and everyone else. I told her funny and embarassing stories and how scared he was of Jen when we were shopping. I may not have known Heeler for a very long time, but I already considered him family.

He was already more of a family than my biological parents ever were.

She just laughed at my stories, occasionally asking questions. I really liked her and she honestly had a great sense of humor. I definitely approve. Her and Heeler deserved each other, they would be perfect together.

As the sun was starting to set we decided to make our way back to the pack house. We had been out for hours and Heeler was probably worried out of his mind.

By the time we were back at the pack house Sarah had completely opened up to me, no more uncertainty or nervousness holding her back. She told me a bit about her experiences but I knew that was for her and Heeler to work through. I gave her the push she needed to trust Heeler, and now he could truly heal her...

Heeler, Heal her. See what I did there...

As we approached the house the sun had begun setting and she was telling me a funny story about her old friends. She as smiling and talking so brightly, no longer the silent shy girl around me. I could tell that Heeler was watching us from his window, I could feel his shock at the immediate transformation but just concentrated on Sarah's hilarious stories.

He watched her in awe for a couple seconds before disappearing. A few seconds later he ws bursting out of the door and embracing her. "I missed you." He breathed.

She tensed up for a moment, looking at me for help but I just gave her an encouraging nod. With that she finally let go. She sighed and wrapped her arms back around him, closing her eyes and enjoying the feeling of being in her mate's arms. She was in the safest most comfortable place possible.

I could feel my body screaming and shaking as I thought about the fact that I'd never have that. I couldn't remember the last time I truly felt safe or comfortable. I'm not sure I ever have. I don't if I've ever let my guard down and let myself be me completely. My walls were built high and strong, sometimes I wasn't sure anything could break them down.

He picked her up an swung her around, making her giggle a little. It was a a beautiful sight.

"Heeler!" She squealed.

After a couple minutes Heeler turned to me. "Thank you Ellie, truly, thank you so much."

"I did nothing. It was all Sarah" I said, giving them a small smile before leaving them alone, heading back into the pack house.

When I did I was met with Chris and a still guilty looking Jade sitting in the living room. I went to my room, changing into my pajamas before going back to the living room to join them.

"Hi" I smiled. I looked outside and noticed Sarah and Heeler weren't there anymore.

"Where are Sarah and Heeler?"

"They just headed upstairs." Chris answered as Jade still looked at me guiltily.

As if on cue Heeler skipped downstairs right to me, swallowing me in a giant hug before settling down next to me with a gigantic smile on his face.

"This girl is amazing!" He exclaimed, pointing at me before turning to a confused Chris and Jade. "I don't know what she did but Sarah's completely opened up! A few hours with Ellie and she's eating, she's talking and she's taking a shower right now! She hugged me back and she's smiling and-"

He turned to me, "Thank you so much." With that he gave me a quick peck on the crown of my head before dashing back upstairs to his mate like a love-struck puppy. Sarah's a lucky girl, she got a pretty amazing guy.

I looked back to Chris and Jade, still smiling at Heeler's joy and they just stared at me shocked.

"What are you? An actual mother fucking saint?!" Jade started, "Sarah hasn't smiled, let alone spoken to anyone in literally weeks and she spends an hour with you and she's basically better! You make everyone smile, you forgave me and you saved Sarah and Heeler, all in the span of a day?"

I smiled awkwardly, "I didn't do much, I just spoke to her about my past, trust me, I am no saint. And as for forgiving you, it wasn't a big deal, honestly, I can tell that you're still feeling guilty and I need you to stop, please. You seem like a great person and I completely understand why you attacked me. No harm done. I think you're going to be great for Chris, he likes em feisty, right Chris?"

I said, winking and giggling at his blushing, referring to what he told us that day in the mall.

Tears formed in Jade's eyes and she came sprung off the couch, over to me, giving me a big hug.

"You're actually the best ever, Ellie. I'd love to meet your family one day! I'd love to meet more people like you!"

Chris and I froze up when she said that.

"No." Chris said firmly. He was briefed on my situation when I came to live here since he was the beta.

"What?" Jade asked innocently.

"You, uh, my parents aren't someone anyone should ever have to meet." I said, awkwardly shrugging.

I watched the panic fill Jade's face as she realized what she'd done.

"I'm so sorry Ellie. I should've told her not to bring it up I just-" Chris started but I waved him off.

"It's totally fine, I'm fine, everything's fine. I lived. I think I'm going to go to bed now though." I said, yawning a little to strengthen my point.

I head up the stairs to bed but on my way up I heard Jade panicking again.

"DID I SERIOUSLY JUST DO ANOTHER STUPID THING AND HURT THAT AMAZING ANGEL UP THER AGAIN! JESUS CHIRST! SHE LIVED WITH ABUSIVE PARENTS AND WAS RECENTLY REJECTED BY HER MATE AND STILL IS SO STRONG AND AMAZING AND HERE I AM, HURTING HER OVER AND OVER! GOD DAMMIT!"

I just laughed as pain swelled in my chest at the reminder of how ridiculously horrible my past has been. Part of me wanted to go down there and tell her not to worry, that I was fine, but then she'd know I heard everything she just said which wold probably just make her feel even worse.

Chris could handle it just fine.

Fifteen

"Don't give up when dark times come. The more storms you face in life, the stronger you'll be. Hold on. Your greater is coming."

—— Germany Kent

My room felt extremely empty without Jen. She left yesterday while I was out with Sarah leaving only a note on my bed telling me goodbye.

Everything was just so different and I was starting to feel suffocated, surrounded by memories that liked to come back and torture me in the worst moments. Everyone in the pack witnessed my most recent and were either sending me looks of pity or disgust.

Jen left, Jack had his alpha duties as well as Jas. Chris had his Beta duties and his new mate Jade, who was definitely a lot to handle, and Heeler had his gamma duties as well as his fragile mate Sarah who really needed him, to take care of.

Jammie and Henry were living their busy lives back at home and I found myself alone a lot, the only thing keeping me company being the horrible memories that liked to haunt me at every chance. Usually I would try and distract myself from my problems by keeping busy, but there was nothing for me to keep busy with.

Sometimes I'd see knives or even something as simple as a plate of strawberries and get flashbacks to memories of the Blood Thunder pack.

Sometimes I'd see fairy lights or even just couples in love and I would get flashbacks to the night I was rejected.

Sometimes I would go for walks and get flashbacks to the night I was attacked and nearly killed by pack warriors.

The days started to pass and I never really seemed to do anything. When my friends had time they'd try and spend time with me, and I'd spend a lot of time with Sarah while Heeler was too busy, but other than that I was alone.

I trained with the guys but none of them could keep up anymore. I would have the three of them fight me at once and still they had no chance. After about 7 weeks I'd had enough. It was time for me to leave.

I only had 9 months left, a simple pregnancy period, and I'd be dead. I couldn't spend the rest of my life like this, I just couldn't.

****

I woke up at 6:00 this morning for training as usual. I entered the gym and no one even really acknowledged my presence. Jack and Jas were sparring on the mats, Chris was coaching Jade on her boxing to help get her aggression out and Heeler was teaching Sarah how to defend herself.

I guess everyone decided to come early this morning and forgot to tell me again...

I went over to one of the punching bags and began hitting it. I let all my anger and frustration out onto it, laying punch after punch, hitting it almost as hard as I could. Next thing I knew the bag was flying across the room. They were supposed to be built to withstand werewolves but somehow I punched it so hard the chain broke and it flew right into an innocent Sarah.

Everyone gasped as we all ran to her side, throwing the bag off of her. I knelt down beside her in panic . "Oh my god Sarah I am so sorry are you okay?"

Next thing I knew I was being picked up by my throat and tossed across the gym into the opposite wall.

Heeler.

Heeler threw me.

My head took the entire impact.

Everyone gathered around Sarah to see if she was okay.

I sat up, feeling dizzy. I felt so terrible that I did that to Sarah that I could barely breathe. Sarah! The most amazing innocent sweet person to ever exist and I hit her with a giant 1000 pound punching bag!

How could I be so careless! So stupid.

Useless, idiot, runt, deformation, worthless, curse, disgrace.

My injuries overwhelmed me and black spots started appearing in my vision as I tried to make my way over to the group but before I could make it they took all left. I passed out, falling onto the gym floor, a puddle of blood forming around my head as my insides screamed at me in shame. I didn't blame them for leaving me here, I would've done the same. Sarah needed help, and even I didn't want to save me anymore.

I woke up with a ringing in my ears. I was still pretty dizzy from the hit. I looked around and realized I was still on the gym floor. I lifted my hand to my head, checking for injuries. When I brought it back into my line of vision it was covered in a mixture of dried and fresh blood. I'd clearly been there for a while.

Since it hadn't healed yet I should probably get it check out. I sighed.

Everyone must have forgotten about me... Its okay, I've been through worse, its just a little blood.

I stood up, swaying a little from side to side as I tried to regain my balance. I slowly made my way to the pack doctor. It took me about 15 minutes when it would usually take 2 to get there because my dizziness tried to bring me down with every step I took.

When I finally arrived my doctor, doctor Hanning I learned her name was, rushed to me. I saw her so much it was only right I knew her name.

"Oh dear Ellie, what happened?"

"Nothing, I'm okay, I just think I need a few stitches" I said, smiling at her.

Doctor Hanning put one of my arms around her shoulder as she led me through the halls.

As she walked me to her room we passed by Jade waiting outside of what was probably Sarah's room.

Jade noticed me, turning to me with a confused look.

"Ellie? What happened are you okay?" She asked, eyeing my now bloody clothes.

"I-I'm fine. How's Sarah? I-Is she okay, I-I." I took a deep breath, "Just tell her I'm so sorry." Tears sprung to my eyes but I tried to smile through them.

Jade ran up to me. "Sarah's fine, the bag just shocked her more than any-thing but physically, there's not a scratch, she's a werewolf after all. Heeler's just being a little paranoid and making them run a bunch of unnecessary tests to be sure."

I nodded, tears of relief slipping down my face. It had been a while since I'd let myself cry but this seemed like good time.

"What happened to you though?"

"Oh, um... nothing I just hit the wall after the incident and it got my head a little, I just need a few stitches." I waved her off, holding back my shrug.

"Holy shit, Ellie I'm so sorry, did Heeler did this? I kind of remember that happening, but I didn't even think I was just so worried about Sarah. I didn't think he threw you that hard and you're usually very strong! Did we just leave you in the gym?" She asked, guilt clouding her features as she processed what happened and saw the extent of my injuries.

"Its fine, I totally understand, I'm fine, I've had worse. Just please make sure Sarah's okay for me? Please?"

"Ya, yeah of course."

"Thanks" I said before Dr Hanning continued leading me to my room. Now that she heard the story she was looking at me, eyes full of pity which is exactly what I didn't want.

Dr Hanning stitched me up and did a few scans.

I had a bit of brain damage and my skull completely shattered. I should have died but my extreme healing saved me once again. I would probably be okay within a day or two, Dr just wanted to keep me to make sure I was doing as well as I should.

When she left that night I finally let myself cry. I couldn't hold it in anymore. I decided to give myself this one night. One night to be weak and then I would be strong.

I cried about my real parents and everything they did, I cried about Jen leaving and the guys getting their mates and forgetting about me, but most of all I cried about my mate rejecting me.

That was the one pain that to this day did not let up. It sat heavily on my chest, crushing me from the inside out, killing me slowly and silently so that no one would know until it was too late.

Everywhere I went there was a reminder, even being in this hospital I remember the pain of waking up after he nearly killed me and rejected me.

The only thing I didn't cry about was the fact that I was dying. Maybe that was the peace I needed. Maybe the only way to be happy again and truly at peace is if I die, but honestly, I don't think even that could rid me of the tragedy that has been my pathetic excuse of a life. What the hell did I do to deserve all this?

After a solid 3 hours of crying I finally forced myself to stop and drifted off into a deep sleep.

****

I woke up to voices, Jack and Chris's to be exact.

"What the fuck? Is that Ellie?" Jack asked as I heard him stop in front of my door.

"Ya, uh, Jade told me she came in last night. Heeler threw her really hard against the wall, apparently she was covered in blood and could barely walk. Apparently we just left her in the gym. I went back this morning and there was a giant hole in the wall and a puddle of blood on the floor..." Chris replied, guilt evident in his voice.

"Fuck man. I was worried about Sarah but how did we not notice this?"

"I don't know I feel awful man. Ellie's been so good to us and our mates and we've been nothing but shitty to her!"

"God dammit. Should we-" He was cut off by Heeler's voice in the halls.

"What the fuck is taking you guys so long?"

I could hear him approach my door.

"Its Ellie, you really hurt her dude." Jack mumbled.

There was a moment of silence and I could hear footsteps approaching me.

"Fuck." I heard Heeler mumble to himself from next to me.

Then I heard Dr Hanning's voice next to me as well.

"She suffered an extremely severe head trauma. Her brain was severely damaged and her skull shattered. Its a miracle she's still alive."

I finally round up enough energy to open my eyes but no one seemed to notice.

Dr Hanning was telling Heeler all about my injuries and the severity of it all.

"I know it was your mate and that you're protective of her, but you almost killed Ellie and Sarah is completely fine. It is very obvious by all the scars littering her body that Ellie's had a hard enough life, you need to think before you act."

"How much longer does she have left?" Heeler asked and Chris and Jack's faces morphed into confusion.

"You know?" Dr Hanning asked, sounding a little surprised, but not as happy as I'd expected considering how hard she pushed for me to tell someone. Maybe it was the fact that he was binging it up in front of the other two like it was nothing that had her hesitating.

"Yes, she told me a while back that she was dying."

Chris and Jack who were standing at the door gasped, looking even more confused than before. I was fuming at this point. I told him that in confidence, he said he wouldn't tell anyone else.

I pushed down the anger and cleared my throat, letting everyone know I was awake.

"10 months." answered strongly.

"Y-You're dying?" Chris asked , making his way over to me, tears springing to his eyes.

"Yes. I didn't want to tell you yet, but it seems I've been robbed of that choice." I said, passive aggressively. I hated how rude and childish I was being but I couldn't help it in that moment. It was all just becoming too much.

"Actually that's what I came in here to talk about. Because of the severity of this injury, and the fact that it was so concentrated in your brain and skull, it seemed to have sped up the process. You now have 8 months left." She said scientifically, but I could see the toll sharing the horrible news was taking on her.

They all stared in shock as I just took it in. I wasn't even surprised at this point. Every time I thought my shit bag of a life couldn't get worse it did.

"Alpha Jack." I broke the silence.

"yes?" He replied.

"I would like to officially inform you that I will be leaving your pack. Thank you so much for housing me, I've really appreciated it, but I think its time that I go."

They all gasped once again.

"Ellie no-" Chris started but I wouldn't let him finish.

"I think we all know I can't stay here anymore. I don't belong here and all I can see are memories of traumatic events. I can't run through the forest without remembering the time I was attacked by rogues and nearly died, I can't go in my room without missing Jen, I can't stand in the fields without remembering being rejected and humiliated and forced to shift in front of everyone and now... Now I can't even train without remembering almost harming Sarah. Its time for me to go. I have to go."

With that that all nodded solemnly. I noticed a few tears trickle down Chris's face. I was about to call him into a hug but I haven't been able to hug him comfortably with the memory of Jade yanking me off of him unexpectedly by my hair while I was still recovering from my coma.

We all just stood there in silence reflecting when Jade came by. "Hey guys, Sarah's ready to go home." With that they all left.

Left me alone.

Again.

I don't know why I ever thought I could be happy. I don't know why I expected more. After all,

I'll always be the deformed runt that ruins everything.

Sixteen

The truth is, unless you let go, unless you forgive yourself, unless you forgive the situation, unless you realize that the situation is over, you cannot move forward."

– Steve Maraboli

After a few more hours of rest I left the hospital, feeling good as new. I only had 8 months left to live and I wasn't going to waste them.

I let myself have the one night of weakness but now I'm back and better than ever, POSITIVITY!

I went straight to my room and packed up all my stuff.

I may not have felt much physical pain but I sure as hell got my fair share of psychological pain from this place. The more I thought about it though, the more I realized that even if all of the shit that went down hadn't, I'd still leave.

I can't let anyone get attached to me. That would be beyond selfish. I couldn't do anything more than hook-ups and short, easy friendships.

I decided to do my rounds and say a proper goodbye to everyone. At this point they all probably knew I was dying and, realistically, this could be the last time I ever seem them. I started with Chris and Jade who were sitting and cuddling in the living room.

I sat on the sofa across from them with a big smile on my face.

"Hey guys, I just wanted to come say bye. I'm leaving today and this, well, it may be the last time I see you guys. I just want you both to know I only want the best for you guys. You've both been amazing, and I appreciate you both so much. I hope when you have children, you tell them stories about their Auntie Ellie, just maybe leave out the whole rejected, abused, deformed, dying bounty hunter thing. " I added with a smile, trying to make light of the situation.

"Look Ellie, I'm so sorry-" They both said at the same time but I stopped them by raising my head, a soft smile still resting on my lips.

"There's no need, all is forgiven and I hope one day you'll be able to forgive me for hurting Sarah. It was never my intention and I will live with that guilt for the rest of my life. I just wanted to say goodbye and thank you for being so amazing to me."

They both got up and gave me hugs, Jade shed a single tear but I wiped it from her cheek and smiled. "Do not cry over me, please don't waste your tears."

I didn't want any of this to drag on any longer than it needed to, so I left the room, leaving the two adorable mates in each other's arms.

Next I found Jack and Jas in the kitchen.

"Alpha Jack, Luna Jasmine." I bowed my head a little.

"I just wanted to say goodbye and thank you again for letting me stay here and showing me so much kindness. I hope one day to return the favor, you have eight months I would start thinking!" I tried to joke but they were not having it.

They both engulfed me in a hug, mumbling their goodbyes.

"In case I never see you again, I just want you to know how happy I am to have known you both. Thank you."

I then walked away to finish off my last goodbye. Heeler and Sarah. They were outside in the fields, picking flowers.

In the beautiful fields I had grown over my time here.

Whenever I had time, which happened a lot, I came out and took care of and planted all kinds of flowers, blooming it into one of the most beautiful pack attractions.

It was my safe haven when everything else felt like it was falling apart around me. The flowers were something that could never betray me. They even seemed to love me as much as I'd always loved them, blooming larger and brighter than I ever thought possible.

As soon as he saw me, Heeler tensed up and went on high alert.

Sarah tried to come closer but Heeler just held her close before growling warningly at me.

He held her tightly to his chest, probably barely able to process my words. All he saw was a threat to his fragile mate, one he would have no problem ending.

This hurt more than a lot of the shit I'd been through in my life. I truly loved and trusted them both and now I've gone and ruined it. There was no doubt in the fact that this was my fault, that I had brought it upon myself.

At least with the abuse I could pretend that some higher powers made a mistake, that it was because of their screw up that everyone hated me. But this was all me, there was no one else to put the blame on.

I made the choice, I punched the bag too hard, I wasn't careful, I hurt an innocent girl and now I have to live with the consequences of my actions.

"I'm sorry. I just came to apologize again and say goodbye." I said. All I got in return was another warning growl from Heeler so I left, letting them spend their time together in peace.

There was an intense burning in my chest as a lone tear slipped through my eyes on my walk back to grab my things. I angrily wiped it from my face. It just hurt so much, I was so sick of losing everyone. Why did I always have to go and fuck everything up?

I grabbed my bag from the porch where I left it and head out. It's time to start over again. I can do this. I need this. A fresh start that I will not let myself mess up.

I ran along the paths and after about a half hour I was finally out of their territory. I decided to continue through the forest and just see what happens. I'd settle down in the first town I came across. I had enough money and if I ever needed more I'm sure I could start the whole bounty hunting thing again.

I'd just spend my last months meeting people briefly and moving on. I'd travel the world and see all of the things I could, help the most amount of people I could.

How much pain could I possibly suffer if I never stay anywhere long enough for people to really get to know me? How can they hurt me if I leave before they get the chance?

I ran for days before finally getting tired and deciding to rest.

I found a hollowed out tree nearby and climbed in. It was the perfect place to have a quick nap.

With that I closed my eyes and fell into one of the best sleeps I'd had in weeks.

****

I woke up to growling sounds. My eyes flew open to reveal a girl getting cornered by a bunch of werewolves.

I wasn't sure what the girl was but I knew for sure she wasn't a were and I knew this would not be a fair fight.

I instantly leaped out of the tree and stood protectively in front of the girl, baring my teeth and letting all of my power leak out of me.

I could see some of the werewolves begin to hesitate and back off instinctively when my power hit them but they were stupid enough to try and fight through it. To resist the instinct to submit to an alpha wolf.

As much as I hated my parents, they're extremely strong and gave me good genes. I wasn't a weak alpha, I was not someone anyone could walk all over.

Not in a fight at least...

One of them lunged at me and that instigated the fight. Within 2 minutes I had all 10 of them on the ground submitting to me, bellies and necks fully exposed. I noticed they were all pack warriors from a nearby territory.

What the hell were they attacking a single girl for? Ganging up on her like that?

I turned around to face her and she was just looking at me curiously, tilting her head a little bit.

"Are you okay?" I asked and she laughed, giving me a little nod.

"I'm Daisy." She introduced and I smiled. She seemed completely fine. She isn't look at all shaken up by the incident, she wasn't even a little wary about the warrior wolves growling as she walked over their submitting forms on her way over to me. "You didn't have to help me you know. They wouldn't have caught me."

I narrowed my eyes a little. I knew all about not underestimating people but that wasn't a situation most people would've gotten out of alive. Especially a non-wolf. I mean, I was pretty sure she was human.

"I hope you don't take offense by this, because I honest to god don't mean this in a rude way, but how? You were cornered and you don't exactly look super threatening is all."

She laughed, shaking her head and crossing her arms, "Neither do you." She pointed out and I couldn't help but see her point.

"Touche." I pointed at her, smiling, "How did you even get into that situation? What are pack warriors doing attacking you? It's very out of character."

"I saw them sniffing around our lands and came to throw them off track. Once they figured out what I was they were all obsessed with killing me" She said, rolling her eyes, confusing me further.

"Huh?" I asked dumbly and she laughed before walking away.

"Bye!" She exclaimed as she walked off confidently, admiring the nature around her as she went.

I'm starting to realize I may have just helped a criminal escape. I started chasing after her, wanting to ask more questions when a loud voice boomed from all around us, not coming from a specific point but instead from everywhere. "Daisy!"

I tensed up ready to fight, but Daisy just rolled her eyes, smiling and started walking a little faster, making me try a little harder to catch up.

I reached out my hand, trying to grab her shoulder gently to get her to stop, but just as my fingers were about to wrap around her someone had grabbed mine and pinned me to the ground.

I instantly reacted, silently throwing whoever was holding me down onto the ground, leaping back up to my feet. I got up to continue the fight and see who managed to pin me but the person had disappeared. Vanished into thin air.

"What the f-" I started but was interrupted by a strong powerful voice.

"Language." He said sternly.

I turned around to see a very large intimidating man standing next to an amused looking Daisy who was smiling brightly at me. He was clearly well built and his presence showed that he was not one you would want to mess with.

"See, what did I tell you? I'm pretty sure she's one of us." Daisy murmured to the man and he had a look of deep thought in his eyes.

He focused his attention on me, "Who are you?" He asked me as I eyed him up, ready to fight if necessary.

"I am not here to fight, relax. I just want to know your name." he chuckled casually.

I instantly relaxed. I somehow knew he was not going to initiate an attack and I had no reason to do so either. I just didn't get any bad vibes from him. I realize that people are conniving and fake and I shouldn't risk my life because I had good vibes, but that's exactly what I did.

I smiled at them both. "Ellie."

"Ellie." He repeated, "I'm Amos."

I nodded, smiling politely, inhaling their scent. It was strange, it was supernatural and smelt like the forest, but it was sweeter and purer. I didn't know how to explain it, I'd never smelt it before.

"Its natural that you've never smelt anything like us before. We don't make ourselves known to many. We are experts at hiding away and keeping ourselves safe."

How the hell did he know what I was thinking? Was I making a weird face or something?

"No darling, we can read minds." He answered my thoughts.

I all of the sudden felt very wary, taking a cautious step back. What the hell are they? Why were the werewolves so hell bent on hurting Daisy.

"That's how I could tell that you are no threat to us. Not yet at least. I can explain everything and I can promise that we won't hurt you, unless it is warranted of course, but we should get back inside the lands. It isn't safe for us out here and I would feel more comfortable having these conversations somewhere more comfortable, like my office. Why don't you follow me?"

I nodded warily and started cautiously following them, constantly being my surroundings, listening to everything and watching for any signs of lies or danger.

We continued in the direction Daisy was originally headed in. I don't remember there being anything around here when I ran through. I got no scent of anything other than forest.

We kept walking until we arrived at a weirdly shaped tree that I had never noticed before. The birds seemed to sing extra loud here and the grass seemed greener.

The tree bent over to naturally create some sort of beautiful arch in the grass.

It was amazing, I couldn't help but marvel at the beautiful sight. The man turned around to face me.

"If you go and tell anyone about our location or security measures or anything that could potentially endanger my people, no matter how close they are to you, no matter how much you trust them, I will hunt you down and kill you. Got it?"

I nodded my yes quickly but actually managed to hut my neck in the process. It got stuck at an weird angle and I had to crack it back into place with my hands, giving the man a sheepish smile as he stared at me, clearly trying to hold back his laughter.

He turned towards the arch and extended his hand towards it. I noticed a small orange glow emit from him before he said the words, "Ouvrirus laba portaiyin."

With that the arch glowed that same faint orange and he turned back to me.

"Follow me."

I followed him through the arch and gasped at what was revealed to me. It was absolutely breathtaking and I had to blink a few times to make sure I wasn't hallucinating. Even then, I couldn't be completely sure.

I was so taken by everything surrounded me that I didn't even notice when Daisy slipped away, probably going back to the lab Amos had mentioned.

There were beautiful little houses built up into the trees and small streets filled with humble looking people. There were colorful little carts lining the roads, selling things raining from fruits and vegetables to little trinkets of all kinds. Everyone that we passed nodded to the man I was following in greeting, he definitely had to be a leader of some sort.

Some looked at me cautiously but after staring for a couple seconds in concentration relaxed and went back to what they were doing, some even gave me smiles.

Suddenly Amos turned to me, stopping and facing me with a bright smile on his face.

"I'm sorry I don't think I've properly introduced myself." He said, extending his hand, "Amos Beaconsfield, leader of the white stags."

Seventeen

"You must make a decision that you are going to move on. It wont happen automatically. You will have to rise up and say, I don't care how hard this is, I don't care how disappointed I am, I'm not going to let this get the best of me. I'm moving on with my life."

– Joel Osteen

"I'm sorry I don't think I've properly introduced myself." He said, extending his hand, "Amos Beaconsfield, leader of the white stags."

"White Stags?" I asked confused.

He just chuckled in response, his deep voice easily filling the space earning ourselves curious looks from people around us.

"Why don't you come to my office and I can explain everything properly there. "

"Sounds good." I responded easily, giving him a smile that he happily reciprocated.

I like him.

I followed him back through the streets, marveling at all the sights.

I smiled at a few people this time and they all returned it. I saw a store selling flowers and made a mental note to come check them out.

After a few minutes we arrived at a large, strangely shaped tree. It was hollowed and carved out to mimic a modern office building with multiple floors and platforms sticking out of it. It was much taller than the rest and seemed to be in the center of the little hidden town.

He led me to the trunk of the tree where there was a wooden elevator that I openly gaped at. This place was crazy.

We rode it to the very top and when we exited I couldn't hold back my loud gasp at the beauty. We were in the middle of a gigantic office floor full of people, but what really took my back was the view.

I large smile made its way onto my face as I gazed out the large, floor to ceiling windows.

"Oh." Was all I managed to get out.

I heard a few chuckles from all around, including Amos Beaconsfield, making me blush a little in embarrassment. Sometimes I just want to shove a sock in my mouth and yell at myself to shut the fuck up.

I continued to follow him through a beautiful light wooden hallway lined with lanterns with white flames with flecks of blue floating in them. Everything around me made me want to gasp and stand around in awe and it was becoming a problem as I tried to keep up with Amos's large steps, unable to concentrate on anything as I took it all in.

If someone were to approach and attack me right now I would have no idea, I was just so wrapped up in the incredible views, crazy architecture, and shockingly beautiful strong flames.

His office rested at the end of the hallway revealing the best view yet. You could see out for kilometers. There were mountains off in the distance and just beyond the village rested the forest that I was just in, they probably even saw me run by.

That reminds me, I wonder if the wolves have been able to shake off my dominance or if they're still on their back submitting in the middle of the forest.

I hoped it was the latter.

"Sit down please." Amos said gesturing to the seat across from him. I obeyed, still marveling at the beauty around me.

He sighed, leaning back in his seat. "Where do I even start? Haven't had to have this conversation before. We don't really get a lot of new people. Like I said I am the leader of the group called the white stags, but you don't know what that is, correct?"

I'm not sure why he asked considering he could read my mind but I nodded anyways, trying my very best to focus all my attention on his words and not let my mind drift off to the view or architecture.

"The white stags are supernatural creatures like werewolves, but we don't have wolves and we don't shift. We have the ability to hide and run better than any other normal supernaturals. We are able to conceal entire civilizations, like you've just seen, and are able to play small tricks on people's brains as well as read their minds. We're very powerful but all around peaceful people. It is part of our nature to be peaceful, never has there been a problematic white stag.

We used to be able to live out, freely among the people. We were beloved by everyone for our calming and gentle nature, but then one day, thousands of years ago, there was a man, a sick man, who got frustrated with our gentle nature. He resented our abilities and turned it into some sort of game for himself.

His life goal became catching and killing a white stag. He eventually even managed to get people in on it with him. It became some sort of competition, a sort of ritual. We were very hard to find and therefore very hard to kill. They started using it as a way of proving themselves as a warrior.

They would try to kill us to simply boost their pride, to gloat that they have caught the uncatchable. It escalated to the point that almost every single person was trying to catch and kill one of us. Because of our capabilities they've never been able to catch a single one of us, but then they started coming after our children. Friends started deceiving friends, neighbors would sneak into our houses at night and try to kill us while we were sleeping.

We had to all move into isolation. I don't believe they could have caught one of us, it is meant to be impossible, but they were tormenting us, we just wanted to live in peace. So, our ancestors created the village you're standing in right now, our safe haven."

"I'm so sorry." That's all I could say, I mean, what the fuck is wrong with people? Damn.

He waved a hand. "It is what it is, we have made ourselves pretty good lives here, we're happy living in peace. We come out for important meetings and such and people still try to catch us but they have all still yet to succeed. Our goddess truly made us uncatchable.

"Look, I have to be honest with you, you are the first non-white stag that we have ever allowed come in here..."

I stayed silent for a second processing his words. "What?"

He just nodded. I sat there, absolutely shocked for a couple more seconds.

"Why?"

"I have no idea." He shrugged. "I was very ready to just leave with Daisy and leave you there but Daisy has a theory and I'm curious to see how it pans out. I don't think what she's saying is possible, especially since you're very clearly a werewolf but it wouldn't hurt to try."

I just blinked at him. "I'm so confused." I said, completely serious.

He laughed a little but I kept a straight face.

"I'm being 100% serious, you've made a mistake. Trust me, I'm nothing special. In fact, you should probably kick me out. I don't want to accidentally ruin the beautiful peaceful balance you guys have. Bad things tend to follow me and I refuse to let it come here."

"White stags don't make those kind of mistakes. You're harmless. Well... harmless to us because you don't want to harm us. If that ever happens, which I don't see ever happening, we are very much screwed" He stopped, staring at the ceiling, thinking for a second before snapping his attention back to me, standing up from his chair. "Come on, its getting late, I'll show you to your room. I want you to stay with us for a while, at least until we figure out what's going on. Sound good?"

"No, I couldn't, I'd be such an inconvenien-"

He cut me off. "Stop right there. You are no inconvenience, in fact, I insist that you stay."

I shut up as he left the room and I silently followed behind him, fighting the large smile that wanted to appear because of his overwhelming kindness.

We walked back into the streets that were now dark and nearly empty, but they were just as beautiful as ever.

He turned to me. "By the way, I just want to apologize for all of the stares you received today. My people were not trying to be rude or hostile in any way, they were probably just shocked to see a newcomer, it hasn't happened in about a century after all."

Is he serious? "Oh, no worries at all! Please, they barely stared and I completely understand!" I waved him off. That's ridiculous, they were so friendly!

He smiled back, seemingly relieved. What an innocent soul.

He led me to another tree that again had something similar to an elevator in its trunk. We rode up it to the top floor again, revealing a gorgeous penthouse of sorts.

"This is where you'll be staying. I hope its to your liking but if you need anything please don't hesitate to call. We do our own laundry and cleaning here but as for food someone will happily deliver your meals to you. They'll place it here."

He said gesturing to a compartment that had a door to the outside as well.

"While the food is in there it will be kept warm and fresh until you're ready to eat it. Once you're finished with the dishes just rinse them off and clean them in here."

He said gesturing to the gorgeous gigantic sink in the beautiful white marble kitchen on the far side of the penthouse. The kitchen had outstanding views on both of the surrounding walls, the view similar to that in Amos' office.

"Once they're clean you can place them in here."

He said showing me a small compartment with a door leading to the outside, "and someone will come and pick them up and bring them all back down to the kitchen. If you are sick or unable to clean your own dishes for any reason you can put them in this compartment."

He showed me one last door at the far end of the kitchen.

"We have no problem washing them if you find yourself incapable."

He continued the tour bringing me to the opposite end of the loft.

He opened a door to reveal a gorgeous, gigantic bedroom. It was all simple and white and had a large closet that was made of mirrors and another door which I'm guessing led to the bathroom.

"Everything in the apartment is yours to use, don't be shy, if you're missing anything just let me know and I'll be happy to help."

"Thank you" I said softly, too overwhelmed by everything to give him the proper thank you he deserved. I'd have to make sure to do that later. I gave him a huge smile as he began his way towards the door.

This is too much. I don't deserve this.

He stopped in his tracks, turning to me. "Don't you say that. I peered into your soul for only a second and I already know that you deserve this and so much more." With that he turned back around and opened the door to the elevator.

"I apologize if I was harsh, please enjoy yourself and feel free to wander the village and do whatever you'd like tomorrow. I'll find you when its time and we can figure everything out. Sound good?"

"Yes sir." I nodded and he cringed.

"Please don't call me that. Just Amos will do."

"Okay, thank you Amos." I said again, as sincerely as possible.

"Anytime." He replied with a smile. "Goodnight, I'll see you tomorrow."

"Goodnight." I replied with a smile.

With that he was gone and I was alone in this insanely beautiful giant luxurious pent house.

I decided to look around a bit. The kitchen was fully stocked with food and drinks. The living room had a flat screen tv and a gorgeous white sofa. The entire apartment's walls were completely covered in windows and the ceiling was littered with sky lights.

I went back to the bedroom to explore. The gigantic closet was filled with beautiful clothes and there was a note taped to the door.

"Dear guest, please feel free to use any of these clothes, just remember to return them washed when you're finished. There is a washing machine in the bathroom."

I went over to what I assumed was the bathroom and was right. It was gorgeous and white marble, matching the kitchen. There was a giant rain shower in one corner and a jacuzzi bath in the other. Along the sink laid a brand new toothbrush and other bathroom supplies I might need. There were fresh fluffy towels and soft robes hanging from the door as well.

I yawned a little deciding it was time for bed.

I quickly hopped into the rain shower, finally removing all of the dirt that I've become caked in from running for the past few days. The water pressure was perfect and I almost never wanted to leave the shower. There was a note on the door explaining that the shower was enchanted and had a never ending hot water supply so I could take my time. I swear this place is heaven.

I had accidentally left my clothes at the tree I was sleeping in and there was no doubt in my mind that it had been snatched and taken by now. I went over to the closet they provided, wrapped in a fluffy towel, and opened up a drawer. There laid several pairs of soft silk pajamas. I looked around for some cheaper ones but these were the only ones I could find.

I carefully picked them up, rolling my fingers over the material in awe. I guess I'm wearing these.

I slipped on the t-shirt and shorts and I swear they were so comfortable it felt like I wasn't wearing anything at all.

I looked at the gorgeous bed and instantly became excited. It looked like one of the most welcoming thing I'd ever seen, especially since I'd slept in a tree last night.

I pushed aside all of the throw pillows and slid into the soft silky sheets. Okay its official. This place is heaven.

I sighed, cuddling into the comforter as I instantly dozed off into one of the deepest sleeps I'd ever had.

Eighteen

"There is some kind of a sweet innocence in being human—in not having to be just happy or just sad—in the nature of being able to be both broken and whole, at the same time."

– C. JoyBell C.

"Count" my father demanded as he hit me with a bat lined with silver spikes that imbedded into my skin on each hit.

I tripped while walking near him and he took it as a sign of disrespect.

He whacked me in the stomach with the bat, hard, puncturing holes all over my stomach and creating a ton of bruising.

"One."

Hit hit me on my back.

"Two"

He moved to my shoulders

"Three."

...

"Forty Five." I barely got that one out, my body shaking in pain, darkness threatening to take over. I looked up with all the energy that I could gather to find Prince Jacob staring down at me with hatred.

"I Prince Jacob Kaden Lunar of the werewolves reject you Ellie Green."

My entire body felt like it was on fire as I experienced a pain equivalent to what I just suffered but in my heart as I felt it shatter.

"Wh-why?"

I passed out. I woke up to see Dr Hanning, Jen, Heeler, Jack and Chris standing over me.

Dr Hanning approached me first. "You're dying. This world will finally be rid of you in just 12 months."

Next Jen approached, "Goodbye, Ellie. I'm finally escaping you. Don't contact me." she said before walking away. I wanted to protest but I was paralyzed, completely unable to move or speak. I just watched her walk away.

Next thing I knew Jasmine and and Jade were standing there.

I smiled at them but they just attacked me, hitting me over and over while I was incapable of moving.

They finally stopped and I still smiled at them. Its ok, I deserved that. I deserved all of this.

Next Sarah appeared. I smiled at her but she fell to the ground in pain. I looked at her, concerned and shocked then Heeler turned to me. Everyone left the room as Heeler grabbed me by the neck and threw me across the room.

He stood over me and proceeded to kick me. "Get away you piece of dying shit. You're a bitch and I hope I never see you again. Stay away from me and Sarah." He then spat on me and joined the others.

My body was now completely consumed by the physical pain I hadn't felt in years and the emotional pain that no matter how long I spent trying to push it away, ignore it and even accept it, never seemed to fade.

I just laid there crying until I finally passed out from my injuries.

All I could think was when will it stop? When will I stop screwing everything up? When can I finally live in peace. I just want peace.

I woke up with a start. It was all just a dream. I'm okay. I looked around as all the events of the last few days came back to me as I felt my body relax and my heartbeat slow.

It was just a dream. I've escaped.

I took deep breaths as I got ready for the day, still a little shaken up by the dream. I hadn't slept deep enough for nightmares in a very long time. Maybe this comfortable bed was only going to cause problems. Maybe this is the universe telling me I don't deserve this.

I slipped on a black tank top and a pair of white flowy pants. I noticed that all of their clothes were of the more gentle and comfortable sort. Lets just say you wouldn't find any tight leather items or anything like that in here. Nothing even remotely intimidating.

I left my room, relaxing as I took in my gorgeous surroundings. The view and simple furniture was even weirdly relaxing.

They must have some really good interior designers, never has a room been able to relax me like this.

The sun was rising as I yawned and walked towards the kitchen.

I checked the time on the phone Jen insisted on getting me to find it was 4:00 am. Well, that's a lot more hours than usual.

The village probably wouldn't be up for a bit.

I checked the food compartment to see that they'd already delivered my food.

The smell of fresh fruits and a pastry filled my nose, making me smile at the beautiful welcoming breakfast.

I inspected the plate to find melons pineapples and strawberries. They all looked like they were just picked and smelt pesticide free.

I found an keurig machine on the counter and decided on a plain coffee. Jammie had shown me how to make them when I lived with her and Henry. I smiled at the memory of them. They were truly good to me.

I tasted it and immediately sighed in happiness. This is the best coffee I'd ever had. This place truly was heaven on earth.

I sat at the beautiful Island in the kitchen and dug into my breakfast as I watched the sun rise. I couldn't relax. Every time I did I found myself left in my horrible thoughts, replaying memories in my mind. Even pleasant memories only led me to ones that tortured me.

Heeler, he was probably my best friend I told him about me dying and I messed it up. He hates me and will never forgive me for what I've done.

Chris and Jack, we had so may good memories together but they also resented me for hurting Sarah. They didn't need me I was just an inconvenience they were happy to get rid of.

Jasmine never wanted to know me, Jade always felt threatened by me I think, but we never clicked.

Sarah, I hurt her. I really messed up she was the sweetest girl and I messed it up. She needed help and she needed to feel safe and I gave her the exact opposite.

Jen, she always had to take care of me, I was always there clinging and annoying her even though she was too nice to say anything. She left and hasn't tried to contact me since. I texted her a few days after she left but she never answered. I understand though, I wouldn't want to keep me around either, she's living an amazing life in England now.

Jammie and Henry, I cost them so much. They were so good to me but I still haven't been able to pay them back and thank them properly. They don't need me around leeching off of them.

My mother and father, well I can't even think of a single good memory with them. As soon as I was able to shift I was nothing to them. Just an annoying pest, a screw up. I understand why they beat me, I deserved it. They didn't deserve a daughter like me.

I finished off my breakfast and made sure to clean my dishes properly. This place was only filled with white stags who were all trustworthy and honest. There were no locks on any of the doors and everyone was trusted to keep things nice for the next guests in the rooms and do their part. No cheating or lying of any kind.

I placed my dishes in the clean dishes compartment. Once I finished my breakfast I noticed there was an adorable blue smiley face painted onto the plates along with the words 'thank you'. This place was just made me want to audibly 'awe' like 90 percent of the time.

I didn't want to be rude and overstay but I was dreading leaving. They don't need me leeching off of them too. I'm done doing that to people. I have money now and I haven't done anything with it. I've got to figure my shit out, I wasn't in a position to easily put things off.

I noticed that the sun was now up and there were people walking around the village. It was about 6:30am. I wasn't at all surprised they were early risers, they probably were awake with the sun and asleep with the darkness, following the natural cycle.

I made my way down in the elevator, smiling at my surroundings.

I decided to go to the village and check out all of the shops and carts placed along the street.

I strolled down the streets, smiling at those who passed by which they all returned. There were carts selling pastries, some selling gorgeous looking fruits. Everyone just looked happy and at ease.

I finally made it to the shop I was dying to go into since yesterday. The flower shop. A gigantic smile made its way onto my face as I walked towards it. I couldn't see the person that owned it but decided to look around a bit. I was marveling at all the beautiful flowers until I saw one of the most beautiful things ever. There was an entire section devoted to solely yellow flowers. There was every kind, most of which I'd never seen before, lining the walls. There were so many that you couldn't see the wall behind it at all.

I walked up to them, bending down to take a good look at some of the more peculiar ones. I felt myself fill with happiness and peace. Yellow flowers, is there anything better?

"Those are my favorites too." I raspy voice said from behind me making me jump. I turned around to see a chuckling old lady and I blushed a little at being caught to off guard. I really went into a trance when with nature. It was portably going to get me into trouble one day.

I laughed with her at my jumpiness.

"Your flowers are amazing, I've never seen anything like this."

She chuckled, "Thank you my dear, are you looking for anything in particular?"

"Oh, no, I don't have any money with me at the moment, I just had to look around I'm sorry. They're just so beautiful it's like they were calling to me."

"Look around all you like, I love it. I'm Rose." She said, tending to a beautiful bouquet of blue flowers.

Well that certainly suits her.

"Ellie."

"Can I ask how you got here? We don't exactly get a lot of visitors. Are you a white stag?"

I shook my head no. "I guess I'm a werewolf of sorts."

"Of sorts?"

"Its complicated." I shrugged.

"Well welcome, I saw that Amos let you in and I trust him completely. You also have a beautiful aura, although I can see it is filled with pain. I hope we can help you with whatever you need. You deserve it."

I shook my head smiling. "I've only spoken to you for a second, how can you tell if I deserve it?"

"I'm a white stag darling, its what I do."

I chuckled at that. Not sure she'd think the same if she knew what I was or what I'd done.

"If there's ever anything I can do for you let me know." I decided to offer.

"There actually might be. I need to leave for a trip for a few weeks. I'd hate to close down the shop, I'm the only flower store in town. It doesn't pay very well but if you could look over my shop while I'm gone that would be amazing. I can tell you love the flowers like me and I feel like I can trust you with it. Even if you're only here for a few days, you can just close it up when you leave."

"I would love to, but you wouldn't need to pay me. I'd be happy to do it for free, in fact I should almost pay you for it."

"Nonsense. I will pay you and I will not accept anything less. Its a deal-breaker."

"Thank you, that would be amazing." I said shyly, still admiring the beautiful shades of yellow surrounding me.

"Of course sweetheart."

Rose then showed me around the shop, explaining what I'd need to do. She was an amazing person, I felt completely at ease with her. How could anyone ever want to hurt these people?

After sitting and chatting with her for about an hour about her amazing life and such I decided to explore the rest of the village. It turns out she's Amos' mother and used to lead the group.

I did notice that they all said lead, not rule over. They weren't anyone's boss or king/queen. They were leaders. They took a large part in the community and helped out wherever they could. They didn't order people around, everyone helped everyone out.

They had a democracy as well, they voted on their leader, it just happened to stay in the family because they were a family of natural leaders.

As I walked I heard my name being called behind me. I turned around to see a smiling Amos.

"You ready to figure this thing out?" He asked.

"Lets do it."

Nineteen

"Learn how to be happy with what you have while you pursue all that you want."

– Jim Rohn

I followed Amos to his office building tree, riding the elevator to the second highest floor. There were people bustling all around in white lab coats and machines of all sort scattered around the floor.

"These are our scientists." Amos explained. "Its very rare for a non white stag to have your kind of aura so we're going to do a few tests to make sure everything is in line. Sound good?"

"Of course," I nodded, weirdly nervous about the whole situation, "do what you need."

He nodded then gestured to Daisy who was standing excitedly in her white lab coat, clutching her clipboard.

"I'm sure you remember Daisy, she'll be doing your tests today. I really have to go but just let Daisy know if you need me and she'll be sure to contact me. Bye Ellie. Daisy." He finished, nodding his goodbyes to each of us.

Daisy suddenly turned to me, her eyes bursting with energy that she didn't have the first time I met her.

"Okay, so let me explain everything real quick. There's clearly something special about you, I could tell by your aura the minute I felt your mind approaching in the forests. It is very very similar to a white stag's which just shouldn't be possible unless somehow your ancestors have been surviving on your own somewhere, although even then we'd be checking in on you, making sure you're okay.

It is a possibility that you have some of our soul in you, that maybe you're half white stag or a quarter and never knew, but I can tell you that you are very clearly not purely werewolf. I'm just going to do a couple simple things to check my hypothesis and then we can figure out what to do from there. Sound good?"

"Yes, of course."

I was shocked at the possibility of being part white stag. There's no way someone like me who seems to bring nothing but chaos and hurt can be like them, but who am I to question them?

She brought me into a separate room where there was a ball of sorts that seemed to be made out of white crystals. It was so large that it took up almost the entire room, only leaving enough space for one or two people to stand.

"This is pretty simple, its the ball of purity formed along with the very first white stag. During the height of white stag hunting we used it as a way to let people into the village or not. If it lights up light blue it means you have at least part of the soul of a white stag within you. Its pretty simple. Once we discover if you have any white stag in you we can then see how much. Just place your hands on the ball and let it do its work. Its as simple as that."

I walked up to the ball, my heart beating strangely fast and my palms awkwardly sweaty. I placed my hands on the ball and it instantly lit up blue. There seemed to be pulses of blue electricity running through the white crystals, similar to the flames I'd seen lighting the halls.

I gasped, staring at the beautiful sight. I hard Daisy giggling from behind me. I turned around to see her smiling widely.

"I knew it!" She exclaimed proudly.

She came up to me and hugged me.

"This is amazing. I don't know how this is possible but I'm sure there's nome sort of crazy story behind it." she gushed but I just stood there in complete shock. What the hell is happening? I'm not fully convinced I'm not dreaming.

I followed her to a separate office where we sat down across from each other.

"Okay so I should explain the results properly. Whenever a white stag places their hands on the ball it always lights up. The pulses of blue electricity will increase in number and shoot across the globe quicker depending on the strength of the stag.

The faster the pulses the more control they'll have over their abilities. They'll be more capable of reading minds and the auras they'll see will be more detailed and a few other little perks.

Mine were fairly quick and Amos' were incredibly fast. Yours, well, I've never seen anything like yours before."

I don't even know whether to be surprised anymore. I'm having a hard time finding a single thing in my life that makes sense.

"Yours were faster than any that have been recorded since the very first white stag ever."

Of course. Because that makes total sense.

Can you feel the sarcasm?

She gave me a huge smile while I looked at her like she'd gone crazy.

"Maybe you should check the ball. I'm pretty sure its broken." I whispered awkwardly wringing my fingers together. God dammit Ellie, what did you do now?

"The ball can't break, its millions of years old."

"Oh my god I broke a million year old ball of crystals! Shit, I'm so sorry! I knew I shouldn't have touched it, fuck."

"You didn't break it!" Daisy repeated, rolling her eyes at me, "Want me to prove it?"

I nodded warily.

With that she stood up gesturing for me to follow. I'm pretty sure I broke it, it doesn't make any sense that I would be a white stag, especially not a strong one. Chaos follows me, not peace. I'm like the exact opposite of a white stag from what I've heard.

We walked back into the room and she placed her hands on the ball. Nothing happened for a second and I almost dropped to the ground in guilt but then lowly the pulses filled the ball. They weren't going nearly as fast as mine, in comparison the ball barely looked like it lit up.

"See? Its not broken, this is how it always looks for me and I am 75llhm white stag soul. Second highest in the village, Amos being first with 77llhm, which was ground breaking at the time."

"But that makes no sense. I'm not nearly as pure or peaceful as you people. How could I have more white stag? I can't read auras or anything like that."

"You have got to gain some confidence. You are very white stag, and trust me, everyone can see it even if you can't."

I really really doubt that...

"We will do a test to find your exact numbers but my bet is its in the hundreds, maybe 110llhm. The very first white stag had 150llhm, so that is the official maximum. As for the abilities, we can train you to use them now that we know you have them."

"You're telling me I'll be able to read auras and people's minds and stuff?" I asked, my eyes widening in excitement.

"Yep!" She said, a giant smile gracing her face.

I like her.

"Well then..." I sputtered out, unsure of what to say. I'm going to wake up back in that tree, trying to run from all my problems, quite literally, watch it happen.

"Follow me so we can figure out your llhm and we can report back to Amos."

I just nodded and followed her joyful figure. I swear if she started skipping down the halls I wouldn't be the tiniest bit surprised.

"A werewolf white stag, crazy." She mumbled to herself, shaking her head.

We re-entered her office and she took out a small crystal ball, probably about the size of my pinky fingernail.

"Each stag gets their own crystal ball. On rare occasions it guides you sometimes and helps you when you need it, otherwise it's just proof you're a white stag and will keep people from questioning you. Once you hold onto it it will give us the number of llhm you have and we can react from there. It will also light up a specific color letting us know what your strength will be, mind reading it will light up green, aura reading will light up purple and mind tricks will light up yellow."

"That's so cool."

"It really is." She smiled, it was clear she loved what she was and she loved her job.

"Go on, take it." She said, placing it in front of me.

I took it from off of the table where she left it on the table taking a deep breath. This is all just completely crazy.

I picked it up and it immediately lit up with a number. It started at 0 then proceeded to climb when it passed 75 I looked up to see an excited Daisy squirming in her seat, at 90llhm she actually stood up dancing a little, at 100 she was squealing. When it reached 115llhm she had gone quiet as a look of shock covered her face but the numbers just kept climbing and climbing. My heart was beating so fast I was sure I was dying, that the doctor had messed up and I'd die before the numbers stopped climbing.

My hands started shaking a little when the number passed 140llhm.

What the actual fuck

It finally stopped when it reached 150llhm.

I looked to Daisy completely calm. "I'm pretty sure its br-"

She shut my up by eying me disapprovingly holding up a hand, "Don't you dare finish that sentence. For the lat time, you can't break it!"

"But-"

"No."

I sighed looking at the ball.

"150llhm." Daisy mumbled to herself. "I can't believe I'm alive to witness this. I feel so lucky, I must've done something right. I just witnessed history! This has never happened! Not since the very first white stag!"

I was just staring at the number trying to breathe.

Holy fuck.

"Okay, it should light up a color soon so we can find your strengths."

I watched the ball and the number started to fade, suddenly it started to glow... white? What the fuck does that mean. Does that mean I have no powers? Daisy gasped. Oh god what now?

I'm having a very hard time believing it's not broken.

I looked up to see her staring with wide eyes. She looked at me and started to laugh. She laughed really hard, tears streaming down her cheeks while I sat in front of her awkwardly, confusion no doubt covering my face. Once she finally sobered up after a solid minute of full blown laughter she looked at me.

"Ummmm, what does white mean?" I asked, trying to break the weird silence.

"Time!" She said laughing.

Nope. Not confusing at all...

"The legends say that the first white stag was, along with everything else, able to manipulate time!" She exclaimed, doing a little happy dance and laughing some more.

That's when I passed out. My brain was like, NOPE NOPE NOPE! TOO MUCH INFORMATION!"

I woke up in the amazingly comfortable cocoon of a bed in the room Amos had let me stay in. There was a note next to me that said, 'sorry for overwhelming you, when you're ready, no rush, please meet me in Amos' office. We'll be discussing a game plan :) -Daisy'

Okay, so it wasn't a dream. Okay... Okayyy... NOT OKAY WHAT THE FUCKKKK.

I sat there for another hour in the bed just yelling 'WHAT THE FUCK' in my head over and over. After that I'd basically processed it as best as I could. I got out of bed and stretched, grabbing a cup of coffee.

"I'm a powerful white stag that can manipulate time." I said out loud to myself, hoping that would help me believe it. I stood there in silence for a couple moments before breaking into laughter.

I dropped to the ground, rolling around, tears streaming down my cheeks. I continued to laugh for another 30 minutes before finally sobering up. I looked outside to find it dark outside.

After another 2 hours of lying and thinking on the floor I'd basically accepted the facts by now. No point dwelling on it.

I looked at the time to find it was 2:00 am. There was no chance anyone else was awake, so I decided to go for a run.

I quickly got ready and head down the path. I decided to run around the entire village territory. If I left I wasn't sure I'd be able to get back in again and I didn't want to risk it or force anyone else out fo their way to come and get me. The track was about 100km long and I ran it exactly 4 times for the next 4 hours.

The sun was finally rising and I decided to head back to my room and have some breakfast before meeting Daisy and Amos.

The run had really helped me clear my mind, and even though the whole idea was weird and didn't quite feel real, I'd accepted all of the information I'd gotten.

Breakfast was one of my favorite meals and often the only one I really remembered to eat. It gave me energy for the rest of the day. I opened the food compartment to reveal fluffy looking Belgian waffles with fresh raspberries, some sort of fruit drizzle on top and some crispy bacon on the side.

I made my cinnamon swirl coffee and calmly ate the amazing breakfast.

I took a nice shower and got ready, wearing one of their beautiful sundresses. I felt good.

I checked the time to see it was already 10:00 am.

I took a deep breath and set out for Amos' office. I felt much better, much more relaxed after my run. I shared smiles with everyone I passed, and even said a quick hello to Rose at the flower shop on my way.

This place is truly amazing but as much as I'd like to, I don't feel like I belong. I couldn't describe or understand the feeling, I mean the place was basically paradise but something deep inside me said I couldn't stay here forever. It was not where I belonged. I needed to see things, experience everything I could before I died.

And most of all, I still craved that sense of belonging more than anything.

Twenty

"Tough times never last, but tough people do."

– Robert Schuller

I knocked on Amos's door and immediately heard a "Come on in."

I opened the door to reveal a smiling Amos and Daisy. They looked pretty creepy, standing side by side with unnaturally large smiles pulling their lips.

I took a seat at the small round table they were sitting around and crossed my legs, trying to get comfortable in the uncomfortable, tension-filled silence.

"Well, its safe to say that your results were shocking, but they do make a lot of sense." Amos started when I got comfortable, "Your aura is very strong and peaceful. We're setting up a training schedule so we can teach you how to use your powers of mind reading, aura reading and mind tricks, but unfortunately, since none of us have any experience with it, we can't help with the time control. It should come to you itself though, don't worry." Amos explained.

"My mother also told me that you'll be taking over her flower shop during the few weeks we'll be gone, we're going to visit some family down in Europe, they've been having some problems with witches breaking into their village. "

Daisy noticed my slightly confused expression and took over, "Witches are the only beings powerful enough to see through and even break a white stag's powers. However, they've been pretty occupied problems with humans trying catch and burn them the past few centuries to bother with trying to catch, us so it hasn't been a problem until now."

I nodded my head in understanding.

"We have trainers that will meet with you every day." Amos continued, "You'll work on aura reading first, once you've mastered it, you'll move onto mind reading, then finally you can advance to brain tricks. With your strong numbers you'll probably be able to master all three before we get back. We're leaving in about an hour actually, you should head down to the flower shop and prepare to take over right about now, I'll send Jeremiah, your trainer down to the flower shop and you can talk about schedules and stuff then. I should probably go pack, it was nice seeing you" With that Amos stood up, giving Daisy and I a quick hug before going on his way.

Daisy had to get back to work so I went down to the flower shop to take over.

As soon as I got there Rose met me outside with a huge smile.

"I heard about your scores, I knew you were special but wow." She chuckled, her voice raspy but somehow simultaneously smooth.

I blushed a little, unsure of what to say, I wasn't exactly used to getting compliments. "Thank you." I mumbled quietly.

Awkward little shit.

"No problem honey, here." She said handing me a bag. I took it a little confused and opened it to see it completely filled with golden coins. There was probably 5 million US dollars worth of coins in here. I looked back to her shocked.

"That's for the trouble of taking over the shop."

I just blinked at her... What the fuck? "Do you want me to give this to someone?"

"No, I'm giving you this money for taking care of my shop. I'm very grateful." She said as if it was the most obvious thing in the world, putting her hands on her hips.

"This is like, 5 million dollars worth of coins in here!" I exclaimed, waiting for her to realize her mistake. Maybe she somehow handed me the wrong sketchy bag of gold?

"Try 10 million, and you deserve it all."

"10 MILLION?! There's no way I can accept this, I was expecting like 20 bucks! 100 max!"

"You will accept it or I will take it as a sign of disrespect. Do you want to be rude?"

"No but-"

"No buts. Its your money now, buy yourself something pretty, do whatever you want with it."

"But-"

I stopped when she gave me the look.

Fuck man, that's A LOT of money.

I teared up a little and pulled Rose into a giant bear hug.

"How can you even afford this?"

"I'm the richest person in town, I've done a lot throughout my life." She laughed, her smile making her face crease in the best ways. "I only opened the flower shop a few years ago as a retirement plan. Trust me, I can afford that."

"Thank you so, so much. Words can't describe how grateful I am right now. This is unbelievable."

"Of course sweetheart, believe me, you deserve it."

I took a deep breath smiling at the money. I would finally be able to help Jamie and Henry out properly. The way they helped me. I'd been sending them money from my bounty hunting gig, but it never felt like it was enough. Jen didn't need any money, she was living a lavish life in England with her new mate. Sidney certainly didn't need any, Jack and Chris either. Alphas and Betas are notoriously rich. Maybe I could give something to Sarah and Heeler. I know I can't buy back their forgiveness, but they'd probably appreciate the money, I remember Heeler telling me he sometimes had problems with that.

****

I was working around the shop when a tall, built, dark-skinned man walked into the shop. He looked around my age and had a buzz cut but somehow with all that didn't look the littlest bit intimidating.

I immediately went over to greet him like Rose always did.

"Hi there, can I help you with anything?" I asked with a smile, trying to sound as welcoming as possible.

"Ellie Green?" The man asked.

"Yes, that's me. And you are?" I said politely, attempting to wipe some of the dirt off my pants.

The man smiled, "Jeremiah Blackburn."

I reached out my hand for a handshake but he pulled me in for a hug instead making me laugh in surprise.

"Nice to meet you. You're my trainer then?" I guessed.

"That's me! I just came here to figure out what schedule would work best. I, personally work best in the mornings but I can happily make evenings work too."

"Morning sounds great. What time?"

"Is 3:00 am too early for you? I'm an early riser." He smiled awkwardly, chuckling to himself and rubbing the back of his head.

"That's perfect for me actually. I'm always awake." I laughed.

"Amazing." He said giving me a hug. "I have to go, I have an appointment. Meet me in front of this shop tomorrow at 2:50am, sound good?"

"Sounds perfect." I gave him one last hug before he left.

Damn, people here are insanely nice.

I spent the rest of the day tending to the flowers and helping people around the shop.

I bought myself a beautiful bouquet of ochna serrulata mickey mouse yellow flowers and a couple of yellow daisies that I braided into my hair, pulling half of it up while leaving the rest flowing down my back.

I closed up the shop at around 5:00pm and spent the rest of the day in the village forests, practicing my fighting skills so I didn't get rusty during my stay.

I realized that I now had exactly 7 months before I died. The time was passing by way too quickly. I tried not to track it but I had so little time and so much I wanted to do. I decided not to sleep that night, I'd been sleeping too much lately. I just spent my time training until 1:30 am when I decided to go back to the penthouse and get ready to meet with Jeremiah.

I quickly got cleaned up had breakfast and made my way to the flower shop. I always had my phone with me, I don't know why but I always felt the need to have it, as if it brought me a type of security. People didn't really bother texting me much, but I thought I should always just keep it with me just in case. What if someone needs me? I'm a fairly descent fighter, I can help.

I arrived at the flower shop at the exact same time Jeremiah did, making us chuckle while we hugged hello.

I followed him to the main tree that held the lab and offices. We road the elevator to the 15th floor to reveal a large white room. It was, of course, beautiful with spectacular views.

"Wow." I said stupidly, marveling at the view for what felt like the thousandth time since I moved here.

"Ya, its a cool room. We make it simple and white because we want the least amount of distractions possible for you. We'll be starting with the aura so you need to be able to notice even the faintest of colors. Come sit." He said gesturing to the ground in the middle of the room.

We sat across from each other, crossed legged.

"Okay, you're going to look into my eyes. Try to relax but focus. I want you to try and see if you can get any colors off of me. Since you're a beginner it won't be strong, and it could take a while but it'll come to you. Just stay relaxed and concentrate." Jeremiah explained, a small smile constantly on his face.

I did as he said, staring into his eyes. He had beautiful blue eyes that complimented his skin perfectly, making them seem like they were glowing.

I could it deep down inside my bones that he meant no harm. I took a deep breath, trying to see any color other than the glowing ocean blue of his eyes.

After about on hour and a half of sitting and staring, trying to relax, I saw a spark of blue fly around him. I gasped, blinking to make sure I was seeing right but there it was.

"Do you see something?" He asked calmly, a hint of excitement lighting his voice.

"I think so!" I said, a small smile making its way onto my face. "I see... a blue spark of sorts flying around you, circling your body."

He smiled large as a bit of yellow added to his, what I assume aura.

"Blue means calm and relaxed." He explained as several other yellows joined the blue.

I laughed a little. "There's also a bit of yellow now!" I exclaimed excitedly.

He laughed some more, "Yellow means happy or excited."

I jumped up in the air, my aura no doubt lighting up yellow.

"I did it!" I exclaimed, making yellow fill out his aura even more, then suddenly there was flash of pink. It was only there for a second, but I didn't miss it, and I was certain I hadn't imagined it.

He then handed me a paper listing all of the different colors and the emotions they reflected. The better you got the more colors you'd be able to decipher.

I was reading the emotions when I came across pink and got curious. Next to pink was labeled... love? It explains that when there are slight sparks it shows a possible interest and if someone is involve the person will glow completely pink when looking into your eyes... Well then. I must've seen wrong.

I looked back at him and saw another small spark of pink.

Shit.

"Come sit back down, we'll try something new. I'm going to tell you stories about my life and you're going to look for emotions, whether its sad, happy, grossed out, excited, bored, anything."

I nodded and we sat back down.

The blue sparks took back over the yellow ones as we settled down. I wonder what my aura looks like.

"This happened years ago. I was about 12 years old, we didn't live in the village yet, we were living among people in a small werwolf pack. My mother, father and I lived together in a small house by a lake and I went to a small school with werewolves.

I knew this pack was problematic, others seemed to hate it, though I never knew why. My mother didn't let me out much other than to go to school. She said that the lands were too dangerous.

No one knew about me being a white stag and my mother had taught me the ways. I decided to go out and explore, figure the pack out, one day. I was able to trick everyone's minds, I walked through the territories but no one could see me.

I heard a crowd and followed it to an open field. Sitting on the field was a sort of platform. I could see a man, the alpha, standing on it with a whip in his hand. He was yelling something at the little girl kneeling beneath him, but I couldn't hear what since I was too far away.

Being stupid and young I decided to get a closer look."

The color of regret started to dance around his aura.

I wrote it down on the white board he gave me and he gave me reassuring smile.

"I got up close to find my alpha beating a small girl, no older than me. Probably about 10 years old. He had given her 25 lashes already and was making her count the rest. "

The color of sadness mixed in with the regret as the calming blue faded and the color of frustration appeared.

After a moment a smile slipped onto his face and the calm colors started to return along with the colors of lust and love.

"I just remember thinking she was the most beautiful girl I'd ever seen,"

Frustration seeped in.

"I remember thinking, how could they do that to someone? I now understood why my mother was so strict. She had every reason to be."

The color of understanding seeped in.

"I ran away, crying to my mother."

His relaxed aura crept back, taking over all of the other colors quickly.

"We ended up moving a couple weeks later and I never saw the girl again, until well."

Realization swept over me and my breath stopped.

"I should probably mention that my old pack was the Blood Thunder pack and my old alpha was Alpha Green."

I looked down, shame taking over me. I had no more tears left to cry over that subject. I couldn't, I wouldn't. But that didn't stop the shame.

I looked up at him. "Yep, that's me. Ellie Green, daughter of Alpha and Luna Green of the Blood Thunder pack. The only child they tortured, thank god."

"Look, I didn't mean to make you upset by bringing it up, but I didn't know how else to tell you. This is an actual exercise we use and you did a fantastic job."

I perked up a little.

"If you continue like this you'll have mastered reading auras within the week!"

I squealed, completely forgetting about the story and jumped into his arms, making him laugh.

"Thank you," I said leaning back, "I really appreciate it."

When I said that more pink sparks flooded into his aura and he hugged me tight. I stiffened slightly but I don't think Jeremiah noticed as he hugged me tighter.

Well, this could be problematic...

Twenty-one

UNEDITED

From here on out this story is completely unedited! If you see any problems or mistakes or anything that can be done better in the writing or the actual plot please let me know and I'll be happy to fix everything I can during editing! I'm currently working through this as fast as I can but it takes time and this is just a hobby. I'm sorry, please be patient!

We'd been working on auras for exactly a week now and today is my graduation day! I've officially mastered them and am now moving onto mind reading. Not gonna lie I'm pretty excited about this one.

I can easily read anyone's aura in a blink of an eye. Everyone around here has calming and happy auras, no surprise but if I really concentrate I can see the most detailed things about their past or any emotion they're feeling no matter how detailed or small.

Jeremiah said he was really impressed. We had someone come in and tell us some stories and we'd see how many emotions I could place. In the end I was finding more than Jeremiah.

The only problem is Jeremiah's aura. I can tell that he's lived a pretty good life but the more time I spend with him the more intense the purple on pink sparks become. At first I thought I was imagining it but now there's not doubting it.

One of the men that came to tell their story even told me that he'd seen em too when Jeremiah looked at me. The only problem is I'm not sure I feel it.

He's such an amazing guy, sweet and caring but to be honest I'm still hurting from all of the rejections I've received throughout my life. Especially my mate's rejection. He was suppose to be the one to care for me and take care of me and love me no matter what but he just rejected me.

I entered the beautiful white training room a little early but Jeremiah was already there waiting.

He immediately lit up yellow with sparks of pink and purple as I entered the room.

I hope he doesn't know that I know. That would be pretty uncomfortab le...

"Happy graduation day!" He exclaimed pulling me into a hug. I'm so proud of you!"

When we pulled back there was even more pink and purple. Oh boy.

"Today we'll start reading minds! This is a pretty fun one to learn and you're so amazing I'm sure you'll pick it up in no time." He smiled.

SEE WHAT I MEAN?! HE'S A SWEETY PIE! WHAT'S WRONG WITH ME!

"This is honestly not my expertise, but I know how to train others. My best is tricking the mind which I'm very excited to teach but I can only read minds if I sit down and really concentrate. I only have a 45llhm so its natural that I haven't mastered all of them like you will.'

We sat down on the floor across from each other like always.

"Okay, its fairly simple. Open up your mind, relax, stare into my eyes. I'll push some thoughts forward to make it easier for you. Just imagine a string connecting our heads. Slide down that string and into my mind. "

I stared into his eyes and imagined the string. It took me a moment to really visualize it properly between us. I had to find the right string. For some reason it didn't feel right until I imagined a glowing yellow biplane of sort between our minds.

I then imagined my mind power sliding across the string and into his mind.

'RAINBOWS' I heard him yell in his mind.

I gasped at the weird sensation of someone else's voice in my mind.

I could feel myself standing at the front of his brain. I knew there was much more to discover and look for but I didn't quite have the strength to do so yet.

"Rainbow." I said out loud and Jeremiah's face lit up.

"That was exactly it, amazing." Pink sparks fluttered in. Shit shit shit I need to stop them.

"THOSE FUCKING BANDANNAS THO AM I RIGHT?!"

Oh my fucking god. Was that really all I could come up with?! WHAT THE HELL IS WRONG WITH ME?!

Confusion clouded his aura and the pink sparks died down.

I mean, mission accomplished tho.

"What?"

"I-I... I don't know I think I need a break... SEE YA!"

With that I leaped off the floor and ran out of the room leaving Jeremiah sitting there completely confused.

Yep. Definitely managed to find the worst possible way to handle the situation.

I decided to go for a run to let all my pent up energy and frustrations out.

Jeremiah taught me how to get back into the village so I was finally able to run outside, get a little fresh air.

I left their territories, taking huge breaths.

Nope. I fucked up. Why do I always do that?! I just left him sitting there! My god I need help.

I continued running for hours. It was Monday and I was instructed to keep the flower shop closed on Mondays so I wouldn't need to worry about that. I had all day to run and think.

I was running at about 250 kilometers per hour. One of the fastest I'd ever run but didn't feel the slightest bit tired.

I gracefully leapt around the trees and over the falling logs truly enjoying myself.

I heard yelling off in the distance though. It seemed like a war cry but I figured I'd go help them out.

I was there in a couple minutes to find about 8 men trying to beat up a man who looked to be about 19 years old.

I immediately read their auras. The group of people beating the kid up all had problematic auras filled with rage, cockiness and the color of sinister, I could tell that they were bad and harmful immediately. The boy had the aura of incense and fear.

I didn't know the situation but I knew that the guy needed help and I was going to give it to him.

I leapt and jumped into action, immediately pinning each of the men to the ground with injuries that would keep them there. Some attempted to fight back and even scratched me a little but over all they had no chance.

I could smell that they weren't werewolves but I didn't know what they were. Then I saw some fangs poking out of one of their lips. Vampires.

I looked to the boy behind me and he looked petrified. He was beat up and clearly underweight. He shivered a little avoiding eye contact with me when I looked at him. I realized that somewhere in the fight I had let out my strong power.

I reigned it back in and saw the boy instantly relax.

I gave a deep low threatening growl to the vampire lying on the floor and they immediately scrambled to their feet and ran away the best that they could with their injuries.

I turned to the boy and smiled. "Hi, I'm Ellie, what's your name?"

He instantly relaxed, giving me an easy smile. "Alex. Th-thank you for saving my life."

"Anytime. What are you doing out here all alone? That seems a little dangerous."

"I-I just escaped my Alpha. I was headed to my sister's pack when the vampires caught me."

"Which pack? I might be able to help you get there."

"Belle Foret."

My breathing stopped when he said that.

"Do you know it?"

I nodded. "Yes, I know it, I can take you there."

The boy's face lit up. "really?! Oh thank you so much!" He exclaimed.

"Of course." I smiled. "Your sister's name wouldn't happen to be Sarah would it?"

"Y-ya, how did you know that, do you know her?"

"I knew her a little yes. "

He sighed out a happy breath.

I could see his werewolf helping already working on the cuts and bruises he'd received. I'd gotten there just on time so he hadn't gotten anything very substantial.

I gave him a hand and helped him up. We fell into a slow jog, which was the best he could do in his condition.

"At this rate we should be there by about 3:00 pm, its 1:00 now."

He nodded. Honestly at my pace I could've gotten there in 5 minutes but I'm not sure he'd appreciate me carrying him.

"Do you live in Belle Foret?"

"No... I left a little while ago. I'm currently living with the white stags."

I could tell by his aura that I could trust him.

He looked shocked then asked, "I thought they didn't let any non-white stags in."

"Ya, the don't..."

It took a second for him to process the information but when he did his face lit up.

"You're a white stag?!" He exclaimed jumping a little as he did.

"Yep" I said, returning the smile.

"Then how did you fight so well? I thought white stags never fought, they're so peaceful they have no reason to."

"I'm also a werewolf and I've got a good control over the white stag thing. It doesn't rule me like it does others."

"That's awesome. Can you like read minds and stuff?!"

I laughed a little, "I can read auras but I'm still working on the whole reading and tricking minds thing. It'll take another couple of weeks to master those."

He nodded in understanding.

"Is that why you saved me? Do I have a good aura?"

I saw sadness and hope fly around him.

"You have a beautiful aura, don't let anyone else let you believe otherwise. You are truly a good person."

He lit up happy when I said that making me smile.

We continued that sort of small talk for the next couple of hours before we arrived. I explained to him how I knew his sister. He's been really strong considering the situation.

We were about 5 minutes away now until we entered their grounds.

I never even thought about coming back here. I don't think I have the heart to be rejected again.

"I think I'll just leave you here, its just-"

"No!" He cut me off, "please come, I could really use the support. Please?"

How the hell could I say no to that? Fuck. I guess we're going to have a little reunion.

As soon as we entered pack grounds I started feeling a little uneasy. I looked over to Alex to see him covered in nervousness.

I took a deep breath. This is not about me, don't be selfish.

I gave him a smile, giving his arm a little squeeze. "Don't be nervous. I'm here with you, I won't let anything happen to you. Just breathe and think about the fact that you'll be seeing your sister."

He instantly relaxed once I said that, the color of excitement filling his aura instead.

I stayed on complete high alert as we entered the familiar territory. I don't exactly trust this place anymore.

I heard an arrow wizzing towards us but it was too late, the one headed for me missed me but there was one headed directly for Alex. Without thinking I grabbed him, taking the hit for him while pushing him to the ground.

A few more arrows hit me but I couldn't feel the pain.

Fuck, I liked this shirt though.

I felt a little dizzy and knew these were covered in liquid silver and poison. It would completely temporarily paralyze any other wolf. This is what they did to unannounced strangers before questioning them.

I knew they would do this which is part of the reason why I insisted on coming with Alex. He didn't need this kind of stress added to him.

"ELLIE!" He yelled, panic overtaking him.

I held out my hand stopping him.

"I'm fine, stay down."

He listened to my as I turned to the guard who shot me.

I raised my hands in surrender.

"Hey Joe." I said, recognizing the guard. "Its Ellie, I'm here with Gamma Heeler's mate Sarah's brother."

He climbed down the tree he had climbed and nodded at me.

I extended my hand to Alex and helped him up. I decided to bring him the rest of the way to make sure he got there safely. We walked the last few minutes to the pack house as I pulled out the arrows lodged in my stomach, watching them instantly heal over.

Alex was very worried and guilty even though I told him I was fine.

The guard had a fairly empty aura, one of a person who's actions are simply an order. It was typical for soldiers warriors and workers.

We entered the pack house and Alex called out "SARAH!"

Immediately Alpha Jack, Jade, Sarah and Heeler were entering the room together.

Sarah gasped when she entered, not even noticing me as she ran to her brother engulfing him in a hug. They both broke into tears, hugging each other tightly.

I almost cried at the sight and noticed around me that everyone was struggling with the same thing.

Twenty-two

After a few minutes their attention started to turn towards me as confusion covered them.

Heeler pulled out a knife defensively making me sigh. Why don't they trust me?

Sarah saw me and pulled me into a hug, shocking me.

Heeler growled lowly but Sarah just turned around and gave him a warning glare effectively shutting him up.

"Oh Ellie I've missed you so much! What are you doing here?!"

God this girl is sweet. I stared into her aura marveling at the beauty. She had overcome such darkness. I was so proud.

"She saved my life and then helped me come here." Alex filled them in.

Heeler put away his knife when he said that.

"What's going on? Why are you all so scared of Ellie?"

Well then Alex, just put it right out there.

They all awkwardly stared at the grounds or the walls.

"I know she's strong, she beat like 8 vampires earlier within seconds barely getting a scratch on her and got shot by 3 arrows and kept walking, but she's so peaceful I mean, its in her nature to be peaceful."

"You got shot by 3 of our arrows?" Jack asked

I nodded my head.

Jade whistled lowly looking impressed, "How are you still awake? Just one of those can paralyze you."

I shrugged, "I've grown a tolerance to poison over the years."

There was an awkward silence at my revelation, everyone understanding except Alex who looked around confused.

"What did you mean when you said it was in her nature to be peaceful? After all, she almost killed your sister." Heeler said bitterly.

I looked at the ground in shame. Heeler's aura was overwhelmingly red, making me eve more guilty and embarrassed.

"That's impossible. It must've been an accident I mean my sister just hugged her clearly she didn't purposely try and hurt her. I mean, white stags don't hurt others. Ever."

"White stag?" Jack asked.

"They don't know." I mumbled to Alex, head still down.

Alex's eyes widened as his aura became panicked. They auras were beginning to become overwhelming so I turned them off, sighing at the lack of aggressive colors.

"Don't know what?" Heeler asked.

I looked up. "It turns out I am a white stag."

They all looked at me in silence before they all broke out into laughter. I looked at the ground in shame and made my way outside. I have no idea why they all hate me but I won't stand around while they laugh at me.

Alex came running after me out the door. "Ellie wait! I'm so sorry I told them your secret I didn't mean it. I don't know why they don't believe that you're a white stag, I don't understand what they have against you but you can prove yourself! Just go read their auras maybe read their minds a little and-"

I cut him off raising my hand.

"Alex, its okay. I cam here to drop you off safely, nothing else." I handed him a piece of paper with my number on it.

"Call me if you ever need anything, I'll come help as soon as possible or help the best I can. I've made peace with the situation here. I don't understand it either but I'm not going to stand here and beg for them to like me. I love them all, they were my family but I won't stay here if I am unwanted."

A tear slipped down Alex's face. "B-but, this doesn't make sense, its so unfair you're such an amazing person and-"

"Thank you Alex but I should go before they kick me out themselves."

After I said that Joe came out of the house growling at me. "Leave rogue or I have orders to kill."

Alex gasped when he said that. I gave him one last sad smile before running out of there. At my speed I was out of their territory in seconds. I ran back home faster than I'd ever run before. I felt a lone tear slip down my face as I wiped at it angrily.

I promised myself I was done being weak. I refuse to break my promises.

I was running at about 51 500 kilometers per hour, letting out all of my frustrations. I reached the village in no time but I wasn't done running. I continued to run as hard as I could for hours, reaching 95 000 kilometers per hour.

At 2:00 am I ran back to the village and got ready for training again.

The run helped a lot, I let out all of my frustrations. I was still sad but sad I can live with. Sad I can power through. As I walked through the village to meet Jeremiah I noticed everyone looking at me then frowning a little.

I knew my aura was depressing so I did my best to try and cover it up. I pushed the depression deep down and brought fourth my happy go-lucky self. I smiled at those who passed and they returned the smiles.

Everyone was happier when I was happy. They don't need to have my problems, I refuse to be a burden to anyone.

I walked into the training room and Jeremiah could sense that my mood was a little off.

We just went right to work, me trying to reach deeper and deeper into his mind.

****

Jeremiah and I have been working on mind reading for about 3 days now. I can easily get the thoughts at the forefront of people's minds. I am now working on diving into the stream that constantly speaks in someone's head, whether they are aware or not.

Subconscious thoughts can say a lot about a person. I'm trying to find the thoughts that Jeremiah has pushed deep down and tried to lock away. Just as Jeremiah was about to call it a day I broke through.

In came a stream of his darkest and deepest thoughts that he'd locked away. I gasped at some of the dark things this man has seen and had to overcome. The dark thoughts that he'd had. It was mostly filled with him wondering why people wanted to kill him, he was just a white stag, peaceful. He just wanted to live in peace.

I then caught another stream that made me gasp all over again. They were all thoughts about me.

My picture ran through his mind as well as specific thoughts and opinions. 'She's so beautiful' 'She's amazing' 'Ellie, what a beautiful name for a beautiful person' 'She's been through so much yet she's so strong' 'I wonder if she can see that I like her... that'd be awkward' ' Oh shit what if she sees that I can't stop thinking about her, I'd be so embarrassed.'

I stopped listening, those words echoing through my head as I concentrated back on Jeremiah's face. He was blushing heavily and looking down embarrassed.

I crawled towards him and pulled him into a hug. I had no words. His thoughts were so sweet and amazing, I was beyond upset with myself that I couldn't reciprocate the feelings. What the hell is wrong with me? I mean he's handsome, sweet and I know he cares about me, and now I'm going to hurt him.

I saw the strong purple and pink that flowed around him as I hugged him and heard his thoughts about how close we were and how perfect I was echoing through our minds as they were still attached and quickly shut them off.

We pulled back as a tear escaped my eye. "I'm sorry." I said and he instantly understood.

He pulled me into a hug, shushing me and petting my hair soothingly as I broke down.

Tears flowed freely down my face as I sobbed into his chest. "You're literally the perfect guy you're so sweet and supportive and you're hot and you have no idea how much I want to want you... But I can't." I sobbed harder.

"I don't know what's wrong with me I'm so sorry."

He shushed me and continued petting my hair.

"There's nothing wrong with you. " He said gently, holding me to his chest as I wet his shirt with my tears.

"Oh my god, here you are comforting me after I just said all that, I should be comforting you and instead I'm ruining your shirt!"

"You're ruining nothing. Everything's okay."

We just sat there in silence and he held me as I cried for the rest of our training session.

Once we finally pulled away I apologized one more time before making my way out.

I sucked in my sadness, letting my happiness shine through my aura as I made my way back to the flower shop.

I bought myself another bouquet of yellow roses and braided a few yellow daisies into my hair. That always seemed to help me feel better when I'd had a bad day. I decided that night to go for another run to clear my head, trying to run faster and faster until it was training time again.

****

Today's my mind reading graduation. I've officially mastered the art or entering someone's minds. I can access their memories all of their thoughts, even those they hide away. I can easily depict a person's brain with just a few seconds of concentration.

Today I'll finally be starting the last portion of training, mind tricks. Jeremiah's very excited about it as its his speciality.

We've been okay since the incident. At first it was a little awkward when I came back but we worked through it. I've blocked out his aura and stayed away from his thoughts about me and it all went perfectly.

I've been running instead of sleeping since the incident as well and weirdly I haven't felt the tiniest bit tired. I felt more relaxed and happy without the sleep weirdly.

Sometimes during my runs I find people in wars or something. If there's a clear good side and bad side I'll help the good side out but other than that I try to stay to of it.

As soon as I entered the training area Jeremiah gave me the biggest bear hug making me giggle.

"HAPPY GRADUATIONS!! Now we get to the fin stuff!" He exclaimed.

We sat in our usual positions as Jeremiah bounced around excitedly.

"Okay, now you now how to read me and see into my mind we're going to work on controlling certain aspects of it. Basically I want you to enter my mind and then find the part that controls my vision. Once you do you're going to remove the part that can see you. Then, boom you're invisible!"

I squealed excited as I tried it out.

I got into his mind but it took me about an hour to finally find the portion that controls what he's seeing.

I looked at it and found the specific portion that saw me. I tried to yank it out but it wouldn't budge.

It took an entire hour of yanking until the part finally came loose.

"You did it! You're invisible!" He exclaimed.

I got up dancing around as he just sat there, portably confused by the noise since he couldn't see what I was doing. I was sweating a little from the work it took to erase me, I definitely will have to work on perfecting this skill.

After replacing the part that sees me in his brain and repeating the process a couple more times I was finished with training.

The flower shop didn't open today so I had the day to myself. I went back to the penthouse, doing my laundry and tidying up a little bit when I got a text.

No one ever really texted me so it took me a second to process what it was.

I opened it up to reveal a text from an unknown number:

Hey Ellie, its Alex. I don't know if you remember me but I have some stuff I want to talk to you about. Can you meet anytime soon? Nothing urgent.

Hey, of course I remember who you are. I can meet you today if you'd like

Perfect!!!

What time and where?

Flower field on the edge of pack territory. How soon can you get here?

I can get there in about 30 minutes

Perfect see you soon!

I sighed heading out the door and began my run towards Alex. I hope he's happy and okay. I hope they're all treating him well, he deserves it.

Twenty-three

I ran to the old familiar territory, the familiar smells that I had tried to push out of my mind filling my senses. I got there in about 20 minutes, a little early. I sat in the flower field, closing my eyes and thinking about everything.

What could Alex possible want to talk about? What if he has turned on me for some reason.

"Ellie" I heard the familiar voice call out from behind me.

I gave him a small smile, quickly checking his aura. It looked calm and excited, not threatening thought a little nervous and secretive. I noticed the smell of the pack on him now, they must have let him join.

"Hey Alex, what's up?"

"Thanks for coming, I just wanted to talk to you a bit, I know some things you might want to hear."

I nodded and invited him to sit with me as I marveled at this gorgeous yellow dandelion that was growing next to me.

"How did you get here so fast? Were you nearby?"

"No, I'm a pretty good runner, but that's not important. Are you settling well here? Are they being nice to you?"

"Right, well they've been amazing to me. They're so nice and they've given me a room and let me join their pack."

I smiled, thankful he was happy.

"That's amazing Alex."

"Ya, all thanks to you."

I just smiled, touching one of the flowers gently stroking its petals.

"Look, I've asked around about you."

I looked at him confused, the smile dropping off my face a little and my body tensing. He looked a little nervous and I checked his aura to confirm my thoughts.

"I figured out what happened between you all and I thought you should know."

I don't think I could take the heartbreak again. I didn't want to hear this. I couldn't handle the rejection again.

"Look, Alex, I don't want to hear this I-"

"No please, you need to hear it. Please."

How could I say no now???

I sighed giving him the go ahead.

"Okay so I talked to them all and they don't resent yo for anything you did specifically. They said you were always sweet and forgiving and you helped Sarah overcome a lot when she got here. Thank you so much for that by the way. But, they said while you were here they couldn't help but notice how powerful you were. They said you were abused as a child which is why you never had the chance to thrive but in that environment you were really becoming powerful."

I sighed, nodding, still confused, trying to hold the tears back. Positivity. I will not be weak. Never again.

"They told me that you managed to throw Alpha Jack across the room without a second thought, they said you could heal from extreme wounds that should kill within a day if not less. They said after one of the most painful things in life, rejection from you mate, you just got up and carried on with life. Each of these things should scar a person for life.

They started to become a little nervous around you. Every time Jade accidentally hurt you everyone was terrified that you'd try to get her back for it or something and if you did, no one could control you. They were scared. You're so powerful. You don't even flinch when someone stabs you or poisons you."

"I can't feel pain anymore." I informed him. "Its not something I like to broadcast but it seems like you should know."

He looked shocked for a second.

"How?"

I sighed again, holding back the tears, ringing my hands together in discomfort.

"If someone tortures you enough that's what happens."

A tear slipped down his cheek when I said that. He was probably thinking about his own experiences.

I slipped into his mind quickly, checking on his pain tolerance. It was pretty high, probably from the years of abuse.

"Your pain tolerance is definitely high too."

"How do you know that?" He scrunched up his eyebrows, a little fearful for a second.

"I've mastered reading minds. I checked on it to prove my point."

He gasped.

"I'm sorry. I should've asked your permission." I lowered my head in shame. "I promise you that's all I looked at."

"Its okay."

I nodded my head, embarrassed.

"Anyways, I just wanted you to know that they don't hate you, they're scared of what you could do. They don't know your limits and they said even the Alpha, beta and gamma had no chance in defeating you.

When you punched the punching bag so hard you ripped it off its chain, that really shocked them. They really saw your capabilities and they felt threatened. They aren't mad for the incident, Sarah was completely fine, they're just scared of what would happen if you became unhinged one day.

Rejected mateless rogues almost always go crazy and even though you showed no signs of insanity they were terrified that it would finally get to you."

All of what he was saying made sense. A tear trickled down my face.

Again, something that's out of my control is ruining my life. Isolating me. I don't belong anywhere. I belong alone. I'm a disgusting deformation and a powerful alpha without a pack.

"If you just proved to them that you are a white stag! They don't believe me for some reason, but if they knew there's no way they could be scared of you."

I don't need to beg for them to like me, I'm not going to try and desperately prove myself so they accept me. They lost that chance when they turned on me. I've given them no reason to fear me. I've always been as forgiving and peaceful as I could be. If they don't want to accept me then then I won't stick around.

"Look I don't want to-"

"Too late, I told them all to meet us here, they should be here any second."

I stood up quickly feeling a little betrayed.

"I won't be ambushed. I won't beg for them to love me back or even like me or hell, tolerate me. If they don't believe your word then they simply don't get to know. I will not let you go behind my back. I really don't want to see them right now, don't you understand its painful for me to see them stare at me in hatred? I can read their horrible auras when they look at me, I know how they feel. I don't need to hear their disapproving thoughts now."

"Well, they're here now..."

"Fuck." I said as they all emerged from the trees confused. Heeler was growling at me and Jack was ready to pounce on me and attack if he needed to. Sarah looked sweet and welcoming like her brother but the others didn't want me here.

I felt a tear trickle down my cheek and I didn't want them to see me. I wouldn't give them see me weak to make themselves feel better about themselves. If they don't like me strong and powerful, then they can't see me weak and vulnerable. I have no doubt they'll use it to make themselves feel better and stronger.

They were clearly searching for my weaknesses and I wouldn't let them see mine. They didn't deserve it.

Before they could say anything I reached into each of their minds and effortlessly pulled out the pieces that could see hear and smell me.

They all gasped as I no doubt disappeared from their view.

I found myself paralyzed, staring into the eyes of those who I loved, my first family.

Alex stood up, shocked. "Ellie?!"

He turned to the others who looked equally confused.

"Where did she go?" Jasmine asked the others.

They all shrugged searching around for me. Some smelt the air, others closed their eyes and tried to listen for me. I just stood there watching them, letting the tears run down my face freely.

Fuck, I said I wouldn't be weak.

Alex turned to them. "If this didn't prove that she's a white stag then I don't know what could."

Fuck, I gave them all exactly what they wanted.

"Do you think she's still here?" Sarah asked curiously glancing around.

"Great, she's even more powerful and dangerous now!" Heeler exclaimed, "How the fuck are we suppose to fight her if we can't see her!"

"SHUT UP!" Yelled Alex. "WHY THE FUCK WOULD YOU TRY TO FIGHT HER?! SHE LOVED YOU ALL AND YOU ABANDONED

HER! WHAT THE HELL IS WRONG WITH YOU ALL THAT YOU CAN'T SEE THAT! SHE DID ABSOLUTELY NOTHING WRONG, EVER. SHE'S LIVED A HARDER LIFE THAN ALL OF US COMBINED AND-"

I cut him off by reappearing, effectively shutting him up.

"Stop." I said. "I don't need nor do I want you pity. If I knew this is why you asked me to come I never would have come. I apologize if I've been an inconvenience."

With that I disappeared to everyone but Alex.

"Alex, the others can't hear or see my anymore. Please, just let this go. Please."

He nodded, a tear slipping down his cheek, he was finally accepting that I wouldn't beg for their acceptance.

The others searched for what he was staring at.

"I'm sorry." He croaked.

"Don't worry. Its okay, I forgive you."

"God you've got to stop forgiving everyone for everything!" He yelled at me, confusing everyone as they searched for me.

"Call me if you ever need anything. I'll be happy to help. You're a great person Alex, but you can't help me, thank you for trying. Even if you just need a friend, I can try my best to get here as soon as possible. I understand that they might convince you to fear me. Know that even if I'd never do it on purpose, they're not wrong for fearing me. I am more powerful than even they know. I could be very dangerous."

"I will never fear you."

"Maybe you should. Bye Alex. Be safe." I gave him a smile and walked off, admiring the flower field. There goes the one place in this pack that I actually liked. Another memory to stain this place. Another place I've shown my weakness that I promised myself I'd never show again.

I looked back to see Alex still watching me, the others trying to get him to go back inside. They were scared because they couldn't see me. I sighed, letting them see me again. They all watched me, my flowy dress blowing gently in the wind along with my hair that had flowers braided into it.

I smiled to them all and waved goodbye before walking off.

It was almost the perfect goodbye, calm and emotional. Peaceful. Then Mother fucking Joe popped out of nowhere and shot an arrow into my stomach.

I turned to him, giving him a bored look as he smiled at me sheepishly, clearly very nervous that I was looking at him.

"God dammit Joe."

He froze up, his skin turning pale as I rolled my eyes.

"This is a borrowed dress!"

I complained. Everyone was still watching me as I pulled out the arrow, throwing it into a tree as I examined the dress.

"No, no, no. Urgh. Its got a hole in it! Can you sow by any chance?"

He just shook his head quickly, looking like he was about to shit himself in fear.

I just sighed examining it.

"Its fine, whatever, I'll figure something out. Just maybe don't shoot me for no reason next time?"

He didn't move, he looked like he was going to pass out.

Yep, there it is.

He fainted, falling out of the tree he was sitting in.

I sighed, catching him and setting him down gently on the ground.

All of the others except Alex were looking at me tensely, trying to see what I was going to do, probably worried I'd kill him or something.

I leaned Joe up against the tree, checking his vitals real quick since they were too busy watching me to come help him.

He's fine just unconscious.

I looked at my dress one more time frowning. I'll go see if the town dress maker can do anything about it when I get back.

With one more look to the tense group of people watching me I ran off back home.

Another useless waste of time.

Twenty-four

Today I am officially graduating white stag training. I am completely able to erase myself from people's minds with ease. I managed to walk through the busy village and block myself out of every single one of their minds. I can make my scent and voice echo from all around people and even create apparitions of myself.

These things are extremely powerful, that must be why they are only granted to white stags. If these powers got into the wrong hands it could be catastrophic. They could easily go on murdering sprees without anyone knowing.

This is why we are considered uncatchable. You can't catch something you can't hear see or smell. Its basically impossible.

Jeremiah has been an amazing trainer, I learned all of these abilities at a new record speed. He's been so sweet. I've noticed that the pink and purple sparks surrounding him have seriously increased throughout the weeks.

I feel really guilty every time I see them so I've been blocking out his aura.

I'm currently working in the flower shop, tending to the flowers and re-arranging things to look a little more organized but simultaneously more magical. I had a way with plants, just nature in general actually. Its always calmed me and I've been told I have a sort of green thumb.

In the Blood Thunder pack I was, of course, inn charge of the agriculture. Thanks to me it has one of the most beautiful landscape around that they were frequently complimented for. Flowers seem to never die or wither with me around weirdly.

One time I passed out in a field of flowers and by the time I woke up every single flower was facing me, as if I was their sun, their source of energy.

I know it sounds crazy and I'd never thought much of it but my life seems to always be crazy now a days. At this point I wouldn't be surprised.

"Ellie!" I heard someone call from behind me. I turned around to see Daisy.

"Hey Daisy" I said with an easy smile.

"I heard you've mastered all of you skills! That's so amazing I feel so proud! I've been researching the whole controlling time thing but there doesn't seem to be anything on it, I don't know where to look anymore."

"Thank you for trying, thats really truly nice of you."

"Of course! Now that you're done with your training do you know what you're going to do?"

"Not sure yet."

"Are you planning on moving into the village?! I know everyone would love that!"

I sighed. "I don't think so. I just, I don't know, I feel like I've barely seen the world and I just don't think I can settle down yet."

"Well maybe you can stay here for a couple of years then start traveling and stuff later? Maybe you can even take over for Amos when he retires!"

"I-I don't know..." She doesn't know I'm dying...

"What do you mean you're dying?!" She burst out.

I looked at her, a little annoyed that she read my thoughts.

"I'm sorry. I could see that something was bothering you and I wanted to see if I could help. How long do you have?"

I rubbed my face. "6 and a half months..."

She gasped.

"My werewolf side is very problematic. My form is small and deformed but for some reason my healing, fighting and alpha powers are much more amplified than usual and my body can't keep up. My doctor gave me pills to curve the side effects, it shouldn't affect me until my last couple weeks."

Her eyes teared up.

"Please don't cry. If you cry, I'm gonna cry!" I said feeling my eyes start to burn.

"How am I supposed to not cry if you look like you're gonna cry!"

"I only look like I'm gonna cry because you look like you're gonna cry!"

"Stop that!"

"You stop and I'll stop!"

With that we both broke into tears hugging each other. We stood there for about a minute when we felt a third pair of arms around us. I looked behind me to see Jeremiah looking concerned.

I just broke out into laughter and Daisy joined me. Crying and laughing at the same time, making Jeremiah look even more concerned than before.

"I have to go. Amos and Rose should be back soon." She sniffled.

I wiped my tears, revealing my probably puffy eyes red eyes as I said good-bye.

I was excited to see Amos again. He brought a good presence to the village and I needed to talk to him about leaving.

"Why were you crying?" Jeremiah finally asked.

Shit. What do I respond to this? I really don't want him to know. He shouldn't have to share my burden.

"Its complicated." I wiped my tears, "Not important."

"Okay." He responded unsurely. "I just wanted to give you this" He pulled out a small jewelry box out from behind his back. "Its a graduation gift"

"Oh, Jeremiah, you didn't have to do that!"

"Its nothing big, really. I would've just gotten you flowers but, well..."

I giggled.

"Here." He said handing me the small box.

"Thank you but-"

"Just open it." He cut me off.

I untied the little string holding it together and slowly removed the top to find a beautiful blue rope attatched sterling sliver dear antlers connected to a small circle that seemed like it should hold something.

"Its to put your crystal ball in."

It would look exactly like this

I looked at it, shocked as it shinned back at me, my mouth hanging open.

"Jeremiah, its beautiful, I love it so much." I said quietly.

I checked his aura to see it almost completely pink now. Fuck, this is bad.

"I-I can't accept this."

"You can and you will. I will not take it back."

"But-"

"No. You deserve it."

"Can I at least pay you back? I'm sure it was really expensive."

"Stop that. You will not pay me back, I will not tell you how much it was, you will take the gift like a normal person."

"Thank you." I gave him a big hug, trying to hold back my second round of tears.

He closed his eyes, resting his chin on my head, breathing deeply.

"I have to start training a new student. I should go."

"Okay." I pulled back, giving him one more fond smile.

"I should close up the shop anyways."

Once he left I slid onto the ground, leaning against the wall with my head in my hands, breathing deeply.

"Hello dear." I heard Rose's familiar voice call out.

I looked up to see the beautiful little woman standing before me, her grey hair braided behind her, her eyes holding calm and gentle feelings. Her aura was inexplicably beautiful. It was different, tough but gentle, as if she's been through a lot and done a lot and now she's completely at peace.

"Rose!" I said, standing up to give her a hug. She just laughed into the embrace.

"You've done an indescribably amazing job taking care of my shop. Its never looked so alive and beautiful. Its as if the flowers love you just as much as you love them. You've got a real gift."

I laughed, "I hope you like the changes I've made. I wanted to do something nice for the amount of money you're paying me. "

"Its perfect. Come sit with me."

We sat on the small table I added to the shop next to my favorite yellow flowers.

"How are you?"

"I'm fine. How are you?" She frowned at my answer, confusing me.

"I'm going to be straight with you okay?"

I nodded.

"I know that you're not fine. You are good at hiding behind you aura, but my strength is reading auras and I know that deep down you aren't fine. Now, you're going to tell me everything and I'm going to help you. Understood?"

I sighed, "Yes."

I told her everything. About my encounters with Alex and everyone at the Belle Foret back, about Jeremiah's feelings for me and about how I'm dying. I even told her briefly about my past at the Blood Thunder pack. It honestly felt really good to just talk to someone freely, not hold anything back. I didn't feel the need to be strong for her, I knew she would never take advantage of my weakness.

"Well darling, you certainly haven't had an easy life."

I laughed at that. Understatement.

"You have suffered many tragedies, each of which alone can break a person, sending them into depression and even suicide. You are so strong and an amazing person. You are not dangerous, no matter what people say. If they don't want to accept that then they don't deserve to know your beauty.

People might say that you are too forgiving for your own good but that is just another way in which you are strong, stronger than any of them. You have been blessed with so much power because those above have seen your beauty and strength and knew that you deserved the gift, but could handle the side effects.

Never be ashamed of what has been given to you, you shouldn't ever make yourself small to make other people feel better about themselves. I like this Alex person. Keep him close and as for Jeremiah. You've let him know that the feelings aren't reciprocated gently and he can read your aura. Anything else is his own fault, you can't beat yourself up over what he feels. I'm sure he could never want you to.

I'm so proud of you sweetheart."

I let the tears flow, giving her a big hug.

"Thank you. For everything."

"You know you can't spend the rest of your life here right?"

I sighed.

"You are made for much more than sitting around this village wasting your talents working in my flower shop. You need to go out. Experience as much as you can so that you can feel satisfied and complete when your time comes."

She's right. I know she is. I can't stay here, no matter how easy it would be. I would never be satisfied with my life. Its time for me to live. To really live.

"But, where do I even go?"

"You're going to start by going with my son to England. He's leaving back tomorrow to negotiate with the witches. As you know white stags can be push-overs. I think it would be good to have a strong-minded person accompany him. From there, you can move on, far away from the Blood Thunder pack, Belle Foret pack and far away from here. Nothing to hold you back. You can even visit Jen and her new mate, I'm sure she'd be so happy to see you. Before you die."

I nodded. That was the perfect idea.

I looked up to her.

"Thank you. Thank you so much. I'm going to miss you."

"You have my number, call me anytime if you ever need anything, and please if you can, come visit before the end."

I nodded. "Absolutely."

I gave her a big hug before setting off.

Its time to say goodbye to everyone here. A final goodbye. Jeremiah, Daisy, Alex, Sarah and all of the Belle Foret group and finally Jammie and Henry.

It was already 2:00. I didn't have a lot of time but it would have to do.

Amos leaves at 4:00 am tomorrow. I wouldn't see them for months, if ever again.

Twenty-five

I cleaned out the penthouse I was staying in one final time. Its time for a change. A new chapter in this crazy life. Hopefully this is the one that will bring me happiness.

I said goodbye to Daisy and Jeremiah. I cried both times. I'd miss them both so much. I'd been crying so much lately it was annoying. But how could I not! I told Jeremiah I was dying. He deserved to know.

Apparently he'd already known. He had read my mind a couple times during training to make sure I was concentrating and accidentally found the thoughts.

I had my necklace on. It was beautiful and I was never planning on taking it off. It had come from someone who truly cared about me, that was really something special.

Next stop was Jammie and Henry.

Running I arrived at about 4:00pm. I knocked on the door, swallowing the lump in my throat. I knew this was going to be a hard one.

Henry opened the door, instantly smiling and pulling me into his embrace.

"Ellie, I missed you kiddo."

"Did you say Ellie?" Jammie called out, hopefulness seeping into her voice.

As I pulled back from a grinning Henry she came running around the corner, leaping at me. She was old but still spunky.

I laughed, embracing her tightly.

"What brought you all this way?" Henry asked.

I have some things I need to tell you about, I figured it'd be better to do it in person.

"Of course. Come sit." Jammie said leading us to the living room.

I smiled at the fond memories I had from this place. I was probably at one of my happiest when I was here.

I told them all about how I left Belle Foret and how I became a White Stag, telling them pretty much everything, saving the depressing details they didn't need to hear.

"While I was working at the flower shop I made quite a bit of money and, well." I handed them wad of cash awkwardly, making them gasp.

"What the hell is this?" Jammie asked, eyes wide as she stared at the roll of hundreds as I placed a bunch more on the table.

"6 million dollars."

They both looked at me, jaws on the ground.

"Ellie, we can't accept this. We never wanted you to pay us back for any-thing, we consider you our daughter, it was our pleasure to help you out."

"I know, but I really really want to give this to you. Besides, I won't take it back. Please? Please take it."

Jammie teared up as Henry remained still in shock.

I knew they had a lot of money problems, I couldn't even imagine the amazing things this money could do for them.

"Honey, shouldn't you keep this? For your future, you never know when you might need this money."

My heart dropped into my stomach when they said that.

"Thats the other thing I wanted to talk to you about actually..."

They sat back down, staring at me intensely.

"You know how my healing is abnormally fast and I am abnormally strong and fast, even for an alpha. Well, there's a reason no one's able to be as strong as I am. My body can't handle it. Its too fragile to handle all of my power and abilities, its decaying, really quickly."

They stayed silent, staring at me taking in what I was saying.

Henry held Jammie's hand to comfort her from what they knew I was about to say.

"I-I, I'm dying." I stuttered out.

They gasped, both of their eyes immediately filling with tears.

"W-what?" Jammie asked.

"I have about 6 and a half months left to live now." I said quietly, looking down. I held in the tears this time. I needed to be strong for them.

They both broke down sobbing. I quickly got up and wrapped them both in a big hug.

"I'm leaving to England with the White Stags tomorrow, and I'm not coming back. I-I" I took a deep breath, "I came by to say goodbye."

They both held onto me crying for about an hour before I had to go. I somehow managed not to cry, I had to hold it in fro them. If I cried I knew it would be a million times worse for them. I needed to comfort them, not the other way around.

It was 7:00 pm when I arrived at the Belle Foret pack. I looked up and spotted Joe in the trees. I gave him a stern look just as he was about to shoot me with another arrow and he immediately stopped bowing his head.

"No need to bow to me! Just don't shoot me! You know who I am, geez!" I yelled up to him and he actually chuckled a little making me smile, pleasantly surprised.

"I need to talk to Alex, Sarah, Jack, Jasmine, Chris, Jade and Heeler, any way you can help me gather them?" I smiled sweetly at him.

He jumped down, seeming a little nervous but gave me a smile anyways.

"Sure, I'll mind link them all to meet us in the pack house."

"Thanks."

We started walking towards the pack house.

"So, you're a white stag?" He asked, his voice full of curiosity making me laugh a little.

"Yep." I checked his aura and it was full of excitement and curiosity, the nervousness disappearing every second.

"Then why the hell is everyone so scared of you?"

I sighed and he started to panic a little, "Oh shit, I'm sorry, that was really blunt."

"No worries, but your guess is as good as mine." I shrugged, probably because I could beat all of you top warriors and ranking werewolves in a battle unarmed." I winked at him, making him gape.

"Ya, but still, you seem nice."

I smiled at him. "Then why the hell do you keep shooting me with arrows?"

He just shrugged chuckling a little, making my roll my eyes.

We walked into the pack house laughing together until I came face to face with everyone waiting for me. I took a deep breath giving Joe a final smile.

"Thank you for everything Joe. I hope I see you again one day."

He nodded before bowing respectfully at his alpha and luna and leaving.

"Well, I'm sorry to intrude, I won't be here for long but if we could go to the living room and sit down. I just have a few things to talk about before, well, you'll see."

We all headed into the large familiar living room. I sat down on one of the couches but the rest all piled up on the other one, some even sitting on the floor to avoid sitting next to me making me sigh a little.

"I am a white stag. You can believe me or not, that's up to you but I'm leaving tomorrow for good. I don't want to leave here with any bad blood I just wanted to clear the air and say bye. As you all know, I only have about 6 and a half months left to live so if you don't want to, you'll never have to see me again."

"What?!" Jade, Jasmine, Sarah and Alex all gasped at the same time, turning to their mates who looked down guiltily.

"Oh... I guess you didn't all know. Well, now you do. My bad. Long story short I have an incurable illness and will be dead soon. I just wanted to say that even though we may not have ended up on the best of terms, I still consider you guys my family. If you ever need anything, you have my number. Just call and I'll come down as soon as possible and help out in any way I can."

I stood up as they all stared at me, their auras surprisingly sad, even a tinge of regret in some of them. Heeler's still hood a lot of fear and a flicker of anger.

"Before I leave, if I could just talk with Heeler and Alex for a moment, then I'll be out of your hair forever."

Everyone cleared the room, mumbling 'goodbye' as they passed me. I smiled at them all, wanting to end on the best possible note.

I looked back into the living room to see a very nervous Heeler and a very sad Alex, a tear trickling down his cheek.

"How can life be so unfair to you?" Alex asked sadly.

I just brushed it off. "I'm completely fine Alex. There is a reason for everything." I didn't believe that but he seemed to like the answer, giving me a small smile.

"Well, there no non-awkward way of doing this so I'm just going to go for it."

I pulled out my bag of money. I pulled out too piles of 1.5 million dollars, placing the rolls of hundreds in front of each of them as they stared at me with confusion and shock.

"This is 1.5 million dollars." I said pointing to the stack in front of Alex. "Alex, you've been such an amazing friend. You deserve the world, but this is all I can contribute. I know you're low on money, use this to get back on your feet and stay strong."

He stood up giving me a big hug. "Thank you so much Ellie. I really really appreciate this so much, I'm going to miss you so much."

I giggled a little, holding back my tears.

"Call me. Would you mind if I had a moment alone with Heeler now?"

"Of course. Bye Ellie." He said sniffling, trying to hold all of the rolls of hundreds as he left the room, making me giggle as he almost dropped a few.

I turned to Heeler who looked at me sadly, though he tried to mask it with indifference when I looked at him.

"I'm going to be real with you Heeler, I can read you aura, I'm a white stag, you can't hide your emotions just let them out on me. Just let it go. I don't want to leave with you holding anything back. If I die before we see each other again, you won't get any closure. I can see that you need it and I need it too. We were good friends. I didn't make that up. Please just hit me with it."

With that I got silent, staring into his pain-filled eyes.

He then burst into tears. Even though I saw in his aura that it was coming I was still a little surprised.

He put his head into his hands as sobs racked his body. I just sat there quietly, staring at my hands on my lap, letting him go through the motions.

After a few minutes he looked up at me, his eyes red and puffy, his aura filled with regret.

"I'm so sorry Ellie." He croaked out.

Once the words left him I let my breath go and sat next to him, giving him a hug as he cried onto my shoulder. Sure I could read his mind and figure out exactly what was going on in his head but I didn't want to break his privacy like that.

"I-I. Your death is going to kill me. I don't know how to handle it. You were my best friend, I care so much about you and just- I needed to push you away. I-I, I couldn't handle the pain of losing you. I thought if you hated me it would be easier. I thought maybe I could convince myself to hate you b-but, you're just so perfect! Like what the fuck! I kept searching for a flaw to hang onto, like you were mean or spiteful or selfish or dangerous but you're not! I'm so sorry I just-"

I cut him off shushing him gently, holding my tears back.

"Its okay. I understand completely. It'll be okay, you have Sarah, you don't need me."

"But, you're my best-"

I shushed. him again rubbing is back. I know, I know. You're my best friend too.

"How are you so good to me after everything I've done? I'm going to miss you so much I'm sorry I'm sorry, I'm so sorry."

I let him cry in my embrace for a few more minutes before pulling back.

"I need to go. I want you to take this money. I know you and Sarah need it and I certainly don't need it."

"But, I don't deserve it! I've been nothing but shit to you for the best 2 months! I shaved 2 months off of your life by throwing you at a wall and almost killing you I mean, my god, you should be hating me not saving me!"

"Its my decision and you're taking the money whether you like it or not. Please take it, for me. I have to go now. Don't be afraid to call or text, I'll always be here for you. Always."

I got up, taking a deep breath and started heading out. I paused at the door, turning around to see a teary faced Heeler. "Goodbye Heeler. I'll always love you, you're my family."

And then left.

By the time I got home it was 11:00pm. I still had a while until we left so I decided to spend it running, but this time it wasn't to let out my frustrations. I ran with a smile on my face because I was finally going to move on. I had finally gotten my closure.

Twenty-six

A mos and I stepped into the airport and immediately all eyes were on us.

All of the women were staring at Amos. I mean, he's tall built and I gotta admit, very attractive. He looked younger than his age because white stags, like werewolves, age much slower. Most living to about 200 years old instead of the usual 75.

Supernatural creatures were naturally more attractive and compelling to humans. We have a sort of glow of power and life that the humans seem to lack, also we're naturally very fit.

I smiled at all of the people that stared at me, even making a few blush. Humans were so funny.

Almost all the men were staring at me with lust in their eyes as well as a few women. This is why most people sprung for private jets and lived in groups away from humans.

Everyone's auras were blindingly purple as they looked at us. I turned off the auras, blocking out the dirty thoughts I was getting bombarded with.

I've heard a lot about humans and seen a few but never this many in one place. It was overwhelming.

I felt a tap on my shoulder and turned around to see a very confident looking human. I smiled politely.

"Hi?" I asked as he just stared at me in silence. I heard gasps and murmurs all around as everyone stared at the man.

"Hi..."

I stared at him in confusion but still smiled warmly. "Can I help you with something sir?"

He looked a little taken aback by what I said, making me look around in confusion. I caught a few people trying to get a picture of the man next to me.

Okay he was pretty good looking with his tanned skin and tall frame but I still feel like I'm missing something.

"You don't know who I am do you?"

I smiled sheepishly at him, shaking my head.

He stared at me a little shocked but then started chucking a little.

"Well. That's never happened before."

"Do you know who I am?"

He laughed a little shaking his head.

"Then how am I supposed to know who you are?" I asked laughing a little.

"I guess you got me there." He extended his hand.

"Prince Xander Abascal of Spain."

I shook it with a smile. "Ellie Green."

"Well Ellie, where are you headed today?" We started walking towards the line to print my boarding pass.

"England. Amos and I have some business to attend to there." I said, gesturing to Amos who was checking our luggage while I printed our passes.

"I couldn't help but notice your one way ticket."

I laughed a little. "Very observant. After the meetings I'm thinking of visiting my sister Jen and then, just see what I'll do from there."

"So, are you with this... Amos?"

I giggled a little. "Why do you ask?"

His face turned a little red while he shuffled his feet uncomfortably, staring at the ground. I checked his aura and it looked extremely nervous and embarrassed. As panic started to seep in I took over.

"No we're not together. I honestly see him as more of a father figure than a boyfriend. Though, he his single if you're interested."

looked up abruptly. Confusion in his eyes. "What, no- I'm not-"

"Ya, don't worry about it, come on I'll introduce you."

"Ellie, I-"

I cut him, "Amos!" I called waving him over with our boarding passes, dragging Xander with my other hand.

"Amos, this is Prince Xander Abascal of Spain, Xander, this is Amos Beaconsfield, leader of the business group, the White Stags."

They shook hands and I pretended to gasp getting their attention.

"Oh shoot, I have to call Jen, its an emergency, you know how it is, boyfriend problems." I whispered the last part, winking at Xander before walking off giggling to myself, not even pretending to take a call.

I'm not stupid, I know he was trying to hit on me, but I just couldn't resist! Amos is straight anyways, Daisy told me when I asked her because when men reach a certain level of attractiveness, you just have to double check, you know?

I laughed as I turned on my werewolf hearing, listening to their awkward conversations while I pretended to look out the window.

"So, uhm, Amos. How-how is it going?" Xander said awkwardly making Amos chuckle and pat him on his back a little.

I let Amos read my mind real quick, telling him to go along with it which he happily did.

"Is there something you wanted to tell me? Am I looking handsome today? I feel like I am, and I feel like you feel that too." He said, winking at me when Xander looked away uncomfortably.

I caught Xander's gaze and he just glared at me as I laughed at his awkward position.

"Uh, look Amos, You're a very good looking guy, its just that uh-"

Amos burst into laughter.

"Ellie, I can't do it, its too mean. Relax kid we're just messing with you."

I walked over laughing. "I'm sorry Xander" I said through giggles, "the opportunity was just right there and I thought" I shrugged, chuckling as he scowled playfully at us.

Since Amos and I are such strong white stags we're able to prank and play jokes on people without feeling too guilty, others would never be able to follow through with it though.

"It was very nice meeting you Xander, but we better get going, there's a dog sniffing everyone to speed up the security line and he just always seems to smell something weird on me and alert anyone. Weird right? Then they have to really check me and all my stuff thoroughly which takes forever." Amos said, sorting our documents.

Its true, Jeremiah told me dogs could sniff out white stags since we have the whole deer scent. They're usually confused by werewolves too, so we'll have to see what happens when he smells me.

"I hope to see you both again soon." He smiled. "I should go too, my plane to Spain should be leaving soon."

"Bye Xander." I said, waving as I walked away.

He bowed a little, smirking. "Bye Ellie Green." He winked

He was pretty charming for a human, not gonna lie. He just had something about him that I liked. He had a nice aura.

We got into the security line and as soon as Amos passed him the dog started barking, trying to attack, making Amos sigh as he got escorted to a private room to be thoroughly checked.

I was next and was prepared for the same reaction. The man gestured for me to walk by them and as soon as I did the dog perked up sniffing the air but he was wagging his tail happily as he did.

He tried to come to me but his handler held him back by his leash. The dog started whining and jumping. He then slipped out of his collar, shocking the man holding him as he tried to catch his dog.

The dog ran over to me and started running around me, wagging his tail and leaping in the air happily.

He walked right next to me licking my hand a little, looking up at me.

The humans obviously found this peculiar and insisted on bringing me to the private room to be checked.

A man tried to gently grab my arm to escort me but suddenly the dog was growling at him, stepping in front of me protectively.

Everyone froze completely confused. Everyone was watching me and they stopped the lines until they had the situation under control.

The human looked petrified and everyone looked nervous. The handler looked scared of his own dog and was absolutely no help so I decided to take it into my own hands.

I looked at the handler. "What's his name?" I asked gently.

"Bacon." The man replied as played with the leash nervously in his hands. I looked at Bacon making him even happier.

I reached into his mind and tried speaking to him.

'Hello Bacon, can you understand me?'

'Yes! Hello! Hello! Hello! I love you! I'll do anything for you! DO you need me to attack someone cuz I will! I really really will! What do you want me to do?! I'll follow you everywhere!'

I smiled at his excitement. Yep. I'm talking to a dog.

'I'm sorry Bacon. I wish I could take you with me but you have to stay with your human.'

He whined, his ears folding back, confusing everyone for sure.

'Please don't be sad. I want you to be happy!'

'Well if you want me too be happy then I will be happy! I'd do anything for you!'

'Okay, go fetch you leash and bring it to me.'

'Okay!' He exclaimed while yipping out loud. He happily ran over to his handler who instantly panicked. He grabbed the leash from his hands sitting in front of me with it in his mouth.

'Thanks Bacon, you did amazing! I'm going to put this back on you and you're going to go back to your owner and continue doing you great job, got it?'

'okay!'

I clipped the collar around his neck and gave him a little rub behind his ear and a kiss on his nose.

'Bye Bacon'

With that I slid out of his mind. He leaped around me, licking my hand one more time before happily trotting back over to his shocked handler and sitting by his side.

I just chuckled turning back to the man you originally tried to escort me before he was attacked.

"What the hell did I just watch?"

I shook my head, giving him a kind smile. "I guess dogs like me." I shrugged.

He just shook his head in shock. "Yeah, I'd say so."

They checked Amos and I thoroughly before finally letting us leave and go to our gate that was already boarding.

People stared at us the entire way and we just smiled gently at all of them.

Amos and I were split up on the plane. I got him a seat a little further forward whereas I had the third to last row.

We walked into the line for the gate, waiting our turn to get onto the plane. There was a teenaged kid, covered in pimples, clearly going through puberty staring at me obviously with his mouth hanging open.

I looked over to him smiling. "Hi." I said. Once I said that he turned tomato red, and just stared at me with wide eyes in shock.

I crinkled my brow in confusion.

Is he going to answer me or? I guess not.

Oh well, I let it go.

I saw what I assumed was his twin sister elbow him a little, laughing at his flustered state. It made me miss Jen. I couldn't wait to see her.

Amos was talking to an adorable couple, they all laughed together. He was a very charismatic guy. He just had an easy vibe to him, though most were a little intimidated by his good looks.

This was my first time flying but I wasn't really nervous. I mean, I really don't think a little plane crash would kill me, it would take a lot more than that.

I made my way down the plane slowly as I approached my seat, waiting for people to settle into their seat and put their luggage into the overhead bins. I noticed an older lady struggling to lift her luggage so high over her head.

I helped her out before making my way back to my seat, making even more people stare at me. I had the middle seat. On one side was larger man who seemed to take up half of my seat as well as his and the other a woman with a baby sitting on her lap.

I didn't have any bags with me, just my phone so I gave my space in the bins to someone else.

Before approaching them smiling. "Hi, sorry I have the middle seat there." I said, pointing.

The woman with the child got up, letting me slide in as the man looked at me nervously and apologetically. He was probably guilty and embarrassed about his weight which I hated.

"Hi, I'm Ellie." I said as I slid in.

He smiled hopefully. "Jean." He responded.

"Nice to meet you." I slid into my seat, having just about enough room to sit without our asses touching.

Twenty-seven

The woman sat back down with her newborn, seemingly a little stressed. I decided to slip into her mind and see if I could help.

'Oh god, everyone's going to hate me when the plane takes off, please God let this be the first time Charlotte is good on the plane! Oh God Oh God'

Her aura was glowing brightly, her nerves flying around her.

I wish I could help her. That's when I remembered one of Jeremiah's lessons. White stags can make you feel calmer through contact. If they touch you they can suck up some of your anxiety and take away some of your worries.

Well, I think its time to test that out.

I extended my hand to her, "Hi, I'm Ellie."

As soon as she made contact with my hand I released my calm, sucking away her anxiety. She immediately relaxed in her seat relieved. It was only a temporary fix but it was better than nothing.

"Marie." She replied.

The seatbelt sign turned on signaling that we'd be taking off soon. The flight attendants were walking around checking everything as our TVs played the security procedures.

The motor started in the plane and we started moving. Instantly Marie tensed up praying in her head.

After about 10 minutes her baby started screaming. I could see people groaning around us, shouting her dirty looks. Rude people. Its not like she was asking the baby to cry.

Marie tried shushing her and bouncing her but nothing was working. She looked exhausted and frustrated.

"Hey, Marie." She turned to me.

"I am so, so sorry." She just said, tears brimming her eyes a little bit.

"Hey, don't worry about it. I was wondering if I could try holding her. I love babies."

She looked a little hesitant at first before nodding and handing her over.

As soon as I had her I sent her calming vibes, rocking her gently. I checked her mind to see that she was just terrified of the engines.

I sent the feeling of safety through her as she calmed down and stopped screaming. She cuddled into my body, yawning gently as she felt the calm and safety I was sending her.

"What's her name?" I asked Marie quietly, settling in comfortably with her in my arms.

Marie just stared at me shocked in silence.

"Ch-Charlotte. H-how you get her to stop c-crying? She always yells on planes."

I just smiled gently shrugging a little. "Babies tend to like me."

Its true I had to take care of a lot of the newborns in Blood Thunder pack and they always seemed to be calm in happy in my presence.

She sighed relieved and I saw her exhaustion washing over her. With a newborn she probably hasn't had a proper night of sleep in a while. I took out the blanket I had brought with me and handed it to her.

"Go ahead and take a nap. I've got Charlotte and I'll wake you if there's a problem." I touched her arm a little, relaxing her.

"Thank you." She whispered closing her eyes, snuggling into the blanket with a faint smile and her face.

I looked over to the window to see the sky and found Jean staring at me. He tried to turn away and pretend he wasn't but his face got red as he knew I caught him.

"Where are you from, Jean?"

I asked, starting a conversation to put him at ease.

He looked at me, a little shocked and flustered but I waited patiently for his answer.

"Minnesota." He responded after a moment. I smiled.

"I've never been. I'm from Connecticut (where Blood Thunder Pack is) and Montreal, Canada."(Where Belle Foret Pack is.)

"I love Montreal, beautiful city. I go there a lot for business, was just there actually."

"What do you do?"

"I'm a pharmacologist. We're searching for a drug to cure leukemia and lymphoma right now."

"Wow. That's amazing. Good for you." I said genuinely. I knew I got a good vibe off of him.

"What do you do?"

"I used to work at a flower shop in my village. I just love flowers and wild life so much it was a no-brainer."

"That sounds really nice. Why are you headed to England?"

"I have some business to attend to with our village's leader, long story, and then I'm going to see my sister Jen. She just moved there." I said excitedly.

I felt that the man had completely relaxed now.

"What about you?"

"Business. Meeting with some potential investors."

I smiled and nodded then I felt a tap on my shoulder. I turned around to see a man. I didn't get a very good vibe off of him. His aura was a little snobbish and resentful.

I gave him small smile anyways.

"I'm sorry ma'am, but I was walking by and noticed your... situation here. I have an extra seat in first class if you'd like it. A pretty thing like you doesn't belong back here with..." He trailed off sticking his nose up at Jean and Marie, grimacing.

I frowned a little at him.

"That's very generous sir but I can't accept that. I'm just fine back here. I'm sure Marie would appreciate it though, extra space for her baby and her, away from the judgmental stares."

He grimaced at the idea, looking taken-aback that I'd rejected him. "No, never mind. Sorry to bother you. Just walk up if you change your mind, the seat is yours. "

I shook my head at him once he left.

"What a dickhead." I mumbled to myself making Jean laugh.

Jean and I talked and laughed for the rest of the flight. He was very nice and good company. We even exchanged numbers as we landed.

Once we hit the ground I gently woke Marie up. She sat up looking much happier and healthier.

She smiled widely, filled with a new energy.

"Thank you so much Ellie you have no idea how much I appreciated that." She said, taking a sleeping Charlotte back as the Motors turned off.

"Anytime." I smiled.

I helped a few people retrieve their luggages as we got off the plane, causing people to stare at me again.

I gave Jean and Marie a hug goodbye, meeting Marie's thankful husband as well before I met back up with Amos who was helping an elderly man get to the attendant with his wheelchair.

I smiled up at him excitedly. "We're in England!" I exclaimed, jumping a little.

He chuckled a little, throwing an arm over my shoulder as we walked to baggage claim.

"I've never been outside of the US and Canada! This is so exciting!"

"Never? Your parents never brought you traveling?"

I shook my head, trying not to let the thought of my horrible parents dampen my mood because IM IN ENGLAND BITCHESSS!

"Maybe I'll even get to see the queen I've heard so much about. I mean she's on the Canadian money! That'd be so cool. I heard she loves dogs and I mean, I'm basically a dog myself!"

Amos just chuckled shaking his head.

Once we finally collected our luggage and went outside we saw a man with a sign with our names on it. I felt so important!

We smiled at the man as we approached him, instantly feeling he was a witch. I guess that was tough for him to believe it was us because he just nodded to us before opening the limo door. I REPEAT HE OPENED THE LIMOOOOOOO DOOORRRR! THAT'S RIGHT BITCHES! YOUR GIRL IS RIDING IN A LIMO!

I leaned into Amos as we climbed in.

"We're in a limo!" I squealed softly. "I feel like we're in gossip girl!"

"Gossip Girl?" He asked, confused.

I just shook my head. "One of the greatest shows to ever grace Netflix!"

He still looked confused but nodded slowly anyways.

I sighed turning to the limo driver who hasn't stopped scowling.

"Have you watched Gossip Girl?" I asked him, hopeful.

"No." He answered tensing up.

I giggled a little. "You know white stags can sense lies right?" I asked as his face reddened a little.

"I don't know why you're embarrassed its an amazing show!"

"I just watch it for Serena! She's hot, okay?" He defended making me laugh harder while Amos still looked puzzled.

"I get you, I mean Chuck Bass!" I replied, pretending to drool.

The limo driver finally cracked a smile chuckling a little. Making a triumphant smile sit on my face.

"What's your name?" I asked him.

"Boston."

For the rest of the half hour ride Boston and I just ranted about the show. Especially when Chuck Bass got shot! Or when we figured out who Gossip Girl really was, I mean, I'm still not convinced. It just doesn't make sense!!!

"Okay, now I have to watch this show." Amos said, looking extremely interested.

"You definitely do." I replied as Boston nodded eagerly from the front seats. He was a completely different person than when we first met him.

He stopped in front of a giant sort of mansion.

"We've arrived at the main coven." He informed us as he got up opening the door for us.

I thanked him as I stepped out excited.

We're finally here!

I looked back at Amos jumping around excitedly.

"I've never actually met witches before... But don't worry I read about them and had Daisy and Rose give me information. I got this!"

I went over to Boston as he chuckled at my excitement.

"Any advice? I've never really met witches before!" I said quietly as we waled up.

He turned to me stopping.

"I guess just make sure you do the touch the foot thing."

"The what?"

He widened his eyes at me. "No one told you?! When you get in there you have to lean down and touch each of their feet as a sign of respect. I thought you were just being rude when you didn't touch my foot."

"Ohhh I'm so sorry." I leaned down rubbing his shoe a little. "Like that?"

"Exactly."

"Okay." I said standing back up, brushing myself off, getting ready to meet the powerful witches of the coven."

I gave Boston a quick smile and met Amos at the door as he knocked politely.

A maid opened the door, smiling at us and taking our coats.

I felt that she was a witch so leaned down and rubbed her shiny black flats.

She gave me a strange confused look but I just brushed it off. Maybe you're only suppose to rub the feet of high ranking members?

Amos tried telling me something but when I turned around to see what he was saying the high ranking members entered the room. I knew immediately, feeling their power.

They nodded in greeting as I smiled at them. Without hesitation I walked forward and rubbed each of their feet.

I could hear someone laughing behind me as everyone looked at me, completely confused.

I looked to Boston to see if I did it wrong to see him crying of laughter though he tried to hide it.

"Uhmmm its nice seeing you all again. This is Ellie, a fellow white stag I brought with me to help out. She is one of the most powerful white stags to ever exist, rivaling the power of the very first one. I thought she could use the experience."

They all stared at me now, furrowing their eyebrows as I looked at Amos.

I went next to him nudging him a little.

He read my mind when I did, getting the hint.

'YOU HAVE TO RUB THEIR FEET!' I yelled in my head, smiling at the witches.

'What the hell are you talking about? I've never seen anyone do that in your life. Who told you this?' He answered as I read his mind.

That's when it hit me. OH GOD IM SO STUPID.

I looked back at Boston, panicking a little.

'I'm going to kill you.' I projected into his mind, dead serious which only seemed to make him laugh harder.

"Well, lets head into the conference room then." One of the witches spoke up, clearly the one in control. He was very large, I could see muscles bursting from beneath his white dress shirt. He had dark brown hair and hazel eyes that stared at me intently.

I smiled sheepishly, completely embarrassed now as I followed them to the conference room, simultaneously shooting Boston a death glare. Oh, I was going to get him back... He messed with the wrongggg person.

Twenty-eight

"Well lets just dive in, us White Stags really just want to live in peace. May I ask the reason why you've been trying to uncover our villages and reveal us to the world?"

The main guy sighed.

"Look, its nothing personal. As you probably know witches pride themselves on being the most powerful creatures in the world, the only thing is that people believe white stags are more powerful. A lot of our members resent that, having never even met a white stag. They want to see you and judge if you're really that powerful, if not, they want to show the world that witches are the superior species."

"What if they met one and were bested?" I asked.

"Then they'll back off. We've been trying too keep the problem under control but witches can be a little... rebellious. Especially the powerful ones, they believe they are indestructible. I have lived in the days when white stags roamed free and am aware how powerful you are, but the rest are not so easily convinced."

"What if I met them then?"

Everyone raised their eyebrows at me while Amos whipped his head in my direction.

"Ellie. If anyone's putting themselves in that danger it will be me. I won't have you risk your life like that."

"Amos, no offense but I am the most powerful white stag to have existed in a long time. This is why you brought me along."

Amos hesitated for a moment before sighing.

"Okay." He said unhappily.

The main witch smirked a little as the others laughed a little.

"No offense little girl, I just have a hard Tim believing you're as powerful as you say."

In an instant I was standing behind him pointing a knife at his throat.

'Don't underestimate me, witch.' I echoed in his mind.

As the other witches got up to protect their leader I disappeared completely. I walked around them calmly as they panicked.

I knocked each of those that tried to stand up to me onto their backs, not harming them but scaring them a little, putting them into their place.

With the mixture of my white stag power and werewolf strength I vastly overpowered them.

I saw some weapons appearing out of thin air as one of the witches chanted trying to disable my invisibility. I just brushed the attempts off, easily dodging and taking control of the weapons. One of the witches set on fire and another had the ground shaking.

I gracefully danced around them, gently knocking them back onto their backs as Amos sat in his spot, shaking his head amused.

"Enough!" The leader yelled and his men instantly stood down.

"Point taken." He continued, "we won't underestimate you again, you have our sincere apologies."

I reappeared, my power oozing from my body. My werewolf side told me that wasn't enough. I would not take their blatant disrespect.

"Bow." I ordered and instantly, against their will every one of them was on their knees bowing their heads to me.

I let them all back up and they retook their seats.

"You weren't lying when you said she was powerful." The main witch chuckled to himself.

He extended his hand to me. "Darius Winter." He bowed his head a little after shaking my hand. I nodded, appreciating his show of respect.

"I should probably tell you all, I am also an alpha werewolf. You will not get away with trying to walk all over me and I will not be disrespected. My white stag was temporarily keeping me from harming you but try that again and I may not be as forgiving." I growled deeply one more time.

Boston looked at me surprised from the door and I could sense his nervousness.

I took a deep breath.

"Is there anything else you'd like to discuss?" I asked sweetly, giving them a genuine smile.

They all relaxed smiling back.

"You can both stay in our community house as long as you'd like. The witches will of course try to challenge you but I have no doubt you will put them back in their place. You will have a place to stay and be fixing your problem at the same time."

Amos and I nodded. "Thank you." We both said.

Darius showed us out of the coven and back to the limo.

"Boston, make sure our guests comfortably and safely get to the community house. If not, there will be consequences."

Boston bowed respectfully before climbing into the limo and beginning to drive away.

"Oh Boston, you're so going to regret what you did because its payback time!" I scolded him making him laugh.

"What are you gonna do?" He asked smirking.

I smirked back instantly noticing him tensing up.

"I don't know I was just thinking that it would be such a shame if you had to tell your boss you lost me... I don't think he'd be too happy about that. Do you? I mean its the easiest job in the world!"

He instantly tensed up.

"I wonder where I'll go... Maybe I'll do some sight-seeing?"

"I won't let you leave this car." He said, his voice wavering a little.

I giggled a little. "Bye Boston."

With that I erased myself from his mind.

No I couldn't teleport but he didn't need to know that.

Amos was shaking his head, looking out the window as Boston started to panic.

I slipped inside his head to see what he was thinking as we started to pull up to the community.

'HOLY SHIT, FUCK, NO, NO, NO, WHAT THE HELL AM I SUPPOSED TO TELL MY BOSS?! HE'S GOING TO KILL ME. I DON'T EVEN KNOW WHERE SHE WENT SO I CAN'T GO GET HER, CRAP!'

I laughed a little. Everyone could see me but Boston, his boss wouldn't get mad at him since I'm right here but he would definitely make a fool out of himself looking for me.

Once we pulled up I heard him gulp as he got out of the car on shaky legs. He opened the door for Amos closing it in my face.

I laughed as Darius gave him a death glare having seen it.

Boston went to talk to him, not noticing the car door opening as I let myself out.

"Um, s-sir, I-uh- I may have-uh- lost Ellie." He said making me laugh out loud as I stood right next to him.

Darius looked confused staring at me. Before he could say anything I reappeared, pretending like nothing was happening. I made it so he could see me but couldn't hear me.

I looked at him seriously. "What are you talking about, I've been here the whole time."

Boston's eyes widened, trying to read my lips. But he just stared at me in silence.

I looked to Darius shrugging as he stared at Boston like he was crazy.

"Well? Answer her." He said to Boston.

Boston gulped looking at me for help.

I projected the words into his head, 'Say, oh you know, just looking around.'

"Oh, you know just looking around." He repeated out loud to me. I just stared at him incredulously along with Darius and Boston's face drained of Colour as he realized I tricked him.

"Are you okay?" Darius asked, looking a little concerned.

"I'm fine!" Boston squeaked.

"Are you sure you're okay? You seem a little off." I asked him, letting him finally hear me speaking.

He relaxed nodding. "Yes, I'm sorry." He said more calmly, his eyes filling with rage and a need for revenge.

As Darius was called away I laughed while Darius gave me the death glare.

"That will teach you not to mess with me."

"Oh you just wait! I'll get you back for that!" I just laughed, shaking my head walking away towards Amos.

As soon as I did there was a scowling witch blocking my path. She really looked like a witch in the traditional sense of the word, long back robe, black hair, tattoo of a spider web on her arm.

"Can I help you?" I asked nicely and calmly since she was staring at me, her aura filled with cockiness and dominance. This girl wanted a fight.

She rolled her eyes. "You're the legendary white stags? Pathetic."

I just remained calm, giving her another small smile. "Anything else?"

I said, completely unbothered.

She spat at me but I stepped to the side, avoiding getting hit. The smile slipped off my face, replaced with one of sadness, but I remained calm.

"I wouldn't do that again." I said calmly but with a warning in my voice.

"Oh ya? What are you going to do? How could someone believe you're more powerful than witches?"

I rolled my eyes as she conjured up fire and a tornado, spears floating in the air above her head threatening me.

"Admit to the world we're more powerful and I might show you mercy."

I sighed, leaning on one hip, bored. This was clearly a strong witch being able to control so many different powers. I was not underestimating her, but I wouldn't let her see that she had any affect on me.

"White Stags don't like lying." I said bluntly.

At that she yelled angrily as a crowd surrounded us, clearly wary of this girl but curious for sure.

She sent the tornado flying my way. I just stood in my place, my arms crossed over my chest as it hit me. I felt nothing, it didn't seem to affect me at all. My hair didn't even blow as the wind picked up, pushing others backwards.

I calmly walked out of the tornado. Her eyes widened a little when she saw that it didn't affect me in the slightest. She then threw her fire at me but the same thing happened. It seemed to go right through me, not harming me or burning my clothes in the at all.

People behind me leapt out of the way as the fire collided with the pavement, burning a hole in it.

The girl gulped, seemingly nervous now. The spears would hurt a little if they hit me but it would take much more than that to kill me, the worst I could get was a little cut that would heal up within an hour, no matter how deep.

The spears started flying at me, probably about a hundred of them at this point. I expertly danced around them, jumping and flipping to avoid getting stabbed. It was very easy with my enhanced speed.

The speed came from the white stags whereas the stamina came from the werewolf. My ability to brush off their other powers came from the mixture of both.

Amos just stood to the side chatting with Darius who was watching me intently.

His stare raked up and down my body as his aura showed he was impressed and was filled with lust and surprise.

I looked him dead in the eye, surprising him and winked a little before turning back to the girl.

"My turn?" I asked.

Her face filled with a panic as she was suddenly pinned to the ground as I held her there with my foot.

I made myself invisible to her to show her she probably shouldn't mess with me. She knew she was being held down by me but had no idea whether I was about to kill her or something. I really wasn't going to, I felt no need but I let her lie there in panic as I faced the others.

I let her hear my voice.

"Anyone else?" I asked the crowd.

Instantly they all started to attack me together.

They were throwing all kinds of powers at me. There were exactly 1042 of them. I picked up from someone's mind that that was everyone that lived in this house. They had planned to ambush me together if things turned south and their most powerful witch couldn't beat me.

Darius and Amos looked a little panicked. Darius stepped forward, ready to tell his witches to stand down. This was such a cowards move. What would they prove ganging up on me?

I stopped him with a wave of my hand, none of their powers affecting me. They started throwing weapons of all kind at me and I expertly dodged them. I could hear their thoughts as a few of them tried to sneak up on me, completely ruining their efforts.

I smiled the whole time, honestly having a good time. Its been a while since I'd had a bit of a challenge. That just seemed to scared them more.

Suddenly there were probably about a thousand spears completely surrounding me. They were so tightly packed together that I couldn't jump between them. They had created some sort of wall all together. I was honestly impressed by their teamwork.

This was no doubt an advanced one, they were certainly powerful. They all came at me at the same time, coming from all directions. I honestly wasn't sure how to escape this one. I was going to get get stabbed a whole lot.

Twenty-nine

Suddenly time stopped along with the spears I thought were going to stab me.

I looked around as everyone was completely frozen, smiling to each other as they thought they'd finally won.

I grabbed a few spears, moving them out of my way easily, making enough room for me to leave the circle.

Amos was looking at me, panicked as well as Darius who also looked shameful. He was probably so disappointed in his community for doing such a pathetic snake move. I mean why would they be proud if the needed 1042 witches to kill a single white stag.

That would just further prove the point that white stags are more powerful, especially me. Honestly I'm not sure Amos could handle all this, he would probably turn invisible and run.

I grabbed the spears, knocking each of them onto their knees facing each other and placing the spears in front of their faces threateningly.

I turned invisible and walked around them, letting time start back up again.

Everyone gasped, going silent, their auras filled with stress.From their point of view they were about to kill me with a whole lot of spears, then in less than a millisecond they're on their knees with one of their own spears floating in front of them threateningly and I'm nowhere to be seen.

I walked around them, seeing if any of them would dare to get up.

After about a minute a guy yelled out, "Fuck this! She's not even here!" He tried to stand up but before he could I kicked him to the ground, a foot on his chest and the spear in his face.

His just widened his eyes in horror.

"Anyone else?" I boomed my voice through the space, making it sound like it was coming from anywhere, everywhere and nowhere.

They all gasped, looking around desperately.

I let go of the guy but he didn't dare move.

I reappeared in front of them all, walking to where they could all see me.

"I'm honestly impressed, that was a pretty cool move! Of course it's going to take a lot more than a few spears to kill me but good effort!" I said sweetly, clapping my hands genuinely.

They all gave me a weird look and I listened into their minds. They were all submitting but one.

'Who does this bitch think she is?! She's actually crazy! We're going to have a crazy person staying at our house.'

I walked over to him, keeping eye contact as he tried to look down and avoid me.

'Maybe I'm crazy, but at least I'm not a coward' I said in his mind, making him shake in fear.

I rolled my eyes walking away.

"Get up." And as soon as the words left my mouth everyone was scrambling to their feet, not wanting to anger me.

"Can someone show me to the kitchen? I'm starving."

"I'd be happy to." Darius spoke from behind me. I gave him a smile as he threw an arm around my shoulder leading me into the house.

"That was very impressive. I've lived a long life and met a lot of people and have never seen your level of power."

I blushed a little. "Your witches are actually very powerful, you should be proud of what they accomplished, even if they were doing it for wimpy reasons."

He laughed. "Thank you, I think?"

I giggled shrugging.

We walked into the gorgeous kitchen and I grabbed an apple out of a basket on the table.

"Do you mind if I have this? I haven't eaten in a couple days."

His eyes widened. "Yes of course! You're telling me you did all that on an empty stomach! I'd hate to piss you off at full strength."

I waved my hand. "I don't think I actually have to eat, I jus do because I like it."

He just stared at me for a second processing. "I'm sorry, but I've never heard of either an alpha werewolf or white stag or any creature for that matter not needing to eat."

I shrugged. "I don't get it either but who am I to complain?"

Suddenly something lit up in his eyes.

"Is there any way you can join the high witches of the community and I in training? Maybe show us a few tips and pointers and we can teach you a few tricks of your own as well."

I leaned on one leg, popping my hip out as I thought. "I'd be happy to." I said.

He smiled. "It starts in about 20 minutes. If you're drained from the fight we can do it another day though."

I waved him off. "Not drained, I'll come."

"Fantastic! We should start walking over now, I'll show you the grounds at the same time."

We walked through the fields. Their agriculture needed a little help... I cringed at the wild bushes and weeds covering everything. Maybe I'll fix it up a little before I go.

After 25 minutes of walking through the grounds, Darius explaining everything we say, we finally arrived at the training grounds. People all over had already started to fight. It was mostly men but there was the occasional feisty girl here and there.

As soon as I entered the grounds everyone went silent, turning to me and bowing. I nodded, releasing them from their positions as they stood and went back to their fighting.

It was sloppy to say the least. Werewolves were MUCH better than witches in hand-to-hand combat, witches only had their magic to rely on, otherwise they were completely human. Contrary to other's beliefs everyone is born with the ability for magic.

What humans don't know is that they exist and therefore the majority of them don't even get the chance to learn.

I walked around, evaluating each of them before walking to the middle platform. Instantly the grounds fell to silence again as they all turned their attention towards me.

"You all are strong with you powers but I am seeing a ton of laziness and sloppiness when it comes to your hand-to-hand combat training. For those of you who are willing and brave enough I will be conducting a training program for the rest of my stay." I said, gently but sternly, keeping a gentle smile on my face.

"All that wish to join must follow me outside the grounds. The training will be rigorous and start immediately. Don't even bother coming if you're not willing to put your all into it." I looked at all of their indecisive faces before nodding, widening my smile and exiting the grounds.

About 45 witches began to follow me out, a few abandoning the idea half-way through, changing their minds and turning around.

Once we were outside there were exactly 38 of them left.

"I believe in competitiveness. I find it one of the main driving factors. I will be ranking you all. The three best witches will win something by the end of the day, and then tomorrow I will completely re-evaluate.

We will start with a run around the entire community grounds. Notice how I said run, not jog, not walk, but do not burn yourselves out by overestimating your abilities. Don't even think of cheating. You cheat you won't like the consequences, and trust me, I'll know."

They all just stood there staring at me making my smile fall a little, scaring them.

"What are you all standing around for? I said run!"

With that they all sprinted off into the distance apart from the couple of people who were smart and ran away at a normal pace.

I slipped into each of their minds, likening for thoughts of cheating, making sure they all stay on track.

'How will she know if we cheat? Come on, lets do it.'

One man said to another, his thoughts flowing out of his mouth.

'I don't know man, she's pretty powerful.'

'Stop being such a pussy. Come on.'

'Shit, I don't want to but he'll never stop teasing me about it.' The second guy finished off in his mind.

I got onto my feet, following their smells and minds to reach them across the territory in exactly a second.

They had just stepped off of the path. As soon as they saw me they gasped, trying to pretend they weren't doing anything wrong but we all knew they were caught.

"You." I said pointing to the second man that didn't actually want to cheat. "Continue running. You." I said pointing to the first man. He was a little bigger but not out of shape per se. He could've definitely competed my run he was just being lazy. "Come here."

He gulped, looking to his friend for help but his friend just bolted off down the path, trying to get away from the situation.

As the witches ran by they laughed at a petrified looking man and a stern looking girl staring at him.

"Come here." I said and he approached me. I grabbed his arms lifting him lightly as I ran us back to the base, dropping him back down after about a second.

He looked even more panicked and shocked now.

I searched his mind for his name.

"Garry. What did I say about cheating?"

I saw in his mind that he could remember my exact words.

"I-I, don't remember. I wasn't ch-cheating."

"Gary. I don't like liars. Hasn't anyone ever told you not to lie to a white stag?"

"I-uh."

"Go home. You are no longer welcome in my training sessions."

"Wait, but-"

I held up my hand to stop him and he scowled at me.

"Bitch." He grumbled so I grabbed him by the colar tightly, bringing him to his knees.

"Say that again. I dare you."

"I said you you're a bitch."

I threw him to the ground.

"Just because I'm a white stag doesn't mean I'll stand for this bullshit. I am an alpha werewolf and I will not be spoken down to by someone I could destroy without even thinking. Do that again and it may not have as good of an outcome. I'm being very generous, walk away."

With that I turned around seeing that everyone was arriving, finishing their lap.

I gave them all a smile and they returned it happily finishing their lap. I noted down who had finished first and was examining their auras to see where we were at and how much farther I could push them.

Suddenly all of their auras turned to panic and fear but before I could figure out why there was a spear through my midsection.

I looked down at the wooden pole coming out of my stomach. Someone had just stabbed me in the back and it wasn't very hard to guess who...

All of the runners gasped, sprinting to come to my aid.

I started laughing out loud at their concerned and panicked expressions making them stop slow down until they were stopped a couple meters away.

I couldn't feel pain so I was completely unbothered by the injury. What I didn't like is that this bag of dicks tried to kill me in the first place.

I frowned, turning around to face him. He was smirking.

"I did it! I've brought down the great white stag! Guys! I did it! I did it!"

His face fell when no one was celebrating with him, but just stood with sadness and anger covering their faces and auras.

Gary's head tilted a little. "Guys? What's wrong? Why aren't we celebrating?"

I took the moment of silence to pull the spear, not even flinching. The wound immediately started closing. Somehow my healing abilities have only gotten stronger these past few months.

I turned to Gary. "Why would you celebrate about murdering someone who was trying to help you for absolutely no reason?"

I lifted up my shirt a little showing that the wound had completely disappeared.

He gasped and started to run but I easily caught him, grabbing his hands behind his back and pushing him to the ground with my foot.

I looked around for something to show people that its not okay to mess with me.

"If I were normal, you'd be dead by now."

"No, if you were normal you'd be dead by now!" He yelled from the ground making me push him to the ground harder as I rolled my eyes.

I mean, he's not wrong.

I spotted the perfect thing to do, smiling at everyone as they looked at me with curiosity.

Thirty

I dragged Gary by the collar to a tree perfectly situated in the middle of everything with strong branches.

I don't believe in torture, not after everything I've been put through but I can't exactly let him get away with this.

I grabbed him and started climbing the tree. He started yelling as I leaped from branch to branch with him over my shoulder.

Once I reached the perfect spot, high enough that he can't get down but low enough that everyone can see him I stopped putting him down on the thick branch.

I had to leap from branch to branch to get here and I knew he wasn't able to get back down without falling out of the tree.

I then removed my white shirt, covered in blood, leaving me in my sports bra and tied it to a lower branch.

I cut my palm and used my blood to write out, 'idiot sighting! Look up!' then stretched it between the branches so you could read it and it was obvious enough.

I sighed in happiness looking at my work.

Gary was clinging onto the branches, terrified of falling and my ruined t'shirt made a very clear sign. Now when people walk by they can look at him being an idiot and I don't have to worry about him stabbing me while I'm training the others.

"YOU FUCKING CRAZY BITCH!" He yelled from the tree, starting to sweat of fear.

I just laughed, smiling up at him and winking.

I walked back to the group I was training and they were all laughing at their friend up in the tree like a dumbass.

I giggled along with them and a few of them gave my high fives.

I could see them all staring at my scars with questioning gazes but I just ignored them walking to the open field.

I was wearing high rise leggings and one of those long sports bras so barely any skin was actually showing, therefore barely any scars.

"Anyone else want to try and impale me?"

I asked, putting my hands on my hips.

They all laughed, quickly shaking their heads no. The man that was with Gary, almost cheating with him seemed to be laughing the hardest.

"Alright, we're going to do some sparring. I want you all to work together and try to pin me. I won't use any of my white stag powers nor alpha powers. I can turn them off rendering me temporarily human. If I pin you, you're out and will go stand to the side. You will come at my maximum 5 at a time."

"All of us together?" One of the guys asked, looking confused. "Wouldn't that be kinds easy since you don't have any powers and no offense, but you're kind of small. "

I pouted. "I'm 5'6 and a half! If you guys can pin me I will cut your conditioning in half."

This got their attention. They all huddled together in their groups of 5 making a game plan.

I fought a lot without using any of my extra abilities when I was training. Its important to be able to defend yourself in all situations. You never know what circumstances might come up.

I'm pretty confident but it still won't be easy.

They finally came out of the huddle, everyone taking their paces surrounding me.

I stood up straight with my arms behind my back, watching all of them the best that I could.

One of them lunged at me but he made it very obvious that that's what he was planning and I was easily able to dodge it, simultaneously pinning him to the ground. The other 4 came at me but I swept my leg tripping them, pinning them one by one as they tried to get up.

Soon enough all 5 of them were out. "Still seem easy?" I laughed, crossing my arms and staring at the now nervous group.

The next group tried to use the element of surprise which worked for a second. They got in a quick it to my jaw but as they tried to trip me I jumped over it, rolling out then once again pinning them all to the ground one by one.

I did that 7 times and was now down to my last group. There were 5 of them and they were definitely the smarter, fitter ones. They knew if they went last I'd be tired out.

They looked very calculating as the tried to read me. I was impressed by that, they were definitely making a good impression.

They all came at me at the same time, working together really well. They got in a few good hits but I blocked out of them. They got close to tripping my but I leaped over their legs last minute.

They were doing really well, seeing my weaknesses and exploiting them. After about 5 minutes the biggest one lunged at me while the others held me in pace. I absorbed the blow, falling to the ground but I continued rolling with him on me, flipping him over my head with my feet.

They almost had me there. I leapt back to my feet pinning each of them, finally ending the long fight.

I finished that one smiling big as the others groaned disappointed.

"I'm very impressed with you 5. Good job today! No ones gotten that close to pinning me in a while. Sadly none of you were able to keep me down which means you will be doing the full conditioning!"

They all groaned as I laughed a little. I rolled my eyes, what babies.

"Drop and give my 25 sit-ups, 25 push-ups, 25 burpees, 25 squats and then a quick sprint to the tree Gary's hanging out in. I want you to touch the tree before coming right back. You will do this sequence again and again. If I see you have pushed yourself hard enough and deserve to stop I will come tell you specifically to do so. If not, keep going. If you don't push yourself I'm just going to keep you going until I feel you have finished. Don't even think about cheating or you'll be kicked out of training or join your friend Gary up there."

They all nodded, getting into position to start.

"GO!" I yelled and the immediately dropped to the ground doing their sit-ups as fast as possible.

They were pushing themselves hard, probably wanting to finish sooner rather than later and I loved it. If they kept this up they would become very fit very quickly.

I let them all do about 3 rounds before I started tapping people out.

I scanned through their minds, searching for the feeling of not being able to do any more without passing out.

I spotted a skinnier woman in the corner, really pushing herself but I could tell that she was finished. Continuing would do her no good.

I walked over to her, searching for her name. "Maria, you're done. You did amazing, I love the way you pushed yourself, go take a break over there. Once everyone's done we'll start the next phase."

She smiled gratefully at me before dropping to the ground trying to catch her breath.

"You have to walk it out otherwise you'll throw up." She groaned but got up, walking through the exhaustion.

She's strong, tough, I like her.

One at a time I tapped them out once they reached their limit until all thirty of them were sitting under a large tree waiting for further instructions.

"You guys have been doing great today! We're about half-way through today's training!"

They all groaned when I said that, probably thinking they were done.

"Follow me." With that I walked off, back to the training area. My students all followed me, dragging their feet and complaining about how tired they were to each other.

We walked into the room and everyone was staring. They had just finished their training and were packing up for the day.

I was happy to have the grounds to myself.

The people already in there were laughing at how miserable my group was, portably thanking god they didn't join them.

There were dummies lined up all along the edge of the grounds for practicing your hits.

"Everyone take a spot in front of one of the dummies and set it to the height of 6'."

They all did so, looking to me for more information.

"We're going to work on kicks first, I want you to do a simple push kick."

I grabbed my own dummy, placing in view of everyone else.

"You lift you knee then kick forward. Make sure you use the ball of you foot, flexing your toes and give the dummy a good push. I want you to try to knock them over. I you can, you can finish training for the day!"

I smiled then demonstrated the kick a couple times. I knocked my dummy right over first try.

I used my werewolf powers to knock it over. It is actually physically impossible for any of them to knock over these dummies but now they'll really kick it as hard as they can.

I walked down the line, critiquing their form and giving them tips for their specific height and body weight.

As I was adjusting someone Darius entered the arena. He burst out into laughter when he saw my utterly exhausted group of students.

"They're brave to let you coach them. I'll give them that!" He laughed as a couple gave him dirty looks. At this point their entire body was shaking. That's how you know its working!

"Well you're welcome to join them!" I offered.

"No, no, that's okay."

"No worries I understand. I didn't really think you could handle it anyways."

That got to him. He was definitely prideful. He looked at me with his mouth wide open before proceeding to rip his shirt off, throwing it to the ground and stepping in front of his own dummy.

I laughed as he gave me a dirt look, starting his kicks.

They are pretty good but need adjusting nonetheless.

"You're standing too narrow, you want to spread your legs a a little." I said, walking towards him. When he did that his hips started to twist.

I grabbed them and jumped a little.

I giggled. "Relax and square out your hips.

He tried the kick again and got a ton of power into it, performing the kick perfectly.

"Perfect! Now keep working on that."

I then left him to kick his dummy and helped some other students.

After that we moved onto the next beginner move, working on their quick jabs.

I walked along, watching them punching their bags, fixing their forms. They were all sweating heavily, and shaking but still desperately trying to kick their dummies over and get out of the torture.

"Okay! Everyone come here!" I yelled when I was satisfied. Darius had now started to breathe a little harder, sweating lightly making his skin shimmer with sweat. At this point everyone one of the have removed their shirts including the girl in their sports bras.

Their bodies were a little weak and lightly overweight. I was pretty excited to see the transformation though.

"Okay! We've finished the basic training and will finish off with one last thing, but as I promised the 3 best witches, will get a little surprise! My number one student today was Maria!"

When I said that she sighed happily, a few of her friends giving her high fives before coming and standing next to me.

"Maria has pushed herself throughout the day and was the most committed during the conditioning. The second best student was Peter!"

Peter laughed a little in relief before standing next to Maria and I. "Peter was the first to come back from the run and was trying very hard the entire day, especially in the kickboxing phase. Third, and last to receive the surprise will be Daniel."

The man came out from the back of the group smiling widely.

"Peter you showed great initiative being the leader of the sparring group that nearly pinned me. You weren't rash and thought everything through and I'm impressed. The three of you are finished for the day and will not have to do the final phase of today's training! Congratulations, you deserve it!"

Everyone else groaned, jealous as the three high-fives each other before making their way out, thankful to finally be done.

Darius was watching me very closely the entire time with a smirk on his face. Before continuing I quickly stopped time for everyone but us and winked at him real quick.

He looked shocked by the entire thing and it effectively wiped the smirk off of his face.

"The final phase, I'll be nice because its only your first day. Give me one lap run around the entire grounds again and then 500 jumping jacks to finish. Don't forget that cheating will not be tolerated."

With that they all groaned and went running around the grounds on their wobbly legs. Darius was the fastest one easily finishing his workout.

"Tomorrow you should join for the entire workout." I told him.

"I'd love to sugar lips." I cringed at the nickname he gave him but brushed it off.

By the time my students were leaving they were cursing and very slowly walking out of the gym. I laughed at their legs that were literally shaking of fatigue.

I'd say first day went pretty well.

Thirty-One

- -

After sending everyone home and getting Gary out of the tree I went for my own run.

I reached 750 000 km/hour. I ran around the entirety of the UK 5 times in about 2 hours.

I was getting insanely fast, not even the first white stag nor the first werewolf had this kind of speed. So, what the hell am I?

Once I returned from my run, a little tired out I headed back to the community house, walking through the beautiful forests, appreciating it.

By the time I got back it was 11:00 pm and everyone was heading to bed. I looked around me at the horrendous agriculture and cringed.

I decided to fix up their property while everyone was asleep.

I spent the next few hours removing weeds, trimming bushes and trees and taking care of the flowers.

I fixed their stone pathways and cut their grass to an appropriate length. I found and unblocked a gorgeous waterfall, refilling the abandoned spring that ran through the property giving the lands a more magical touch.

I rearranged some trees to make some archways over the entering roads, restoring it to its original glory allowing flowers to spurt.

Because of my super speed I had finished their entire property by 6:00 the next morning.

When everyone walked outside they were gasping, shocked at the over-night turn-around. I looked around, satisfied and headed back inside to take a shower, leaving them guessing as to how it all happened.

They property looked a million times more welcoming and magical. I even fixed up their training grounds, making the footing better and made a small path through the forest perfect for their runs.

I walked into the gorgeous guest bedroom they showed me, taking a nice relaxing bath. They even provided body scrubs and bath bombs.

I exited feeling completely refreshed and smelling it too.

I got changed into an easy black shirt tucked into my high-rise jean shorts and braided my hair into two long French braids.

When I headed downstairs the house was filled with people bustling around, a buffet set up against one of the walls.

I grabbed a croissant from the table, looking around to meet eyes with Darius and Amos.

I walked up to the smiling largely.

"Hey guys, what's up?"

They both gave me a look that said, 'cut the bullshit' confusing the shit out of me, as I chewed my croissant in confusion.

"Did I miss something?"

They both laughed than walked away.

Ummmm what the fuck?

I just stood there, croissant still in my mouth as I watched them walk away, starting conversations with other people.

"I saw that and I'm just as confused." A voice said from behind me.

I turned around to see Peter, making my smile.

"Thank God I thought I was going crazy!" I threw my hands up into the air. "I almost dropped my croissant I was so confused! Imagine the tragedy!"

He laughed shaking his head.

"Are we training again today? Everyone's so sore and dying from yesterday."

I shrugged, "If they want to get better they're going to have to suck it up. Training starts at 4:00 pm sharp."

He sighed a little. "I was afraid you would say that, but if it makes us as good as you its worth it."

I laughed a little. "Kissing my ass is not going to get you a spot in the top three Peter."

He pouted making puppy dog eyes but I just laughed at him shaking my head.

"Nope! That won't work either!"

He sighed giving up.

"Fine, I guess I'll just have to impress you with my amazing fighting skills again. I'm going to pin you today! That's a Peter guarantee right there."

"I'm holding you to that."

"What are you planning on doing today?"

"Well, I have hours to kill before training so I was going to go visit my sister, she lives here somewhere. She just married Brian Adams. "

"Delta Brian Adams of the Greenrock pack?"

"Ya do you know him?"

He nodded quickly eyes wide. "Everyone knows the Greeenrock pack, they're the most influential pack in England!"

"Woah, go Jen! I was planning on surprising her, I feel like it would be more fun. I've been talking to her today and she told me she was doing nothing but hanging around her house today."

"They're never going to let you in there, they're so overly protective even people they know are considered threats the minute they step into their lands unannounced. "

I shrugged, "I'll figure it out."

"How the hell are you going to get there and back in time for training? Its a 4 hour drive."

"I wasn't planning and driving."

He scrunched his eyebrows together.

"Don't worry about it." I said, walking off as he stood there confused. I could practically see the wheels turning in his head.

I turned on my phone's GPS, quickly memorizing the best route to take to get there. 65 km/hour, 4 hours is 260 kilometers. I run 750 000 km/hour or 208 kilometers per second.

It should be about a 1.25 seconds before I arrive. I laughed to myself. This is probably the best part of my powers, its just so useful!

I dashed off and as I calculated, 1.25 seconds later I was at their palace. I turned myself invisible as I walked through the grounds, looking around for Jen.

I boomed my voice throughout the entire grounds, they didn't know where it was coming from but everyone could hear it.

"I'M LOOKING FOR JENNIFER ADAMS. PLEASE MEET ME IN FRONT OF YOUR PACK HOUSE."

In a matter of minutes almost an entire army was guarding the house, the majority guarding the front of the pack house.

Yep, I should have thought that through a little better.

I reappeared in front of them smiling.

They all got into their defensive stance, all aiming guns at my head, a helicopter thing flight and watching from above. I put my hands up in the air smiling sheepishly.

"My bad, that was my mistake I'm sorry I should have been more clear and less ominous and creepy! I regretted it the moment I said it I was like - uhhh that wasn't a good idea but it was too late! Right, shut up Ellie, get to the point! I'm Ellie Green, Jen's sister, I came to visit from Canada. I wanted to surprise her but I see now I did it the wrong way."

I saw Brain, Jen's mate walk out of the crowd to see if I was telling the truth. As soon as he did he sighed in relief and dismissed the army.

"Sorry!" I called out again as they all gave me dirty looks for causing a really unnecessary false alarm. Shit I probably scared Jen half to death.

"I mind-linked Jen, she's on her way now." Brian said, coming and giving me an awkward hug. I laughed a little giving him a good hug.

"How'd you do that anyways? You scared the actual living shit out of me."

I smiled guiltily. "I'm so sorry about that, I didn't really think, but it turns out I'm a white stag! Its one of the perks."

Before Brian could answer Jen was bounding out of the house towards me. I turned around and ran gently towards her as we tackled each other in the middle in a giant bear hug, laughing and rolling on the ground.

"I MISSES YOU SO MUCH BITCH WHY DID YOU HAVE TO SCARE ME LIKE THAT?! I THOUGHT I WAS GOING TO DIE!"

We both just laughed at hugged each other for another few minutes before finally getting up, both of us with tears of happiness in our eyes.

We went inside where people were still giving me dirty looks. Jen would tell off anyone who did and they had to listen to her since she's delta female. She seemed more confident and self-assured since the last time I'd seen her and I was so proud.

I told her all about the belle foret pack and becoming a white stag to finally meeting the witches and everyone here. She told me all about her mate and becoming a delta female to one of the strongest packs in the world. It just felt really nice to finally catch up. I missed her so much.

After hours of talking and gossiping I looked at the time and saw it was time to go back to train the witches.

"I gotta go get back to training the witches. I'm sorry."

"Come back once you're done, I'll wait for you just outside the palace. I have a preposition" She said bouncing in her seat a little.

I smiled at her. "Of course."

I gave her a quick hug goodbye before running back to the community.

I arrived in seconds startling everyone who hd gathered.

Peter put a hand to his chest breathing hard. "Jesus Christ where did you even come from?!"

I laughed shrugging, "I told you I was with my sister Jen."

"How fast exactly can you run?" He suddenly asked a little skeptical.

I gave him a sheepish smile, "Well, my best was 755 000 km/hour."

Everyone gathered around went silent staring at me in complete shock.

Peter burst out into laughter making me frown, tilting my head.

"I'm not kidding."

"No way. Not possible."

"It is possible apparently since I can do it."

"Prove it."

"Okay what do you want me to do?"

He thought for a second.

"There are these flowers that only grow a few towns over that way." He pointed in a direction.

"If you continue straight you'll hit their gigantic fields of flowers. It is a 3 hour drive. Go get a flower and bring it back."

I shrugged, "Okay."

"Okay, want me to ti-" Before he could finish his sentence I had gone and come back with the ugly little blue flower.

"This?" I asked but he just looked at me with his mouth wide open, blinking and trying to figure out what just happened.

He gulped, "well. "

The last of the group arrived with Darius. I giggled a little when I saw him.

"Alright now that everyone's here we can begin! We'll start with the same warm-up, one lap around the territory. Remember not to cheat, don't want to repeat Gary's situation do we? There is now a clear path that you can follow so no excuses will work."

They all headed out beginning their run, some of them clearly still sore from the day before, but that's the best time to work out, it really builds those muscles!

I listened into their minds, checking for cheaters or dickheads. 'I wonder what will happen if I cheat?' I picked up from Darius.

'She can't really do anything, I don't know what happened to Gary but I'll be a lot more careful. She'll be so impressed when I get there first and not even that tired... Okay I'm doing it I'll just cut through the forest and be careful and quiet. No way she catches me.'

As soon as he takes a step off the path I'm standing in front of him with my arms crossed shaking my head. The people that ran by laughed at the familiar situation, making Darius blushed a little. They knew what the consequences were.

"Darius. I'm very disappointed! Of course I was going to catch you!" I shook my head some more, making him look down a little in shame. My god it was like scolding a puppy! I have to do it but I hate to do it.

I smiled a little as an idea came to mind. He looked terrified as he took in my excited features.

I picked him up running him to the field, getting there in less than a millisecond. He gasped, looking a little panicked.

I was still listening into everyone's minds to make sure no one was cheating. Damn this is a lot of work.

I set him near a wet patch of dirt.

"Stay still or you'll be kicked out of my training group or hung from a branch for all to see like Gary."

I grabbed a big handful of mud then rubbed it all over his body and clothes.

"Lie down." He listened, pouting trying to wipe some of the mud off.

He laid down in the grass, belly down.

I giggled a little as I stood up and sat down on his back, legs crossed underneath me.

He groaned a little, clearly embarrassed as the others came in, laughing really hard as they saw their leader covered in mud and a small girl sitting on him smiling.

"Okay, I deserved this." He mumbles grumpily making me laugh little patting his head.

They all formed a small semi-circle in front of me.

"When will people start listening when I tell them they can't cheat!" I exclaimed throwing my hands up into the air.

"You all did great, I'm proud at the effort I'm seeing, keep this up and you will no doubt see results! For our next exercise you will all be chasing Darius, trying to hit him with mud. Once you have you can come to me. You will then try to tag me. Again I won't be using any Alpha or white stag powers, I'll make it fair. If even just one of you can tag me I'll cut today's conditioning in half. Go!"

I exclaimed jumping off of Darius. He instantly leapt off the ground giving me a dirty look as he ran away from everyone trying to hit him with balls of mud.

God I love this job.

Thirty-two

I had just finished another great day of training witches!

After everyone chased Darius hitting him with mud, leaving no clean space on his body, they all tried very hard to tag me.

Unfortunately for them they were not able to catch me. I climbed trees, leaped over their arms and ran faster than all of them laughing the entire time.

They did a similar conditioning to the day before but I noticed them all pushing themselves even harder. They really wanted the reward of being top 3.

I taught them a few more self-defense and kickboxing moves before letting them do their last run. The top 3 were three completely different witches. I liked that. They all put so much effort they were making my choice hard.

I took a quick shower before heading back to the Greenrock pack to meet Jen.

As promised she was waiting outside for me, her leg bouncing up and down. She always had so much energy it was crazy!

"Hey Jen" I ran right up to her, startling her.

"Hey I wanna talk to you about something."

"That's why I'm here." I said with a smile, settling in next to her.

"Well, Brian and I are going on a trip to Spain and I really want you to come!"

"Spain?"

"Yes! It would be so fun! Brian has a ton of work to do while he's there so you and I can hang out and explore Spain! What do you think?"

Without even thinking I leaped onto her, wrapping her into a bear hug. "OF COURSE I WANT OT GO TO SPAIN WITH YOU!"

She laughed out loud. "OH THANK GOD IT'LL BE SO MUCH MORE FUN WITH YOU THERE! We're leaving in twenty minutes though..." She said, giving me a sheepish smile.

I laughed. Of course she waited this last minute to ask me. I have no idea why she couldn't have texted me this or asked me when I was here earlier today. Whatever, she wouldn't be Jen if she didn't do stuff like this.

After squealing about how excited I was for a few more minutes with Jen I ran home to grab my things. They were all still packed since I hadn't moved into the room they gave me yet.

I ran down to talk to Darius and Amos who were hanging out in the common room with a group of people. Amos and Darius had girls literally drooling over them making me roll my eyes. They could be so oblivious sometimes, I've been in their minds they have no idea that these girls are trying so hard to get their attention.

"Hey guys!" I called walking into the room. I spotted Boston and Peter talking with a couple other guys I'd never met and waved at them.

"Amos, I'm going to Spain with my sister, like now. Just text me if you need me to be back, I'll come back every day for training anyways."

"Okay, have fun, just be safe." He's so cute I swear.

I waved bye to everyone before heading out. I haven't actually tried running on water yet but I'm sure it'll be fine.

When I got back to Jen's her and Brian were packing up the car, getting ready to go.

"Hey." I said popping up behind them. Immediately they all jumped around, facing me in a defensive position, a few guards running to me.

I put my hands in the air laughing.

"Maybe I should pop up a little further away and then walk to you."

They instantly all relaxed, Jen holding her heart taking deep breaths.

"I think that would be a good idea." Brian chuckled, amused by Jen's flustered state.

We all climbed into the car but I was already itching to get out. These last few months I have been gaining so much power, strength, speed and energy. I would have to sit here for 30 minutes and then on a jet for another 2 and a half hours.

My leg was already starting to bounce and I was playing with my fingers.

Jen noticed this and raised an eyebrow. "Are you okay?"

"Yeah, totally fine."

She gave me an unimpressed look. "You would think being a white stag would make you better at lying."

"I'm not lying!" I exclaimed in a weird high pitched voice making Jen role her eyes at me.

I sighed, "Okay fine, I've just had a hard time relaxing. I have so much energy all the time!"

Jen frowned. "How is it you're getting stronger? Shouldn't you be getting weaker since, you know, you're... dying" she whispered the last word, tears welling up in her eyes a little ass she fidgeted with her fingers.

I sighed, "I don't know Jen."

"Maybe you're not dying! Maybe you're okay! Maybe the doctor was wrong!"

I've been thinking this a lot too lately but I didn't want to get my hopes up at all. I shook my head looking down. "Jen, please don't get our hopes up. I've already accepted I don't have much life left."

"But-"

"Jen." I cut her off, "Please, just leave it."

The tears finally trickled down her face and I pulled her into a big bear hug. I will not cry, I have to stay strong, for Jen, I repeated in my mind.

I took a deep breath before pulling back and shooting her my best smile. "Jen, we're going to Spain."

She instantly perked up, her sobs turning into laughs as she smiled and her tears slowed. "We're going to Spain." She repeated, taking a deep breath.

When we finally arrived at the airport Jen was jumping around happily. She kept kissing Brian and leaping on the guard's backs yelling in excitement, making them groan in annoyance.

I decided to look around at auras and they were all extremely happy and excited. Some were a little annoyed by Jen but it was mostly positive.

We were led to a special entrance to the tarmac where their private jet was parked.

I climbed up the small staircase to see a couple workers lined up to greet us at the top. I was the last to get on the plane and everyone seemed to just ignore them. Rude.

"Hi, I'm Ellie" I introduced myself once I got on, shaking each of their hands. Both of their auras lit up a little in gratitude making me smile. Sometimes the smallest things can make people's days.

"I'm Genevieve and this is Tom." The flight attendant responded gently.

After that we got into a conversation a little about their lives and their families. I don't even really know how but we were talking until I got pulled away by Jen.

I could see in their auras that they like that I acknowledged their existence and didn't treat them like they were beneath me, not to mention how happy they got when they started talking about their families, especially their kids which they both had.

Jen sat me down in front of a giant tv and we started watching a movie. It was frozen 2 and honestly, not a fan.

Jen seemed to love it, she thought Elsa was super badass, but the entire movie I just kept thinking, why the hell is she pushing away the ones that love her?! AGAIN?!

I was getting super fidgety and uncomfortable after the first half hour. It took us an hour to actually take off since there was a small technical problem they had to fix. Genevieve had gone to sleep, cuddling with Brian. I admired what they had and wanted it so badly, but I knew I couldn't. My mate rejected me and I'll be dead in 6 months.

Both of my legs were bouncing all over the place, my hands were gently tapping my thighs and I was chewing on my tongue in frustration.

I felt a tap on my shoulder and turned around to see a concerned looking Genevieve.

"Hey Ellie, are yo okay?"

"Ya, I'm totally fine I tried to lie."

She gave me a look that said, 'cut the bullshit'

Damn my horrible lying skills!!

"Sorry, I just don't like staying still for so long. I'm a little uncomfortable."

She nodded in understanding putting her hands on her hips in thought.

"Want to come for a walk? I can show you the plane."

"Oh, I really don't want o be a bother."

She scoffed, "No bother at all, come on."

I stood up and she showed me around, telling me about the job.

Finally she brought me into the cockpit where the pilot was sitting. He noticed we walked in and put the plane an autopilot.

"Hey martin, this is Ellie. She was getting a little uneasy sitting still for so long so I'm showing her around, I hope you don't mind." The pilot had old graying hair and I could see he had a beautiful and gentle soul.

I giant smile filled his face. "I don't mind at all, would you like to learn about flying a plane?" He asked hopefully. It was clear that he was bored too.

"I would love to."

His face lit up when I said that. He was clearly happy to talk about something he was so passionate about.

I sat down in the co-pilot's seat and he taught me all about the plane.

It really took my mind off of sitting still. If my body wasn't active at least my brain was.

"It's time to start descending. Would you like to do the honors?"

"You want me to land the plane?! What if I crash it!"

He chuckled.

"You won't crash it I'm right here just in case but I believe in you."

I squealed a little, jumping in my seat. SO COOL I'M GONNA LAND A PLANE!!

I put on my serious face and concentrated.

After 15 minutes of descending I had landed us safely on the runway.

Martin Genevieve and Tom were cheering for me and I was smiling widely.

"Thank you so much you guys this was amazing!" I exclaimed giving them each a big thankful hug before heading out to meet the others.

When I entered the main area Jen looked at me relieved.

She came up to me and whacked my arm.

"Ow! What the hell!" I yelled jumping back, giggling a little.

"Oh shut up, we both know you can't feel pain."

I shrugged a little, as she was steaming next to me.

"WHERE THE HELL HAVE YOU BEEN?!" She yelled.

"Oh, I was flying the plane! I just landed it." I said excitedly.

"you were flying the plane?" She asked in a deadly calmness, making me tense up. Calm is as bad as it gets with Jen.

"uhh, ya I-"

"YOU. LANDED. THE. PLANE?!" She screamed cutting me off.

"Umm, yes, I did."

"Oh my God. What am I going to do with you? Who gets on a plane having no prior knowledge about planes or the people flying them and after LITERALLY 2 AND A HALF HOURS IS FLYING AND LANDING IT?!"

I just shrugged giggling a little as she rubbed her eyes.

"Jen, we're in Spain."

That seemed to snap her out of it again.

She smiled at me. "Shut up." She said through her smile hitting me on the arm again.

We made our way out of the plane and Jen went to Brian, ranting about me flying the plane. Whoops, sorry Brian.

They seemed to fit perfectly together. Brian was quieter and more of the listening type whereas Jen was the loud talker.

They were really cute. It was amazing seeing each of their faces lighting up while they were in each other's presence and how they seemed to be slightly less bright when the other was away.

They were truly in love.

Thirty-three

We've been in Spain for about a week now. I run back to England every day to check on the witches. I am now able to run 60 000 000 km/hour. I somehow just keep getting faster and faster and I have no idea when it will stop.

Jen said she has a surprise for me today. I decided to be polite and not read her mind, I mean where's the fun in that?!

We climb into the car but weirdly Jen's aura is very nervous and a little scared.

"Jen, are you okay?"

She sighed. "I'll tell you what's bothering me later okay? Please for now just let it go?"

"Okay." I understand where she's coming from, I'll give her some space, its not exactly fair that I could read her aura so easily.

We drove a few minutes until we pulled up to the side of the road in the middle of the city in Spain. We were surrounded by giant skyscrapers and nice buildings.

Jen looked even more nervous her hands were even shaking gently.

I looked at her, concern covering my face. She lifted up a blindfold confusing me even more.

I put it on and felt her anxiety relax a little.

She grabbed my hand and led me into what I assume is a building. She talked in hush voices to someone before leading me down some echoing halls.

Finally we stopped and she took a big shaky breath.

"Can I remove my blind fold?" I said, a little excited to see what all the fuss was about.

"One more minute."

We stop there in silence for another couple of minutes before she spoke up again. "Okay, go ahead and take it off."

I removed it to reveal a doctor's office. What the hell?

I turned to Jen questioningly as her anxiety peaked. She was literally sweating visibly as she avoided eye contact with me.

The reality came crashing down on me as I realized what was happening. But I couldn't be right. Jen wouldn't do that would she?

"Jen?" I asked, "What the hell is this?"

She just looked down avoiding eyes contact when a man walked in in a white lab coat.

"Ellie Green?" She asked.

"Yes, that's me."

"I'm here to test to see if you are indeed dying from what your other doctor believes. Her diagnosis is not one I'm familiar with but I called her and we discussed it a little. What she says makes a lot of sense but I'd be happy to double check for you guys, making sure everything adds up."

I smiled Kindly at the doctor, Jen still avoiding eye contact. I can't believe she brought me here against my will.

I sat on the examination bed as she took a couple files of blood.

She did a full physical. I could see her aura darken as she took in all of the scars that littered my body, what she doesn't know is that the majority healed, only the deep ones were still there.

Jen stood in the corner, watching her diligently.

"I am going to go get the tests to confirm your doctor's suspicions, but from what I've seen so far, it looks like she is correct."

Jen broke into tears when she said that. I looked at the ground. I felt guilty. I hated that she refused to listen to me. She did the exact opposite of what I wanted.

I just wanted to live all of my days being happy and making the most out of life. I wanted to forget about my illness, I didn't want anyone crying over me. I didn't want their pity. I just wanted to be happy, for once in my life. That's all I want.

After about 15 minutes of silence the doctor returned looking grim.

"I have bad news. You are dying, but you doctor was wrong about how long you have left. Since your powers and strengths have increased so exponentially, she couldn't predict how much strain it would actually take on your body. It looks like you now have 4 months left to live."

My heart dropped to my stomach. I just lost 2 whole months. Jen started crying harder. I wanted to comfort her but I was too angry right now. I didn't need to know this, I could've lived being oblivious.

The doctor told me a little more about my disease, I have to continue taking my pills every day, she warned me not to miss it.

He left the room leaving Jen and I to process the information.

"Ellie, I'm so sorry I just-" I waved her off, looking down.

"Its fine Jen. I'll see you tonight at the hotel." With that I left, trying not to let the tears escape. I have to be strong. I have to be strong. I never should have left the white stags. Why couldn't I have just let myself live out my days peacefully with Daisy, Rose, Amos and Jeremiah. Working at the flower shop and going for runs.

I ran back to the witches to do our daily training. They have made so much progress. They often worked out shirtless and you could definitely see the results forming. They are tiring much less quickly, getting much closer to beating me in their groups during sparing and doing the runs in half the time.

When I arrived back at the community the group was talking and laughing together. A few more quit and there exactly 30 of them now. I smiled at them proudly as they made their way over to me, smiles plastered on their faces.

I could see people watching from afar full of envy. I'm sure a lot of them regret letting the opportunity of being trained by me pass.

"Before we continue I wanted to see how you're all felling. You're no doubt feeling the changes that I can definitely see."

I was still a little down about the events of earlier today, it would be nice to hear some success stories.

One guy decided to speak up, "Our entire group has risen to be the best fighters in the entire community in less than 2 weeks! I personally feel amazing."

Others nodded along, agreeing happily. This brought a smile to my face.

"A lot of people are asking if its too late to join." Maria spoke up.

I shook my head, "They can come and see me personally during training sessions if they would like to join. I'll give them a chance to win a spot but they'll have to be convincing. Now, lets start with 2 laps around the community grounds."

None of them groaned they just leapt into action, running at a quick pace around the grounds. I could tell that they all were much more energized. They were starting to get hooked on all of the physical exercise, soon it will be a part of their routine that they are dying to do.

I smiled to myself as I sat on the grass, relaxing under the sun, listening for cheating, although they all know not to cheat and I trust them.

I felt a presence next to me and looked over to see Amos and Darius. They sat down on each side of me while I closed my eyes, letting the sun seep in.

"I can see that there's something bothering you." Amos said after a couple minutes of silence. "You know you can tell me anything. Is there anything I can help with?"

"I don't feel like explaining it, feel free to look for yourself." I said, opening my mind to him. It was too painful and raw to explain for today.

He looked inside and I knew when he saw it. He instantly tensed and his aura became sad.

"I'm so sorry Ellie."

I nodded in appreciation. I could tell that Darius was very curious and confused but he respected the fact that I didn't want to talk about it.

I leaned my head on Darius' lap and my legs over Amos.

"The students should be back soon." I said quietly.

"Please don't make them chase me with mud again." Darius said desperately.

I let a small laugh escape my lips, feeling a little lighter.

"I make no promises."

He groaned nervously making Amos chuckle as well.

Boston had joined my training group a couple days in. He was easily my strongest student and becoming a good friend.

I could see him leading the group back, finishing it off in a dead sprint, a huge smile on his face.

I opened my eyes when I felt something under my head star to become a little harder, getting a little, excited...

I sat up quickly blushing a little, leaning more towards Amos.

Darius just winked at me, trying to play it off cool but I could tell he was mortified at wha had just happened.

I laughed a little, awkwardly confusing Amos.

He looked over to Darius and immediately burst out into laughter. He laughed harder than I've ever heard from him before, his whole body shaking, tears streaming down his face, further embarrassing Darius.

Boston laughs along with us while Darius awkwardly stood up, walking into the forest.

"I wonder what he's doing in there." Boston said suggestively, waggling his eyebrows, earning a whack to the chest by m as I stood up.

Once everyone was back from the run they all tried to pin me again in their groups of 5.

At least 4 of the groups got very close, making me fall to the ground a couple times. I was so proud. Their kicks and punches were coming stronger and more precise, their form becoming almost perfect.

Soon they would be able to beat my human form in their groups and I was honestly excited for the day. There was a very large crowd when they fought me now, they all cheered and amped up both the group and me.

After that we did some conditioning, we did a simple hiit workout before moving onto fighting techniques in the arena again.

When we arrived there was a very large group, waiting to watch, again. I would be teaching them some tackling techniques.

We started with leaping onto your opponents shoulders, wrapping your thighs around their necks and throwing them to the ground without falling yourself.

This was a very advanced move and took a lot of time to teach. They were definitely struggling but I was confident they would start to get it after a couple weeks of practicing.

After training I ran back to Spain. I stood in front of the hotel we were staying in, debating with myself whether or not to go in.

I decided I need a little more time and decided to go for a walk. I walked the beautiful bustling streets of Morella. The streets looked magical under the moonlight and the walk was slowly relaxing me.

I smiled to myself as I watched an adorable couple and their little daughter. She was in the middle holding onto both of her parents hands, jumping around excitedly as her parents gazed into each other's eyes lovingly and happily.

I sighed knowing I could never have that. 4 months. I have 4 months left. I will never fall in love, never even have my first kiss!

I grew up in such isolation and hatred. Once I finally escaped I was rejected by my mate and feared by my family.

I felt a tap on my shoulder.

When I turned around I gasped a little in surprise at who was standing there.

"Ellie? What are you doing in Spain?"

Thirty-Four

There smiling down at me was Prince Xander Abascal, I forgot he was the prince of Spain, but something felt different about him, he didn't feel human, he had that paranormal glow to him.

"Xander?"

He smiled nodding.

"What are you doing I Spain?" He repeated.

"I came here to keep my sister company while her mate does some business with some people here."

"Is she here? I'd love to meet her."

I shook my head, "No, I'm not sure where she is right now."

He raised his eyebrows questioningly.

"Its complicated."

He nodded in understadning.

"Can I join you on your walk then?"

"Of course."

"So, how do you like Spain so far?"

"Its beautiful." As we walked down the streets everyone was staring at us again. "I'm sorry, but you seem different..."

He laughed a little, "Yes, I'm a werewolf. I cover that up while I'm traveling."

It all made so much more sense now! I was wondering how a human could be so attractive and just generally big and strong.

"That makes so much more sense."

"Are you hungry?"

"I could eat."

"Great, I live near him and I have just made the best paella you've ever had."

He took my hand and had me down a few streets. We were laughing and joking the entire way there. There was just something so likable about him.

He brought me up to a giant castle, making my eyes widen. I completely forgot he was the prince of Spain. Well...

We passed a few guards who bowed to him in respect.

I smiled to each of them as we walked past. I would've stopped and said hi but Xander was pulling me really fast.

"Come one Ellie! The food's gonna get cold!" He started into a run, pulling me behind him giggling.

We came to a GIGANTIC kitchen full of people. As we walked by they bowed deeply, sending me a confused look.

He brought me up to one of the stoves where there was a pot of paella.

He pulled out a little bottle of seasoning out of his pocket.

"We ran out of my favorite seasoning so I ran to the market to get some."

I was surprised that he didn't make some servant or something go for him, hell I was surprised he could cook! He was definitely not what I expected from a prince.

With the whole prince thing I couldn't stop thinking of my mate. He was the prince of somewhere. I honestly knew very little about him... Realization hit me... No, he can't live here. Xander is the prince of Spain, not werewolves.

"So, have you found your mate yet?" I asked curiously while he plated the food for us.

"Not yet." He said dejectedly, "Still waiting."

I nodded.

"Its so annoying, I would kill to find my mate. I would do anything to find her, but when my brother gets gifted with the arrival of his mate he rejects her!" He exclaimed, throwing his arms in the air in frustration.

I gulped, "You have a brother?"

"Ya, my twin brother. I swear he's such a dick, but he's next in line because he was born like, 2 minutes before me!"

It can't be. It can't be, shit, no."

"Enough about him, so, what exactly are you? You don't smell like a pack, actually you smell a little like the jungle and weirdly, peace. I've never smelt someone who smells like peace, didn't even know that could be a smell but that's what you smell like."

He picked up our plates bringing it to the empty table that looked out over the beautiful city.

"I'm white stag and, uh, sort of werewolf."

He stopped halfway through sitting down, awkwardly hovering over his chair, shock covering his face.

"What?"

"You know," He started, sitting down and recovering a little from his shock, "there isn't a single part of that sentence that I don't need explained."

I laughed a little, pushing the possibility of my mate being here out of my head.

"Well, I don't know what to say. I was born a werewolf, well sort of, that part's kind of hard and weird to explain, and then a couple months ago I discovered I was white stag as well. I stayed with them and trained for a while. "

"Wow. That's amazing. I've never met a white stag before, I've always wondered..."

"Amos, the man with me at the airport was a white stag as well."

I dug into the food and moaned as I chewed it.

"Oh wow, this is amazing. You have a gift."

"I know." He winked at me.

"So do you have any special powers, being a mix and all that?"

"Well I'm an extremely strong white stag, as strong as the very first there was. I have completely mastered reading people's auras, reading people's minds, playing tricks and people's brains and I've been working on controlling time. I can also run about 75 000 000 kilometers per hour and stronger than the average werewolf."

He whistled lowly. "Well shit."

I giggled a little nodding my head.

we talked a little more when suddenly the most amazing smell entered my nose. I inhaled deeply, closing my eyes, trying to get as much of it as I could in.

What is that? Oh shit. Oh shit.

My eyes flew open in panic.

"Xander, you're not the prince of werewolves are you?"

"I am, why do you ask?"

"Fuck." I mumbled under my breath as I heard footsteps approaching.

"Xander? What is that amazing smell?" heard the familiar voice call out. My heart fell to my stomach as I gulped in panic.

I could feel myself paling.

"I made my paella!" Xander yelled back. I put my fork down slowly, not daring to turn around.

"No its something better than that. Its kind of familiar."

Soon he was standing in front of us, his eyes on mine, shock covering his face. I could hear is heartbeat pick up as we made eye contact.

"What the fuck?" Xander broke the silence.

My mate growled lowly.

I stared at my plate. The pain of the rejection washed through me again making my stiffen up. I could feel my heart literally tearing and throbbing in pain as I tried to hold back my pain.

Memories of that night flew back to me and I closed my eyes to try and push them away.

I closed my eyes and took a deep breath, finally relaxing when I smelt the most amazing smell in the world. What the fuck?

I opened my eyes as I sniffed it again. Words couldn't describe the smell it was so amazing. It was familiar but I had never smelt anything like it before.

Then I met eyes with the most beautiful man in the world.

What. the. actual. fuck?

He came running towards me but all I could do was stand still.

He immediately embraced me, putting his face in the crook of my neck and inhaling. My heart was beating so fast I'm sure he could hear it.

I looked at his face up close and I almost fainted. It was perfect, looked like it was sculpted by the god of beauty himself.

I ran my finger along his sharp jawline resulting in a deep growl from him. I looked into his eyes and felt complete. the word echoing through my mind. I knew what just happened, I just found my mate. FUCKKKKK

I knew I should tell him to get away from me, that he couldn't want me and should begin moving on but I couldn't. I felt selfish and couldn't tell him. Somehow I already felt like we were one and to take him away was to rip me apart slowly and painfully.

He stroked my cheek then spoke to me in the most soothing voice I've ever heard. "What's you name?"

"E-Ellie."

"Ellie. Absolutely perfect. Ellie, what?"

I don't know why but I felt compelled to tell him the truth.

"Ellie Green."

As soon as I said that he took a step back, a look of shock covering his face.

For some reason everyone was staring at us now.

"You're Alpha Green's daughter?" He asked, disgust lacing his voice.

"Y-yes."

"Shift."

"What?" I asked, panic starting to set in.

"I said shift. Now."

"B-but"

"GUARDS!" Next thing I knew there were 8 guards on me, grabbing me and pinning me on the ground. Then I felt a sharp pinch in my arm and knew exactly what just happened. He was forcing me to shift.

Not only that but I knew exactly who he was. Only one man had that many guards following him around listening to his every order, and only one man could invite this much attention.

He was the prince. The one everyone was dying to meet, the one everyone wanted to be made to was my mate.

I started shaking, trying to hold back the shift but they just just injected my three more times until I couldn't hold back anymore and was forced to shift.

Normally shifting this way is extremely painful, some people die, their hearts not able to deal with the strain of the torture. One dose could do that, three you couldn't even imagine.

My pain tolerance was EXTREMELY high, I hadn't felt any kind of pain in years, but this I could feel. It was a whole new level of torture that I had never experienced before. All I could see was bright white as I felt a scream leaving my mouth. My body felt like it was burning from the inside out. No one had ever survived this high of a dose, no one has ever lived through such torture.

I could feel my body shaking and my mouth fill with bloody foam.

When I stopped shaking I was in my form and I cold hear gasps and even crying all around. I was still in an insane amount of pain, unable to move or even see.

I could only hear one thing, one voice that could cut through anything. The voice of my mate

"I, Prince Jacob Kaden Lunar of the werewolves reject you, Ellie Green, rogue."

I started hyperventilating as the memories flooded me and I stared into his face.

I couldn't breathe. I looked around in panic, Xander looked confused and concerned as he stared at my panicked state.

"Ellie? ELLIE! Are you okay? What's going on?"

I wanted to answer him but I couldn't find my voice.

I just looked back at my mate who hadn't taken his eyes off of me.

After another minute of hyperventilating and I felt black dots begin to take over my vision. I felt my head getting dizzy.

In a panic I tried to stand up, I made it a couple steps before the darkness took me and I fell to the ground. I felt arms wrap around me at the last minute and the feeling of tingles shooting through my body indicated exactly who had just saved me.

****

I started coming back to consciousness slowly. I could feel that I was laying in a bed and my hearing was staring to return to me, though I still wasn't able to move or open my eyes.

"What the fuck is going on Jacob?"

"That is Ellie Green."

"Yes... your point?"

"Green! Alpha and Run Green of the Blood Thunder Pack's daughter!"

"Urgh, I hate those people."

Jacob growled, "Hey, they are a strong pack, I respect them."

"They tortured their own daughter for everyone to watch! They're sick!"

"Besides the point, do you remember why they tortured their daughter?"

There was a moment of silence. "Oh. No! Ellie's the deformation!"

"Yes..."

"Wow. I did not see that coming, although it adds up with the whole 'I'm sort of a werewolf' thing. That still doesn't explain why she literally passed out by just looking at you."

Jacob growled in frustration. "She's my mate."

Another minute of silence. "WHAT?!" Xander screamed.

"You heard me."

"HOW THE FUCK COULD YOU REJECT SUCH A CRAZY AMAZING PERSON?!" Awww, he's adorable, I love Xander, why couldn't he have been my mate!

"You heard yourself! She's a deformation, she certainly isn't fit to be queen of werewolves."

"So what if her from isn't great! She's a white stag who's powers rival those of the very first! She can read auras, minds, trick minds and even manipulate time! She's stronger than every other werewolf and can run 75 000 000 kilometers per hour! You're the one who doesn't deserve her you dick head!"

More silence.

"What?"

"You didn't know?!"

"No."

"HOW?!"

"We didn't exactly talk."

"Wait a minute, you just met her, and rejected her without talking to her. You could not be a bigger ass head if you tried."

I was finally able to move and opened my eyes, stirring a little.

They went silent and turned to me.

I instantly leapt to my feet in a defensive position.

I put a mask on my face, not letting them see my pain.

I stood up straight, staring them each in the eye.

"I'm leaving."

Thirty-Five

"I'm leaving." I said.

I started towards the door but was blocked by an angry-looking Jacob.

I growled lowly. I let out just a sliver of my power, not wanting to start a fight but having a hard time holding back my anger.

"Where do you think you're going pup?"

"I. am. leaving."

"No."

I growled stronger now, more of my power accidentally slipping out. I don't like being intimidating so I always keep it inside to let people be comfortable around me.

"What the hell do you mean no?"

"You're not leaving me again."

I put my hands on my hips. This guy cannot be serious right now.

"You rejected me! Now let me leave! If I knew you were here I never would have agreed to coming!"

"Oh, please, you're clearly obsessed with me."

I stood there for a minute. This is a joke. I smiled, then started laughing but when I tried passing him again he blocked me.

I let some more of my power slip. I saw his eyes widen and he took a step back when it did. He could feel it. Even Xander widened his eyes and tilted his head to reveal his neck in submission.

I could feel Jacob trying to push his power through but less than half of mine was still too overpowering.

"Let. me. go." He said calmly, my hands turning into fists.

I need to relax. If I don't I'll turn into the master they were all scared I'd be. I need to keep my control or I'll prove them all right.

I closed my eyes taking a deep breath when I felt something metal wrap around my wrist. My eyes flew open to reveal a pair of hand-cuffs around one of my wrists.

I looked up confused as I felt all of my power and extra energy leave my body. What the fuck?

"These cuffs make anyone human. Like I said, you're not going anywhere."

My heart beat sped up intensely.

I ripped my hand from Jacob's grasp, getting into a fighting position. I was still strong as a human, I trained for this. I didn't have my strength or speed but I could use theirs against them.

I looked to Xander who was just watching from the corner.

He came to object but one look from his older brother had him submitting and backing off. He avoided eye contact as he tried to grab my arms.

I brought them out of his grasp, ducking under his arms and sped to the other side of the room.

Jacob started approaching, a sick smile on his face.

He lunged at me but I easily ducked sending a kick to his 'little Jacob'. Oops? Thats gotta hurt.

He fell onto his knees for a moment cupping his crotch as he turned to me, eyes swarming with range.

Xander came at me again. He reached for me but I leapt onto his shoulders, wrapping my legs around his head. I did a sort of back flip, landing him on his back as I stood above him. He tried to get up but I stood on his chest, one foot lightly resting threateningly on his throat. I didn't really want to hurt Xander.

Jacob lunged at me, causing me to fall of balance but I quickly recovered sending him a big kick to the face while I held his body in place. His neck snapped backwards before flying forward. I gave it one last punch, sending him to the ground with my okay strength.

Suddenly countless guards swarmed in.

A fuming Jacob sat up, holding his now bleeding nose.

"Inject her." He said.

I turned around in a panic as they took out the force shifting serum.

I don't know what it would do to me since these cuffs were making me human but I didn't have a good feeling.

I fought back the best that I could, rocking about 17 guards out but I was tiring out and there was a never ending supply of guards flooding in. I was severely outnumbered, I had no chance.

A small woman managed to get through and stabbed my with the needle. I immediately tensed up as the liquid filled my system, my body going into shock. I stopped fighting as I just looked around in panic.

"Give her 2 more doses. She's a tough one." I heard Jacob say from the ground. I felt two more pinches and my body filled with that familiar torturous pain. The worst pain I'd ever felt was back as I fell to the ground, feeling the foam filling my mouth, blood dripping from my eyes ears and nose.

My body started convulsing uncontrollably, there was nothing I could do as Jacob hovered over me, smiling, still holding his bloody nose. Out of the corner of my eye I could see Xander's tortured face.

A guard came forward, picking me up following Jacob out of the room as my seizure died down. Now all I got was the occasional shock going through my body. The foam and blood was now socking into mine and the guard's clothes.

He looked down at me with pity but I hated it. I'm so sick of getting everyone's pity!

They walked down many staircases until I could tell we were deep deep underground.

They led me through the halls and placed me in a prison cell. Surprisingly this is my first actual prison cell. So there's that...

I just lay there, my heart and body on fire.

They chained my wrists, upper arms waist, thighs, ankles and neck up and attached me to the wall. I could barely move I was strapped in so tight, not that I could move anyways I was in so much pain.

I never let a tears slip down my face though. I never showed him my weakness. Even if I die here, I won't let him see my weakness.

After a few hours the bleeding and foaming calmed down, drying up on my face. I must look really disgusting right now.

After another hour the pounding in my head and the pain in my body started to dull and I found myself able to move and think again.

I sat up, the best I could being so locked up at least.

I blinked through the darkness as my eyes adjusted.

Across from me sat a curious looking asian man. He had black hair and bright orange eyes that seemed to glow softly.

"She's awake." He said calmly.

I wanted to respond to them but couldn't find the strength yet. I leaned against the wall, trying to regain my strength.

"What do you think she did?" another male voice asked from my left.

"I don't know, she doesn't look that evil." A female voice answered from the darkness.

"Well clearly she's evil to get locked down here, just like the rest of us otherwise she wouldn't be here." The male voice snapped back. "We haven't had anyone new down here in 200 years, is it bad that I'm excited?" The man finished.

My heart stopped when he said that. What the fuck? There's no way I heard that right! How old are they?!

"Wh-what?" I managed to croak out making them all gasp and look at me.

"I honestly don't know what part you're confused about." The male voice answered.

"Shut up Donny." The female voice answered. Okay, so that one's name is Donny.

"ME?! WHAT ABOUT AIMOTO?!" I guess that's that asian dude's name.

"Hi dear, I'm Elizabeth, but you can call me Elle. What's your name?" She said softly.

"My name's Ellie."

I answered, smiling at the darkness.

"OH MY GOD SHE'S ADORABLE CAN WE KEEP HER?!" Donny yelled, making Aimoto roll his eyes as Elle groaned.

"I am Aimoto." he said, nodding his head in greeting.

"Hi, its nice to meet you."

"I'M DONNY!" Donny yelled from next door so loud it made us all cringe.

"Shut up Donny!" Elle yelled.

"What do you guys mean there hasn't been anyone new in 3 000 years?"

"Well," Elle started, "Donny got here 200 years ago, I got here 250 years ago and Aimoto has been here for 500 years now. This is the deepest part of the prison where only the worst of the worst come, so that doesn't happened too often, but when it does, we're pretty much stuck here for eternity."

I blinked, trying to comprehend all the information. Aimoto just continued to stare at me, seeming to analyze quietly. I noticed he didn't say much."Do you mind me asking what you guys did to get in here for that long?"

Donny started laughing, "mines kind of a funny story. So I was visiting my sister in Spain, I'm originally from Australia, and this guy was just being really annoying. SO, I decided the only way I could deal with his irritating ass for so long was to get drunk as fuck! The only problem is when I got drunk it turns out I had even less patience for this annoying ass kid. Anyways, at the end of the night I may or may not have ended up throwing him off of the roof. Well, I probably should have mentioned that the kid was actually the prince of werewolves at the time and I had just killed him. I know, not that bad but, the problem is that when they tried to arrest me I was still pretty drunk and ended up burning down the entire castle and everyone in it since I shift into a Phoenix... Not my finest moment but its been 3000 years! Can't they let it go yet?!"

I was shocked. Well, shit, that's pretty bad. How the hell did I end up down here? Is what I did really that bad? What did I even really do?

"I lost control of my powers." Elle started, "I am a powerful witch, most powerful that they've seen in the last 500 years. I got angry when my... when my mate was killed. I accidentally summoned a tornado that wiped out an entire country... There weren't any casualties because at the time people had shelter for these types of situations but it was close to being really really bad. I wiped out all of their building and homes and not everyone was exactly happy with that. They let me off with a very serious warning but later that day I accidentally summoned a tsunami. There were many casualties the second time around so they locked me up here."

Well...

"I got too powerful." When Aimoto started talking everyone immediately shut up. "I was stronger than their king after he killed my mate. I went to visit him and reached into his mind. I slowly pulled his brain apart, dismantling who he was without even touching him. I did that to everyone involved. They began fearing me because I gave them a reality worse than death. They became powerless potatoes basically. They could carry to their basic functions, breathing and such, but otherwise were completely brain dead. All they could see was their nightmares replaying for the rest of their miserable lives."

Well that one was intense and unexpected.

"What are you, if you don't mind my asking."

"I am an Abura-sumasha, spirit of the mind. "

"What did you do to get down here sweetheart?" Elle spoke up after a moment of silence.

"I-I'm not exactly sure..." I told them the entire story, for some reason I felt like I could trust them, even after they told me about the horrible things they've done.

"I don't get it. Am I missing something?" Donny spoke up once I was finished.

"I don't think so." I giggled a little.

"Let me get this straight," Elle started, "This Jacob dude rejected you then proceeded to lock you up for absolutely no reason."

"I guess you could put it that way..."

"How did you fight off that many guards anyways? You must be strong if they locked you up like that, not to mention you just took three full shots for force-shifting serum and are up and talking within a few ours. I mean, you smell like a human which makes this even more confusing." Donny rambles on.

"I'm actually kind of a werewolf and a strong white stag. They put cuffs on me to make me essentially human and weak but I had already been training for a while and managed to fight them anyways. If I had my full powers though, there's no way in hell they could have caught me. I let me guard down. I trusted him because he was my mate. It was stupid."

I liked Donny, Elle and Aimoto. They were super down to earth and nice. I know they've done bad things but that's in the past. Everyone's got a dark time they've overcome and if they haven't had it yet its coming. I thought I had escaped mine but I guess I haven't. I'll just have to keep waiting for my moment of peace.

But I know its coming. It has to be coming.

Thirty-Six

I've been in the dungeons for about a half-hour and I already feel much better. I feel almost completely healthy although the chains are making me feel a little weaker.

"You're healed?" Aimoto spoke up again making everyone go silent.

"Ya I feel much better thanks. "

He nodded his head, seemingly observing me again. His evaluating eyes were making me slightly uncomfortable. I felt like he was looking into my soul, although, he probably was honestly.

We heard foot-steps coming down the hall and everyone quieted down. Xander came around the corner surprising me. I had a hard time looking into his eyes. I know he didn't want to lock me up, he didn't have a choice but it was still hard to see him.

"Ellie..." He said, stepping in front of my cell looking at his feet.

"Xander." I said calmly, finally looking at him.

He lifted his eyes and they looked full of pain and regret and I felt myself instantly soften.

"I'm so, so sorry."

I sighed, shifting as much as I could in all of the chains. Xander eyed how locked up I was and his frown deepened. No one else was chained up at all and I was covered in them.

"It's fine Xander, don't worry about me, I've probably been through worse."

"It's not okay, but I- I can't help you." He said shifting from foot to foot.

"My brother knows we're friends so he he's given me direct alpha orders to not let you free, I physically can't help. If I could do anything trust me I would have by now! Its just-"

"Xander. Relax. I'll be fine." I won't be here any longer than 4 months anyways.

"I'll figure something out. I have to. This is all my fault." He mumbled the last part to himself and walked off before I could say anything else.

"I always liked that kid." Elle speaks up and the others nodded along.

"Every once in a while when his brother is being a dick he sneaks down food to us. Good guy."

Every time someone brought up my mate I flinched a little, feeling another strike to my heart.

After a couple minutes we heard another set of footsteps approaching.

I could already feel by the shivers arising on my body and the large presence exactly who was coming.

A smirking Jacob stepped in front my cell. I stared him right in the eye, showing no submission or signs of hurt or pain. He would not see me weak. He will never see me cry.

Hr growled threateningly, incorporating his king powers to force me to listen but I just brushed it off staring directly into his eyes.

"Ellie." He snarled.

I stayed calm and silent even though everything inside me was screaming at me to jump on him and kiss him and kill him and wipe that stupid smirk off his arrogant face.

Aimoto didn't even acknowledge his presence, still staring me down but I could hear Donny growling from next door.

"I've decided to keep you. I've heard that sex with your mate is as good as it gets."

"I will never sleep with you." I said calmly.

"We'll see what you say after a few days of isolation without any food or sunlight, suddenly you'll be begging to be my sex slave."

Donny was snarling and banging on his bars at this point and I could see Elle's eyes begin to glow in anger through the darkness.

I just stared back at him calmly, giving him no reaction. He knows that if he unlocks me to fuck me I'll just beat him the fuck up, human or not I can fight back. He's going to try and break me, little did he know that I am very very stubborn. I would wait here for the rest of my short life if I needed to.

I snarled one more time, "You might think you're all strong and almighty now, but just wait until you see what I have in store for you."

"Do what you gotta do." I said, giving him a fake smile that said 'fuck off'.

He walked off in a huff punching a wall on the way out, creating a small hole in the brick.

It was so annoying because as much as I hated him I still felt the pull to him. He rejected me so we could live without each other but we'll always have the mate chemistry and attraction. It isn't the mate bond that makes us attracted to each other, its our attraction to each other that makes the mate bond.

I guess I understand why I was mated to him. He'll never have the joy of loving and living the rest of his life with his mate. I'm strong enough that he can't make me a slave to him and I'll be dead before he can truly break me down.

"Well he is just one of the biggest assholes I have ever seen." Donny spoke up making me smile slightly, taking a big breath and trying to let it go.

****

I've been in the cell for a day now. It's pretty uncomfortable and I haven't had anything to eat. The guards have finally been switched out for the first time. The one that was there before was really unfriendly and was hell bent on ignoring me.

"Hi there." I said to the dark silhouette of a female guard I saw resting opposite me.

There was a moment of silence before the silhouette moved towards me carefully.

I watched curiously as she stepped into the light. Her face was covered by a mask or helmet of sorts so I couldn't see what she was thinking. If only I had my white stag powers. It'd be very helpful to be able to read their auras.

As the figure came forward it stopped and I heard a small gasp from it. It then ran up to my cell, bending down near me.

"Ummm" I said as she just stared at me for an entire minute.

She reached up and removed her helmet but this time it was my turn to gasp.

"Ellie?" She spoke up, "Ellie Green?"

"Sidney?"

Memories swarmed back to me.

"Hi there!" She said as she came in, taking a seat in the chair across from me. I was shocked by her sweet attitude.

"Uhhhh hi?"

"You must have a lot of questions."

"Well, ya actually."

"Okay, well basically your father, Alpha Green put a bounty on your head, its worth a five hundred thousand dollars! Can you believe that?!" She said, with the same cheery attitude.

I knew I should be scared or shocked but her voice was just too nice.

...

She stocked over to me, holding a collar of sorts in her hands with gloves on. Must be coated in silver. She slipped it over my head. Silver was known to be deadly to wolves but to be honest I've never really been affected by it. Just another way in which I'm different, although I must say, I didn't mind this one.

The collar was connected to a rope which she led me by, like a dog. She unlocked my cuffs and started leading me out of the room into some hallway. We were walking through the dark, stone halls. There were old light bulbs flashing above our heads, making me get a bit of a migraine. Every once in a while the brunette would turn around and smile at me.

To be honest I kind of liked my kidnapper. I knew it was weird and she was like the 'bad guy' and all that, but in a way I get it. I'm just a runt, I mean, they are getting A LOT of money from this. She just had good vibes I don't know, I feel like we could've been friends.

...

"This is weird, usually my prisoners are terrified of me or yell at me or something." She laughed again. "I mean, I am about to torture you but you don't look even a little nervous. You're strange, I like you."

I just shrugged a little, "Hit me all you want, the only thing is I really like this shirt." I said, frowning down at it.

"Oh honey, I got you." She replied, immediately turning around. "Quick detour!" She sang, skipping a little, making me laugh some more.

...

"I just canceled the meeting with Alpha Green. "

"Wh-what?" I was shocked.

"I cannot let you go back to them. Raping is where I really draw the line. I don't care about killing and torturing, especially people who deserve it, which I assumed you did but, you're just a runt! You're not bad! Plus, I like you and it would be hard to be friends if I turned you in. "

...

"Hey, what's your name?" I finally asked.

She giggled, "Sidney"

"Sidney!" I exclaimed, a smile slipping onto my face.

"Hey girl, I missed you but we have got to meet under better circumstances please."

I giggled a little, "That would be nice, ya."

"What the hell did you do to get yourself locked up this time?" She said, sitting crossed-legged in front of me.

"My mate is Prince Jacob." I shrugged.

"Urgh, that dick? I'm so sorry, why do these shitty things happen to you?"

"If only I knew."

"He is such a dick ugh!" I heard Donny scream from next door.

I giggled and Sidney rolled her eyes, obviously used to hearing his bullshit from having guarded him before.

"Since when do you work here? I thought you were a bounty hunter of sorts."

"I pissed off some powerful people, now I'm laying low and I thought I'd get a job."

"I missed you."

"Me too, babe."

I spoke with her for a while, telling her about everything I'd been up to since we last met and she told me all about what she's been doing. Everyone else had gone to sleep since it was night time but I still didn't really sleep.

"God, you could not be more unlucky if you tried!"

I shrugged, "It could be worse."

She gave me a look, "At this point I'm not sure it could."

I rolled my eyes smiling, "Shut up, it definitely could be and you know that. I can handle it, its fine."

"You realize they're going to start torturing you starting in about an hour right?"

I nodded, "I'm not surprised, but you remember I can't feel pain right?"

Her eyes widened, "rightttt I forgot about that part." She looked down at my clothes and frowned.

"That's a nice shirt, its a shame."

I nodded, "Definitely still the worst part." I said frowning.

She smiled at me before standing up, "I have to go, my shift is over. I'll be back in about a week, I'll try to brainstorm ideas for breaking out."

"Talk to Xander, he's doing the same."

"How do you know Prince Xander well enough to convince him to break out?"

I waved my hand, "Long story."

"You're telling me next week." She said, pointing a finger at me.

"Sounds good."

Once she left I waited a half hour before a man walked up to my cell, opening it up.

He unclipped each of my chains from the wall, holding them as leashes, a whip in hand just in case.

I laughed at his nervous face, making him tense up further.

I decided to be good, there were too many guards around at the moment to escape, they would just lock me up even further. He led me down the dark and cold halls to a separate room.

He chained me up to a post and began whipping. I felt nothing of course other than a slight tickle letting me know he's ripping my skin open.

I didn't flinch or give any reaction which seemed to confuse and frustrate the man. My blood was pooling the floor under my knees but I still gave no reaction. He poored a bucked of salty ice water on my head and wounds but I still refused to flinch.

They would not succeed, they would not see my weakness.

The guard growled and picked up a bad covered in spikes. He began shaking my stomach and already injured back with it, splattering blood across the room but I still refused to react.

I could feel the slight tingle of pain when he poured the poison over my wounds but it quickly faded and I could feel my skin begin to reform, knitting back together.

"What the fuck?" The man asked and I just smiled at him before turning back as he tried a multitude of new things.

Thirty-Seven

Its been 3 weeks now I've been in the prison. They have tried almost every kind of torture method but have landed on injecting me with the shifting drugs as it had the most results.

They're up to 10 injections at once to get the reaction they want. I'm in hell, constantly paralyzed in pain, mouth dripping with foam eyes ears and nose dripping with blood. My cell is now covered in nasty substances.

With the combination if the drug greatly weakening me and the complete absence of food I've been losing weight and strength extremely fast.

These days with the cuffs sucking out all of my powers and the drug running through my system I've barely been able to move let alone talk.

Aimoto is watching me carefully almost all the time and Donny and Elle are talking to me, telling me stories and trying to distract me from my reality.

They come in every few hours, once they notice the drug's effects lessening and inject me again so that I'm in constant pain.

It has been getting easier and easier to handle the pain but the weakness is hard to look past. I can barely keep my eyes open most days but I can't sleep either. I'm just stuck, feeling and suffering.

"Hey Ellie." I heard a soft voice above me. I forced my eyes open to see a very very concerned looking Sidney.

I managed to force out a reassuring smile before closing my eyes again.

"I'm going to get you out of here El, I promise, we're trying so hard and we're close. We're going to figure something out."

She reached through the bars and grabbed my hand in comfort, I managed to give it a weak squeeze before going limp again.

I heard Sidney sniffling above me, she was trying not to cry.

I opened my eyes again with a frown. There were a couple tears running down her face.

I fought against the cuffs' magical sucking properties. My body might be weak but my mind was still going strong. I fought and I fought until I broke through.

I let my body fill with that amazing feeling of magic running through my veins. I found Sidney's mind and reached out to it, placing a message in her brain.

'Please don't cry, I'll be fine.' I placed in her brain.

She gasped for a second, getting used to the unfamiliar feeling before more tears fell down her face and sobs racked her body.

She was so sweet, I didn't even know her that well. We've been talking a lot in the last few weeks, I just lost the ability to talk about a week ago so she's started talking to me while I listen.

It was amazing how much she could care about someone she barely knew, she did the same for me the first time we met, when she kidnapped me then ended up saving me from my father.

"How is she?" Donny asked softly.

Sidney just cried harder, unable to answer.

I reached to Donny's brain. 'I'm fine, don't worry.'

'Ellie?' He replied in his mind.

'Who else.'

'How are you doing this?'

'You know I am a white stag.'

'Yes, but you're locked up in those cuffs, not to mention this entire prison suppresses any extra abilities.'

'I know but I'm fighting against it, I can't do much but at least now I can speak.'

I heard Elle crying and switched into her brain.

'Why would they do this to her? This is so unfair. Is she dead? Why isn't Sidney saying anything. Oh god what if she's dead, god dammit I can't see her.'

I cut off her stream of thoughts, relaxing her gently. I heard her sigh.

'What the fuck is happening?' She though.

'I'm just helping you relax, I'm fine, don't worry about me.'

She sighed in relief and pushed her to sleep into a peaceful sleep. I noticed by being in their minds that they all experience intense nightmares of their past. I gently blocked the nightmares from ruining her sleep and she fell deep into unconsciousness. I could tell that it was the first good sleep she'd had since the incident which is ridiculous considering how long she's been here.

I jumped to Sidney's mind, comforting her and slowing her cries, making her calm. It felt good to finally do something with myself.

I heard her stop crying and relax, walking back to her post to avoid suspicion in case someone else walked in.

I jumped back to Donny and he felt exhausted. He too had been suffering from nightmare this entire time. I pushed him to sleep gently and blocked out the nightmares letting him sleep properly.

Once I was finished with them I decided to try Aimoto's mind. See if there's anything I could help with.

My breath stopped once I entered.

All brains have a certain level of chaos, some worse than others, but Aimoto's was completely organized. There weren't random thoughts constantly flowing through his subconscious, it was peaceful.

'Hello little one, I see you've pushed past the magic barrier. Very impressive.'

'Wow.' Was all I could manage to say.

'This is what happens once you've reached complete peace with yourself and everything around you.'

'This is amazing.'

'This is the brain of a abura-sumasha. This is why we are able to manipulate other minds so easily, once you have reached a peace, you can be properly observant and complete much more multitasking. It is organized instead of a big mush of madness.'

'I see why they were scared of you. With a mind like this you could accomplish so much.'

'I'll teach you one day.'

'Really?'

'Once we're out of here.'

I felt my hope deflate. 'If we get out of here.'

'Have faith young one, now return to your mind and save your strength, you're going to need it.'

'For what?'

'Good bye.' With that he gently pushed me out of his brain and back into my own. Once I was back in my own body I felt how tiring that really was. He was right, I should save my strength.

I let my mind wander wherever it wanted to, trying to drift off to sleep even though I knew it would never join me.

A few minutes later they were back with a glass bucket full of needles.

The man opened my cell but I just watched him, trying to keep my eyes open.

The guard actually frowned at me, seemingly a little guilty.

I quickly pushed through for a moment to see his aura. It was good, he felt guilty, he had an innocent soul despite the hardships he's faced.

I relaxed. I trusted him not to kill me. He has direct orders to keep going until I'm on the verge of dying then stop, he couldn't stop if he wanted to.

One injection. I counted.

Two.

Three.

Four.

Five.

Six.

Seven.

Eight.

Nine.

Ten.

He paused, nothing had happened yet.

"Shit." I heard him curse under his breath.

Eleven.

Still nothing.

Twelve.

More swearing.

Thirteen.

Still nothing was happening, I didn't feel any worse than before, if anything I felt slightly better as the effects started to lessen.

I looked behind the guard to see a small smile lighting Aimoto's wrinkled face.

Fourteen.

Fifteen.

"Hey Carl" The man called the head guard. He sauntered over looking annoyed.

"I'm sorry sir but I've given her all 15 injections and nothing's happening. "

"Let me see." He snarled before stepping into my cell. "

He roughly inspected the injection spot, usually it swells and turns slightly blue but nothing seemed to be happening.

"Fuck." He mumbled.

"She's immune now, isn't she?"

Carl sighed, "Yes. She is, she's immune. God fucking dammit, Prince Jacob is not going to be happy." He ran his hands through his hair nervously, "I'm going to go talk to him, you watch her."

The kind-hearted guard nodded, standing up straight into a guard's position.

Once Carl left he visibly relaxed.

"I'm so sorry Ellie." He whispered.

I got enough energy to smile gently and slipped into his mind.

He gasped stepping back a little when I soothed his mind, comforting him. 'Thank you, John.' I found his name in his mind.

His eyes widened but he relaxed when I soothed his mind. Again I pushed away his nightmares, his thoughts were riddled with guilt from his job. I didn't make him emotionless he'll still feel the pain of the job, but I made it slightly more bearable, I made him more at peace, happier.

He smiled softly at me, thoughts swarming with admiration.

Suddenly Jacob walks into my cell.

"What are you smiling about, guard?" He snapped, making John wipe the smile off his face and become an emotionless pawn again.

"You're saying the bitch is immune?"

"Yes sir." Carl responded.

"How is this possible?"

"We don't know sir, it shouldn't be. You mate is very strong."

Jacob growled sharply, making Carl's heartbeat fly through the roof, tilting his head in submission, falling into a slight bow.

Not gonna lie, its kind of hot when Jacob does that. I mean I hate him but damnnnn.

NO. SHUT UP ELLIE.

I felt my energy slowly returning, I should be able to talk again any minute now.

I smiled at Jacob, enraging him further.

He gave me a big kick to the stomach, making me fly into the opposite wall.

I just smiled and laughed, blood flooding my mouth,

All three of the looked at me terrified as I sat up, spitting the blood out and laughed. God they look hilarious, they're so scared of a little girl who's poisoned and locked up! How am I supposed to respect this pussy.

This little jack ass can't just lock me up in a cell and expect me to surrender just like that.

"Are you ready to submit?" He asked, a slight, barely noticeable, shake in his voice.

That just caused me to laugh harder. I coughed out some blood and I was dizzy but I laughed through it.

I haven't been able to take my pills in weeks, I'm feeling all of the symptoms of my disease making me even weaker.

Fuck it, I'll be dead soon anyways. I'm done being careful. I would enjoy my last days even if I was just here sitting in this dirty cell that was somehow always slightly wet.

I looked at him in the eyes as he approached me.

'Submit.' I ordered in his mind.

His face turned to shock and panic as he tried to fight against my powers. I easily pushed him to the ground so that he was kneeling to me, revealing his neck in submission.

The other guards panicked, Carl running away, probably to get back up.

"Awww look at you big bad alpha prince kneeling to a little girl. How cute!" I exclaimed laughing.

He growled in protest so I pushed him harder. He was unable to make eye contact or do anything I didn't like as he sat there, submitting to me.

Suddenly I felt a gigantic presence enter the room. I masked my power from everyone else, only letting Jacob feel it, making him look weak.

A man, who I assumed was the king burst in with Xavier and an endless supply of guards following him.

I made myself look as weak and innocent as I possible could as I pushed myself into the corner, putting a panicked look on my face.

He observed the scene with his eyebrows furrowed.

"Son, what the hell do you think you're doing."

I let him answer, lessening my powers over him only slightly.

"I-I c-can't-t" He stuttered out, making everyone else confused. Aimoto across the the hall looked amused as he watched everything. I could feel Donny and Elle were still asleep, they were really tired.

"Wh-what's happening?" I pretended to stutter out, putting on a terrified look.

"Stop submitting, royalty does not bow." His dad growls out.

I felt my weakness return, I couldn't hold him much longer in this weak state.

The king walked into my cell carefully but I just widened my eyes at him, pretending he intimidated me.

"This little girl is making you submit." He sniffed the air.

"What are you?" He asked.

"I-I'm a white stag and a werewolf runt sir." I said avoiding eye contact to show my submission.

He looked at his son.

He grabbed his son's arm pulling him to his feet but Jacob's body fought against it, needing to bow to me.

Thirty-Eight

The king growled, putting on his alpha voice. I pretended to cower in the corner.

"Is it her that's making you submit."

"Yes." He said in frustration.

"The white stag werewolf runt is making you submit. Are you sure its her?"

"Yes."

"Xander come here." Xander walked into the room and I gave him a small mischievous smile when no one was looking, making him chuckle.

"Does this little girl make you want to submit?"

"No sir." Xander answered amused.

"My sons are not supposed to be weak. Stop embarrassing me."

My powers were pretty much drained so I decided to let him go. I would have to save my strength.

The king looked down at me and a little pity filled his eyes. "You're a white stag."

"Yes sir."

"Strong or weak?"

"My powers rival those of the first whit stag. If I hadn't trusted your son, he never could have caught me."

"Why would you trust my son so much? What landed such a peaceful creature down in the worst part of my dungeons?"

"I'm his mate, your majesty." He frowned deeply.

"He locked up his powerful mate in the dungeons. Why?"

"I wish I knew." I said simply, true sadness filing my features as I fiddled with my fingers.

I could feel that the king had a good soul, just like Xander.

"You can all leave." The King dismissed the guards as Jacob stomped off.

Only Xander and the King remained.

"I am truly sorry for what my son has done to you." His eyes filled with pity.

"Thank you sir, but no need to pity me, its nothing I can't handle."

I heard someone scoff from the corner and there was standing Carl.

"You have something to say Carl?"

Everyone seemed fairly relaxed around the king and Xander, much more than Jacob, they knew he wasn't a total irrational dick.

"This girl can definitely handle it. We don't know what to do with her anymore."

"What do you mean?"

"She doesn't react to any torture methods and we've tried them all. She doesn't flinch when we whip her and douse her in poison, she doesn't make a sound as we tear her skin apart and her body heals completely within minutes if not less. We've been giving her force-shifting injections for the last few weeks but even those have stopped working. We just gave her 15 full doses and nothing!" He threw his hands up into the air.

"Its true, I've spent a good amount of time with her. She's my friend which is why I brought her here, neither of us knew that her mate was my dick head brother.

The king sighed, running his hands through his shoulder length grey hair.

"What are we going to do with him? I thought once he met his mate he would soften but he goes and does this?! I'd like to retire one day but I can't pass the werewolf population over to him. I can't do that to my people. What is he even keeping you here for?"

Xander flinched at the question, looking to his feet in shame.

"So that I submit and become a sex slave to your son." I answered him, nonchalantly, even though the fact that my mate would betray me like that was tearing me apart.

"WHAT?!" He growled and even the quiet Xander and Carl growled at this.

"Did you both know this?" He asked, sounding defeated.

"Yes. We were ordered to stay quiet and follow his decisions." Xander filled in.

The king rubbed his face.

"Please release her from all of those chains at the very least. If I let out his prisoner it will make him seem even more weak in front of his future kingdom, I can't do that but at the very least make her more comfortable. You are to stop torturing and get her some food and water regularly." Whatever the king orders goes, they had no choice but to obey but they didn't seem to fight against it.

I smiled widely. Fuck it, I thought and stood up warily. I walked over to the king and gave him a big hug. He stiffened up at first, shocked, but soon hugged me back.

"My son doesn't deserve you." He muttered lowly "If he would have accepted you he could've really changed into a better person. That is going to be the biggest mistake of his life but you deserve better. I know it is in a white stag's nature to forgive, but he doesn't deserve it, you understand?"

I nodded before giving him one last squeeze and pulling away. Before I could even do anything Xander had pulled me into his own embrace.

"Why couldn't she have been my mate?" He pouts while I giggle and the king smiles rolling his eyes.

"You don't deserve her either." He said, making Xander gasp in fake hurt.

How could 2 such amazing people be related to such a monster. How could such a monster be my supposed other half.

"Hey Xander, is there any way you could tell my sister Jen that I'm okay. Don't tell her I'm locked up or anything, she doesn't need that worry, just tell her I'm okay."

He hesitantly nodded his head before heading out, following his father.

I felt my strength return quickly without the hand cuffs. My magic and power swarmed me, healing me properly. I felt alive again as I just sat there smiling.

I'm a little upset about the state of my shirt though, I'm pretty much exposed to everyone. Now that I feel better its all I can think about.

Aimoto had gone to sleep once everyone left and it was just me and the guard, John.

"Hey John." I said peppily as he took over his post.

He smiled at my new energy.

"I see the king liked you. He's a nice guy isn't he?"

I nodded my head laughing, "I wish he were my father." I said daydreaming about how much better my life would be.

"So, distract me, tell me about yourself, how's your wife, May?" I saw that in his mind.

His aura turned to one of deep love and admiration. "She's amazing. She's pregnant with my first pup."

I smiled at his excitement.

He begun his little rant about his family, a few of the other guards joining in, talking about the ones they love. I just smiled the whole time, happy to listen.

"What about you Ellie?" A guard I learnt was named Derek piped up.

I smiled at the memory, "I have two people I consider my parents, Jammie and Henry. They sort of took me in about a year ago and have treated my like their own daughter ever since. They're so loving and generous, even though they don't have much they gave me everything they could.

Jen, their biological daughter, I consider my sister. She's so sweet and caring, always able to make me laugh. She's a little crazy but I love her to death, she's actually the reason I came to Spain.

I have friends who I consider a weird kind of family back in the belle forest pack in Canada. Jack, Chris, Heeler, Sarah and her brother Alex. Although the last few times I saw them were a little rough, they were there for me when I first go there and I really appreciated that.

Amos, Daisy, Rose and Jeremiah from the white stag village. They all took me in when I had to leave Belle foret for reasons I don't really want to talk about. They all brought me more confidence and taught me to use my white stag abilities. They never resented me for being powerful and I always appreciated that.

Darius, Peter and Boston from the witch community. I haven't known them for long but they all impacted my life and were good friends as long as I knew them, always making me happy.

Sidney, Donny, Ellie and even Aimoto and Xander here have helped me through a lot.

A lot of people have helped me and made me who I am and, even if I don't know all of them that well or for that long, I love them all and if any of them ever needed my help I would give my life for theirs. "

When I finished my little monologue I looked up to see looks of happiness and relaxation on their faces.

"Sorry I went on a little rant there." I giggled a little and they all chuckled with me.

We all knew Jacob would not be coming back down here for a while after the incident so everyone was much lighter and more relaxed.

Although I desperately wanted to be free, it wasn't that bad. It could always be worse.

Even if I never see them again I still have a very long list of people I care about, I've lived a pretty good life in the end, though I don't feel complete yet. I'm not ready for it to end.

"What is all of this laughing? I'm trying to sleep." Donny croaked out from next door.

We all burst out into laughter again, accidentally waking the others.

Aimoto simply sat up and opened his eyes, going back to his crossed legged position.

He gave me a small nod, which for him is a lot of emotion, and I returned it with a huge smile.

I felt so much better.

"Good morning Donny!" I chirped out.

"Ellie?"

"Why do you always ask that. Of course its me."

"But you don't sound like a dying ball of crickets."

I rolled my eyes, "Gee, thanks."

"You know what I mean." He said through a yawn.

I giggled, "The king stopped the torture and uncuffed me. This is the real me."

Elizabeth gasped, "Oh Ellie, I'm so happy for you."

I giggled, "Thank you Liza."

"Liza?"

"Ya well Elle and Ellie are really similar, I figured I'd call you Liza, you know, Elizabeth, Lizabeth, Liza."

"I like it." Donny piped in.

"Me too." Liza added.

I smiled widely.

Then slid into all of their minds, 'You guys wanna get out of here?' I asked.

Thirty-Nine

They all went silent and I took that as a yes.

I was still severely under weight but the weakness had faded away with the poison and cuffs. Its time they see what I can really do.

I entered the guards minds, making them see us all sitting in our cells calmly. I broke the bars off my cell and they had no clue.

I walked over to Aimoto who was giving me a small smile as I ripped the door off his cell. He got up, not even bothering to stretch as he stood and waited as I walked to Donny's cell.

There was standing a jumping excited little ball of blond joy. He had short but floppy hair and bright blue eyes, freckles dusting his cheeks and nose.

When I ripped his cell open he enveloped me into a big bear hug, jumping slightly.

He then switched his attention to the oblivious guards, he furrowed his eyebrows standing in front of them, waving his hand in front of their faces.

"They can't see or hear you, they think you're still in your cell, don't touch them though." I warned sternly.

"Wicked." He mumbled, dancing in front of them goofily.

I went over to the last cell to discover Liza. She looked around my age even though I knew she was hundreds of years older.

When I opened her cell we hugged, squealing and jumping a little.

"Thank you so much Ellie. You didn't have to save us."

I scoffed, "You guys have paid your dues, just don't go burning down buildings, okay?"

Donny stomped huffed throwing his hands in the air. "I only did it the one time!" He wined.

Liza gave him look.

"Fine, 3 times." He pouted, making him raise my eyebrows and giggle. He's honestly adorable.

Aimoto nodded at Liza and she nodded right back. It was strange but not surprising that this is how they greet each other after all these years.

"Okay, lets go!"

"Allons-y!" Donny echoed following behind.

Aimoto followed silently in calm silence with amazing posture while Donny leapt around from thing to thing in excitement and Liza observed everything she walked by, a light smile lighting hr face.

We walked out of the halls past all of the guards as I searched for minds, blocking us from view.

I could easily run out and be gone in less than a second but the others can't exactly do that. It was definitely a lot more work to bring them with me but I couldn't leave them behind there.

We walked out of the dungeon area and I made sure no one could see or hear us opening and closing the doors. I noticed Sidney's mind walking around the corner, it was her shift next.

I let her be able to see and hear us as we walked towards her through the grand halls.

When she turned the corners and saw us she stopped in her place. Her eyes widened and she blinked. Blinked again. Looked at each of us, blinked.

"Okay, I'm going crazy." She whispered to herself making us laugh. That seemed to confuse her more. She looked around as other guards passed by giving her weird looks.

"They can't hear or see us." I filled in.

She nodded slowly, "So I'm hallucinating?"

Donny groaned from behind us.

"Sid, pull it together, she's a white stag, this is what they do! This is not a hallucination, we're really leaving if anything everyone else is hallucinating." He explained quickly, bending forward like he were talking to a child.

"Oh fuck off Donny." She growled.

I wanted to tell them to shut up as I felt a familiar presence coming around the corner but I didn't do it in time.

I cringed as Xander walked around the corner looking and Sidney and in front of her where there was nothing.

I sighed, I wasn't gong to let him see us just in case, but I guess that's out the window.

"Ummm, are you okay?" He asked Sidney and her cheeks lit up red like a Christmas tree at night.

"Ummmm, yes?"

"Who's Donny?"

I made us visible in that moment.

"I'm Donny Bitch, geez, I'm like this close to throwing another prince out of the window."

He said sassily as I gave him the death glare.

"Donny, what did we agree to?"

"Hey! You never said I couldn't throw a prince out the window, you just said I couldn't set it on fire!" He said, putting his hands up.

"Don't throw any princes out of the window."

He sighed, "Fine whatever, you saved me I guess I can hold back."

I rolled my eyes turning my attention back to Xander who was looking at us confused. It was definitely hard to concentrate on everything at once, the conversation the countless people I have to make us invisible to.

"You're not hallucinating." Sidney filled him in as another guard walked by not seeing us at all.

"White stag, right, never experienced it for real, caught me off guard for a sec, but okay, I'm good now." He said nodding his head.

"At least he got it faster than Sidney." Donny grumbled earning a whack from Liza.

"Ouch!" He exclaimed jumping in the air, giving Liza the death glare.

"I can't even say how long I've wanted to do that." She sighed, looking more complete.

"Hey, I said I wouldn't throw PRINCES out of the window so unless you grow a penis and a crown you should watch yourself." He growled out making her roll her eyes.

"We should get going, it is a big strain on Ellie to keep us all invisible for so long." Aimoto spoke up.

They nodded, instantly listening to Aimoto as we considered our walk.

"I'll come see you tonight Xander, you too Sid, meet you in the kitchen?"

"I'll be there." He responded and Sidney nodded happily.

We walked the rest of the halls, carefully avoiding bumping into guards on our way out. Once we were out of the castle everyone sighed in content, happy to be outside.

Donny bent down looking at the grass. He picked up a handful taking a good whiff. "God I missed the smell of grass." He said closing his eyes in content.

Even Aimoto was taking especially long breaths, closing his eyes, all signs of tension leaving his body as a small, barely noticeable smile, lifted onto his face.

Liza was squealing, doing cartwheels and rolling around in the grass. It has been so long that each of them have spent in the cells, I only spent a month I couldn't imagine how they stayed sane the whole time.

We kept walking until we came across a small garden of yellow roses.

A huge smile made its way onto my face.

I picked it up, giving it a good smell. I felt myself relax completely as my mind relaxed and my entire aura calmed.

I even noticed everyone around me had calmed and looked happier, feeding off of my aura without even knowing it.

I kept the flower, twirling it in my fingers as we continued our walk. 3 months left.

"So where do you all want to go?" I asked.

"I want to go to a coven and witch community. Any of them really would be nice, its pretty hard to get into one, especially with my level of powers, they're very wary."

"I actually know a great community. I've been training some of the witches in combat and in exchange they'll teach me a few basic witch tricks. I could ask Darius, I'm sure with my recommendation they'll consider letting you in at the very least. But I can't promise anything."

Her smile covered her face, "Oh Ellie, you've already done so much, thank you."

I nodded.

"I'm going back to Japan." Aimoto spoke up.

"Ellie, I would love for you to stay with us for a while, I can teach you like I promised."

I lit up this time.

"That sounds so amazing Aimoto, thank you." I said calmly even though I was dying of excitement inside.

"Hey Ellie, do you think I could just, stick with you? I don't really know anyone, like anywhere and I think we could have fun traveling the world together. We'd be an unstoppable duo!" He said confidently but I saw a lot of insecurity in him.

He was scared of being along, everyone he knew is dead and he's scared he'll mess up again and be locked up again. He knows I can help keep him in check.

"I'd love that Donny." I said giving him a big smile.

He returned it, just as wide, before jumping on me and hugging me.

He lifted my up, shining around.

"YES! Donny and Ellie! It even sounds good!"

"Ellie and Donny." I corrected.

He scoffed, "In your dreams."

"You wish you could be in my dreams."

"Not even if I died."

"Not even if you died?"

"Okay, over my dead body, but my body will be high because I'm a pheonix so good luck with that."

"I'll fly if I have to!"

"Hey! I'm the only one who can fly here!" He then leapt into the air, his Phoenix wings materializing and spreading as he stuck his tongue out at me.

I ran to the top of a tree before he could even blink so that I was higher than him.

"Then how come I'm still above you."

Donny flew higher but every time I'd climb on something higher until he was flying over there trees.

"Oops." I said, letting myself fall off the top of the tree. He panicked and flew down to try and catch me but before he could I grabbed onto one of the last branches at the bottom and sprint climbed back up the tree so I was above him.

"Told you." I said smirking while he huffed, crossing his arms.

"WHAT ARE YOU GUYS EVEN SAYING?! This is the worst argument I've ever heard oh my lord." Liza burst out, "Literally none of what you just said made any sense, I worry for wherever you both visit together."

We both stuck out our tongues at her as I leaped back down from the tree.

"No need to hate on us because we're young." Donny said, putting his arm around my shoulder giving Liza a disapproving look.

"You're literally hundreds of years old! You're way closer to my age than hers!"

"I'm still younger though."

She rolled her eyes, "Come on, lets go." She stomped off deeper into the woods.

"I totally won that, look at her." Donny whispered in my ear as we laughed together at Liza's flustered state.

We walked the rest of the way to the hotel I was with Jen at, hopefully they haven't left yet, if they stayed on schedule they should be leaving tomorrow so we should just be catching them.

Luckily the castle wasn't too far because the entire walk Liza was shooting death glares towards Donny who kept laughing at her. Even Aimoto's lips twitched sightly when Liza started screaming in frustration, pulling on her hair as her face got red.

I honestly have no idea how they handled each other for so long.

We reached the gorgeous hotel and I finally let my illusions drop. They would now be able to see none of us were in the cell. I wish I could've held off a little longer but it was too much work and I was having a hard time concentrating on everything.

I was so excited for Aimoto to train me, I needed a lot of help with my multitasking.

3 months left and I am going to live it. I'm not going to hold back at all, there's no time for that anymore. Its the last stretch and I am going to go out with a bang.

Forty

Once we entered the beautiful hotel I waved to the receptionist who somehow remembered me and headed into the elevator.

I took it up to Jen's room, crossing my finger that they didn't leave early.

I knocked on her door. We waited for a couple of tense seconds as I heard footsteps approaching.

"Can't you see the do not disturb sign?!" She burst out angrily, when she met my eyes she stopped in her spot for a second before flying onto me, knocking us both over as we hugged.

"Holy shit Ellie, you have so much explaining to do. I told you to stop fuckign scaring me and you gave me the most stressful month ever. Then some random ass guy who apparently is the PRINCE OF MOTHERUCKING WEREWOLVES comes to tell me that you're fine although I could totally tell he was lying which just stressed me out even more and-"

"Jen!" I cut her off finally getting off the ground, laughing as she blushed a little at her outburst, finally noticing the other people.

"Jen, this is Donny, Elizabeth or Elle or Liza and this is Aimoto."

She just crossed her arms raising her eyesbrows.

"Guys, this is my sister Jen."

Jen turned to me, "You have so much to explain, AND NOW PLEASE!"

I nodded as we all headed into Jen's room.

I told her all about the last month, leaving out the gory or depressing details of course.

"HOW DID MY AMAZING ASS SISTER GET MATED TO SUCH A DICK?!"

Jen's been yelling that sort of stuff ever since I finished my story. She's been ranting to the point where even Donny was overwhelmed.

Finally Brian came walking through the door, finally shutting Jen up as she leapt into his arms.

"LOOK YOU SHOWED UP BRIAN YOU WOULDN'T BELIEVE WHAT HAPPENED!"

Brian chuckled, clearly used to her craziness, "Calm down and tell me about it."

"Actually I need to go, I need to go talk to Xander and Sidney and I need to get these guys a room for tonight." I cut in, standing up and heading to the door with the others behind me.

Jen pouted but I knew she needed to time to explain everything to Brian.

I head down to the front desk buying a couple rooms for the night.

I decided Liza and I could share a room and Donny and Aimoto could share.

Donny pouted a little at getting put with 'the man who never speaks' but after a quick slap across the head from Liza he was quick to listen.

I had to explain the whole concept of the hotel key since they were invented while they were still in jail, I had a feeling I'd have to explain a lot. They'd never even seen a car before.

We walked down the streets, Donny bouncing around from thing to thing, excited about everything new.

I lead them to a cute little homey restaurant. We walked in and the little bell rang signaling we'd arrived.

A man come out with a welcoming smile and I knew they'd be safe here.

I sat them down at a table and gave them money, explaining how the restaurant works before heading off to meet Xander and Sidney.

I easily avoided the guards that seemed to be in a state of chaos with all the missing prisoners that literally just disappeared out of nowhere.

I strolled into the kitchen, admiring the beautiful moldings on the walls and found a tense Xander and Sidney talking.

"What if she doesn't make it?" Sidney asks in a panic, "Everyone's looking for her."

"I don't know, do you think its a possibility that they catch her? She never gave us a specific time what if she meant like midnight when there are less people."

I popped up, making them jump as I was standing right next to them. I felt like a midget next to the two of them. Sidney was 5'10 an Xander was 6'2 whereas I was only 5'6.

"Its eight o'clock I think this counts as 'tonight'."

"Jesus Christ, you scared the shit out of me." Xander said dramatically holding his heart.

"We could've met you somewhere else, what if you get caught?" Sidney asked, still panicked.

I waved them off, "I won't get caught, don't worry."

Sidney nodded though she still seemed tense.

"I just wanted to thank you both. You guys made this whole thing a little more bearable and I know you guys had tried to get me out too. Even though I beat you to it I'm still so grateful."

They both pulled me into a group hug though I saw them both flinch when they touched each other. I eyed them suspiciously. As they both blushed and seemed to panic slightly.

"Something you want to tell me?" I asked, putting my hands on my hips.

"Umm, no?" Sidney answered as Xander swore quickly under his breath.

I scowled,"Don't make me read your minds."

They both froze, looking at each other guiltily.

"XANDERANDIAREMATES." Sidney yelled out, making me step back, my heart beating a little faster.

"What?"

"Xander and I are mates." She repeated more slowly, cheeks going red and eyes going wide.

A gigantic smile made its way onto my face as I leapt on both of them, pulling them into another group hug.

"OH MY GOD MY BABIES HAVE FOUND EACH OTHER I'M SO HAPPY!"

They both sighed in relief, laughing a little at my excitement, their on smiles slipping onto their faces.

Then I froze and stepped back crossing my arms.

"How long have you known?"

I asked and they both gave me sheepish smiles.

"Ever since we met 2 weeks ago passing on the way to your cell..." Xander mumbled.

"TWO WEEKS?! AND YOU ONLY TOLD ME NOW?! Actually, you didn't even tell me! I practically forced it out of you!" I threw my hands in the air in frustration.

"Well you were going through a lot and we didn't want to throw it in your face and then um, we were nervous because we thought you'd react like this when you found out we didn't tell you."

I was fuming. I gave them each a slap across the head.

"Stupid cows." I mumbled.

We spent a couple more hours talking and catching up properly, they'd already announced it to everyone and Sidney was going to become the new princess of werewolves.

The door to the kitchen flung open and in walked the king in only sweats, his shoulder length hair in a bun on the top of his head.

He yelped a little and jumped when he saw the three of us. Putting a hand on his chest.

"Ellie?" He asked, confused as hell.

I nodded happily, laughing at his flustered state and outfit. He looked so much more human, less regal and intimidating.

"Didn't you escape the dungeons, why would you come back?"

I shrugged, "I wanted to say goodbye."

"But what if you get caught."

I laughed a little, "You guys can't catch me."

The three of them growled a little playfully.

"Please I don't even have to leave the kitchen and I bet you guys still wouldn't be able to catch me." I said, brushing my hair over my shoulder leaning back on the counter.

"Okay, bring it on." The king spoke up.

I giggled, "Its on."

"You won't leave the kitchen?"

"I promise. 1... 2... 3... Go!"

With that I turned invisible completely and moved out of the way as they all lunged to where I was standing.

They all stalked around the kitchen, lunging at air, trying to listen for sounds they'll never hear.

"Just let me know when you give up." I echoed around them, laughing at their frustration.

When they didn't give up I took a bowl of cookie batter I found on the side and the spatula and sat in the middle of their kitchen island, having a little snack while watching them leap around confused.

It has been going on for about 20 minutes now and I could see they're all getting frustrated.

I decided to mess with them a little since I was getting bored. I froze time, leaping off the counter and opened all of the cabinets before sitting back down.

I unfroze time and watched as they all jumped in surprise at the now open cabinets.

While jumping backwards Xander tripped over his own foot falling to the ground.

"Graceful." I echoed.

I decided to mess with them more, walking up to them and taping them on the shoulder.

It was hilarious watching them whip around, grabbing at the air letting out sounds of frustration.

"Okay! I give, you win!" Sidney said, putting her hands in the air.

I reappeared to only her and she looked at me with a death glare as she saw me sitting on the counter.

"She's there! Get her!" I giggled at their little plan as they both lunged at me.

I once again froze time going to stand next to Sid watching them leap over the counter.

When Sidney saw me standing next to her she just sighed.

"We're never going to catch her." She mumbled to the as they got off the floor, rubbing their butts.

"Fine, you win." Said Xander followed by the king saying, "Okay, okay, point proven."

I reappeared standing next to Sid, still picking on the cookie dough.

"How did you move that fast? Or do the cabinet thing?" Sidney asked.

I shrugged a small evil smile gracing my face, "I just froze time for a bit."

They all groaned in annoyance. All thinking, 'well not shit we couldn't catch her if she can freeze time.'

I felt a familiar presence sneaking up to the kitchen. I made myself invisible to only him trying not to let how much his presence bothers me show on my face.

I gave them a sad smile, "I should probably go." I said quietly making them all confused until Jacob walked in.

He came in like he ruled the place. He looked really hot though, his hair messy and his arms on show in the tight t-shirt and sweats he was wearing.

"What the fuck are you all doing in here?" He huffed out making the king scowl and Xander roll his eyes.

When Jacob saw this he pinned his bother to the ground by his neck.

"Watch your attitude." He growled out making Xander submit. He spat at Sidney, what is this little weak bitch doing here, I told you to reject her."

I saw red. Now he was taking it too far. I let myself be visible and let all of my power leak out of me making Jacob stumble backwards.

"What the fuck?!" He spat but when he made eye contact with me he smirked.

I walked up to him slowly growling lowly as I pushed him to the ground with my powers.

He couldn't even struggle as he Aly completely exposed to me.

I grabbed Jacob by the throat picking him up.

"Enough." I said calmly but with a deathly tone.

He was shaking slightly in fear as I stared into his eyes.

I was about to close my grip, effectively ending his life when my white stag stone started glowing.

'Leave him, you will get a much better revenge, be patient.' It whispered through me.

I closed my eyes taking a deep breath as everyone watched my carefully.

I walked out of the kitchen down the halls, dragging Jacob by his neck.

Even if I can't kill him he can't get away with treating Xander and Sidney like that.

My mate needs to learn his place. It physically hurt me having to treat someone that is suppose to be my soulmate like this but he didn't give me much of an option.

The others followed behind together. As I passed by guards they all fell to their knees submitting to me, bowing respectfully. My power was out for everyone to see and I couldn't even care.

I walked to the dungeon, down the familiar halls to my cell.

I threw him in there, he played on the floor unable to move. I locked the doors and turned to the small crowd that had gathered.

"Keep him in there for a week, give him food and water but nothing more. If you let him out before then you'll have to deal with me personally." I growled out, "Understand?" They all nodded quickly and I relaxed.

I closed my eyes for a second, all of the tension leaving my body.

I gave them all a soft smile.

I gave the king Xander and Sidney a big hug, "I should go, call me if you need anything and I'll be here as soon as I can." I said softly. I saw a few of the guards that I spoke to the last day join in looking confused as they took in the scene in front of them.

I gave them all a smile before walking out. I let everyone see me as I left, the all bowed to me as I calmly walked out of the castle.

I kind of hate myself for doing that, to my mate too, but it needed to be done.